All she needed now was for her own father to take her down...

"COM CONNECT CDR21!" RETT OPENED the pcom to the 21st command channel, almost snarling into the pickup. "Fang leader to 1-21!"

"Fang Lead, this is 2-21, what's up?"

Shit, Rett said to herself as the strong alto voice of SubColonel Nauskova answeredinstead of Reve's. *He would make me talk to his second!*

"Damn it, clear your flaming targets! You people aren't alone up here. We've crossfire patterns going! What's up over there, anyway?"

"Fang leader, we have a supply jumper down and civilians in the trough, sector eight. Coalition's cutting them off. We're hot here—and 1-21's with patrol and cut off with them."

Sector eight? They'd moved fast. *No wonder . . .*

More Books by Terry Roy

~ ~ ~ ~

Science Fiction/Action

Convergence – Journey to Nyorfias, Book 1
Gravity – Journey to Nyorfias, Book 2
Stratagem – Journey to Nyorfias, Book 3

NYORFIAS UNIVERSE STORIES
Carakenne (Supplemental novella to JTN2 Gravity)
Kyarta Girl (Supplemental novel to JTN3 Stratagem)

~ ~ ~ ~

Sff-Romance

Discovery – A Far Out Romance

~ ~ ~ ~

Romance

Crash Into Me (Romantic Suspense)

~ ~ ~ ~

Humor
as Terran Moffat
First Bass and Other Stories

Visit
teryvisions.wordpress.com
for the latest news, updates, sneak previews, and more!

To contact, please email:
terzap@gmail.com
Please write with any comments, concerns, or questions

STRATAGEM

JOURNEY TO NYORFIAS, BOOK 3

TERRY ROY

ISBN-9781937899820

CONTENTS

AUTHOR'S NOTE: THIS IS THE third book in a three-volume story arc, with two supplemental novellas. Together they create one epic story that is simply too long to put into one book. (Even cutting some parts out.) Like its predecessors, *Convergence* and *Gravity*, *Stratagem* is composed in a series of connected episodes rather than conventional chapters.

You might be able to muddle through without having read the first volumes of Rett and Pam's adventures, but I highly recommend reading them all in this order: *Convergence, Gravity, Carakenne, Stratagem,* and *Kyarta Girl.*

ACKNOWLEDGEMENTS

TO ALL THOSE WHO'VE ENCOURAGED, discouraged, inspired, been around, were gone, listened, ignored . . . I thank all of you. Really. It's helped shape me and helped shape my stories. A great big shout out to authors LK Rigel, Deb Martin, Sandra Edwards, K.C. May, and J.C. Phelps . . . who listen to me whine, bitch, and moan, and who help me keep things in perspective. My past and recent editors: Sara, Karli, Mary N., Cathy, Debra, and Linda. Most of all to my family, my brother Tim; my sisters Cathy (a different Cathy), Nancy, Sharon, Maria, and Laura. Parts of all of you are thick in this story. Especially Sharon, who perhaps gave many qualities to Rett.

STRATAGEM

JOURNEY TO NYORFIAS, BOOK 3

TERRY ROY

"**W**HAT'S THE POINT? NO MATTER how long I look at them, the words don't change."

Rett shoved her Omni back into its belt holder and lengthened her stride. Normally she wouldn't think twice about the half hour it took to cover the distance between Special Forces operations center and the AirSpacefighters headquarters. Now, every step she took seemed to take her farther from her goal.

~I'm sorry Jaq's message was such a downer, Rett,~ said Pam. ~Especially after Olvero's had put you in such a good mood.~

I shouldn't have read either one. I should have kept them for later, after the mission.

~No,~ said Pam.

Pam was right. There was no putting things off for later, not when it came to the people Rett loved, to the fragility of life during wartime. They might have thrown back the Coalition and gained ground, but all that could change in an instant.

She didn't need to hear it and wasn't in the mood to be pacified. Physical activity would make her feel better. She sorted out her thoughts better when she was doing something that didn't require much more than reflex action, be it walking, working out, or maintaining her gear.

Her young cousin's most recent letter had made things worse. Rett had felt so warm and happy after reading it, had even failed to smother her giggles a few times, earning strange and amused glances from passers-by. It filled her with energy and hope. So when she saw Jaq's code pop into the message alert on her Omni as she was closing Olvero's note, she'd been stupidly optimistic.

Why should I have expected anything different?

Waves of supportive energy lapped out from the spot in Rett's mind occupied by Pam, the alien mindforce from some planet called Earth. Support was good, but it wasn't what Rett wanted right now. She wanted to take her frustrations out on something. Something to break, or kick, to reduce to particles. A rock, a frozen chunk of soil, anything.

Of course, in the spotless corridors of MainCommand there wasn't much, unless she wanted to start taking out her frustrations on important pieces of equipment . . . or people. Neither was an option.

The pain left by Jaq's parting had never abated. Loneliness gnawed deep inside, a hunger she couldn't seem to satisfy. Damn it. Despair and anger twisted more knots in her belly. She still couldn't believe it had happened—and that she had just sucked it all in like the good little soldier and let Jaq leave thinking he was in the right and everything was her fault.

So here I am thinking that since F-troop and Easy Force are running so smoothly again, other things would be easier to handle.

~Other things like Jaq.~

Rett answered Pam with a grunt mental and physical. She'd thought that when Pam came back, she'd feel better. She had—for a while. Despite Pam's familiar, supportive presence inside her, even despite Captain Etron's tireless and friendly attention, Rett didn't quite know how to feel anymore.

Jaq is gone.

Three simple words haunted her day or night, on duty or off. Only on active combat assignment was she safe from the gut-deep ache. She thanked all good deities that missions with the 2023rd and flying with the 114th AirSpacefighters had kept her hands full lately. As if her present thought had widened a crack in a frozen waterfall, more followed in a hot, hurting flood.

Jaq is gone. For four months, all she had from him were letters. He sounded happy. He had lots of friends. He felt, finally, as if he were making himself useful in a direct and practical way. What, as if his time with the 2023rd and F-troop wasn't at all useful? Maybe Jaq would be so damn happy he'd make that open transfer into a permanent one.

Just thinking about the flaming letter brought everything to the surface again.

I've a mission to fly, she reminded herself. *We're going to take out those coastal defense systems, go after those big guns and air bases they have farther inland, and make sure our invasion for Aurora continent is going to make landfall. After that, when we get back, we'll be getting the rest of the invasion going. I don't have time for anything else.*

For fifteen strides she went over the mission details in her head. For the next ten, she started a mental checklist of what would happen after those heavy weapon emplacements were destroyed. Her next visit to Aurora wouldn't be made above ground level. Ground, sea, and air units were being gathered from all over for a massive assault on the continent that was the Coalition's last supply of fuel insystem.

Rett growled softly under her breath. Her thoughts of the other troops being pulled in for the Auroran operation brought up another possibility she didn't want to consider. Like the fact

3

that the 21st Infantry, her father's unit, was being positioned as one of the first wave divisions for the invasion. It was inevitable that she and her father would end up in shouting distance of each other. The Nyorfian military was small, and this push was important, almost as important as the one for Circle had been.

And if the 2023rd and the 21st end up on the same base, Ariam will be sure to try to get us together.

Rett pushed back a fresh ache and let out a long sigh through her nose. *Can't decide what's worse now. Jaq's not giving me a chance, or Dad telling me I didn't stand one.*

Sinking back into her dark thoughts again was too easy. The Transportation and Supply unit Jaq'd taken a position with had just been redeployed, probably to the far north of the Epnocian main continent. When he wasn't actively 'porting supplies, he did work for MainCommand on the technical-mechanical things he was so good at.

Does he ever mention anything when I write back and tell him I miss him? He can't even write "I miss you too". He signs off by writing: "Tell everyone I said hi. More later, Jaq."

~At least he writes.~ Pam inserted her thought cautiously into the opening.

Wonder if he'd do it at all if I didn't write him first.

~Maybe it's all censored out or something,~ said Pam. ~You told me that sometimes the TRANS units go almost completely incommunicado when they're moving troops and supplies.~

That's not it. Rett knew what Jaq wanted of her, what he was holding out for. Obviously, he wasn't going to turn one wild hair on his head in an effort to consider her personal reasons about the situation.

~I know he didn't make much of an effort to talk to you and left things for granted,~ Pam said, ~but have you considered that maybe he's hurting as much as you?~

Rett growled. *I didn't accuse him of an offense he didn't commit. I didn't try to hide anything away from him—*

~You hid me.~

Go away, Pam. I think my life was better before you or Jaq came into it. It didn't hurt so much inside, just the outside.

~You were smothering yourself and well on your way to a breakdown before I got here.~

Like your life is so perfect? Rett thought. *Why don't you take care of that before you go off trying to fix mine?*

Pam's temper spiked. ~Like I went looking for some super-powerful godlike alien being and asked to be plopped into the middle of this?~ Instantly she felt guilty. Rett didn't need her anger. Rett needed support and understanding. She thanked goodness that Rett had other people around her who weren't shy about getting hardnosed when she started shutting herself off: Ariam, F-troop, Major Yidnar, Sergeant Semage, and Lieutenant Evetez—when he wasn't being a bubblehead. Rett might have her individual tiffs and quarrels with them all, but they were the people she loved and respected the most in two worlds. For the past decade or so, they had been Rett's family.

Pam tried again. ~Rett, I— ~

Oh, don't bother. Things will even out, they always do. As you like to say, been there, done that.

Rett's thought was harsh and bitter on the surface, but carried so much sad, weary forbearance that Pam's throat ached in empathy. Pam withdrew into a deep private level, wondering how to approach this. In spite of the outlets and diversions Rett had now, the morass of dark nightmares, repressed memories, and current heartaches managed to creep in with insidious tenacity. It simply wasn't normal.

The depressing stuff is hitting her more than ever, Pam thought on her private level. Making it worse was Rett's growing capability of blocking Pam. Pam couldn't buffer negative thoughts without Rett's cooperation. It was as if her Nyorfian friend was being attacked from the inside out.

Pam sat back in her corner, chewing on her imaginary finger-nails. What if it was her? Pam? What if she got put here in Rett's head to screw stuff up? No! She refused to believe that. Whatever pushed Rett's deep black moods came from *outside*. If Pam had been merged with Rett for an evil purpose, Ariam, Rett's sister, would have been able to tell. Pam was positive about that. Hell, Pam herself would have known. It wasn't as if she hadn't had plenty of chances to take Rett over completely and get her into horrible trouble.

Causing Rett harm was the farthest thing from Pam's mind. She had to believe she was put here to help. Her need to help was strong enough to risk Rett's tiff. So Pam left off her private musings and edged out farther into Rett's public mind. Maybe she could try a diversion.

~Say, you never answered why there wasn't a special holiday to mark a new year. I asked that the other day when you mentioned the date.~

I don't know why. Maybe because we're on GTC Standard time and not on a time system based on how long it takes either Nyorfias or Epnoce to complete an orbit around our sun. You know that. Rett's return thought was short. *Please, later?*

~Later. Later. Always later. I'm here now, Rett. I've been back more than two months since the drop on Complex 412 and only gone again for two days—your time—during Complex 63 and that fiasco with Avok not too long ago. You keep saying you want to talk to me, but you keep putting me off. Oh, we talk and all, but none of it has been deep, and you're all ripped up inside. You know talking it out helps to put things in perspective . . . ~

I told you, I haven't had time. Deities, you should know how busy I am, Rett thought.

~Sometimes I think this extra duty is only adding to your problems.~ Pam took another step out, even though Rett's retaliatory backlash had nearly flattened her and stung with every ounce of hard anger the Nyorfian had shown on discovering she and Pam were the "victims" of an ego-merge.

You're the biggest flaming factor adding to my problems! I don't need you telling me how to run my life. Just back out, okay?

Rett didn't need help from a dimwitted alien from a culture that regarded graphic reenactments of extreme violence as popular entertainment—even as games for children! She felt her lips and nose wrinkling in a sneer, but didn't try to stop it. No one was around to see, anyway.

Earth. It sounds like a place that would get along really well with the Yixolryn Coalition.

Those thoughts slipped right out from Rett's private level to the one she and Pam shared as if shot from a missile launcher. Rett tried to intercept them, but it was too late. Pam's mental presence flinched as if physically struck. Then her mental companion backed off so fast Rett thought their merger had broken.

She shook her head in self-rebuke, sorry for the harshness of her thought. Why was it so easy to slam Pam with all her bad feelings? Pam had nothing to do with this situation, with any of it. All the time her inner companion had been gone, Rett'd missed her as much as she missed Jaq. So why was she whining and blaming stuff on her ego-merge friend? Worse . . . insulting her. Pam had only been trying to be helpful.

Rett peeked quickly into Pam's place, just long enough to pick up that her normally cheerful and upbeat alien friend was in anything but a coherent or sociable mood.

She puffed out a breath, noting with irony that the instant she was going to need more time to make up for her actions with Pam, she had arrived at her destination. She was early, so as soon as she checked in here, she would find a quiet corner for a talk. Rett made the left into the AirSpacefighters flight operations center.

Time to shed her normal identity as Sergeant Rett, commando, Special Forces, to become Sergeant Rett, fighter pilot,

114th AirSpacefighters. It always seemed that the ID check from military police team on duty made the transition complete, just as her return to Section C put Rett the pilot away again until the next time she was scheduled for the flight line.

Right before Rett could make the change, Pam exploded.

~You know, I put up with a lot from you, because I consider you a friend; I know you're under the worst kind of stress, and I care about you. But I'm not taking this. For all your harping about Nyorfians having open minds, I'd think it impossible for you, Sergeant Open Minded Nyorfians Aren't Like That, to make such an outright, snobbish, *bigoted* comment. I hope it felt good.~

Pam's mental voice sounded as angry as Rett had ever heard it, her energy dark and edged with fiery reds and oranges. The emotion was so strong Rett's breathing quickened in response, her teeth ground together.

~If you want to talk to me in a *civilized* manner, you know where to find me. But probably by the time it is convenient for you, your Majesty, I may not be here any more. Not that you would care anyway. I mean, deep down, you've never stopped wanting me gone forever. I wish I could oblige you!~

Deities, Pam, I didn't mean—

~Piss off, Rett.~

Pam. I'm sorry!

~Fuck you, Rett. See this? The Kick Me, I'll Understand sign—the one that says I have to take everything you throw at me, deserved or not, and be understanding about it—is coming *down.* Now and forever.~

Following Pam's tiffed thought was a very graphic, detailed mental image of a great big muddy boot kicking shut the mental door. Hard. The impact almost knocked Rett right off her feet. If she hadn't been within arm's reach of a corridor wall, it would have. Making it appear as if it had been her intention all along to choose that moment to lean into the wall, Rett grabbed her

Omni from its belt pocket with one hand, scraped the other through her hair. Although she pretended to be staring at the device as if her life depended on it, she didn't see anything but the backs of her closed eyelids.

I deserved that. The familiar, sick churning started deep in her guts again. *Why am I acting this way?* Here she was, still angry with Jaq for having a similar attitude. Not to mention that she should have learned her lesson about allowing things to build up, not communicating. The not-communicating thing had caused the mess between her and Evetez. Caused her suspension.

How stupid can I get? Swallowing back her frustration and blinking back a sting in her eyes, Rett recovered her balance. Returning her Omni to her belt, she let out a sigh and continued to FlightControl.

I know you can hear me Pam. I apologize. I was way out of line. Rett didn't try to maintain any sort of blocks or barriers, not even the normal ones. She left all her defenses wide open so Pam would know how she really felt.

The door opened a little. Rett waited for it to open the rest of the way. It didn't. Instead, a clear image emerged: that of a stubby, freckled hand making a very peculiar gesture with one finger. Whatever that meant, Rett understood it was not complimentary.

The hand withdrew; the door closed with a tight bang once more, sending the ache in Rett's heart right to her head. Again, in a habitual reaction of agitation, her right hand went for her hair. Since coming to Epnoce, she'd let it grow out a little more, but it was still much too short for the really good yank she wanted to give herself right then.

Maybe it was just as well. *Ow!* She had to shake the headache, and fast, or she was going to have to sit out this mission. *Great. Just great.*

At least the argument with Pam got her mind off Jaq.

3.1.1 UNSPECIFIED AIRSPACE OVER AURORA CONTINENT, EPNOCE
0536.01.04 (LOCAL RECKONING)

"FANG!" THE VOICE OVER HER headset was urgent. "Two coming behind. You'll have to hold them. I'm a little busy!"

Rett peeled her fighter away from the pair of sleek, space-black Coalition pursuit craft and climbed into clear air. Using a new maneuver, she kicked the craft into a gut-wrenching loop that placed her above and behind the paired enemy fighters. The guns blazed and the tight formation of Coalition aircraft vanished into fireballs and fragments.

She maneuvered her fighter around to get back into a covering position for her wingpartner. Asherle destroyed another tandem pair seconds later. Rett cringed as a piece of something pinged off her canopy.

"They're all over the place—" another voice said, cut short, replaced by static as his craft exploded from a direct strike.

A fleeting thought, a name, a face was all the time she had to grieve. "I have this one, Skyfire," said Rett as another black fighter headed straight toward them, apparently intent on a collision course. *Must be out of ammo.* "Hold him . . . hold him . . . break down now."

Ash's craft dove, and Rett's shot blew the left side of the enemy ship into fragments.

"Thanks, Fang!"

"Ten more marks coming in fast." Captain Etron sounded calm, but his words were clipped. "Watch the deck! Divert them off!"

Rett shook her head and followed Ash's lead. She didn't know where all these enemy fighters were coming from. She didn't think they had that many left. They were coming in as fast as the squadron could take them down.

It made sense, she had to admit. They were seeing smarter fighting than ever before, more good strategy. As the pompous and foolish Coalition commanders who spent time trying to intimidate and prove their superiority were killed or captured, the smart ones who survived were finally allowed to plan and execute some hitherto unseen master ploys.

It was a little late in the war for that, especially now that the GTC forces had arrived to help the Nyorfian system.

On the other hand, it wasn't so late that it didn't present an immediate problem right this minute. The GTC was busy in space, most of them on the system's borders, some insystem with Nyorfian Spacemarines and AirSpacefighters, hunting down evasive Coalition troop carriers that still posed a significant threat should they get an opportunity to land.

She felt a stir from Pam's corner and despite the situation outside didn't try to push back or repress Pam's tentative emergence into her public mind.

~It doesn't look good right now, does it?~

No. Rett took a breath. *Pam, about before, I have to say I'm very sorry.*

~It's my turn to remind you that this isn't the right time and place for that, Rett. Wrong time for thinking about GTC troops that aren't *here*, too. Right now you need to fly.~

Although Pam still gave every impression of being hurt and angry, Rett sensed something else. Pam wasn't about to desert her. She was there to support her now with everything she had.

Outnumbered three to one. Rett kept one eye on her targeting display, the other on her ship's fuel reserves. *This is becoming suicidal.*

"This is suicidal," Captain Etron said. "Skyfire, Nightwing, Sharpeye, Kennet, make a run for it. Fang, you're with me. We'll decoy until they clear. Break off, the rest of you—now!"

She guessed he picked her to stay back with him because she wasn't as critically light on fuel as the others. What fuel she had wouldn't last very long. "Can't stay with you, Raptor One, I'm going to break starboard. We're about to get pinched in the middle of ten more problems otherwise."

Etron's fighter broke left the same instant she kicked hers to the right. Rett saw the black Yixolryn craft likewise divide forces. Shaking this bunch was going to take a little bit of finesse. She wished she could figure out how to divert and decoy up here as well as on the ground.

A soft chime alerted her to a call coming in on a different frequency. "We're still on for dinner, I hope?" Etron wanted to know.

We didn't have any plans. Rett tilted her head briefly in the direction of Etron's fighter as she switched frequencies to match. *What's he thinking, using an insecure frequency? No one uses this channel any more. Coalition pilots still monitor it—*

~Think the man has a plan,~ said Pam.

I hoped he clues me in to it before it's too late, Rett thought back.

"Shit, you have to ask? It's mushroom day," Rett said aloud. "You know it's going to take something big to make me miss any meals on mushroom day, especially dinner."

"And . . . later?" There was no doubt whatsoever what he meant. Even though they had never been lovers, Etron still made her want to think about the possibilities.

Which, she realized as she rolled her craft from a missile, *is exactly what he wants now. For the Coalition pilots.* She had to smile. It just might buy them some precious time.

"Later?" Rett made her voice as slow and smoky as possible. "You had plans?"

She hit a switch to spit a reflector at the missile before it turned back on her. Then she nudged Pam, who as always was ready with enough ideas to leave an unbroken string of them across the known galaxy. Maybe farther. She hoped she had pegged Pam's willingness to pitch in and help, despite her tiff, because Rett really needed Pam's help now.

Pam? Feeling creative? Think we can work tandem, like we did with Commander Stinky back at Complex 142?

~Let's go for it.~

Not to mention, Rett dared to add, *that I think you fantasize more about Etron than I do. He's all yours.*

~You don't know what you're asking me to do, Rett.~

Yeah, I do. Thanks, Pam. Rett started the cooling systems in her flightsuit and helmet. She'd need them. *Let's hope most of them are humanoid and this gives them something to think about besides shooting us down.*

"Mmm," Etron said. "Was hoping to convince you to participate."

Hoping the Coalition pilots were hanging on to every word, Rett said, "I have some ideas of my own about later." Then she let Pam take over the talking while she concentrated on everything else.

Rett was glad she wasn't paying attention to exactly what Pam was saying, but it had to be good, because right after a few of those ideas for later started coming out three of the Coalition ships collided with each other. Four others were so distracted by the collision they never noticed Rett or Etron get the drop on them. Some things only went so far, however, and while the humanoids were most affected, the non-humanoids remained dangerous, distracted, but not carelessly so.

Their ploy was enough to allow the remainder of the squadron to fall out of the battle and speed for home without pursuit. Rett kept enough attention on the secure channel to hear them call in. She let out a soft breath of relief they managed to escape and hoped those who'd taken damage made it back to Base.

13

Her thumb had barely depressed the fire control for the main gun when her fighter lurched and bucked. She fought it steady and hauled about to get a look at her pursuit.

"How bad are you hit?"

Pam drew back immediately. Switching her voice com back to their secure frequency, Rett answered. "Minor damage, electromagnetic shielding is down." She managed to get another Coalition fighter out of the action. "Toasted the port wing a bit. Nothing serious. Yet."

"The others are clear. If you can maneuver, run. I'll be right behind you."

"Not if you don't break straight up and spit some deflectors right now."

His hissed curse boomed in Rett's headspeakers. His fighter went vertical, the missile nearly clipping his rear stabilizers. The sparkle of the deflector attracted the heat-seekers attention, ending that threat.

Rett ignored the chorus of protests from her wounded machine and coaxed it into clear sky, keeping a sharp watch for potential threats. She glanced up a second before her proximity alarm went off—two coming at her from overhead. Damn. She targeted one and barely avoided a collision with the second. Didn't help that she was rapidly losing power and control response. A light haze of smoke from overheating or shorting-out instruments hung inside the cockpit.

Etron sounded rough. "Okay?"

"I'm fine." Rett eyed her instruments and returned most of her attention outside the cockpit. Nothing she could do for anything in here. "The ship's taken all it could handle. I've no control response. Everything's jammed, including the manual overrides. Anything moveable is locked tight—or getting that way."

She felt as if it was the strength of her body that kept the ship aloft at this point. For a brief moment, she was reminded of the shuttle trip from Nyorfias, when she and Ariam had wondered about the Spacemarines losing the mechanized control of their heavy armored shells. Wasn't much difference, she mused philosophically, between that and this.

Well, there is one important difference. She twisted her lips into a one-sided grin. *Gravity.*

"Come on, ship, you can do it." As her hands and feet kept busy on the ever-stiffening controls, she watched Captain Etron find another target and send it into fragments.

His voice cracked into her headspeakers. "I told you to run, damn it! What are you waiting for, written permission?"

"Raptor One," she said steadily, "I said everything was jammed. Systems are shorting out all over the place. In another minute I'll have no control at all."

"Try the manual eject."

"I am." Her left hand had been locked around the manual control for several minutes. "I've tried every means of opening the canopy. I'm not suicidal. Seems to be locked up as well." She'd already considered breaking the clear material somehow. The stuff was as strong as azurium-alloy deck plating. It would be easier to put her foot through the side of the ship than to make a stress crack in the canopy.

Well now, there's an option. But by the time I make it big enough for the rest of me, I'll just be a frozen smear on Aurora continent.

With her other hand, her feet, brute strength, and will, Rett fought her craft steady, forcing it somehow from what would have been a direct hit. The fighter's sluggish response wasn't enough. Once again, the craft lurched. Flames erupted along the fuselage as her left airfoil disappeared. Nothing would keep this machine aloft now. The crippled fighter tilted abruptly into a nose-first plunge toward the far below, frozen surface of Aurora continent. The whooping of the stall warning was lost in the babble of the other alarm signals.

Pam, thought Rett, *I'm sorry I for being such a logheaded jerk to you. And not making the time to talk.*

~Yeah, well—me too. I should have taken the opportunity to kick the snot out of you for saying what you did before. You really hurt me.~

Rett laughed. "You can go ahead and do it now," she said aloud. "It won't make much difference in how I'm handling this ship." Rett couldn't help but feel the leakage of disbelief and fear from her friend and appreciated Pam's effort to keep it locked up. She took a breath and applied both hands to the frozen manual eject control.

~I'll wait,~ said Pam. ~You're not getting off so easily. I'm getting out of the way so you can concentrate. Once we get to the surface . . . I'll finish kicking your ass from the inside out, and then after that, you just might have plenty of time to tell me *everything,* from the first time your people arrived in this system.~

Sounds like a plan. Aloud, she said to her com, "Well, Raptor One, not going to be able to make it for dinner tonight. Maybe another time." Jamming her feet against the cockpit deck so hard she was surprised they didn't puncture through the hull, Rett threw everything she had into her effort.

She detached herself from the intense, forceful, gut-twisting gyrations of her doomed fighter, closing her eyes to dismiss the sight of the wildly spinning planet's surface looming closer with alarming speed. Ignoring the smoke and flame, she wrapped both hands on the lever that would blow the canopy and eject her from the fighter.

I sure hope you're going to wake up in your own bed, Pam.

~Don't think that way. You're going to unstick it.~

Then Rett thought of Jaq. *I love you, Jaq,* she told his mental image. *I always did. I just needed to find out that it was real, not because you showed up at the right time and said or did the right things. Now I can't even tell you that.*

Sucking in a deep breath, Rett dismissed her interlude, focusing her full effort through her hands with the breath she expelled.

Pam wondered how this situation could feel even more unreal than the first time she discovered herself merged with Rett. She was glad Rett had closed her eyes—Pam didn't want to see. Not to mention it blocked any sensation of movement from outside. She couldn't help thinking . . . if Rett dies, what about me? Then she tried to imagine the stuck control coming loose under the Nyorfian's straining grip.

And it did.

~It moved! Try it again.~

Rett held the rest of her breath even as she imagined Pam's thought was true. Had there been some motion under her hands? Was that a clicking noise and a hiss of air from a slight motion of the canopy overhead?

More likely I broke it, Rett thought. Probably now the damn lever is going to come apart in my—

3.1.2 SECTION C MESS AREA, MAINCOMMAND, EPNOCE
0536.01.04 (LOCAL RECKONING)

SEMAGE SPUN AROUND AND CLOSED his fingers around his second-in-command's shoulder harness as she lurched sideways. The tray she'd been carrying crashed to the floor.

"Ariam, what is it?" Semage got his other hand on her. From behind, a wide-eyed Junior Sergeant Rimms had managed to thrust his own tray at a comrade and move swiftly enough to catch Ariam before her body crumpled to the floor. Rimms supported most of her weight now, craning his neck over her shoulder to peer anxiously into her face.

"She's out, Sarge. Down like someone shot her."

"Ariam." Semage felt for her pulse, puzzled and a little frightened.

Med Shenyver shouldered her way through the handful of B-troop personnel who had closed protectively around them. Semage sent one significant glance to the concerned and curious faces of the rest of his troop, who faded back to continue with whatever they'd been doing.

"What happened?" asked the B-troop medtech.

"I don't know. She just . . . went out." Semage had Ariam now and adjusted her in his arms as he looked helplessly at his third-up. "Went out like she caught a stun. Did you see anything, Rimms?"

Rimms poked at his glasses and shook his head. "She was reaching for a roll and . . . passed out. No sound, no gasp, no glance around."

Shenyver compressed her lips and made a humming sound. "She seems simply to have fainted, but what triggered it—I have no idea. Let's get her to Medical."

Semage started for the door, then stopped in his tracks. He turned his head first toward Shenyver, and then Rimms, who had taken a half-step after them. "Rimms, the 114th went over to punch some targets on Aurora this morning, didn't they? Find out if Sergeant Rett flew with them."

"I believe she did. Ariam mentioned it earlier . . ." Rimms' eyes went wide behind his corrective lenses. "Sarge—"

"Find Sergeant Trebor," ordered Semage. "Tell him to meet us in Medical. Then find Lieutenant Evetez and ask him to contact FlightControl and get an update. I'd prefer it if we kept off the com channels. I want to find out what's going on before everyone else knows."

Rimms nodded, spun on his heel, and left them. Settling Ariam more firmly against his chest, Semage continued into the hall, his teeth grinding together so tightly his jaws ached.

He'd heard, and noted on her record, that Ariam was prone to some sort of reaction when something extreme happened to her sister. Nowhere did it state or even hint that the effect was this abrupt or dramatic. If she passed out every time her sister was wounded or faced extreme danger, Ariam either would be dead now, or transferred off a combat Active position into one where such a reaction wouldn't endanger anyone else.

Whatever happened to Rett this time had to be . . . He let out a breath. Not much choice of conclusion there. He hoped he was wrong.

* * * * *

ARIAM MOANED SOFTLY AND DRAGGED her hands to her face. "What happened? Did someone hit me from behind?" She didn't realize she'd asked it aloud until a voice answered her.

"You would have been pretty focused on those fruit rolls to fall to an attack from the rear like that." A lame-sounding laugh followed. "We were hoping you'd tell us."

She blinked. Something was wrong. She saw Semage's freckled face nearby, heard his voice, felt the warm pressure of his hand. But . . .

19

"I can't feel you," whispered Ariam.

One of the hands that had pressed into her face reached to Semage's, spreading flat against his skin. Nothing. Just skin, the slight rasp of whiskers, flesh, warmth. Her only clue to his inner feelings was the deep furrow in his brow; the anxious concern in his hazel eyes, and the tightness of his mouth.

"We were getting lunch. You collapsed. Do you remember anything, Ariam?"

"I can't feel anyone." Ariam's voice rose slightly as panic gripped her throat.

"Your psi is down?" Med Shenyver moved into view, her hand cool on Ariam's wrist, her neck. "Whatever made you pass out probably shocked your system. I'm sure it's temporary. I'll have Rhozev check you to be sure."

Ariam moistened her lips and pulled her focus inward. Shenyver was right, her psi wasn't gone, but it was knocked out. The terror eased, allowing the return of rational thought. "Rett . . ." she said, her breath catching.

"Something happened to Rett?" Semage's hands tightened over hers. "Is she dead?"

"I don't know." Ariam closed her eyes. She remembered now. She'd been preoccupied. She always was when Rett was flying a mission with AirSpacefighters. Even so, she wasn't about to pass up those freshly baked rolls at lunch—there were big, sweet and chewy chunks of dried fruit just popping out all over them. But Semage was right—although she was enamored of her favorite treat, she hadn't been so taken with them that she would have been oblivious to anything tangible coming at her. Still, the moment she'd touched one, there was something like a big, bright flash in her head.

She woke up here, in Medical, with a worried Semage and a puzzled Shenyver hovering over her.

About Rett she felt nothing. Her psi was down, bruised, leaving Ariam as handicapped as if deafened by a loud noise or blinded by a bright light. Without a doubt, something had happened. Something extreme.

I refuse to believe she's dead. Ariam clenched her teeth. *I have to wait until I can concentrate on her.*

"Talk to me, Ariam."

"I'm all right." Ariam slid her hands free of Semage's grip. She pushed herself into a sitting position. "There's nothing wrong with me. It won't happen again." She sent a smile she didn't feel to the B-troop leader.

Semage didn't smile back. He moved one of his displaced hands to her shoulder. The other blocked her from swinging her feet over the edge of the bed.

"I'm *fine*," Ariam said.

Semage shook his head. "That's for Shenyver to decide."

"It might be best she keeps busy. But I don't want to pass her full combat Active until Med Rhozev has a look."

"Med Rhozev?" For a moment, Semage's puzzled frown increased. "I keep forgetting F-troop's medtech has direct specialty in the psi-talent department," he admitted.

"I don't need to see him," Ariam said. Her head was clearing with every passing second, the emotions of those around her seeping into her awareness like water from melting snow. "I'm fine. I—" *Shenyver's been hanging around Med too long,* snarled Ariam to herself in frustration as she saw the uncompromising face of the B-troop medtech.

"You're cleared for anything but combat until further notice, Sergeant," Shenyver said. "Since you're on free time, if you don't want to stay here, I suggest you await Med Rhozev in your billet or in the common area."

"Yes, Med." Ariam looked down, her fists clenching the material beneath them. Ignoring Semage's offered hand, she swung her legs off the bed, and left the Medical section.

"Ariam." Sergeant Trebor, stepping aside to avoid a collision with her, pivoted instantly to fall into step alongside. "Semage asked me to come here because something happened to you. What's up?"

"Keep walking, Trebor," Ariam said through clenched teeth. "If I stop . . ." She shook her head, unable to continue as her throat closed. In the next second, she stopped anyway and gripped Trebor's arm with intensity enough to make her sister's second-in-command hiss a protest.

A familiar figure in AirSpacefighter colors closed distance between them, accompanied by the rangy length of Major Yidnar on his left, Lieutenant Evetez on the right.

"Deities, it's the Sarge." Trebor's deep voice had gone so low Ariam wasn't quite sure if she had heard the words.

Ariam saw the same understanding in the bleak hazel eyes of Semage as he caught up with them. By the time the officers were in range, the three of them were at attention and showing nothing more than they were supposed to.

"At ease," said Major Yidnar. He gestured with his chin toward a break room the medtechs and assistants on duty often used. Ariam stood aside to let the others pass ahead of her, but Major Yidnar put a hand on her shoulder, the pressure indicating she was to go ahead. "Everyone take a seat at the table."

Ariam was about to take a seat. Instead, she put her hands flat on the table and leaned toward the battalion commander. "Sir, I already know Rett's in trouble. What happened?" She shifted her attention to Etron, who appeared drained but composed.

What Ariam sensed from inside him was a different matter.

Etron cleared his throat and took a deep breath before answering. "Sergeant Rett's fighter went down on Aurora."

"What happened—exactly?" Trebor's voice was just a little stronger than before.

"My wing encountered overwhelming resistance after we accomplished our objective and left our target area," Etron said. "I lost more than half my people. I would have come to you sooner, however—" His voice faltered again.

Ariam sat down and reached toward the hands the pilot held clenched in front of him on the table. Captain Etron was as closeknit with his group as any good leader, and despite his outward control, his personal pain and grief for his squadmates and friends was raw and strong.

"We understand your priorities, Captain," Ariam said with a gentle squeeze over his fingers. "And we appreciate you taking even more time away from them to come to us. I'm sorry for your losses."

Ariam's sentiment was echoed from Semage and Trebor. The Major and Evetez more than likely gave him some condolences earlier, for now their support was silent, visual, but to Ariam as tangible as more spoken words.

Etron didn't withdraw from her light touch. Instead, he bowed his head over the hand Ariam had placed over his. She willed him to accept the sympathy and strength she offered. As if awakening from a dream, he shook his head slightly and straightened in his seat. When his gaze lifted again to hers, there was puzzled wonder and deep respect in his regard.

"Go on," said Ariam softly. She withdrew her contact, but kept a mental finger on him, just as she had one on everyone in the room.

"Since we had more fuel to burn, I kept Rett back with me and sent the others left to make a run for it. Her ship took several critical hits and her last report was all systems had locked and failed."

This time, Ariam's head turned a little to her left to watch Trebor. His lean, hawklike face broke composure for one eyeblink before returning to a mask of such tight control it might have been carved in basalt. Above every other emotion that displayed on that fierce, craggy countenance for that tiny space of time was disbelief.

Ariam managed to catch his glance.

You said she was in trouble, not dead? Trebor mouthed.

Ariam nodded once. *I'm sure of it.*

"She couldn't get out?" Semage sounded ill. "I thought those fighters ejected pilots automatically when they were hit that bad."

Under the table where no one else could see, Ariam slid her right hand into his.

"Coalition has been using an electromagnetic pulse on a new frequency lately," Etron explained. "Normally our ships can block it. However, hers had already taken some damage, possibly those sensors. She said everything was jammed. That includes the manual systems, which definitely meant she took a good hard pulse, maybe two. Shot like that will lock everything mechanical or manual as if it was welded in place. She took another hard hit, and that was it. I flew back over when I could." The pilot's voice cracked slightly, steadied. "All I saw was pieces of the fighter. No life readings, not even the ident pulse from her locators. I'm sorry."

"She's *not* dead," Ariam said. "Whatever happened—"

"Shit, Ariam," snarled Semage with sudden heat, "whatever happened knocked you unconscious, right off your feet! That never happened before. Did it, Trebor?" His voice snapped and rumbled like flame given liquid fuel. "All those times things happened to Rett, every nasty episode, was Ariam ever incapacitated by them?"

"Sergeant Ariam wouldn't be with us now if that was the case." Major Yidnar cut short any possibility of discussing that aspect.

Ariam felt fine now, truly, her empathic sense as normal as ever. She wisely kept her silence, absorbing the wide range of emotions from the others, glad of them. Like her sister, she knew a diversion when she saw one. Putting her natural and trained abilities to the task of easing some of the more painful emotions and moderating the hotter reactions of her comrades helped to push back her personal fears and misgivings.

Knowing in her heart that her intuition was true, but unable to dismiss an all too humanoid shadow of doubt, Ariam lifted her chin. "EM pulse can knock out our locaters, too. She's not dead. I would know."

Etron shook his head. "As much as I want to believe that, there's just no way she could survive the impact, Ariam, unless she ejected. I saw no evidence that happened. No matter what strings Colonel Centra or Major Yidnar can pull, a recovery won't be authorized without verified readings. We already tried."

Evetez nodded. "MainCommand wouldn't budge."

Ariam turned to Major Yidnar. "Sir—"

"Ariam," Major Yidnar said gently, "even if Rett survived the crash, the possibility she made it through the next few hours is minimal. Especially considering she may have been injured. Last met reports said it was fifty below freezing, that's without adding the wind factor to it."

"We do carry emergency survival gear," said Etron, "and the flightsuits—"

Yidnar interrupted the pilot with a gesture. "Sergeant Trebor."

His face as frozen as glacial ice, Trebor fixed his attention on his commander. Ariam's heart went out to him, knowing what was coming. "Yes, sir?"

"You are in front of F-troop now, until further notice. Do you accept the command?"

As Ariam had maintained in her past as F-troop second, the last thing Trebor wanted was a sudden elevation to platoon leader. Not even if Rett had been right there and Yidnar was offering him his own troop. Ariam also knew Trebor would accept, without question, for love of his platoon sergeant. As if that familiar voice spoke right out: *Don't disappoint me, Trebor,* like any of F-troop, he'd answer instantly, *Never, Sarge.*

"I have command, sir. Sergeant Worren will second; Sergeant Nerrah will be acting third-up." His gaze slid toward Ariam, went past her to Semage. His query was plain.

Ariam sent encouragement in her return glance. She didn't have to look at Semage to feel his answer. He held on to hope, but his conviction wasn't too strong now.

Yidnar did not miss the subtle exchange. "Ariam, I do know that cold-climate survival skills are something you and Rett have practiced most of your lives as you grew up. But we can't do a thing right now."

"As Captain Etron said, we already asked. We were turned down so fast . . ." Lieutenant Evetez sighed, his blue eyes troubled and dark, the fingers of his right hand restlessly tracing circles on the slick surface of the table.

"We're still on to invade Aurora continent in three days. MainCommand also refused to move that up, or send Easy Force in to punch some preliminary targets. If Rett lives yet, and has her survival gear intact, she'll just have to hang in there until—" The Major left it unspoken. "You brought the chart, Captain?"

"Yes, sir." The pilot picked up the notepad he'd brought.

"Do you want to get back to your squadron?" the Major asked suddenly.

"I've time to go over this. I'd like to." He took a notepad marker from his sleeve clip, hesitated for a breath, and glanced at Ariam before turning toward the Major and Lieutenant Evetez. "I should contact Jaq Pym and Colonel Reve, since normally, if Rett was a full part of the 114th, I would have. Before I went that far, I thought I'd check. I'm not sure those people know she's on dual status."

Ariam dismissed her momentary peeve for being left out: honestly, she didn't have a real say in the matter at all. Despite that, she spoke up before her seniors could answer Etron. "Lieutenant, Major, I'd like to take that responsibility, and request that we keep the status as missing in action."

Evetez's hands stilled. She couldn't detect one hint of the usual mischief or humor in him. "Sergeant Ariam, as dependable as your psi talent is, we can't rely on it exclusively for confirmation of Rett's present circumstances."

"I understand, that, sir."

"What if we get confirmation and it doesn't align with your instinct?" Major Yidnar leaned back in his chair with his arms crossed.

He wasn't closing himself off, as his body language might imply. He simply didn't know what to do with his hands. Ariam saw that he tucked them beneath his upper arms, fingers clenched.

"Major, unless the confirmation provided is her physical body or a part of it that she can't exist without, I'd like to think that those who know me, and know Rett, will believe me." She then fixed Lieutenant Evetez with a challenging stare. "As far as relying on me for confirmation, Lieutenant: Rett's my sister. She was a part of me even before I was born. If I were GTC adept level, my feelings about even a stranger would be valid in a court of law."

"But you're not an Adept, Ariam," the lieutenant pointed out quietly.

"Someone needs to retest her," said Etron under his breath.

Again, Yidnar spoke up, getting them back on track. "Sergeant Ariam, no matter what, there's no denying you have the right to make the request, since you're Rett's closest relative and she's authorized you to make decisions on her behalf. All right. We'll hold back releasing this to the general record altogether for three days," he said. "I'll let Colonel Centra know as soon as we're done in here. And after three days, or until we hear otherwise, or are provided undeniable proof, we'll keep the status as missing in action."

27

Ariam agreed instantly. Holding back a known casualty or MIA from the general record even for a day was a huge concession, usually only made for personnel on covert operations. It was more than she'd expected. "Thank you, sir."

He nodded once but didn't look happy about it, nor did Evetez or Captain Etron. Ariam didn't blame them. She rubbed at her temples with the fingertips of her left hand. "Let me explain my reasoning. First of all, there's Jaq Pym. Everyone here understands his . . . feeling towards Rett. It goes deeper than any of you understand. If he hears some rumor that Rett's dead, or if it's made official because no one will believe my feelings on the matter, he might take his own life. That's part of his Zetinorian nature, and something no one can change."

Major Yidnar raised his eyebrows. "I didn't know that."

"Labonne explained a few things to us while we were at Complex 63," Ariam said. "And speaking of Complex 63, that's my second reason. Olvero and Aunt Valera. Aunt Valera is an Adept level Talent and precognitive, so it's possible she had some idea and was prepared enough to buffer for Olvero what happened to me. But I'm not sure how either she or Olvero would take hearing Rett was dead if their Talent told them otherwise."

Everyone except Etron, who didn't know about Olvero or Valera, nodded now.

"And then there's Dad—Colonel Reve. In any case, whatever the status was going to be, I'd like to be the one to tell him—to tell any of them— first."

"I'm sure you know best, Sergeant Ariam," Etron said.

The words he never added, "*But if it were me . . .*" went unsaid, but Ariam caught his context.

"I'm sure," added the pilot, "that with the permission of your seniors—Colonel Centra will allow me to transport you directly to wherever you need to go so you can deliver this news personally."

Ariam emptied her lungs in a long, soft exhale of gratitude. The best she had hoped for was a few tightband com messages. "Captain, if my seniors will clear me for such a thing I'll be in your debt."

Etron gave her a quick, small smile, a flash of his usual warmth easing the lines of tension around his silky brown eyes. For a moment, he looked as if he wanted to say something in return. Instead, he let his breath out slowly, swallowed, and after another brief smile glanced at his notepad for a moment.

"Sergeant Semage?" inquired Yidnar.

The B-troop leader's gesture of agreement was curt, but his agitation had nothing to do with what Ariam wanted to do, or with Etron's offer. "It's fine with me. Lieutenant Evetez?"

"I'll clear Sergeant Ariam as soon as you get permission from Colonel Centra, Captain," said Evetez. "Since the Aurora penetration is all-go, anything taking her elsewhere will need to be done with by tomorrow midday."

Etron nodded and gestured with his marker to the notepad. "So let me get on with this. The Major wanted me to show you this since he's fairly sure the 2023rd's trajectory will take you near this area." Captain Etron had uplinked his notepad to the big wall display in the break room. "She went down here." Etron circled the area on his notepad, added a cross-mark. "This is all forested, with a few remote tracking stations—lightly staffed, heavily armored, all equipped with anti-aircraft batteries." His marker made quick symbols in precise spots for each object as he spoke. "Coalition's dug in all along this area to hold onto the pipeline."

"If she survived, it's likely she was or will be picked up by a patrol," said Evetez. "Intelligence says they're scavenging all they can, even hunting."

Ariam growled. "I've seen what they consider *hunting*," she said. Visions of partially butchered animals, great destructive scars in stands of food-bearing plants, huge tracts of forest burnt to the ground just to drive out a few animals, fish hunted with explosive—with only a few taken, the rest left to rot, or fish traps filled with dead and dying fish and water creatures rose along with her temper. "If they're doing the same thing here, it's going to take the Auroran ecosystem decades to recover—if there's anything left of it. Look what happened on Nyorfias." Then she swallowed. "I apologize. I didn't mean to go off topic."

"Any Nyorfian, especially those used to living off the land before this war, completely agrees with you, Ariam," Yidnar assured her.

Yes, well, she shouldn't have let her outburst get the better of her. She felt better for venting, though. Calmer. Angling her position toward Etron, she reached again to make a soft contact, laying her fingers on his wrist. "Captain, is it possible any of your other pilots ejected safely and might get captured by a patrol?"

"Of course it's possible." Etron's eyes closed for several seconds. "However, among those of us who are left, none of us who saw the others get hit saw any of them make it to the ground. Those who ejected were shot down just as quickly. I had one pilot's locators tagged for a while, but the signal went flat after a few minutes."

Ariam bit her lower lip from the inside. The locators that most military personnel wore into combat sent a strong active signal only when the bearer was alive. The device continued to transmit even after it was removed, but only for a short time. However, once body temperature went below a certain level, the signal changed and diminished, ranging only a matter of a handful of miles and broadcasting a different frequency, which most referred to as "going flat". Not once in the short time the devices had been in use on Epnoce was any soldier found alive after their locator signal had gone flat.

Etron was taking this hard. She couldn't help but be reminded of Rett after the battles for the Wide River Gap and Circle. He was hanging on to himself by remaining focused on his tasks, but he was hanging on by his teeth. Ariam decided it was time to end this meeting.

"Captain Etron," Ariam said, "if you flew over here in one of those little jumpers, one of us should take you back now. Lieutenant Evetez is qualified for shortrangers now, as is Sergeant Semage. That way you can be with your squadron, get some rest, and at new day tomorrow, we can get started on the trips I must make."

Evetez rose instantly, taking the cue, sending Ariam a glance of approval. "Good idea. I'll be happy to take you back, Captain."

To his credit, Captain Etron didn't argue. He slid his marker back into a sleeve clip, tucked his notepad beneath his left arm, and pushed back his chair.

"I'll go with you part of the way," said Trebor. His hand squeezed Ariam's shoulder as he stood, reinforcing the bond of trust between them. Of anyone present, Trebor had the most faith in her feelings about Rett. His lips formed words no one could hear, but that Ariam interpreted as easily as if he'd whispered in her ear. *I'm putting every credit on you being right.*

"You've really grown into your Talent, Ariam," said Major Yidnar after the others left. "Very well done. Etron's right, maybe we should have you re-assessed." He stood and came around the table, pausing at her chair. "For right now, though, come here." He opened his arms, and Ariam didn't refuse the offer. It wasn't the first time the Major had taken one of them into his embrace as if he was their father instead of their commander.

Ariam leaned into him and closed her eyes. Letting go any pretense for those few moments meant a lot to her, to any of them. She tightened her arms around him in silent thanks before stepping back and taking her seat again. Yidnar brought some water bottles from the cooler unit and took the seat Trebor had vacated, handing a bottle each to Semage and Ariam before drinking off half his own.

"You know, this isn't very far off the coast," Semage said as he studied the map display of the area Etron had indicated on his Omni. "Only one hundred and eighty miles or so . . ."

Water bottle halfway to his lips, Major Yidnar sent a sharp glance to the B-troop leader. "Sergeant Semage."

"Sir?"

"*Don't even think about it.* I've already had to give Evetez a warning. I don't need to lose any more of my lead people—temporarily or otherwise. This invasion is far too important to be put at risk for a rescue mission. When you go to Aurora, it will be with the rest of the battalion."

"It was just a wild thought, sir," Semage said, his gaze dropping back to the Omni.

Ariam again reached beneath the table to slide her hand into his, gripping it tightly in a blend of appreciation and support.

3.1.3 UNSPECIFIED LOCATION, AURORA CONTINENT, EPNOCE
DATE AND TIME UNKNOWN

. . . I THOUGHT YOU DIDN'T feel anything when you were dead. I thought it would be . . . well—nothing. I was dead before, and that's what it was. Nothing and painless. Then again, maybe I wasn't really dead before . . . I'm freezing! Pam . . . ? Are you dead, too?

Pam?

Shit.

Pam was gone.

Deities. Whatever had jolted her thought processes spread with quick agony to every extremity. "If this is being dead," Rett said, clenching her teeth, "someone has to set the record straight. Being dead hurts!"

Her head felt as if she'd caught an entire drill's worth of SMG with it. Someone had used her body to bludgeon a mature longcone to splinters. She tried to move her hands. Just thinking about that brought more pain and, despite her present chilliness, the oily-slick, cold sweat of nausea.

Then Rett remembered, and she forced her eyelids open, hissing as her eyelashes stuck together. From blood or ice, or both, she didn't know.

"I'm not dead." Coherent words or groan, she heard them over the pounding buzzing in her ears.

She and Pam hadn't imagined the eject control moving or coming apart—it *had* moved. She had been blown out of her fighter at treetop height. The whirling impression of snowy tops of trees flared stronger than her headache. She'd seen them for less than a second before blacking out.

But wait . . . am I sure? I saw trees from inside the cockpit, too. My chute didn't have time to open . . . I don't even think the fighter canopy opened completely . . . She thought hard, as painful as it was, but couldn't remember. Anyway, that would explain part of the pain in her neck and head. There was no way she could have gone through the canopy material and survived. *As hard to break as I am, I know my limits.* She kept her laugh short and inside, since the rest of her hurt too much to risk a real laugh. *Face it, I'm dead.*

Arguing with herself made her feel even worse. She identified the pain in her jaw and forced her teeth to unclench. Her head ached, throbbed, felt five times its normal size, and she moved it, hoping to ease the pressure. The deeper flash of pain that ran the length of her semi-frozen body suggested she was indeed alive.

Her surroundings came into a fuzzy focus. Tree limbs and branches were broken and scattered on the snow around her. She started to shiver.

No wonder . . . she'd had the cooling ability of her flightsuit turned on, and having that cold air trapped next to her now wasn't a good thing at all when even colder air was attacking her from all around.

I have to get up. Not safe. Any movement of her head was agony. Her nausea spiked; only determination kept the light meal she'd had inside her where it belonged.

"I think I'm in trouble." She focused again on her personal inventory. Forcing down her headache and nausea, she flexed and checked muscles and limbs, searching for damage, assessing her condition with a minimum of movement. She was bruised, cut up, burned, scraped; her breathing fast and shallow . . . probably due to shock; she had a fierce, pounding headache.

Yeah, I think I remember hitting the fighter's canopy with it, she thought wryly. No doubt knocked down a few trees for good measure. She squinted at her helmet, half buried in snow. The fastenings hadn't broken—a tree branch or something must have scraped it off. Lucky she hadn't broken her neck. Lucky for her the strap had been loose enough to yank the helmet off, or she might have.

Concussion, yes, definitely.

She was freezing cold, getting colder by the second. Other than that, her injuries were minimal. The crash left her too cold, dazed, and stiff to move on her own. She wasn't going to think about her impaired vision right now. If she lived long enough and it still didn't clear up, then she'd start to worry.

She forced her hands to move, running them over her body with sharpening awareness. She managed to roll to her side, regretting every agonizing increment of motion even as she channeled the pain into sources of the energy she lacked. Her helmet was right there, but it seemed a mile away as she reached for it. She flipped it over, hands and fuzzy vision examining the surface for clues. The face shield was gone completely; the front, top and left side so dented she was surprised her head hadn't been pushed down to the level of her navel.

"Deities, no wonder my head hurts."

More surprising, the padding within seemed dry and cushiony instead of hard and frozen with blood. She supposed that was a good thing, and dismissed the matter. She had to get up, no matter what condition her head was in, or she wasn't going to have time to worry about anything.

A length of tree branch assisted in getting her partway vertical. Despite the bone-numbing cold, her face felt hot and flushed. Her breaths came in short, hard gasps. She fought the urge to vomit and made herself relax. The blurry forest seemed to be spinning slowly around her, and that didn't help matters any. Even after she closed her eyes, she could still feel the planet revolving beneath her knees.

Then she heard them. The sounds were more chilling than the frigid air, some deep and bellowing, others high-pitched and yelping. At once unfamiliar and familiar. *Growtus.* They weren't the Nyorfian variety Rett was familiar with, the species her mother had made an area of special study. These were Auroran growtus, unique to Epnoce.

"I'm not going to get out of being lunch this time," she said. She gripped her branch hard and pushed herself up. Her hands slipped before she found any balance and she fell heavily to her knees, the impact causing her to bite her tongue. "Ow. Damn it." *It's the little things,* she thought as sudden tears of pain formed in her eyes. She forced them back ruthlessly before they froze. *I guess that answers the next question. There's no way I'm going to be able to climb a tree.*

Her body simply wasn't cooperating. Its movements were as sluggish as the controls had been in her crippled fighter.

She tried to peer in the direction of the sounds, despite the real danger, curious for a glimpse of the big predators. She remembered that Pam had, at first, thought the growtus were like Earth animals called "wolves". After Rett showed her images on her Omni, Pam had changed her mind. *"Not wolves. Those things are more like bears. Cougar-sized bears that live and hunt like wolves in packs."* And of course, Pam had to make mental images of the Earth animals she was comparing them to, most of which were mammalian and quadruped, but looked like nothing Rett had ever seen before.

What was coming for her wasn't anything like a Nyorfian growtu. These were twice as large and, at least among the Coalition troops on Aurora, regarded as more dangerous than the freezing cold.

"Stop dreaming," she said to herself. "Get focused. Maybe you're on the menu for lunch, but you're not going without a fi- *huuh!*"

Something huge and heavy slammed into her. The very last of her energy went into taking the force of her fall with her shoulders instead of her abused head. After that, she couldn't move to defend herself even if she wanted to. She stared in awe at the massive animal that snarled over her trapped form. The gleaming, bluish-white teeth were as long as her fingers. She had a good view of them as they rushed toward her, droplets of saliva hitting her cold skin like points of fire. The snarling, snapping jaws closed on the collar of her flightsuit and two mighty shakes shredded the strong material as easily as a knife blade.

For the very first time in her life, Rett surrendered, completely, without reservation. She'd learned from infancy that nature could not be forced, that it had its own balance, and one had to work with it rather than against it, no matter how hard it seemed. Like fire, floods, and earthquakes, the growtu was a natural, elemental force of nature, as much a part of her worlds and the ecosystem as she was. The strong survived, the weak were lunch, and no amount of canny instinct or human ingenuity was going to change that, not for her, not at this time and place.

She counted herself lucky to be killed this way, thanked all deities for it. Better the Auroran growtus than the Coalition. At least the growtus belonged here; they were part of her, part of her worlds, a part she never wanted to change. It felt right. For a brief second, her blurred vision locked with that of the slavering predator standing over her. Then she turned her face aside and relaxed her taut body, accepting whatever it willed.

Please make it quick, growtu. She felt only weariness as the powerful animal, still gripping her ripped flightsuit, shook his head again, rending it further. Its hot breath smelled of blood.

A great weariness washed through her, and warm wave of sleepiness. Part of her argued that was wrong, that it was dangerous. Rett dismissed the warnings. It was far too late to resist or worry. It would be better this way . . .

3.1.4 UNSPECIFIED LOCATION, AURORA CONTINENT, EPNOCE
DATE AND TIME UNKNOWN

THERE IS A CHANCE TO save her. It would push the rules of this Game, but I will still be within bounds.

As other growtu shapes gathered around their leader, their icy eyes alert as they waited for him to make the kill, Pheasyce flickered into their sight, creating a scent marker they would also recognize.

Hesitating, the giant silver growtu ceased his snarling. He turned his head, fixing frost-pale eyes on her visible form, which actually cast a shadow. The other growtus of the pack flattened to the snow, silent, waiting.

"Neophyte, you go too far! I protest this move!"

That she had agitated Xonomer was plain—and surprising. Then the enormous presence of another life force surrounded them.

"Pheasyce, you must not intervene." The Voice was as passionless and cold as the void of space.

Pheasyce acknowledged the reminder of the Arbitrator, but didn't look away from the growtu leader. "I must not directly intervene with my key Player. My influence of peripheral Players, however, is allowed, provided I limit it to suggestion."

"Those are not *Players*, those are *animals*." Xonomer sneered with contempt.

"Every molecule, every rock, every grain of dust and pollen, plant and fungus, every creature of these worlds are my Players."

"You will force these creatures to go against their nature?" Xonomer laughed. "Then you forfeit your key Player. We shall end not only the third level, but the entire Game, here and now."

"And what do you know of their nature?" Pheasyce asked. "You know not even the natures of your own Players. Even they are driven by something far greater than any of us." Pheasyce gestured toward a distant Coalition patrol trudging through the snow. "Look well at your creatures."

The only thought on the minds of the patrol was their need for warmth, food, and shelter. They had only performed a cursory inspection of the burning wreckage of the fightercraft, not bothering to confirm if the pilot had been inside. Instead, they had agreed to say the pilot was dead, no remains were found.

"And yet you," added Pheasyce in measured reminder, "demand their compliance, force some of them constantly to go against their natures. Despite all that, it seems their need to survive the conditions of this world are stronger than your demands, than the fear they have for their commanders."

"My Rules for the Game are not the same as yours, neophyte. I have no precious Balance to maintain."

The Arbitrator spoke again. "However, you took your move, Xonomer, and you cannot change it. Pheasyce, tell us of your intentions."

Pheasyce said, "I ask the growtus not to go against their natures, rather to go with them. If nature takes a small step sideways, the choice, as ever, will still be theirs."

"The attempt will be allowed," said the dispassionate tone of the Arbitrator.

Before Pheasyce could make her suggestion to the growtus, however, the snowy landscape itself offered a solution.

And when the outcome was observed, Pheasyce remained in place, frozen with surprise, while Xonomer disappeared in a rage.

3.1.5 UNSPECIFIED LOCATION, AURORA CONTINENT, EPNOCE
DATE AND TIME UNKNOWN

FIGHTER GOING DOWN. EJECTING RIGHT above treetop level and slamming into a formless blackness. Freezing. Fingerlength fangs about to rip her throat out . . .

Something wet was spreading over her chest. Rett tried to move her arms, but her movements were hampered. *Did the Coalition find me?* Her mind came fully alert in time to stop her body's trained defensive reaction. *No. I'm in no condition to attack or defend right now.*

Bewildered, she thought hard. What happened? She had to remember. Hadn't she been attacked by growtus? Eaten? If so, what was this?

Where am I?

She didn't bother trying to use her ability to scope energy auras, her head hurt too much. She concentrated on her body. She was still very cold, but not freezing. The still-spreading spot of cool dampness on her chest brought her attention to the fact that a great deal of her shoulders and chest was missing flightsuit. Even the inner uniform was ripped open to her waist. The only thing between her and the air was her breast support, left whole by virtue of its skintight fit and the attacking growtu's mouthful of insulated flightsuit and inner uniform. The sturdy material of her support wasn't very good protection from the cold, but Rett was glad of even that thin barrier when something else wet and icy cold landed with a plop over her upper body and face.

"Arrgh!" Rett snorted her nose clear, kept her eyes and mouth shut, and concentrated fiercely on continuing the assessment of her body. It hurt, a stiff, achy soreness that movement would ease; her headache was moderate, and she had an incredible thirst. The icy stuff on her face was melting, tempting her. Not yet. Not yet.

She cautiously flexed every muscle from toes to shoulders: everything worked. She didn't feel any body parts broken or missing. Her vision had cleared—for that she felt a profound relief. The shock of wet cold brought a sharper awareness to her limbs, and she realized her arms and legs were not restrained by anything artificial. Tree limbs and branches entangled them. This only added to her confusion.

She shoved that aside for the moment.

A sweet, clean scent filled her nostrils. Alien, but with familiar undertones. The air temperature was cold, but tolerable.

Not tolerable enough, however, to merit remaining motionless and half-exposed. She recognized that even if she was no longer in danger of frostbite, she was still in danger of hypothermia. With great caution, she lifted her head and shoulders in hope of making sense out of the situation.

She lay half in, half out of a pile of dead and dying limbs, branches, bark, and twigs. On either side, frost-coated earthen walls, rough with exposed tree roots and stones, extended upward to a pale, translucent roof broken only by a single hole, through which she glimpsed more branches and a darkening cloudy sky.

I fell. Something . . . She closed her eyes again, fiercely trying to remember. Yes, there had been another falling sensation, but at the time, she'd been past caring.

Serendipity? Or . . . A deep shiver started at Rett's feet, shot up her spine, and spun around a few times in her head. Too easy, too convenient, to forget she was already a target of personal interest by powerful paranormal beings. They didn't arrange her ego-merges with Pam for nothing. And if they were powerful enough to merge minds without regard to space or time . . .

What do you want from me? I wish you'd let me in on it. Oh, and by the way, make up your minds if you want me dead or alive. Pam might say I've never a dull moment, but damn it, I would like a nice interval of dull moments to break up the monotony of always being in a life or death situation. How about it?

Blinking the last of the haze from her vision, Rett took a more detailed look around her surroundings. The light filtered through the hole and a forearm's depth of loose snow over a more tightly packed bottom layer. Probably an icy layer, if it held her weight for any amount of time after that growtu knocked her over what . . . a ravine? Ditch? Old creek bed? A crack in the planet's surface left by an earthquake? Whatever it was.

The crack was narrow, barely wide enough to lie flat. Right now, she was semi-inserted into a deep bed of plant debris. She struggled to pull herself out, a feat not at all simple. Dry twigs and branches snapped into powder as she moved, sinking her deeper.

"Okay, then deeper it is." Instead of trying to go up, she concentrated on clearing a space around herself. At first she moved slowly, soreness and cold-stiffened limbs preventing any other kind of movement. As she got closer to what looked like the floor of the crevice, she realized more than her upper body was warming—so were her legs, which had sunk into the loose, powdery material beneath all the dead tree branches.

"Of course." The decomposing organic material gave off heat. Rett knew right then she'd found her key to survival.

Her hands went to her head. "Of all the strange things that have happened to me," she said, "this has to be the top. I mean, I would have expected an ego-merge before I expected to survive crashing a fightercraft into an arctic continent and falling into a crevice where it's warm . . . well, warm compared to outside. Much less fall into the crack while a giant snow growtu was trying to rip my throat open. I should be grateful the growtu didn't fall in here with me."

She kept talking aloud, not quite trusting that her hearing wasn't going to act up on her again. Not to mention that after her brief activity, her head was sore enough—inside and out—that tuning out her own thoughts would be too easy. Maybe it was weird, but it hurt less to talk her thoughts aloud than think them in silence.

While her hands and fingers were on her head, she explored that area, probing carefully. There was still a tender, mushy swelling the size of Centerland Lake over most of it. Some lesser bruises and cuts all over her head and face. She was grateful none of her cuts and scrapes showed any telltale sign of infection. She might have inherited a formidable immune system from her offworld mother, but she wasn't impervious to infection.

Pulling off her supple, insulated leather gloves and thanking all deities that she had them, she examined her hands for signs of frostbite, then checked again over her exposed skin and felt her face. It felt sore and puffy, but not as bad as she'd expected. A bit of frostbite on her nose and cheeks, lower face. She laid her hands flat over those parts now to warm them. "How long . . . ?" Her breath deflected off her palms, making her skin tingle and sting. "How long was I down here? Hours? Days?" Not days—more of her would be cold damaged. How long then? Where was her chrono? *Oh . . . broken. And not my wrist or hand?* She made a face. *Lucky. I was lucky.*

She brushed away itchy particles of detritus from torn clothing, even into the close fit of her breast support. Removing the irritating bits gave her the opportunity for another careful, close look at herself. Her skin was chapped, cracked in places, reddened, cold-damaged certainly, but nothing serious or permanent. Yet. She'd have to figure out something to do about the cracking, which might lead to nasty complications.

She draped the slashed material of her flightsuit over her exposed portions, wondering what she could use to repair the damage. If she had ejected properly, a survival kit would have accompanied her. Wherever that kit was now, it sure wasn't in here with her.

Rett pondered for a moment. "Of course, all the sense *was* knocked out of me." She reached into her flightsuit, into her inner uniform. Brightening, she started to empty the contents of her pockets. Feeling as if she discovered fire, she withdrew an assortment of items and laid them carefully in a row for inspection.

"Camo tape—never leave home without it. Markers. Omni. Sidearm. Knife. Pocket med pack—couple roll bandages, medicated wipes, a gelpack, burn stuff, and antibacterial ointment. Better save that for emergencies, there's not much. A water bottle. Four packs of nuts, two fruit bars—a bonanza. Yum, my favorite kind. Forgot about those. A handful of cording. Perfect."

She beamed at her bounty, especially the camo tape. Etron had laughed at her for carrying it, made a habit out of teasing her about transferring the tape from her Special Forces uniform to the jumpsuit she wore while on duty with the AirSpacefighters. Having not been introduced to the many uses of camo tape in his profession, he didn't understand the stuff could be used for so much more than making things blend in with their surroundings.

After testing the solidity and depth of the material below her feet, she took advantage of the space she had cleared to stretch. She relished the pull, tug, and tight pain of her muscles . . . she was *alive*. Didn't matter what was responsible: the grace of whatever aliens, gods, or deities, or sheer luck. She was alive, grateful for it. And she was going to stay that way.

She began applying tape to her torn clothing. Body heat was her most precious resource now. She'd been lucky to escape severe frostbite and hypothermia this long. This was Aurora; the warmth inside the crevice was deceptive. Although snow had fallen and definitely had melted on her body, the lack of icicles along the snowy ceiling of the crevice was proof enough that both temperature—and humidity— were low.

"There. That should hold." She gathered the rest of her things and carefully stowed them in the outer pockets. What next? She eyed the frost-lined walls of the crevice.

"I don't think I should try climbing yet. But if I'm going to be stuck down here . . ."

The thought produced an instant cramping in her guts. Not from her fear of tight spaces or confinement: from a need to relieve herself. She glanced up at the gray sky visible through the opening in the snow. Was it getting dark or getting light? How long had it been?

She frowned as she realized she had forgotten an important part of checking her other technological assets: to see if they were functional. She already knew her chrono was useless. The locator . . . she couldn't feel it through her flightsuit. She stuck her hand inside and dug around beneath her right arm, where it should have been adhered to her skin. It was gone, but something else was in its place, a huge bruise that had simply been waiting for her to dig at it that way so it could explode into full fury.

"Probably coming down through those tree branches." Rett winced. "Ow. Well, locator's probably in bits. I'm not stripping down right now to find it." Next, she took her Omni. It powered up, but she could only access her local files, and she didn't dare try to access the networks, not even to find her position. Not until she knew what was out there.

She stared at its time display. "Fifteen hours since I last remember checking time." That had been sometime during the battle in the sky. "Fifteen hours. It's not getting dark up there, it's getting light."

"Ariam will know I'm not dead . . . the problem is that only people from F-troop will put any real faith in that."

Her head hurt too much to speculate on what would be happening back at the Base.

She sighed. Again, she eyed her shelter. Yes, shelter, she had to think of it that way. Now favoring her right arm, she half pushed, half dug her way through the dead limbs and detritus a body length toward one of the narrow ends, and took care of her bodily needs. Then she returned to the larger clearing she had made. Remaining directly beneath that hole in the snow wasn't an option.

45

After some rearranging, she settled deep into the warmth of the decomposing layer, arranged a shielding weave of larger branches and limbs over her, and settled back with half of a fruit bar and some water. Nibbling, she filed the points she knew as fact: she had crashed on Aurora, had the clothes on her body, the handful of items from her inner pockets, her renewed sense of survival, and this unexpected shelter.

Rett thought about that, and smiled. Other than the lack of warm clothing, she had a lot more now than Special Forces allowed in survival training. "All I ever had then was me and uniform. And whatever I could find . . . rocks. Sticks. Bugs. This should be like . . . going on leave." She chuckled and took a final sip of water before returning the flexible container to a spot next to her skin. Settling down as comfortably as she could, she decided that maybe between now and the time she was ready to try going outside that she could figure out why being unconscious was so exhausting.

3.1.6 NEAR COAST ON MAIN CONTINENT, EPNOCE
0536.01.05 (LOCAL RECKONING)

ALTHOUGH THE FIGURE APPROACHING THE mobile office was covered head-to-toe in insulated outer gear, Ariam knew it was Jaq. She'd know him even psi-blinded. She waited as the big Zetinorian shook snow from his hood and jacket.

"Ariam?" He paused in surprise, one foot still outside the door. "Ariam, what are you doing here?"

"Hi, Jaq. Come in all the way."

"Is this allowed? I thought—" His glance went past her to the dark fighter pilot, and the Zetinorian's eyes seemed to get laser-bright as his pupils contracted to nearly invisible points. At the same time, his platinum crest lifted.

"Jaq," Ariam said in a sharp tone, going to his side. His attention shifted back to her, and the flash of aggression receded. She took his arm, nudging him towards a chair. "Sit down." She slid her grip to his hand, taking it between both of hers.

"It's Rett?" The blood drained from his face, leaving his ruddy skin looking like rusty ash.

"Jaq, listen. You trust me, remember? *Listen* to me." Ariam squeezed his hand tighter. "Yes, it's Rett. Her fighter crashed on Aurora and no one knows where she is. But she's not dead. No, look at *me*, not at him. Captain, if you don't mind—"

"I'll be outside."

She didn't turn to acknowledge Etron's exit. Instead, with her left hand she threaded her fingers into Jaq's sensitive hair. That got his complete attention. "Captain Etron knows what he saw, but *I* know what I'm still connected to."

Some of the deeper color started to come back to his face.

"As for being allowed to visit an active TRANS unit, I received special permission. I wanted you to hear this news from me."

"What does it matter what I heard, anyway? Etron—"

"Jaq, *stop* it." Ariam twisted her fingers in his wild locks. "Ow!"

"I can't *believe* you're still feeling sorry for yourself. You still think *you* were the one who was wronged, don't you?" Ariam compressed her lips for a moment and shook her head. "Oh, Jaq. If only you open yourself to the truth. It's there, down inside you. You always had the truth from Rett, too."

"It doesn't much matter now, does it," he said, looking away.

Ariam groaned. "Listen to me. She's *alive*. No matter what you might hear, unless you hear it from me, Rett's still alive." She let the few multihued strands in her grasp loose, smoothing them, letting her hand rest there on his temple as she encouraged him. "She loves *you*, and she *needs* you, no matter what you might still think. And Jaq—if you take your own life, it would kill her: from the inside out, in the worst possible way. Do you want that?"

"No." He swallowed and closed his eyes.

"I can't stay much longer. Please tell me you'll be all right."

Jaq smiled, wan and pale, and maybe only halfway, but a smile all the same. "So, should I still plan on coming back in two months?"

Ariam threw her arms around him. "You'd better. Please try not to worry. Remember, no matter what you hear, unless you hear it from me, or hear it from someone with irrefutable evidence, she's still out there, and there's always a chance. We're set for the invasion, and we're going to find her. I'm sure of it. And I've already asked for a message to get pushed through to you as soon we know any good news."

Jaq hugged her back. "Thanks, Ariam. Does Rett know how lucky she is to have you for a sister?"

Ariam kissed his cheek. "Yes, she does. And I'm counting on having you as a brother. It's been my hope since the first time I let myself see you for who you really are. So don't let me down, Jaq. Don't disappoint me."

His little smile grew more as she used Rett's familiar maxim. "I'll do my best."

"I've already stayed longer than I should." She hugged him again. "Take care, Jaq. We'll see you soon."

3.1.7 **Unknown location, Aurora continent, Epnoce**

As RETT STUCK HER HEAD into the open, the colder air hit her like a physical blow. The inner lining of her nostrils shriveled in protest and she went into a hard, short fit of coughing. She had to look at the good side of that instantly: her bruised ribcage was feeling much better after sleeping for so long.

Damn, but the reality of the harsh temperature was daunting. She made herself stay in place and listen hard. Not even a breath of wind . . . all quiet. She gathered herself so that she could push the rest of her body from the opening, but before she could take a deep breath, her vision grayed and her hands lost their grip. Hissing in pain and vexation, Rett slid partway down the wall, fell the rest of the way to the bottom. She thanked all deities for the way the dead plant material fractured beneath her weight and the forgiving powdery surface below that.

Damn it, Pam!

~I'm sorry! I'm not the one that does this!~

Rett clamped both hands over her head and squeezed her eyes closed. *Ow . . . ow, ow, ow. I'm not going to throw up. I'm not. I won't . . .*

~This is one hell of a headache. No fracture?~

I don't think so. Concussion . . . yes. Rett pulled herself together, willing the moment of intense nausea to pass. She pressed her upper arms to her sides, where fresh aches kept her from taking the deeper breaths she longed for at the moment.

~My God, Rett, you're just one giant bruise from top to bottom, inside and out, feels like. Anything broken?~

No bones, anyway, thank all deities. Can't vouch for anything else. You should see my helmet. It's a good thing I had one on. It's out there somewhere, with my survival gear. I was going to try to find it until you decided to crash into me. Are you okay? Were you gone long?

~Three days this time . . . I'm all right—now. It's been driving me insane, not knowing what happened to you. What's going on here? How long for you?~

Rett updated her ego-merge companion swiftly. She was really glad of Pam's return, but wished the re-mergers weren't so abrupt. She sat up, groaning, keeping her arms tight against her sides.

I need to go out and scout around. Try to find my fighter, my pack, check the area. If I can't find my emergency gear, then I need to think about food. And water . . . getting enough of it is going to be a problem. I'll have to eat snow, and it takes a lot of snow to get a decent amount of water.

~Well, there's plenty of snow. It's okay to ingest, right? As long as it's not yellow . . . ~

Although Rett had to chuckle at Pam's allusion, she had to take her water issue seriously. *That's not the point. I have this little water bottle, but it doesn't hold enough. I'm constantly packing new snow into it, keeping it next to me to melt. Which makes me colder from the outside in. To stay decently hydrated, I'm going to have to start eating it instead of waiting, which can bring my core temperature down. It's not impossible; I just have to be careful.*

When her breath came back, she stood up and eyed the wall again. There were plenty of toe and handholds from the living tree roots that wove through the soil. She started up with determination.

~They're warm.~

What?

~The roots. Didn't you notice?~

I noticed that the decomposing stuff was warm. Nyorfian longcones are warm to the touch, too—the older they are, the warmer they feel. I'm not surprised at the roots feeling warm, but I am surprised I didn't notice until you brought my attention to it. Rett paused. The roots were warm, and what gave off heat, she could track with her energy sense. She pulled off one of her gloves to lay her fingers over a thick root nearby. *I'm going to try to sound it.*

She was glad she was on a steady perch. She sent her awareness along the root, and what flowed back staggered her. The unusual arctic trees were all connected. It made sense . . . perhaps the temperatures were never warm enough, the ground never open enough, to allow any seeds to germinate. So the trees had found another way.

"Wow." Rett patted the root and returned her hand to her glove. "Pam, when this is over, I have to come back here."

~Has the eco-biologist forester part of you all juiced up, does it?~

Yeah, actually. Continuing her climb, she reached the new hole she'd made and cautiously emerged.

The wind had come up, biting and painful, sending snow into her face as sharp as specks of quartzite sand. Encouraged by the performance of her energy sense below the surface, Rett sent it out once more. Small telltale spots of warm-blooded creatures, most small, on the ground and in the trees. The trees themselves. Nothing larger and nothing that was sparking her combat sense.

Be nice to have some VARs. But I don't. "If onlys waste time." Shrugging with that familiar reminder, Rett levered herself the rest of the way from the hole and rolled away from it, toward the nearest tree.

She waited a few seconds for her head to clear. Soon she was standing, leaning close to the tree trunk for support as much as for cover. She pressed her face against it, trying to find the warmth she'd felt below the surface. The tree betrayed nothing. She would never have known, or guessed, from a surface examination alone. The bark was thick, fairly smooth. How strong were those branches? *I'm not up to finding that out just yet. I don't need to fall again.* Instead, she scooped up a handful of snow and nibbled. It had a faint metallic taste, less pronounced in this state than it was as a liquid.

51

~Maybe there's a river or creek nearby,~ suggested Pam.

With liquid water?

~Well, yeah, under the ice.~ Pam sounded defensive. ~Why do you think that's so amusing?~

Rett smothered a chuckle. *Because I'd probably need a grenade to crack through the ice. Maybe more than one. And while ice will give me a better yield than snow . . . it's harder to melt. Yes—if I were camping out here on an environmental survey, and had the convenience of thermal storage units, I'd use ice.*

~So I'm not an arctic survival expert. It was just a thought.~ Now Pam was disgruntled.

It was a good thought, Pam. Just because I say why I can't or won't use one of them— don't stop with them. Rett took her water container from underneath her clothing and packed the snow into the empty space. *It's a bit more than surviving the climate, as well. Don't forget this entire continent is under Coalition occupation . . . at least until the invasion, if it's successful. Even if I had a grenade, or an ML-12, or anything else techy, they'd be sure to send people out here to investigate.*

Now . . . food. Three and a half fruit bars were great, but wouldn't go far. She didn't need carbohydrates for short-term energy. She needed something that would keep her body from eating itself in an effort to stay warm. The survival rations the fightercraft had carried were made specifically for cold weather, higher in fat and protein. She didn't have those, so she needed alternatives.

Recalling what she'd learned of Auroran flora and fauna, there was plenty of small game active all year round. Her energy sense confirmed it. Many of those animals lived off the continually peeling bark and twigs of these unusual trees.

Rett supposed she could try eating the green twigs and stems as well, but again, that wasn't what she needed in this environment.

~What about the colored snow?~ Pam asked. ~You were telling me that the parts of the snow that looked tinted—blue, violet, even a bit of green and pink—were plankton. Or algae. Or lichens. Something. Microscopic plants or animals that lived in parts of the snow. Aren't certain ones edible?~

Rett took a shallow breath and let it out in a long white jet of vapor. *Thanks for the reminder.*

~Hah, at last, an idea you can use.~ Pam's relief was evident by the brightening of her energy.

I'm glad you remembered. Because that was knocked right out of my head. I hope I didn't forget anything else important. Let's see . . . yes. The violet and green parts are safe, but not as they are. Not for humanoids. They need to be heated because of some other organism that lives in there as well, or all I'll end up with is gut cramps and the runs.

~Not a good idea, until you find a way of making fire.~

But the pink sections are supposed to be safe, in small quantities. H'tenneck told us in his district it's considered a treat.

Pam's mental laugh tickled an answering smile from Rett. ~You know, I used to think only places like Japan or some Scandinavian country would consider a . . . plankton-flavored snowcone a treat.

Yes, well, the way I see it, your planet still beats mine for strange. And, Rett was quick to add before Pam could protest, *I don't necessarily mean that in a bad way.*

~I understood your context, this time.~ Pam couldn't quite hide the residual sting she still felt from Rett's pre-crash remarks.

I am sorry, thought Rett, wishing with all her heart that scene never happened.

~I forgive you,~ said Pam. ~But I expect you to make it up to me. When we get back, we hit the books in your free time.~

More research, I guess. All right. When we get back, I'll read for you until my eyes cross. Just don't ask me to write anything down. My spelling has never been a strong point.

Pam awarded her a light mental smack. ~I need you to read because I can't read the language you use in the first place, silly. ~

Rett took a few steps away from the tree, scanning with both her sight and her energy sense. *I need to be like the growtus, a predator.* She had a knife; she had some cording for a net or some snares. All she had to do was take some time to study the game situation.

But deities, she couldn't stay out for very long like this. She needed more clothes. Or fur. Reaching the spot where she crashed, she knelt and brushed the snow away. Nothing was there. Nothing but broken branches and limbs. The helmet was gone, no signs of anything.

Except for what had to be a humanoid-sized bootprint in the leeward side of a large boulder.

She glanced into the direction the bootprint pointed. Despite the accumulation of drifted snow on the ground, she traced a definite path marked by broken branches, limbs, even entire tops of trees. The path her fighter had taken. *It must be there—yes, there.* A tiny yellow spot of mechanical or electrically generated energy flared into her awareness.

She took a few steps more in that direction, tempted. Then reason reasserted itself.

There are Coalition troops in the area . . . quite close. They've already tracked and marked the fighter—and now they're searching for the pilot. For me.

~It's a good bet anything useful that survived the crash is already salvaged. You said their supplies were starting to run short, especially on Aurora,~ said Pam.

"Yeah," said Rett aloud. Outdoors, her voice didn't seem to go very far, as if the cold instantly froze her words and took them crashing into the ground. "Oh well." She shrugged, hugging her arms around her body. It was too cold to stay out here any longer, anyway. "Hopefully, they'll think I was dragged off and eaten by the growtus." She continued in her thoughts. *Time to see if some of that tree dust will insulate me just as well outside as it does down at the bottom of the crevasse. If that works, I'll be able to stay outside long enough to get something done.*

3.1.8 COMMUNICATIONS STATION, MAINCOMMAND, EPNOCE
0536.01.06 (LOCAL RECKONING)

"Colonel Nauskova."

"Sergeant Ariam. Colonel Reve isn't available—"

"I know. I can't wait for him. Can I ask your favor then, this is sensitive. A family emergency."

SubColonel Nauskova, second-in-command of the 21st Infantry Division, looked a bit preoccupied and impatient to clear the com, and Ariam couldn't blame her. The 21st was also part of the Aurora invasion, part that was going to hit a different part of the continent. Lightning Force had been assigned to them, and they were scrambling with last minute preparations.

The heavyset woman with the short coppery curls changed her expression in seconds after Ariam's words. "It's Rett?"

Ariam nodded. "She's going to be listed as missing in action—and she is. On Aurora. About one hundred and eighty miles behind the lines, we guess. There might be scuttlebutt that she's dead—from us, or from the Coalition. I want you to tell my father that *I* said she's *not* dead. If she is, he'll hear it from me, or it'll be backed up by absolute proof. He's all right, though?"

"Yes. But he's been particularly concerned for a couple days now."

Ariam wasn't surprised. Her family had always been strongly bonded, Talented or not. She knew her father didn't hate Rett, hadn't written her off. The fact that Nauskova had been so quick to mention Rett's name—and mention her father's concern—was proof enough of that.

"If he gets a chance before we go to com blackout—"

"Hold on a moment." Nauskova glanced over her shoulder, and then moved out of range of the video pickup.

Dad.

Colonel Reve's tall figure, still clad in heavy outer gear and dotted with unmelted snow, stepped in front of the camera. "Ariam? What's this about Rett?"

She repeated what she'd told Nauskova, aware that the technician had work to do, and the five minutes she'd begged on tightbeam were nearly gone.

Her father's expression didn't change. "What do you think the official word will be?"

"Her squadron leader is convinced she didn't survive. Her fighter was locked from an EM pulse blast. She couldn't get out. All he saw was wreckage and nothing from her locator."

"So officially, it hasn't been anything hopeful. Thanks for making this effort, Ari." Reve stretched a hand toward the video pickup, just as Ariam did on her end. "What about Olvero and Valera—"

"I've seen them. They're all right. Valera is confident and Olvero puts his trust in his mother's feelings." Ariam wished she could go into more detail, but time was tight. "My seniors gave me permission to visit you, but getting to you in person didn't quite work out. This is the best I can manage."

Her father nodded. "I'm glad it worked out."

"I have to go. I love you, Dad." She willed her love through her fingers, that the transmission carrying her words would also carry her touch to him. "Take care."

"I love you, Ari. You take care, too. And we'll hope for the best."

"I'm sorry, Sergeant," said the communications technician as Ariam pushed herself away from his workstation. "I shouldn't have been here for that—"

"Please, don't worry about it. You wouldn't be on tightbeam if you were someone who went around telling other people what you've overheard. But all the same," Ariam said with a stern expression, "if anything I've said about Sergeant Rett gets out, you'll have me, Rett, and Colonel Reve to deal with."

3.1.9 UNKNOWN LOCATIONS, AURORA CONTINENT, EPNOCE

RETT DRAGGED HER KILL THROUGH the snow, hoping it didn't freeze solid before she managed to get it into the relative warmth of the crevice and section it into more manageable chunks.

She often heard the roar of aircraft overhead and several times had come dangerously close to passing Coalition columns as force deployments were rearranged. She hoped that meant the invasion had gone well for the Nyorfians. It wasn't exactly going well for her.

~You're surviving,~ said Pam.

I should be elsewhere. I should be with my troop.

~You weren't exactly able-bodied for a while, either,~ said Pam.

Rett compressed her lips. She hadn't been in any condition to travel for the first five days. During the past four, she was able to move around, range out, and learn the area around her—at least for the short periods of time the temperature allowed. To travel any distance, she still needed to prepare a little more.

I wish there was some way I could pass information at least, maybe send coordinates for AirSpacefighters to hit those columns we've seen.

Rett was glad she was almost back at her shelter. Any light in the sky was rapidly disappearing as a storm front approached, and she hoped her shelter would hold up to whatever was coming. She had no way to check the met updates even if she wanted to. Her Omni was blocked from any outgoing connection, a routine precaution in case it fell into enemy hands.

The skin between her shoulder blades prickled. Rett slowed, getting her knife in hand, extending her energy awareness around her.

Growtus. Thirty lengths from her shelter, and there were four very large predators between her and the safety of the crack below the snow.

~Will they attack?~ Pam asked.

Depends how hungry and threatened they are, I guess.

A massive shape emerged from the tree line ahead. Two flanked it on the left, one to the right.

~Holy crap, they're way bigger than I expected.~

I showed you Nyorfian growtus. These are Auroran snow growtus, Rett clarified, not taking her eyes from the lead predator. It took two more steps toward her, head down, fur bristling, a threatening, rumbling growl coming from behind those finger-length fangs.

~How did they get from Nyorfias to here, or here to there? There aren't other similar species between these two plan—~

Pam, now is not a good time, they're way too close. Rett averted her gaze, watching sidelong and wishing she could interpret the fluctuating energy of the big hunters the same way she could humanoids.

"Hello," she said, pitching her voice lower than normal. "Look, I didn't mean to trespass on your hunting territory. And . . . sorry for depriving you of your dinner the other day, but I didn't plan on falling into a hole, either."

~What are you doing?~

My mother said they're intelligent. Not in the same way we are, but they can read nuance. I'm not afraid of them, Pam. There's a chance that they'll go on their way, and let me go on mine.

~What about that meat you're dragging?~

Rett had completely forgotten her kill. Maybe it would be taken as a peace offering. She dropped the hold she had on the single spatulate horn of the cotos and slowly stepped backward a few body lengths.

All four of the animals were in the open now. The leader's icy eyes remained fixed on Rett; the others watched the leader.

The lead growtu took another step forward, the fading light glinting from its thick silver fur. Rett was envious of it, envious of them. She pushed the thought from her mind and took another step backward, avoiding eye contact.

"Go ahead, take it. It's fresh. Might not even be frozen yet. On the other hand, I'm going to be frozen in another minute. And hungry," she couldn't help adding as a loud protest came from her belly. She ordered it to hush.

The growtu cocked its head. The snow squeaked as the animal's weight shifted on massive paws.

"That wasn't me. I mean, it *was*, but I wasn't growling at you."

But something had changed. The bristling fur smoothed. The lowered head came up slightly. The animal came forward.

Rett dropped into a crouch and remained in place, head down, hardly daring to breathe. The big silver growtu reached the carcass of the cotos, sniffed it, never taking his unblinking stare from her. She didn't have to look at the growtu to feel the impact of those eyes. She felt them right down to her skin.

When she dared to look again, they were all gone, including her hard-won cotos.

Rett swallowed and didn't waste any more time going to her shelter. The wind was picking up. She'd have to hunker down, sleep it out, and hope to find more game after the storm passed.

She was settling in to the spot she called her nest when her combat sense alerted again. Now what? She remained still, listening, extending her awareness through the darkness. The growtus again. They were moving up there . . . two of them, carefully pacing the length of the crevice to the narrow end she used as her entrance and exit. They wouldn't try coming down, would they? They were far too large, even if they came through the wide part.

Snow sifted down, glittering in the faint light from the snowlit world above. Snuffling sounds. Rett stood up, reaching for her knife. She could smell musky fur, blood, and meat. Something was dropped through the opening.

She felt toward the spot. Her uncovered hand touched something furry and partly frozen.

It's a piece of the cotos. Rett was stunned.

~Is this normal?~ Pam asked.

I don't know. My mother said Nyorfian growtus were known for some unusual behavior, but no one knows too much about the Auroran growtus. Including how they got here—much less how different species of them came to be on both planets. She was hoping to study them. I'm not going to think about it any more. I'm just going to take it as luck.

~It just might be that they want to keep you fresh, fat, and happy for emergencies.~

Rett chuckled. *Maybe.* The portion was small, but for tonight and tomorrow, it was enough. She used her knife to take off the bit of fur and hide still attached, cut the remainder into strips. Folding most of them back into the hide, she tucked the package into the loop of a tree root just above her head level, where it would stay very cold but—hopefully—not freeze solid.

3.1.10 UNKNOWN LOCATION, AURORA CONTINENT, EPNOCE

"IT' A GOOD THING IT'S so cold." Rett smeared grease from her latest kill over her face, ears, and neck. It was all she could do to try to protect her skin from the prolonged exposure. "I'd probably smell just as bad as that Coalition commander back at Complex 142 if it decided to warm up suddenly."

Skin taken care of for the moment, she gnawed on the remainder of the raw fat and turned her attention to the gray and bluish hides she'd collected over the past two days. She'd become expert at catching these small, tree-dwelling creatures.

Pam's constant attempts to compare them to creatures from her planet were amusing, especially since Pam had no single Earth creature to compare them to. The latest: *cat-pig-chipmunk-flying squirrel creature thing* was a thought concept enough to give Rett a headache. She didn't care what the animals were called. They were plentiful, they were food, they were clothing, they were protection from the cold. Perhaps most importantly, the growtus didn't seem to mind how many of those she caught. They just showed up when she found larger game, such as the cotos and dubok.

Rett managed to skin her last cotos, too, but using the thick, slightly greasy hide as an extra covering while outdoors hadn't proven successful. Instead, it had incited an attack from the local growtu pack. She hadn't been hurt, just knocked down and shaken, but her cotos hide had been taken aside and thoroughly consumed.

"I have enough of these now, and the fur is incredible." Rett had started scraping the inside of the skin, but she had to turn it over and run her fingers through the thick, glossy fur that blended in so well with the snowy landscape. The tree creatures became very still and looked like lumps of snow in the branches when they felt danger. That was enough to keep them safe from some predators, but not from her.

She used sections of her cordage to piece the small hides together. There. Now she had something to go over her head, neck, and face. She turned the fur side in and pulled it over her head, feeling the difference almost immediately.

~Any reason you're still avoiding fire?~

Rett had to laugh aloud. "Think about it. I'm sure this stuff would burn readily enough . . . but I'm behind enemy lines here. They're scanning every fingerlength of this territory—most general, broadrange scans based on heat sources. The heat sources get interpreted as biological, mechanical, or geothermic, to name a few. "

She pulled off her new hat to make some adjustments. "Fire is generally grouped with mechanical, so it will merit a closer look, especially if combined with a biological reading. Most especially if those readings show up with metal and weapons. That's when the scans start going for more detail."

~Is that why you've been going out lately with only your knife?~

"Yes. I don't think my sidearm would raise any alarms on a broadrange scan—it's just a stunner. Combined with my knife, and moving with a human sized heat source, it just might get me some unwanted attention. I'm pretty sure the Coalition scanners aren't looking for combinations of factors as insignificant as I am right now, or they would have found me by now. It doesn't take them very long. They vectored on my initial crash position fairly quickly—both of them—and I was less than three body lengths away down here when they were up there picking up my stuff."

~I'm really glad the growtus don't care for those blue raccoony-pig blanket things,~ came from Pam, trying out another nickname for the creatures as Rett re-tested the fit of her hat. ~You'd stand to get your head taken off the minute you stick it out of your hole if they did~.

I can't figure that out, either, Rett thought. *The tree creatures don't taste bad. Maybe it's just too much effort for the growtus to get enough to satisfy their needs, so they leave them alone.*

Rett's alliance with Aurora's apex predators remained a mystery. Since the first time she went out, they had followed, maintaining just enough distance to let her know they were nearby. Every once in a while, the big silver leader would move into sight and keep pace with her. If she made a kill, she backed off and let them have it first—there was always a piece left for her. Likewise, if they made a kill, she would emerge from her shelter to find an offering nearby. The one day she hadn't taken possession of the meat soon enough for the growtus' liking, it had been reclaimed.

63

She liked knowing they were out there. It made her feel connected, like the arctic trees, to the landscape, a part of her environment instead of just in it. She repacked her flight suit with fresh tree dust for its insulating qualities.

~Maybe one day they'll reopen that study your mother and brother were going to be part of,~ suggested Pam. ~And you can come back.~

"Maybe. It would be a lot more fun to stay out here for an extended period with the right equipment, too. But you know I don't speculate too far into the future." Rett slipped off her boots and wrapped two other furred skins around her feet. "Right now, let's just worry about me getting back to our own lines. I'm going to need three days off to bathe, you know that? I stink. No wonder the growtus don't want to come any closer." She pulled the boots back on and wiggled her toes, more than ready to travel.

"There are ditches and depressions filled with the dead material those trees cast off. I know how to find them now, so I should be able to find enough shelter along the way."

~Too bad you had to find that out by falling into each and every one of them,~ said Pam with a chuckle that Rett echoed aloud.

"At least until I learned how to focus my energy sense to find them." Rett checked her shelter a final time to make sure she wasn't going to leave anything useful behind, and then climbed to the surface. After one long, last look around at the place she had spent the last tenday, she started off through a fresh layer of snow.

* * * * *

"Faugh—what's that reek?" The more humanoid shaped Coalition sentry jerked his face coverings over his nose and gave his partner a shove. "Did you eat those roots again? You know your kind can't digest them."

"Shut up, human, it's not me." The second guard turned slowly, sniffing the air. It took three steps toward the big snowdrift on oddly jointed legs. "There must be a dead animal in here."

"Dead animals freeze or get eaten before they can stink on this iceball," the humanoid said.

Rett waited in her snowdrift. She didn't think she smelled that bad, but what mattered was the guards were distracted. It was time to move. She exploded from her hiding place and laid them out in short order. The humanoid trooper would be unconscious for a good long time, and she could only hope his alien comrade would, as well. She raided their weapons belts and harnesses for what she needed and slid beneath the nearest big supply rover.

~What's that . . . what are they doing?~ Pam thought.

Rett's gut twisted. Damn. She'd forgotten about her escort of growtus. The sounds coming from the place she'd left the unconscious troopers were more chilling than the frigid air.

Oh, the growtus wouldn't *eat* the Coalition guards, she knew that much. She had to remember the growtus were at war, too. They hadn't hesitated to attack a few of the smaller patrols she had avoided so far on her trek.

With the way the Coalition had decimated the balance of animal and plant life on Nyorfias and Epnoce, Rett couldn't say she blamed them.

I guess we don't have to worry about them regaining consciousness.

~I wonder, though, if their hatred extends to your people as well,~ Pam thought. ~After all, your first encounter with them would have ended badly if you hadn't fallen into that ditch. ~

I don't know. Rett scrambled beneath another rover. *I do know a Nyorfian wouldn't kill them outright, only in defense. Coalition troopers, on the other hand, come out shooting just hearing growtus howling from a distance.*

~The bunch that followed you . . . it's as if they're protecting you.~

They're probably curious more than anything. I'm glad to have their company. I'm only worried they might be killed because they chose to follow me. The pack has young . . . the ones who stayed behind have to fend for them. I don't see how they could spare their senior male and half their hunters.

She quickly worked her way along the file of vehicles. Already the larger impressions she'd made in the snow were filling in, thanks to the sharp wind. As she moved away from the column, she kept any footprints she had to make in those already made by troopers. Shouting and commotion erupted from the place she had left the unfortunate guards, and she dove headfirst for the nearest snowbank.

~You're good at this sabotage stuff,~ said Pam as Rett wriggled deeper into the powdery crystals. ~You think anyone will guess it's you?~

65

Rett cleared a small opening so she could breathe and pushed her energy sense to check for movement outside her snowbank. She couldn't stay in here long.

I'm hoping Nyorfians might, because no matter how much Ariam might deny it, I'm sure they think I'm dead. I don't have any other way to let them know until I actually find them. But overall? It doesn't matter. The only thing that matters is that the enemy can't use this stuff against us.

The rumble of engines was muffled through her snowbank, but enough of a warning for Rett to emerge from her hiding place and break into a lope through the deep snow. It was about to get very hot, very fast.

3.1.11 UNSPECIFIED LOCATION, AURORA CONTINENT, EPNOCE
0536.01.24 (LOCAL RECKONING)

SEMAGE AND B-TROOP FOLLOWED THE dry creek bed back to their temporary headquarters.

"Think there's anything to that story going around that the growtus are sabotaging Coalition patrols just west of here?" Semage shrugged deeper into his jacket and pulled his breath muffler higher on his face.

"I don't know, Brown Lead."

The voice that sighed over Semage's pcom was muffled, partially from the speaker's face coverings, partially from the low moan of the wind. Ariam was at point, six body lengths in front of him. He studied her back, her pace, the way she moved. She seemed fine, alert and energetic, not slouched or dragging. He knew she was sleeping, when they had time. Yet she sounded so utterly exhausted.

It's this worrying about Rett. She can't let it go. It hasn't affected her performance yet—but I can't say it won't in the future.

"It's possible," Ariam was saying. "Mother always said the growtus were intelligent, and the way the Coalition's been slaughtering the game, shooting more than they need and just leaving the animals lying dead, and ruining this—"

"Brown two, come on. Are you saying there's *organized animals*? Hold on, I'm coming up there." He closed the transmission and stretched his stride to catch up with her. "These aren't Nyorfian growtus."

"They're related."

"So . . . yeah, maybe Auroran growtus are attacking Coalition patrols because their normal prey is disappearing. But from what those prisoners said, the attacks are—"

"Feels wrong." Ariam raised her hand with a sharp, sudden motion. "Something's out there. We're well inside our own lines, I know, but we're being watched."

Semage gestured for his platoon to stand by on full alert.

"Don't do it, Ariam, don't push. Rimms and the squadleaders are on the VARs. If anything is out there, they'll spot it."

Ariam made a face, and Semage had to harden the sympathy he felt. Ever since her collapse, he, Shenyver, and Lieutenant Evetez—even Major Yidnar—had absolutely forbidden her to stretch her talent seeking Rett. Ariam's ability was needed now, here, for B-troop and the 2023rd. Rett would tell her the same thing.

"Brown Lead," said the voice of Junior Sergeant Rimms over the pcom, "I'm reading four large and one humanoid size heat source paralleling us behind the treeline. Big ones are likely growtus, the mass and temperatures are in the right range. The humanoid's very lightly armed—knife and a small stunner from what the VARs can tell—moving toward us."

Semage halted his platoon, the barest motion from him dispersing his people into defensive positions into whatever cover was available between them and the wooded tract.

"Ariam, what's wrong with you—come on." Semage had to smack her shoulder to get her to move. She was facing the treeline, had even taken a step toward it.

He closed his hand around her shoulder harness. Then a questioning, piping whistle cracked through the frigid air and shivered against his ears. Ariam staggered, and Semage was quick to yank her back. He shifted his hand to her arm, steadying her even as the familiar group of notes lingered.

"Let me go. It's Rett."

"Can't be." Semage swallowed his astonishment. He felt Ariam's pulse pounding through the thick material of her sleeve.

"Let me go, Semage!"

"There's growtus out there."

"I don't care."

Semage tightened his hold and gave her a shake. "Sergeant, get yourself together. Let's do this the safe way. One more minute isn't going to hurt." Signaling B troop to stay wary, he pushed aside his breath muffler, pursed his lips and returned the correct response.

A tall, somewhat lumpy figure in a patched and dirty AirSpacefighters' flightsuit emerged from the ice-coated brush near the creek bed.

"Good gods and deities." It was Semage's turn to feel off balance. He stood frozen in place as Ariam slipped out of his grasp and ran forward, dropping her weapons.

"Growtus are leaving, Brown Lead," reported his third-up over the pcom as Semage watched Ariam throw herself onto the newcomer so hard they both fell into the snow.

"Leaving! What were they, the escort detail?"

"I'll guess we'll have to wonder, Brown Lead," Rimms said.

Semage shook his head and went forward to join the two women. He couldn't begrudge them their reunion, but they had five more miles to cover before they met with ground transport, fifteen more after that to Base, it was getting dark, and another storm was coming in.

Hmm. "Com connect Brown Three. Relay back Sergeant Rett is recovered, maybe we'll score some faster transport."

"Excellent, Brown Lead. Will do."

Semage crouched near Ariam and Rett.

"Shh, Ariam. Stop crying," Rett was saying. "Your face will freeze."

"And that's not all," Semage said. "Come on, you two. Up. We have to keep moving."

Ariam sniffed and rolled aside, coming easily to her feet. She reached down to help her sister.

Semage stepped closer for his own hug. "Gods, Rett, you stink," he said.

Rett's familiar warm laugh filled him with energy. "I love you too, 'Mage. Thanks for stopping."

"You feel strange." Semage squeezed the arm closest to him, and then felt along the tall woman's back and waist. "What do you have going on under there, Rett?"

"Don't ask. It helps insulate."

Ariam gave a watery hiccup. "Are you hurt? Do you need a medtech?"

"I'm fine," Rett said. "Nothing a couple showers and a good soak won't cure. Come on, you two, you don't need to hang on to me. I'm not going to try to escape or anything."

Semage stepped aside, but Ariam wasn't about to let go. Semage shouldered her weapon with his. "By the way, Rett, nice hat. Is that what stinks?"

70

"Partly. The rest is me. Twenty days . . . Honestly, it didn't seem that long. Good deities, what you must have gone through. I'm sorry. I did try—"

"We'll talk about all that when we get back to Aurora Base," said Ariam firmly. "But I'll bet it wasn't growtus wreaking havoc with Coalition patrols out here."

"Well . . . I did my part, the growtus did theirs. I was looking for a way to communicate. But I figured depriving the enemy of some fuel, transportation, and ammunition was a good thing to do, too."

"It was," said Semage. "It gave aerial recon something to target; we made a lot of progress in this sector the past tenday." He let out a soft whistle. "No one made the connection with you, though. This is going to be an interesting debriefing."

Rimms met them as they joined B-troop. "Glad to see you, Sergeant Rett, and there are a lot of people at Aurora Base who are quite anxious to get you home. They're sending us a troopjumper."

"I can hear it," Rett said, and after a moment, Semage heard it too. He was relieved they'd have a short, fast trip into Base.

"I need to say something before we go another step." Semage waved B-troop on. "Ariam—I'm sorry I doubted you. I think we all did, to various extents. It won't happen again, even when something goes on as long this did. I should have listened to Trebor's advice. I think he and Major Yidnar were the only ones pretty much sticking with your opinion."

Ariam's smile could have melted the snow around them to bare ground. If anyone else had anything to say, it was lost in the roar and sudden whirl of snow as the troopjumper came in low over the ridge ahead.

3.1.12 AURORA BASE, EPNOCE
0536.01.28 (LOCAL RECKONING)

THE FIRST THREE DAYS AFTER B-troop had brought Rett back had been spent, at Med's insistence, going from a bath to one medical test to a bath and to another medical test, and so forth. The process left Med so exhausted he made Rett spend the next two days in bed, with full access to bathing facilities, away from the others, until he satisfied himself she wasn't carrying some sort of disease or had permanently frozen an important brain cell or two.

Or, as Pam so wickedly suggested, Med simply was keeping her away from everyone until Rett brought her body odor under reasonable control.

Whatever the reasons for her medtech's strange behavior and conclusions were beyond Rett's understanding, since aside from an above normal appetite for things fatty, green, and starchy, she felt fine.

Now, released, debriefed, and passed to full Active, Rett made her way to the new AirSpacefighters' area, into Flight Operations, and found the familiar smile of Chihakiru greeting her from over the banks of computer video consoles.

"Good to see you back, Sergeant Rett. Colonel Centra has you back on active, but you're not on the flight schedule for the next two days. I can put you on standby if you're free."

Rett nodded. "Any chance of getting a trainer and instructor for a while? I've done some sim time, but was told I need to get out and rechecked as soon as possible."

Chihakiru started to look doubtful as he studied his readouts, but then the uncertain lines on his forehead smoothed, and he grinned up at Rett.

"T234C just came off Maintenance. I'll tell them to prep for you. Go get geared up and come back here for your new log. Captain Teague is also available. I'll let him know."

Rett pushed herself away from the counter and headed for the pilots' kitting area. It would be nice, she reflected, to see Etron, if only to thank him for freighting Ariam around to see Jaq and her father. Unless someone was used to being around Talented individuals, accepting an empath's non-tangible feeling about someone out of normal reach—like Rett had been—was truly difficult. Etron's offer was a gesture that went far beyond the normal boundaries of thoughtfulness.

He'd sent her several handfuls of messages since she'd been back, three or four a day sometimes, telling her he was glad she was back, alive, safe, and he couldn't wait to see her. Squadron operations kept him busy, however. And of course, he couldn't get past Med. Not surprising. As outrageous and daring as Captain Etron could be, he had limitations. Besides, the only two people in two worlds she knew with the guts to try getting Med when he became insistent over leaving someone undisturbed was Major Yidnar, and possibly her father.

~Etron is a very nice, very sweet guy,~ Pam reflected.

And good-looking.

~No argument from me.~

You know, you came up with some real wild thoughts during that conversation to distract the Coalition pilots. I'm glad I wasn't focused on those—I might have crashed a lot sooner.

~And crashed thinking about doing them with someone other than Etron, like a certain bubbleheaded Zetinorian,~ teased Pam, then gave a sigh Rett nearly echoed physically. ~I wish I knew someone like Etron back home.~

If there is someone for you, you're not going to find him in the pasture with your horses, thought Rett, giving her friend a mental poke.

~Maybe, maybe not. I just might, I've met some very nice farriers and vets. Then again, I have enough problems being single.~

Chicken.

73

~This is not the time to get into the very strange, convoluted peculiarities of dating and courtship in the society I live in. Zetinorian territoriality looks positively simple in that light.~ Pam rolled mental eyes and promptly changed the subject. ~It's a good day for flying.~

Rett agreed. *But you said chickens don't fly.*

~You should know, being the exception to the rule, Sergeant-Too-Chicken-to-tell-Jaq-to-get-his-big-carcass-back-where-it-belongs,~ Pam returned smartly. ~Because as good a friend; as sweet, good-looking, and thoughtful as Captain Etron is, we both know damn well Jaq's the man you're in love with.~

Rett gracefully admitted defeat at her own game. *Okay, all right, you win. Just don't kick me, whatever you do.*

After finding her new locker, she started to gear up. A muted giggle and a low, soft, male voice drifted to her ears from another part of the room. Rett stiffened in absolute surprise for a moment. She knew that voice. She didn't even have to verify it with a deeper sounding of his aura.

Her surprise turned into tiff. *No time to see me in person, huh?* Movements automatic, she continued to settle her equipment, carefully arranging the shoulder holster, knife in boot sheath, markers in left sleeve clips. She made sure her handy roll of camo tape and emergency supplies were tucked deep into an inner pocket, checked her new helmet, pushed her pcom patch in place, picked up her gloves, gave a savage tug to her shoulder belt, and exited the locker as quietly as she'd entered.

~Ooh! What's this?~ came from a highly amused Pam. ~Jealous?~

Why should I be? Rett retorted sharply.

~No reason. But you're——~

I know what you mean, and I am not!

~Oh, yes, you are. You heard someone who's flirted with you flirting with someone else and were overcome by pure, unadulterated, green-eyed monster jealousy.~

Good deities. Is that what it feels like? Rett had no idea at all what to name the awful sensation that put every nerve ending in her body on alert, raising her hackles like a growtu sensing a threat. On the other hand, imagining making Etron suffer for making her feel whatever she was feeling right now felt just fine.

~Seeing how you never even made love with him, the only reason I can imagine why you have such strong feelings about it is that maybe you're jealous *because* you've finally admitted to yourself that you're truly in love with Jaq.~

I don't see how that can make me react like that.

~Being in love does odd things to people.~

Rett raked a hand through her hair. *Whatever, wherever this is coming from, it has to stop. It really didn't matter. We both can see as many people as we like. Deities, I know he's seeing at least a handful besides me—has been ever since we met. It's never bothered me before. Why now?*

~Do you want more of my opinion?~

Rett shook her head angrily. *I don't want more. The bottom line is, I don't own him, and he doesn't own me. I'm not going to ignore you anymore, Pam, but please leave my personal life alone!*

When a moment of stillness answered, Rett was quick to amend her statement. *At least leave it alone when I'm working. I can't be thinking about stuff like this. But I might want to go into details later. Just don't knock me unconscious.* Rett stalked back to FlightControl for her new logs.

~I won't. I think I need this flight as much as you do.~

Pam quieted, but Rett could still feel an odd blend of amusement and sympathy leaking from her corner.

Chihakiru glanced up and started to hand over the log. His hand froze midmotion and his heavy eyebrows pulled together over his nose. "Sergeant? Anything wrong?"

~You've got your war face on,~ Pam said.

Rett relaxed the tense muscles in her face and flashed Chihakiru a smile. "No, but if I've Teague and arrive there two seconds off the chrono, I'll never hear the end of it."

Relieved, Chihakiru handed over the log. "I could only get you forty minutes, but your ship's warmed, checked, and ready to go, so that'll save you some time."

"You're worth three times your weight in azurium, Chihakiru. Thanks."

In the hangar area, Captain Teague, who'd been one of her instructors, fell in step with Rett. "Hey, Rett," he said. "You're exactly on time for once! We didn't expect you back on Active so soon. I've done the external check already—Chihakiru told you, good. Assigned a new one yet?"

"Not yet," said Rett. "I didn't know we had any new ones." She eyed the trainer as they neared. She trusted Teague, of course, but habit and her own pleasure at admiring the sleek lines of the aircraft held sway, and he didn't protest when she detoured to walk around the craft.

"Oh, we do. While you were gone, two GTC carriers made it in. Gave us a hundred new Valier class craft."

"Shit, I *have* missed a lot. I'll have to grab the specs on them before I leave. Are they on the line?" As tempted as she was to look around and spot one, Rett kept her attention on her inspection.

"All those designated to the 114th are at the far end. Colonel's assigning them as I speak. Maybe catch a glimpse of one when we come back in. Speaking of new, you have a new call name now, too."

This time she glanced at the older man. "Oh?"

Teague grinned. "Weren't you told that?"

"No, this is the first I've been back in this section, and Captain Etron or Colonel Centra didn't mention it—or the new ships—in their messages."

"Not surprised, things have been crazy for us since coming across to Aurora. Still, it's odd Etron didn't tell you, since he was the one who came up with it."

"What is it?"

"You're Snow Growtu now. Fits, I think. Do you like it?"

"Yes, I do. I like it a lot."

A wash of deep color started flooding the skin beneath and around Teague's close-cropped beard, going right up to his hairline and creeping down his neck.

"Did I say something wrong?"

He cleared his throat. "Not at all." He turned and jerked his head toward the cockpit. "Let's go, we've only forty minutes and we've wasted enough time." His usual crisp and crusty manner was back.

What did I do, Pam? I didn't have my "war face" as you call it, on that time.

~You smiled at him,~ said Pam. ~Some people seem to have strange reactions to you when you smile in certain ways. Like Med and the guys did at Complex 63?~

I smile a lot, Rett protested.

~Yes . . . you do—on the inside. And maybe around F-troop or the 2023rd, and any kids or old people you happen to meet. But you've made this little habit of not showing too many others what or how much you really feel on the outside—although you might be feeling it inside—and they get used to it. So, when one of those big, gorgeous, drop-over-dead smiles you get sneaks out from behind your Special Forces face, people react to it. Know what I mean?~

No clue.

~You're such an idiot, Rett.~ With a mental motion as if to flip her hand at Rett's head, Pam pulled back to her place with a huge sigh of amusement and exasperation.

"By the way," called Teague from the back seat as Rett settled in, "I'm glad you're back safe. Real glad."

"Thanks." Rett slid down into her seat, snapped the safety harness and various hookups in place. *At least,* she thought as she started the onboard check, *some people really did miss me.*

Pam's mental snort and short thought, ~yeah, you are jealous,~ came back at this so loudly inside Rett's head she thought Teague overheard. Pam was back in her corner before Rett could think to warn her into it.

"I'm just here for the ride," Teague told her as they received clearance for takeoff and the trainer moved into position. "Just pretend I'm not here at all. Do what you want . . . well, crashing is an exception. I have a lesson scheduled and need to get back in time for it."

"I'll make sure I crash near the base this time, just for you," Rett assured him, nudging up the throttles.

She felt a light thump on the back of her helmet and Teague's snort in her headspeakers. "I need to use *this* trainer for the lesson, if you don't mind. Let's go."

She then concentrated her full attention and energies on flying. The intense feeling of powerful freedom made her tension vanish. There weren't very many sensations that compared to that of streaking through a clear sky five times faster than the speed of sound . . . and she found herself thinking about Jaq again.

She had no idea where Jaq was now. At some point during her absence, his unit had been relocated. Since Nyorfian supply units went into total communication blackout while they were moving, there was no telling when she'd get to contact him. Not even text-based messaging made it past the routers all military mail went through when addressed to anyone on such an assignment.

It was mind-boggling that Ariam had managed permission to visit him in person, however briefly.

"Back to business," Rett ordered herself. To keep her mind from wandering again, she executed combat-speed maneuvers as if an entire Coalition squadron chased her through the clear, cold sky. She managed to forget all about the instructor in the back seat until her aircraft touched down on the runway. Teague didn't say a word, which usually meant everything was just fine with him.

After a "See you later," from Teague, who shooed her out of the cockpit and promptly took the trainer off for refueling, she almost ran over Captain Etron. She recovered her footing and reached a quick hand to steady him, then stepped back swiftly.

"Rett! Deities, it's good to see you." Etron was genuinely warm, a bit amused. The wide smile on his dark face came right from his guts. "I saw you were out with Teague. I was hoping to run into you here, but not quite this way."

"Hello, Captain." She kept her own voice neutral and friendly. "Check went well?"

"He signed me off," said Rett, indicating the status monitor on the far wall of the bay. "So it must have."

"I'm really glad you're back," he said again. "Were you looking for me? If you have some extra time, there's a stack of hardcopy updates and specs we need to go over."

She glanced at her chrono. "We'll have to schedule that, Captain. Maybe I can pick up the hardcopy, go over it later, and get with you about it tomorrow?"

He whipped out his Omni and studied his schedule. "That'll work."

"My second's waiting for me right now, I've some platoon work to get to. Hello, I don't think we've met." Rett looked beyond Etron to a rather petite woman with captain's rank insignia. The captain returned Rett's salute, the slight downward curve of her full lips turning into a warm, friendly smile.

"Oh, right—how thoughtless of me. I was so glad to see you I forgot all about Briealun." Etron grimaced in charming apology and made the introductions. "Briealun, this is Rett. Rett, this is Briealun. She arrived a few days before . . . before that mission, and has just been assigned to wingsecond for Group A."

Briealun's older than she looks, guessed Rett. There was a bit of silver in the hair of pale red-gold; small lines around eyes the same blue-violet color as Nyorfian sky. *Like Carakenne's.*

~Matches the uniform, too,~ observed Pam, referring to the black and sky colors of the AirSpacefighters uniform.

"So you're Snow Growtu," Briealun was saying. "I've heard so much about you."

The captain offered both her hands to Rett in greeting, which was a surprise. Rett hadn't encountered the two-handed greeting much outside of friends, family, and the closeknit community in which she was raised.

"I hoped to meet you."

The familiar accent—or lack of one, to Rett's perception—in Briealun's voice suddenly registered. The warmer greeting suddenly made sense. She didn't hesitate to return the gesture and gripped the other woman's hands firmly.

"You're from Treetop! What district?"

"Wind Valley." Briealun's smile made deep laugh lines around her eyes and mouth. "And we've some common interests, from what I've heard. My secondary study was eco-biology, too. We really should get together soon and talk," the pilot said.

"Practically a neighbor," said Rett happily. The Wind Valley district began a mere three hundred miles south of Treetop-town. "I'd like that."

"I *knew* you two would take to each other." Etron beamed.

Ignoring Etron, Rett continued to address Briealun. "I'm really happy to meet you, but I have to run. Let's try and hammer out a time when we can get together, though, but it might not be for a few days." Her glance swung toward Etron, cool again. "I'll get those files, and see you tomorrow, Captain. Let me know if your schedule changes before then so I can make alternate plans?"

"Of course." His lush brown eyes a little puzzled, he gestured Briealun to go ahead without him and moved off with Rett. "What's up, Rett?"

"Nothing. I've been gone for a while, have a lot to catch up on, back at my section as much as here. It's a bit frustrating." She shook her head. "I'm sorry about that mission, losing half your squadron, your friends, like that. I can really relate. Not to mention they were my friends, too."

"Thanks. It was hard, for all of us. I've been keeping busy. It helps."

Rett nodded. "I know that. But it doesn't help for long. You're going to have to let it go. I'm sorry; I was a bit of a jerk just now. I don't know what flew up my butt."

"Don't worry about it. I'm just so glad you're okay. I mean that, Rett."

"And thanks for all you did. Taking time to explain things to the 2023rd, taking Ariam around."

"It was nothing. I just wished that I had more faith in her at the time. And in you." He let out a short laugh, looking a little shamefaced. "No wonder your Sergeant Trebor worries about his gray hairs. Rett—now that medtech of yours has let you loose, can we get a few minutes to talk about things other than business sometime soon?"

"Sure. But honestly, time's going to be at a premium for both of us the next few days. We can just keep trying, I guess." Her bad mood had passed. When Etron took a half step closer, she did, too. The hug was brief, but enough for her to know for sure all was forgiven.

Rett was two steps short of making it into the corridor outside of the FlightCenter when the 114th's commander, Colonel Centra, called to her.

"Rett—glad I caught you!"

The officer's words tumbled out in such a quick, breathless manner that Rett turned with a frown of concern. "Colonel?" *No, she's all right, just Centra as usual—in a rush and busy as a kurra gathering nuts.*

81

Centra's plump arms were piled high with of thick binders and file folders and even as Rett took a step toward her, the entire mountain of them shifted alarmingly to starboard.

"Ohh!" wailed the 114th's commander as she desperately tried to keep the stack from sliding. "I hate not being able to use our Omnis! Ohh—damn!"

Rett sprang to steady the slithering pile with one hand, the other rescuing several folders right before they hit the floor.

"Can I help you with these, sir?"

"Oh, no, thanks, dear, but if you would adjust this a bit, I'm sure I can manage. These file folders and binders are just so slippery—" Her complaining ceased as Rett balanced the load. Centra beamed at Rett. "That's so much better. Yes. Thank you."

Rett smiled back at her. She'd liked Centra from their first meeting, just as Major Yidnar had said she would. Centra's physical appearance, however, was totally at odds with her reputation for brilliance and innovation. A very plump, frazzled-looking woman of middle age, Centra baffled many with her ability to get things done, since it appeared her thoughts flew in every possible direction at once. Which they did, but Centra was in complete, methodical control of each of them. Her inherent ability to multitask herself gave her a formidable edge as both pilot and commander.

And the people under her command adored her as much as Rett and the others in the 2023rd loved and respected Major Yidnar.

"Oh, no, dear, I'm far too old," said Centra suddenly with a very girlish giggle. "Although that's an interesting prospect—"

Rett groaned inwardly and clamped a tighter hold on her thoughts. Centra was an Adept level empath with, as Rett found out, a trace of mindspeaking ability as well, especially in proximity to another person. The Colonel had lifted that fleeting thought right out of Rett's head before she even realized she had it.

82

"I can take some of those," Rett offered again. "We *are* going the same direction." Centra's office was near the main access of the AirSpacefighters' section.

"Oh, no, we aren't. I've assigned you a new ship. Just two minutes ago. Brand new. Number 198V. Teague reported you checked out fine, and Yidnar said I could plan to put you on the flight line for the next few days, so I did. FlightOps have changed—so you have to check with Chihakiru again before you leave, okay?"

"Yes, sir."

"And Rett, dear—try not to make a hole through the canopy of this one with your head." Centra's pale blue eyes twinkled at her. "The new ships use a reflective azurium coating on all outer surfaces, it'll be expensive to replace. Not to mention you would look very strange with your head pushed down somewhere between your shoulder blades."

Rett winced and laughed. "Yes, sir. I'll try."

Placing her round chin atop the formidable stack of hard-copies in her arms, Centra added, "Is that problem you had with Etron something you want to talk about now, dear?"

"I think I'm past it, sir, but I do need to think about where it came from," Rett said in complete truth. With Centra's talent, there was no sense in answering otherwise or making an attempt at evasion.

"Feel free to talk to me any time. You know where to find me," the colonel said, and with another smile for Rett, tottered off toward her office.

Rett sighed and addressed her pcom. "Com connect Fang Two," she said as she turned and retraced her steps. "I'm going to be a bit late."

"Don't worry," said Trebor. "I'll make sure none of this stuff escapes until you can review and sign it—it'll be hard, but I can do it."

"Smartass," grumbled Rett after she signed off.

83

* * * * *

It seemed like forever, but Rett managed to complete her business with AirSpacefighters and return to the section of Aurora Base assigned to Special Forces. She stopped short when she turned into the side annex they usually worked in and burst out laughing. There was Trebor, weapon at the ready, as promised, successfully preventing the escape of the forms and reports that needed her attention.

~He's been a bit punchy lately,~ said Pam. ~Silly with relief you're back, I guess. ~

I suppose. But Trebor's always had a playful side. We just haven't seen very much of it the past year or so.

Rett settled down with him to complete the forms and reports. At least her second was cheerfully inclined to take the bulk of F-troop's busywork upon himself, unlike Ariam had been. Ariam had resented it with the same intensity she'd shown her schoolwork and constantly needed prompting. When Kraym was alive, there wasn't any problem, but afterward . . .

Rett shook her head. She'd never made much of an issue of Ariam's slacking with the less physical side of platoon management since Ariam had more than made up for it in so many other ways. Despite that, Rett hadn't needed extra work, either.

Trebor needed no such prompting. He loved the busywork and took great satisfaction in making sure the platoon's records, forms, reports, and schedules were in perfect order. Most of the time he not only did his share of the work, but most of hers, and all she had to do was review and add her personal code.

Maybe it's all for the best Ariam is in B-troop now, she thought, and wondered if Semage was having any problems with Ariam doing this part of her job. Probably not! Rett did miss the nightly chats with her sister before bed, now more than ever. Ariam always knew how to handle—man problems. Trebor . . . well, they talked a bit at night before dropping off to sleep, but about other things.

~And Trebor isn't your sister,~ added Pam.

Can't have it all, Pam, returned Rett with a wry mental smile.

About an hour later, Trebor cleared his throat. "That's the last of it, Sarge." He entered the final scrap of data into the computer. While the machine compiled, saved, and spat out the hard copy, he straightened the worksheets neatly and dumped them into a recycle chute. "Want to talk about it?"

Rett stared at him for a moment. "About what, Trebor?"

"Whatever it is that's bothering you. After four years, don't you think I can tell? Ever since you've been back, you've been so far away. What really happened out there?"

Rett smiled a little. "Survival," she said.

Trebor looked puzzled.

"I guess in some strange way, I felt I belonged there. I was happy. Living. Surviving. At the same time, I missed everyone. I did a lot of thinking. But today, Trebor, something happened to me that never happened before." She looked down at her hands. "I heard Etron talking to one of the new pilots. I felt . . . I don't know what I felt. Or where it came from. It was awful."

"Territorial. Possessive."

"Yeah, I guess."

"Jealous."

Rett winced. "You were there? Is it curable?"

Trebor leaned back, the hard planes and angles of his face halfway between sympathy and amusement. "Rett, you spent all that time in a totally different world. You're still partway there."

"I suppose . . ."

"And this jealousy . . . yes, it's irrational. However, might it be simply for the fact that Etron has no shortage of lovers, and you're missing yours? You thought about him a lot out there, didn't you? Jaq."

She chewed her lower lip thoughtfully. "I guess I'm being stupid about it."

85

"Maybe, if you let it continue. Not if you let it go. Now you know what Jaq was feeling. That kind of territorial jealousy is a fairly alien concept to us native born Nyorfians—the humanoid ones—but as you know it's not so unusual out there among our animal friends."

Rett nodded.

"Or," said Trebor, "people from outsystem, humanoid or alien."

"That makes sense."

"Not that I'm excusing the way Jaq handled things, mind you. Not at all. Can I ask you a favor, Sarge?"

"As long as you're not asking me to pass out on demand—name it."

"Tell Jaq to come home—but only after you yell at him for being an idiot."

"What? You don't think it was my fault he left?"

Trebor made a rude noise. "If you don't know by that I—and the complement of F-troop—is one hundred percent with you, Sarge . . . then maybe it's time I apply for transfer."

"Deities forbid." Rett actually had to suppress a shiver at the thought. "I'm sorry. But after a few people on this base thought I drove him away by flinging myself at Etron—"

"Don't worry. I get it. It's been tough to talk about. When he comes back, it's not only you he's going to have to make up with."

"You think he'll come back?"

"Ariam seems to think so."

Rett made a face. "I don't know how Ariam managed to see him. They usually don't budge on anyone making contact with the TRANS people on active missions. But I'm glad she did. You know, I've tried to contact Jaq since I came back. His unit's completely incommunicado right now."

"Keep trying. And, Sarge?"

She raised one eyebrow.

"Don't ever disappear like that again. I think I lost ten years of my life when I saw Captain Etron coming down the corridor with Evetez on one side and Major Yidnar on the other. I'm still in shock over it. I think I need at least a tenday off to recover."

"I can imagine. If there's anything I really feel bad about from that crash, it's stuff like that—what it did to the people left behind." She frowned and studied her Omni, then leaned forward and accessed the Battalion's schedule on the workstation they used. "A tenday, huh?"

"I wasn't being serious."

"*I* am." She scowled at the display, punched in a few combinations with the touchpad. "Shit." She scratched her cheek and tried again. "I can't get you a tenday right now—"

"Sarge, I'm not due for time yet, I'll take it when it comes up."

"I can get you five days, with Nerrah, starting at new day."

He stared at her. "What?"

"Five days, with Nerrah, starting end of this shift at new day." Rett hoped Nerrah, Trebor's longtime lover and one of F-troop's squadleaders, wouldn't have a problem letting her juniors run the squad for half a tenday.

~I think she'll be thrilled,~ thought Pam.

I hope so. "Well, Trebor? Take it or wait until your regular time. Guaranteed no one will bother you unless the base is attacked."

In the five years she'd know him, Rett had never known Trebor to make a single impulsive action. Until now. She was so taken aback she didn't move a muscle as he leaned toward her, took a firm grip on her upper arms, and kissed her until her eyes crossed.

"I'm not even going to ask how you managed that." He pulled back. "I don't want to know." He dropped his hands and let out an incredulous laugh. "I'll take it."

"Wow. Deities, Trebor." Rett touched fingers to her lips. "That's some talent."

He gave her an impudent smirk. "That's not talent. That's a natural gift." He reached to touch Rett's left ear. "Shooting Avok through a tiny gap between your ear and shoulder and only taking off this little bit of you, now *that* was talent."

Rett couldn't argue with that. "All peripheral talents and gifts aside, Trebor, you've always done a good job for me. Beyond good, no matter where you were placed. Ever since you've been second, those times you filled in for me when I've not been around went as smoothly as if you'd been born to it. Are you sure you don't want the troop? Or your own?"

He shook his head. "No. Very honestly, no. Of course, if there were no acceptable alternative, it would be different. But I've no desire to fill your headband—I'm not wild about that much responsibility. I'm happy where I am—and where you are. Have been since C-troop. I can speak for Nerrah as well."

"Thanks. That means a lot to me," she said softly.

"I'm good handling kids." Trebor always referred to anyone younger than himself that way. Except for Pipano—at fifty-seven the eldest of the platoon—that meant the rest of F-troop. "I'm a good sharpshooter, it was okay when I was a squadleader, and I hope I'm a good second."

"I wouldn't trade you for all the roasted mushrooms on Nyorfias," confirmed Rett with a smile.

~Especially now you know how he can kiss,~ added Pam.

He chuckled. "Thanks, Sarge. Coming from you, that's solid. But, like Ariam used to say, 'I'm not too anxious to make platoon leader!'"

Rett shook her head. Feeling her mood lighten, she invited Pam to come forward slightly and help her give Trebor a few more parting shots. "Nobody wants my job," she said, and stood up. "I don't know why! Why not?" She took the reports and DSU from Trebor. "Hours aren't great, but what about the benefits of being on the enemy's most wanted list?"

"I'm already on it," said Trebor in a sour tone. "But at least I'm a little farther down than you are."

Rett stepped aside, Pam adding a suitably dramatic huff. "Are you sure?"

"I have never," said Trebor with emphasis, "been so absolutely sure of anything in my life, Sarge."

"Gee, thanks. Chicken," said Rett. Inside, Pam gave a funny little jump that nearly cracked Rett into a giggle. She pivoted on her heel to hide her sudden grin from Trebor. *Wasn't that the appropriate context?* she asked Pam.

~It was fine,~ Pam said. ~It was just weird to hear you say one of my words aloud without me putting it in your mouth.~

Rett pivoted on her heel to continue on her way. "Oh, Trebor. Anything you need for your downtime, whatever it is, if it's on this base you'll have it. Someone in Supply owes me a few favors, and I'm calling them in right now. I'll tell him to expect you."

The pleased, astonished look growing on her second's face filled her with warmth. "I'll also let you have the opportunity to surprise Nerrah with this. I'm off to see if I can run down Etron for a few minutes, he should be at some busywork himself for a while yet. See you later . . . if I don't, see you in five days."

She exited, aware that, for the moment, he remained seated in the attitude of astonishment and surprise. Right before she turned into the outer corridor, she heard him say in a bewildered tone, "What in two worlds is a chicken?"

HER HAND WAS SLIPPING.

Rett tightened her fingers and fought her instinct to drop what she held in her right hand to save herself from falling. Gritting her teeth, she pulled herself and her burden upward until her collarbone was level with the rail. Then she swung her right arm, slinging what it carried to the platform overhead.

"That's enough of that," she said aloud, although no one was around to hear. "I'll do the reps without the sim-body for a while."

~You'd better hope Med doesn't come by and see you're not wearing your support bandages.~

The interior voice of Rett's ego-merge companion blended impressions of warning and complaint.

"Med, thankfully . . . has enough on his agenda . . . setting up the new medical area . . . to sneak around spying on me." She completed five more of her torturous pull-ups and switched arms, swiping sweat from her face in the process. "Trebor, however, is a different matter." She raised her voice to a normal level. "Minute, Trebor."

There was a level of their ego-merge on which Pam couldn't interface. Rett's trained ability to sense and interpret energy emissions. She felt her mental companion make that funny little jump, like a shiver, that always followed the announcement of something the mindforce from Earth couldn't see or sense, almost as if Pam actually tried to get Rett's head to turn so she could see for herself. Pam knew better than to try that by now though, involuntarily or not. At least, most of the time.

~Here we go again. Something else to interrupt. You promised me, Rett. You said that you'd go look up some historical pictures and read some stuff for me from the earliest settlers in the system after your workout *for sure*.~

Pam, I'm sorry, but you know I can't just tell Trebor to go away because I have an appointment with an invisible friend who lives in my head.

~I know,~ Pam allowed grudgingly. ~But I'm getting a little antsy. You gave me so much to think about while you were downed behind the lines; left so many gaps open. If I can't get answers from you, I'll just have to use my imagination. I'd hate to have to imagine the wrong stuff for that journal I've started when I get back.~

I thought you said you were writing all this as a story, thought Rett with a huff of exasperation inside and out. She didn't like the idea. There was enough speculation in her own homesystem about her and her alleged exploits since the war began. Adding Pam's imagination to that . . . good deities.

~Gee, thanks. I'll have you know I don't *have* to exaggerate very much when it comes to your exploits.~

Rett sent her an apology. *It isn't something I like to think about.*

~Then don't. He's been a bit down lately, don't you think?~

Trebor? Rett frowned as she held her position and Pam squirmed with the effort not to react to the strain that Rett's personal thought processes so easily bypassed. *He hates being cold. Since we've transferred here to Aurora continent, it's been nothing but dark, cold, and nasty outside.*

~But we're all indoors.~

It's still not normal for us. Maybe I can arrange more time off for him.

Aurora Base, like Epnoce MainCommand on the big continent, was once a freighterport servicing ships loaded with trade commodities bound for other parts of the galactic quadrant. The ambiance here, though, was a lot different. Rett liked it. The smaller, looser-knit series of buildings made it seem more similar to the small backcountry communities on Nyorfias. In contrast to the base, the complexes of the main continent, with their unending miles of corridors and levels, had always made her feel as if she needed to find a place to hide. Aurora Base was as cozy as it was possible to get in such an arctic region.

For Trebor, Rett thought with an inward sigh, it would be the opposite. He was urban through and through, used to an active social life, university campuses bustling with students, and lots of warmth and sunshine. No amount of combat training or time away from home had taken what they'd grown up with away from any of them.

"What's up, Trebor?" Rett said aloud as she dropped to the floor and picked up a towel to mop her sweaty face and body.

"You're pushing too hard, Sarge," Trebor said, his judicious golden eyes raking her from boots to hair.

Stop that, Rett warned Pam as her friend squirmed.

~I can't get used to being naked or half-naked in front of people like you are.~

Rett picked up her breast support with a sigh inside and out. She'd worked up such a sweat Pam was lucky that she hadn't shed *all* her clothes, let alone anything from the waist up.

"Any trouble with that arm?"

Trebor's query startled Rett, who paused to sharpen both visual and mental focus on him. "No, other than the usual aches when the weather changes, like the rest of me."

~You were making these terrible faces,~ Pam said helpfully.

Ah. No wonder. "*You* try getting back into one of these when you're all sweaty and it's still wet, Trebor." Rett adjusted herself and the tan colored material.

Her second-in-command chuckled and handed her a frayed, sleeveless overshirt—also damp from the exertion that had caused her to shed it. "Should have stripped off to start with. Or found something less strenuous to do on your free time. And your wind?"

"Fine. Do you hear something wrong with my breathing?" For a moment, real worry filled her.

"No, just asking."

"Not that I don't appreciate it, but what's up with you?"

93

Trebor's amusement disappeared. "Did you have these on at all? Or did you bring them along so they could watch?" Fixing her with his sternest glance, he held up her forsaken support braces and wraps.

"Oh."

"Oh? *Oh?*" He glared.

"I'm eating, I'm resting, I feel great, none of you have indicated there's a problem, and Med's not complaining. Or is he?"

"No. No complaints. Not from him." Trebor folded the elastic material and stuffed the entire handful neatly within one of the wrist braces. "But from me. Don't forget who has to fill in for you when you're laid up. So *next* time I catch you out, I'll make a note of it and make sure it gets dropped in Med's queue first thing."

"Shit, why not kick me in the ass instead," said Rett. "All right, all right. I'll keep them on. What's up, anyway?"

"I came to tell you Major Yidnar wants to see us to discuss Complex 117. F-troop's supposed to punch it for the 21st Infantry."

She held her outward expression, but inside, a jolt of acid fire hit her belly. "The 21st, huh? I suppose it was only a matter of time."

"Colonel R—"

She cut him short. "I *know* what his name is. However, is the good Colonel of the opinion F-troop is good enough to point for him?"

"What's the problem, Sarge?"

"Tell me you don't know?" Rett looked hard at her second.

"All I know," Trebor said, "is that he's your father. I've only known *that* since Complex 63, when the children asked about it. And, Major Yidnar mentioned you and Colonel Reve didn't get along too well."

"Ariam never mentioned anything?"

"Not a word, Sarge. Maybe she had at one time to Kraym. Ariam never discussed her family in any detail with any of us, before or after we even knew you two were sisters. Just as you never have."

Seeing Trebor was telling the truth, Rett softened. "I didn't mean to get so defensive, but lately it seems as if everyone knows everything about me, so why not this as well?"

"I understand."

Leaning against the bars she'd been working out on, she explained. "Colonel Reve and I had a falling out some eleven years ago. It seems I was a useless, no good, backwoods mountain kid who'd never be of any use to this war; much less make it through Basic without making a fool of myself in the process."

Trebor's mouth opened in astonishment. Rett saw the switch as his body energy went almost completely neutral, than flared into a hard dark reds and oranges she associated with both anger and combat tension. "What gave him the right to say that?"

"Who knows? Maybe he was mad because I didn't speak up and tell him I had enlisted sooner. Maybe nothing. Or, maybe again he figured being my parent gave him every right." Rett turned aside, picking up her black headband. She grimaced as she ran her fingertips through her damp hair, and then sniffed critically at her upraised arm. "Ugh. When do we have to go?"

Trebor glanced at his chrono. "In that singularly famous word of our matchless commander: 'Now'. We'll just make it on time."

"Great, no help for it then." She settled her headband in place. "Deities forbid if we're a second late!" She tucked her shirt in and snapped the catch on her weapons and utility belts. "No time to clean up and change. I hope my sweaty self doesn't offend the Colonel. Let's go."

"Does Major Yidnar know?"

"That I stink? He'll figure it out."

Trebor wasn't amused. "That Colonel Reve said *that* to you?"

"Deities. If I can change anything about that day, it would be that Reve and I were alone and not at a meal with Ariam and four strangers. It wasn't for lack of trying to get him alone for a talk. Although I suppose I might have been more insistent." She shook her head. "Believe it or not, the Major was one of those four strangers, along with Mahrhys and two infantry officers. If ever I wanted to be struck dead by lightning or have a tree fall on my head, it was then."

"Shit."

"Of course I didn't know any of them at the time. I still don't know who the other two were. All I knew was they were our guests, up on a few days leave for the steelhead fishing." She took the package of support wraps from Trebor and rolled them inside her towel. "I was seventeen. I saw Reve once more after that day. I visited Ariam right before my first assignment to C-troop. He wanted to surprise Ariam and had no idea I was there. For a minute I hoped . . ." Rett shook her head. "But again it was very nearly a disaster, thank all deities it was just for a few minutes. And, after Special Forces training, at least I didn't let him see any reaction." She shrugged. "I've not seen or spoken to him since."

3.2.1 CONFERENCE ROOM, AURORA BASE, EPNOCE
0536.02.04 (LOCAL RECKONING)

HAVING GONE OVER THIS DATA before and knowing he'd be going over it several times over again, Major Yidnar took the opportunity to keep most of his attention on Colonel Reve. Without being obvious, of course.

No doubt, Reve was an imposing figure. A thick, healthy crop of sun-gold hair was caught at the nape of his neck in a short, wavy tail. Already tall, the bright hair made him look a lot taller. The cool gray depths of his large eyes arrested one's attention immediately. His infantry uniform, in Epnocian shades of building grays, was worn enough to be comfortable. The uniform and the accessory gear, however, were so neat and precisely fitted to the hard strong body beneath that one almost looked for the dress uniform instead of the dreary camouflage.

Giving the total impression of a man relaxed and in control, Colonel Reve, along with his second-in-command, listened attentively as Captain Mahrhys, Lieutenant Evetez, and a civilian advisor went over building schematics on the large display board.

He hadn't changed one bit since Yidnar saw him last. Just the attitude about Rett. Reve didn't seem to think he needed any help on this mission, especially not from F-troop. There wasn't too much to be done about that—MainCommand wanted the job done. With Mahrhys and Evetez, Yidnar had tried to suggest another unit be assigned to the 21st.

The attempt didn't get far. The 2023rd was tied up in so many directions they could only spare one unit, so MainCommand insisted it be F-troop.

Yidnar, irritated, worried the inside of his lower lip with his teeth. He didn't like it. He also had to admit he wouldn't be griping if it were anyone other than Reve.

Knowing the both of them, there would friction if they were related or not. They're both professional enough that they won't let this interfere with the completion of the mission. At least I hope not.

He saw the civilian was about to conclude the discussion for the moment, and the instant the opening came, he spoke. "Thank you. Mahrhys?"

The quiet, silver-haired man signaled his understanding and withdrew, taking Evetez, SubColonel Nauskova—Reve's second—and the civilian advisor with him. They didn't need to be here for this, and Yidnar wanted any initial blowups between Colonel Reve and Sergeant Rett to stay within this room.

Reve elevated a sandy eyebrow in mild surprise, as if he'd expected those already here would remain, but didn't protest their leaving. After a glance at his chrono, his gaze met Yidnar's.

It wasn't hard to imagine the words the infantry officer did not utter: *Your commando has forty seconds to get here.*

Instead, Reve asked, "Is F-troop as good as all the reports say?"

"F-troop's one of the most effective units under my command, Colonel Reve, and as far as I'm concerned, the best fighting unit in the galactic quadrant." Yidnar held the Colonel's gaze. "I hope the success of this mission will take priority over any personal matters," he added.

Reve's face remained impassive. "I was unaware personal matters were involved, Major Yidnar."

At that very moment, Sergeant Rett and her second entered the conference room. *Eighteen seconds to spare,* Yidnar noted with satisfaction. Trebor had obviously pulled her from an intensive workout. Despite the sweat-stained, threadbare old fatigues, Rett was every inch dress uniform formal as she moved inside and acknowledged her commander with a crisp salute, then the infantry officer. Yidnar didn't expect any less. He could count on any of his people to show the normal, properly respectful, formal, and proud attitude of any Special Forces operative in the presence of ranking officers outside their own Battalion.

On the other hand, Colonel Reve's polite coolness became a hair short of outright condescension and open hostility. The single glance he gave Sergeant Trebor would have flattened any five ordinary soldiers, produced a flinch or a blink among the tougher ones.

Trebor's fierce face didn't rearrange a single molecule. He inquired instead if there was anything they needed him to procure, automatically placed a filled water bottle in front of his platoon leader, and then took a formal stance slightly behind and to the right of her chair, ready to produce anything she might ask of him.

There wasn't any reason Rett's second couldn't take the chair next to hers. Of course, no one outside Special Forces knew that, they assumed it was all part of some mysterious rules of conduct. Well . . . so it was, but not in the manner anyone would think. The second's position would be proper if this was a formal meeting or hearing of some sort, not a pre-planning discussion of a target area. To anyone from Special Forces, Trebor's taking the more formal stance at this meeting clearly indicated his high respect for his platoon leader and scorn for the attitude of the officer. Not to mention it made the Colonel the slightest bit uncomfortable.

Good for you, Trebor, Yidnar allowed silently, and then opened the meeting, feeling hopeful things had a chance to go smoothly.

At least, that was until Colonel Reve started talking.

* * * * *

GOOD GRIEF, THOUGHT PAM ON her deepest private level.

Rett had begged her to sit deep for this one, so Pam was as closed and tight as she could possibly make herself. That didn't stop her from experiencing every sensation her host did, from observing every expression, and hearing every word and shade of nuance. She didn't have to use her imagination to fill in the blanks here.

Yet, despite the man's insufferable attitude, Pam liked what she saw. Most of Rett's recollections of her father had been deliberately hazy, so seeing him in person was a pleasant surprise. Reve's features weren't exactly handsome, but they were arresting. Rett certainly had his height and build, some of the same angularity of feature. The man's eyes and wavy golden hair, though, were Ariam's.

Physical features aside, it was the impact he had on Rett that sparked Pam's concern—even raised her mental hackles a little. If she were physically separate from Rett right now, she'd walk right up to that guy and . . . No, she wouldn't. Rett would have kittens.

Rett appreciates the sentiment and support.

Pam sent quick apology for "leaking".

Well, since you feel everything I do, I'm not surprised, since I've had similar thoughts a few times.

Pam settled back, wondering what was going to happen.

As you said earlier, Pam, he's just another infantry officer we're being temporarily assigned to. I can put up with it.

With that thought firmly in her grasp, Rett was comfortably able to do whatever she needed. Trebor's obvious show of support was heartening, as well. She composed herself, sitting still and attentive, listening as the infantry officer spoke. Well, at least she listened for the first thirty seconds. After that, she had to divert energy into controlling her temper and impatience.

~Is he for real?~ Pam's astounded thought broke from the thick muffler she'd drawn around her space.

Rett narrowed her mental eyes while retaining the expression she had on the outside. *He should know better than that.* Hitting that refinery with Reve's approach would totally disable her platoon, along with half his infantry.

~He's baiting you, Rett. Don't give in to it.~

You're right, I think, thought Rett. *He wants me to blow up, use that as an excuse not to have us. He doesn't want F-troop to point for him any more than I want us to.*

~Then you have two choices.~ Pam didn't detail what they were.

With a mental sigh, Rett took the opportunity for a fast look at Major Yidnar while Reve was glancing at his Omni. The Major's attention was on Reve; his only sign of strain the position of his eyebrows and the deepened furrows and lines around his rugged-featured face.

Only one choice would have acceptable results, Rett thought. She owed it to the Major to do this right.

So she sucked it in, vowing neither Reve nor her commander was going to suspect that she had one fingertip of personal feeling about any of this.

Rett was familiar with Aurora Complex 117, both from intensive study and flying aerial reconnaissance with the AirSpacefighters. The massive refinery was one of the best-defended Coalition positions on Epnoce, let alone Aurora, because it supplied fuel to the land vehicles of the remaining Coalition forces on the continent.

I am doing this because if I don't, it will reflect badly on Major Yidnar. Plus, gaining the refinery would expedite the Coalition's downfall. There. She'd made her statement, now she'd stick with it. *Besides, I've taken baiting and condescension and things far worse than anything the likes of Colonel Reve could give me.*

~You were better off thinking of him as just another officer, period,~ Pam thought.

Yeah, I guess you're right, Rett had to admit, and did just that.

Finally, when Rett was asked to comment freely, she did. With a polite, acceptable, half-medium smile in place, she said, "Colonel Reve, sir, your plan stinks. Like shit. Sir."

Rett didn't bat an eyelash as the Major sent her a narrow-eyed glare of warning. *Hey, he asked for my free comment,* Rett thought inwardly for Pam and indicated in her posture and expression for Major Yidnar.

Don't push it, her commander indicated in return.

"Excuse me, Sergeant?" Her father's cool gray eyes were hard as Reve nailed his focus on her.

Rett pushed aside the memory of the last time she and her father had been eye-to-eye. "Colonel, did I understand correctly that you wanted my honest words and free comments on this?"

"Yes, I did." Reve's tone was flat. "I'm also not quite sure I heard you correctly before, Sergeant."

Rett raised her volume a notch and enunciated her words with care so there would be no mistake. "My apologies, sir, allow me to repeat my statement. I said the plan stinks like shit, sir."

101

* * * * *

TREBOR'S GUTS HAD SHRUNK IN an instinctive biological protection reflex with the sergeant's first remark. The rest of his internal organs shrank now, all of them trying to hide behind his breastbone. He felt them strangling his heart, which had apparently dropped toward the spot his stomach used to be.

Any minute now, he thought, *Med will show up. Because if she comes out with another remark like that, my balls are going to be stuck behind my kidneys. Nerrah could forget about us having any kids when this war is over.*

The glance he exchanged with Major Yidnar wasn't too encouraging. Either the Major was going to start cracking some molars, clench his fingers hard enough to break bones in his hands, or make a more physical movement and simply tear his hair out.

"Would you care to elaborate, Sergeant?" Colonel Reve asked.

"Yes, thank you, sir, I would."

Trebor closed his hand around the empty water bottle the sergeant handed back so casually. He didn't remember seeing her take a sip, but then again, from the heat he felt in her fingers during the exchange, maybe the water had simply evaporated.

"Your plan will get us and half the infantry into the refinery very quickly—yes. Meanwhile the rest of your division will still be outside, with nothing between F-troop and your people but the full garrison of Coalition troopers. No way in for support troops, no way out for us if things go wrong. We can't attack like that, Colonel. It's suicidal, and stupid."

"And what did you have in mind, Sergeant Killer?" asked the infantry officer.

From his new vantage point at the water dispenser, Trebor watched with his peripheral vision. His platoon leader gave no indication she'd even heard the hated nickname or the tone of voice in which it had been uttered. Her acceptable, polite smile remained in place and her dark eyes held their expression of alert attention as she gave a brief outline of her own proposal.

Returning to his place, Trebor sternly told his innards to report to their usual positions and stay there. Then he gave most of his focus to the conversation, the small part he held in reserve wishing he could knock that big chip off Colonel Reve's shoulder. He couldn't wait for this uncomfortable session to end. Although Rett still appeared cool, relaxed, and confident, the heat radiating out of her body from all that stored up anger was making Trebor glad he hadn't worn the extra layer he had longed for earlier.

In the end, Colonel Reve accepted the sergeant's plan, with a few little modifications. They made no difference. As long as the infantry didn't get in F-troop's way, the attack should be successful. Trebor thought he saw the barest gleam of approval in the man's luminous gray eyes and wondered to himself if the officer's original, senseless plan had been a deliberate test for Rett.

Must have been, thought Trebor, *since Reve's command record as a field commander is nothing short of brilliant. He's the one who came up with the plan to sneak three divisions here from Nyorfias before we even sent the GTC-Nyorfian task force in. No, if Reve were that much of a bubblehead, he wouldn't even be here.* When Trebor glanced to the colonel again, the man's expression was every bit as coolly emotionless as the platoon leader's.

Soon afterward, the Colonel left; Rett and Trebor stayed, and for a few eternal moments, there was complete silence in the conference room.

Trebor took the opportunity to move a safer—and cooler—distance away from the sergeant. Even Major Yidnar eyed her warily. Rett sat back down, resuming her apparently relaxed position. She reached for her replenished water bottle and drained it. Trebor had his hand out before she turned around.

"Thanks, Trebor." She hesitated before letting the bottle go, a grin twitching her lips. "Maybe you'd better sit down. Let me get you a drink, instead."

He snatched the bottle and sidestepped over to the water cooler. "It's not water I'm wanting right now," Trebor said, shaking his head.

"Mind sharing what you found so amusing about this meeting, Sergeant?" Major Yidnar asked.

"It's just that you and Trebor were so *obvious*. Especially you, sir, trying to mediate between Reve and me. Then after he left, you two looked so funny I just couldn't help it."

"Funny?" said Trebor. "*Funny?* Excuse me, Sarge, but speaking for myself, that look wasn't amusement, it was sheer terror." He set her replenished bottle down with a *thunk* at her right elbow and sank into the nearest chair.

"I was wondering why all your hair turned gray—just kidding," she said as he sent a significant glance toward the bundle containing her unworn workout braces.

103

"We were only trying to keep the roof on Aurora Base, Sergeant," said Yidnar in an injured tone. "You do realize he was testing you? What we had discussed with him and the others earlier was directly in line with your proposal, almost verbatim."

"I did, Major. Appreciated it. The support from the both of you boosted my morale tremendously. However, sir, there is nothing to be concerned about. Permission to be dismissed, sir?" She stood up, still smiling. "Trebor and I have to brief the platoon."

Yidnar regarded her with a sour expression. "Get out of here. Now. Go."

She made good her escape, Trebor on her heels.

"All that redirection of energy and I'm *starving*." The sergeant pressed a hand over her belly. "I wasn't about to blow up in front of Reve—or Major Yidnar. That's what Reve wanted. I let him know I was aware he was setting me up with his stupid plan. I'm sorry you . . . uhm . . . took the heat in there—he simply hated it that you stood. It put him at a strategic disadvantage, especially since he didn't have an assistant or a second."

"Does that make you feel better?"

"Hmm. Does it? Actually . . . yes. In some perverse way, it does." She hastened to explain. "It wasn't the same as what happened with Etron, something that just blurped out of me because I was feeling out of sorts. Not like that. I didn't take one step out of line—"

"Sarge, if you'd been a bullet, Colonel Reve would have needed a medtech."

"Come on, Trebor. I've taken that stand with others. You've seen it before. There is no difference between Colonel Reve and any of them. Besides, Reve's feelings weren't hurt, he wasn't humiliated beyond belief, and I didn't bite him in the ass or anything, either. He was simply disadvantaged for a minute or two."

She took a breath, puffed it out from her lips. "But for the long run, I'd as soon rather not feel this way, that way, or the other about any of it, and just have things be normal."

Trebor nodded, satisfied she had a clear view on her actions. He took the hardcopies of the planning sheets from her hands. "Go get a shower and something to eat, Sarge." He cleared his throat. "I'll take care of this for you. I've been told the woods just east of here are full of cotos and burrowers, since the mess hall doesn't seem to keep your latest diet handy."

He waited for the usual reaction to that. Rett—like almost any other Nyorfian who'd been used to living off the land—went off into passionate tiffs about the Coalition: how they were wiping out complete ecosystems with their pollution or by shooting down entire herds just for a few hunks of meat, or completely wiping out a stand of food plants, leaving nothing to propagate. Completely prepared to endure some variation of that tirade, her actual response took him by total surprise.

"Good idea, Trebor! How did you know I was craving some raw meat with the fur still attached? Especially after that meeting! I never would have thought of it! How far east? Can I run there and back in time for the briefing, you think, or do I need to sign out a shortranger or rover?"

For a second or two he had to wonder if he had to be concerned. Then he started to smile. "You know, I hate to say this, but I think stress is mellowing you. Ever since that ambush at the Circle bridge I've noticed a change. You're still wound pretty tight sometimes, but other times I see flashes of the kid who was my squadleader back in C-troop. The one who liked to relax and tell jokes and every once in a while—a crazy story."

"And that's a good thing?"

"Yes." He gave her a gentle push ahead. "Go take a shower and change, I'll schedule the briefing. Go on—after your workout and that meeting, you stink almost worse than Colonel Reve's test."

3.2.2 COMMON AREA, AURORA BASE, EPNOCE
0536.02.04 (LOCAL RECKONING)

"Sᴇʀɢᴇᴀɴᴛ Aʀɪᴀᴍ, sᴏʀʀʏ ᴛᴏ ɪɴᴛᴇʀʀᴜᴘᴛ your free time."

Ariam studied the young GI. "What's up?"

Semage and the handful of other B-troop members with her likewise fixed curious attention on the messenger. Ariam felt the GIs nervousness escalate and extended reassurance.

"Colonel Reve of the 21ˢᵗ Division requests some of your free time, if you're available."

Dad! She had been expecting his arrival, of course, but she also had expected to feel him nearby a lot sooner. *He must be locked tight for a reason. And not because of me.*

Ariam turned to Semage. "I missed him by three hours at Complex 63, and only got to speak with him on com when Rett went missing—and now he's here."

"See you later, Ariam. You're on free time."

"But we scheduled that meeting—"

Semage made a shooing motion. "Go. I'll explain."

Flashing him a grateful smile, Ariam turned to the messenger.

"I have a complex rover in the main corridor, Sergeant." He looked a lot less nervous than before.

"Let's go."

* * * * *

"Ariam."

She flung herself in her father's arms. "I missed you!" She burrowed close as his embrace tightened around her.

"I missed you more. Let me see you, Ari."

They stepped apart. Ariam eyed her father up and down with the same careful assessment he was giving her. Nothing telltale, except a new scar along his left temple and some fresh silver in his hair.

"You look fit, Ariam."

"You look good too, Dad. Aunt Valera said she enjoyed your visit." She mentioned it with a bit of guardedness, since her mother's sister looked enough like Tonia to have been her twin instead of three years older. Ariam didn't want to push at Reve to gauge his mood, not at the moment. He was still so tightly shielded.

To her vast surprise her father smiled, the expression not so much sad as merely wistful. "Yes. I enjoyed seeing her and meeting Ulorath and Olvero." He chuckled. "Valera hasn't changed much, at least from what I remember of her from twenty-four years or so ago."

"Dad, why were we never told she's an Adept?"

"That's something you should ask Valera. Let's sit." He took her arm and indicated a couch in the corner. "That Olvero—he's quite a kid. I'm glad I was forewarned of his abilities."

"He must have pushed whatever blocks you set to the limit."

"It wasn't that bad. It sure reminded me of what your mother and I went through with you and Tova."

His smile wasn't forced. It pleased Ariam right down to her toes. Her father had somehow found peace with the deaths of Tonia and Tovadan that had all but devastated him so many years ago. Maybe his visit with Valera, Olvero, and Ulorath had given him that breakthrough. She wasn't going to argue the instrument; she was going to appreciate the result. All she hoped for now was that her father was ready to move forward and make peace with Rett.

"Besides, he spent most of the time talking about you and your sister." Reve sent her a sideways glance, one corner of his mouth lifting in a familiar manner. "I was introduced to his friends not as his Uncle Reve, but as his *'Cousin Rett's dad'.*"

"Serves you right." Ariam tossed her head, added an unsympathetic and amused sniff, and took her opening. "Does Rett know you're here?"

"I've already seen her," said Reve as he seated himself, his smile fading.

Ariam sat alongside him. "And the Base is still in one piece?"

"We discussed preliminary attack plans for Complex 117, since MainCommand told Major Yidnar to loan me F-troop to spearhead."

"You're getting the best, Dad," Ariam said. Inwardly she cursed MainCommand, who must have insisted on F-troop, completely unaware of the situation between the commanders of the Special Forces platoon and the 21st Infantry division.

A heartbeat later, she was thanking all good gods and deities for it. This was an opportunity too good to let go. She just wished B-troop was in on this too, but they were already scheduled to head off with the rest of Easy on another target—which was the context of the meeting she was, hopefully, going to miss all or most of for this visit.

"I know that, Ari."

Reve leaned toward her. She closed her eyes and tipped her head into her father's hand, enjoying the tactile contact. He tucked her hair behind her ear, cupping her jaw and cheek in his palm for a moment before letting his hand drop. Then he sat back, and she opened her eyes to see him looking three times older than his years.

"I'm sorry I couldn't see you in person last month—but I appreciated hearing that sort of news from you, rather than someone else."

"That's how it goes when we're on combat assignment. But why didn't you try to contact Rett when you heard she'd been recovered?"

He didn't reply right away. When he did, it was with: "Rett looked fine." He sounded as if he wanted to go on, but lapsed again into silence.

Ariam nodded and slid closer against him, leaning quietly against his side with her head on his shoulder. Of course his arm came around her then, his cheek rested on her hair. She nestled in comfortably and for a minute she kept still, listening to him breathe, to his heart beat, looking for and finding the strength she'd always took such comfort in as a very small child. Reaching gently, she encouraged him to relax, let down his defenses.

The physical contact helped. That, and the natural link she shared with her father, just as she shared with Rett. From the jumble of emotion she felt in him, Ariam began to make some sense out of the situation.

"Dad?"

"Yes, Ariam."

"Don't you think this has gone on long enough? A little too long?"

His body stiffened a little and he lifted his head. Ariam was quick to slide her arms around him, without the slightest force effectively preventing any evasion.

Reve just shook his head.

"It's been *eleven years*. You two were so close, closer than anything, yet in less than a minute you contrived to alienate yourself from someone who still loves you so much the pain will never leave."

"Ariam—"

This time she had to tighten her arms around him, anchoring them both in place. "You have no idea. You can't even begin to imagine, no matter how many reports you read, on any level, what Rett's been through. I can't even do that. She's blocked most everything up so tight I doubt she can ever get in touch with those things any more without losing herself completely."

"I've kept up."

"Through what, personnel records? My letters, what you've heard from me? Those don't begin to scratch the surface. On top of all that . . . she's had a hard time of it personally just since we've been here on Epnoce." Ariam scooted back just enough so she could angle herself toward him.

"Are you blaming me?" Her father's tone was quiet, his curiosity genuine.

"For what happened to Rett? No. What happened would have happened anyway, because Rett would have done the same things, the same way, no matter what you said to her the day she left. No matter what happened after that."

"Then what are you looking for?"

"I'm looking to get my father and my sister together again, because they both need each other, and I need them."

Reve closed his eyes. "Ariam—"

"No, *you* listen. Whatever happened in the past is gone. But we're all still alive *right now*. After all these years, and having people that we love dying, being hurt so horribly, don't you think it's time to stop being so logheaded and put something right again, before it's too late? How would you feel right now, for the rest of your life, if Rett *had* died in that crash? Or at any other point over the past few years? Or if you both had to face each other in a meeting because *I* had died?" She had to look away then. That scenario was part of her personal heartaches. Not the dying part. Not that. The part where her death might be what it took to bring Rett and Reve into sight distance of each other.

Her father slid his free hand beneath Ariam's chin, lifting her face to his. "Listen—"

"You said the words, Dad. Rett did the best she could. I know it. She tried, so many times. And when you told her to go ahead and she did—you said those horrible words." She blinked back tears. "I can still hear them, and I can still feel what Rett felt at that moment." She moved her chin aside, piercing her gaze deep into his. "And I can still feel what you felt before you said them. I know why.

"You were scared. You knew it was coming, and when it did, you were terrified. You were hoping Rett would wait a while longer, take care of me, and be safe, because you know damned well we would have signed up together once I was of age otherwise."

"That's for sure," he said under his breath.

"And then you probably would have hoped we would have chosen the infantry and somehow wrangled us to be assigned to you, was that it?"

"I expected Rett to go eventually to AirSpacefighters. But I never dared to plan beyond having both of you stay right where I knew you would have safety and close family friends for assistance and support," said Reve, and she knew he was telling the truth.

"I can understand your fear and lashing out because of it," Ariam said. "But not hanging on to it the way you did. You wronged her, and now you have to make the first move, don't you understand?"

* * * * *

REVE CLOSED HIS EYES FOR a second, letting a long breath out through his nose. He didn't know why he did it that way, either. He didn't dare admit—even to himself—that he hadn't been in complete control of his actions. Of course he'd been. He remembered having some very clear, deliberate thoughts on them at the time—but he couldn't recall any bit of them now. One thing he would never forget was the expression of complete betrayal and shock in his firstborn daughter's eyes. As long as he lived, he'd remember it.

"And why just Rett?" persisted Ariam. "Why didn't you do something like that to me when I enlisted?"

Reve rubbed his hands over his face. With a sigh he let his head drop back to the material behind it. "How do I explain something I'm not sure of myself?"

The extremely capable young woman alongside him resettled herself on the couch. *That's my youngest,* thought Reve. *My baby. Look at her. She's grown, her Talent has grown . . . and she's not going to let this go.*

"Start at the beginning," she suggested. "It'll come. Then, when you've finished telling me, you can go tell Rett." She crossed her arms over her chest and glared. "Damn it, I want this thing resolved once and for all!"

"Ariam, Rett would never listen to me or believe me now.. It's been far too long."

"You'd be surprised."

"And I wasn't exactly . . . cordial . . . in the conference room."

"I'm sure that wasn't exactly the best forum for what I had in mind." She wasn't backing down one fingerwidth.

"You talk about *us* being logheaded. You are still the most outspoken—"

"The cone doesn't fall far from the tree, Dad," Ariam said. "Please promise you'll try, *really* try, to clear this up. If not for you, for me. Please?" Uncrossing her arms, she twined them around his waist. Leaning her head on his shoulder again, she sent him an honestly pleading glance through her eyelashes. "*Please,* Dad."

"That's quite a weapon you have there, Sergeant." Reve had to admit defeat. He slid an arm around her again. "You can thank your mother for it. When Tonia looked at me like that, I'd do anything for her, even if it was wrong. Fortunately, she never asked that of me."

"What I'm asking is far from wrong, too."

He dropped a kiss on her forehead. "I'll talk to Rett after the mission."

"Why not before?"

"Don't push any more than you have already," said Reve. "I need time."

"There might not be time afterward," Ariam said.

"Ariam—I will talk to Rett when *I* feel right about it. Maybe in a day or two, after I've been around her a bit more. I don't know—something about that damned commando attitude. It just shuts me out. I don't know Rett any more. I'm glad you didn't pull that stuff on me on top of everything else you've hit me with. Do you use those eyes of yours to set off your explosives, Ari?"

"I don't give away trade secrets," she said.

He let out a short laugh and shook his head.

"You were going to explain something to me, Colonel Reve, sir?" Ariam instantly adopted the attitude he claimed to find so disconcerting.

"Ariam—" said Reve.

"Oh, cool off. We're *supposed* to be that way around people outside our own Battalion. Excuse me." She touched her left ear to let him know she had a com. "Ariam."

From the disappointment that flashed across her face, and the confirmation she gave that she was on her way, Reve knew their visit was at an end.

"I guess Semage ran out of excuses." Ariam stood up. "Dad—"

He got up, hugged her, and kissed her forehead. "We'll talk again. I love you."

"I love you too. And we'll get back to this."

"We'll see," said Reve, walking her to the door. He stood in place for a long minute after it closed between them. Valera had told him, too, it was time to move forward, that she felt it was urgent to do so.

Those with precognitive Talent weren't always right—there were too many constantly changing variables for complete accuracy. But still . . .

"We'll see," he said.

3.2.3 ISOLATION WARD, MEDICAL SECTION, AURORA BASE
0536.02.05 (LOCAL RECKONING)

"WHAT ARE YOU TELLING ME, Med?" Rett planted her feet as Med tried to push her through the opening.

"I'm telling you she'd be all right, in a tenday or so. No one else seems to be infected but even so, I'm cooking immunizations for the rest of you as well as the Base."

Rett cast an anxious glance over his head. Through the haze of a sterilization field, Carakenne's deep, dark skin, shiny with fever, looked as if it were coated in glowing blue slime.

She wasn't at all certain about the med assistant hovering so solicitously near the delirious little commando. "Does *he* know what he's doing?" Rett had never seen him before.

~You don't make the medical area a habitual stop, either,~ said Pam.

Med growled. "Good*bye*, Sergeant."

"Wait a minute—"

"If you must know, he has been a med-assistant longer than I have been a doctor. All right? Out!"

"But—"

"This is supposed to be an *isolation* area. Quarantine, get it? Or do we run ourselves through these radiation fields and risk mutating future generations for the fun of it. You might not get sick—but you can carry germs." Med took her arm in a firm grip, kicked her left ankle, and pivoted her toward the door. "Carakenne is not doing very well at this point in time. True. However, the treatment and medication takes a few seconds at *least* to even get circulated through her bloodstream, a few hours to really start working, and I have complete confidence she'll pull out of this in a tenday or so."

"She took a hard fall, are you sure there's no other—"

Med's grip turned to a shove and Rett found herself talking to a closed door. "—injuries. Damn." She leaned against the wall outside and raked her hand through her hair.

Carakenne's unexpected collapse, which happened right out of nowhere in the middle of drill, left her shaken.

"Rhozev, like Ariam, is usually right about these things."

Rett spun to the left in surprise. Major Yidnar stood there, his features drawn with deep concern. "Come on, walk with me. This leaves you short a demolition team leader, doesn't it."

"I didn't think of it that way yet, but you're right. It does."

F-troop had taken casualties in the invasion of Aurora, during which time Rett had still been missing behind enemy lines. Junior Sergeant Nitraym, since F-troop's formation a squadleader and the leader of special demolition and chemical teams, had been one of them. He was back on Nyorfias now. Rett just thanked all good deities both Nitraym and Darbey were still alive and going to recover. In time. In any case, Corporal Carakenne replaced Nitraym as head of the chemical and demolition team.

"Do you have someone else in mind?"

"I'm running short on experienced people in that department," admitted Rett. "Those I have can handle themselves, but the main advantage I had with a team leader who knew a lot of tricks was making up something on the spot if we had to. Too bad H'tenneck doesn't have an affinity for chemicals."

"He has his own squad to look after now. I think I can resolve this issue. Ariam's experienced, knows a lot of tricks, and you know firsthand she can make things up on the spot, with or without chemicals. It'll be a bit inconvenient for Semage, but he won't need Ariam for Easy Force's assignment as much as you will for yours."

Rett chewed her lower lip, scrambling for alternatives, for all the reasons this temporary transfer shouldn't happen.

"Any problems?"

"No, sir. Thank you."

The Major thumped her shoulder lightly in encouragement and support. "As soon as the medtechs can assure us no one else is going to go down to the illness before we all get immunized, I'll meet with Semage and Evetez and arrange for it, then. I don't foresee any problems—from any angle."

I'm glad someone has a positive outlook, thought Rett to Pam.

Even if only for a few days, it would be nice to have Ariam on the same schedule. Rett only wished it wasn't because poor Carakenne was back there in Medical practically in convulsions from a fever.

3.2.4 AURORA BASE, EPNOCE
0536.02.06 (LOCAL RECKONING)

"I JUST CAN'T HIDE FROM you any more, can I?"

Ariam slid down the wall to sit alongside Rett. "I know it's the first time you've had to yourself since this latest craziness started, but I needed some time with you, too."

Rett smiled at her sister and leaned into her for a moment. "It's really about Dad, isn't it?"

"I've been watching you two pretty closely since he arrived. I'm glad you're managing to keep your differences from the troops. But I've been asked why Colonel Reve's being so high-handed with you."

"Who else have you told then, Ari?"

"No one," said Ariam, sounding hurt. "I just remind them that everyone handles pressure differently and Reve doesn't want anyone to think he's showing you any favoritism because we're family. I mean, we can't hide that much of it. I reminded them how hard you were with me once everyone knew we were related. Of course they couldn't remember—"

"They couldn't remember because I was never that hard on you. Not any harder than on anyone else, anyway."

"In any case, they stopped worrying about it." Ariam pulled her knees to her chest and wrapped her arms around them.

"I'm sorry, Ari. None of this has been easy." Rett sighed and rubbed her forehead. Of course Ariam would never spill such a sensitive topic. "So you know, in F-troop, only Trebor and Med know we had a falling out."

"What does Pam have to say about all this?"

~About the problem you have with your father?~ thought Pam

"I don't have a problem with my father. The problem IS my father!" said Rett aloud so forcefully that she startled Ariam.

"Sometimes I really regret not being a mindspeaker," said Ariam. "Look, Rett. Pam usually has good insights, right? Please talk to her. I want my family together again. It might be too late for anything before the mission, but maybe after. Please?"

"I can't promise anything, Ariam."

"Please think about it. Go back to that time in your head with Pam and let her think about it, too. At least that much." Ariam turned and hugged Rett so fiercely it was hard to breathe.

"All right. That much."

"I'll leave you two alone, then." With a final squeeze, Ariam jumped to her feet and slipped away, leaving a cold spot against Rett's side.

I'm sorry that I've been ignoring you again, Pam, thought Rett.

~That's all right. I've been trying to stay out of the way. You've really been so busy—inside and out—lately I didn't want to be a distraction,~ Pam said.

Thanks. Thanks for understanding. I appreciate it. Rett was determined to never take a chance that Pam would be whisked away again without knowing how much Rett truly appreciated her: as a friend, advisor, and . . . a soul sister.

~I know you do, but it's still nice to . . . er, hear it.~

Rett leaned her head back to the cool, smooth wall behind her. *Talk to me, Pam. You usually have good ideas. Especially about people. Wild and unlikely ideas, but usually good.*

Pam wished she could fix the fresh surge of hurt and confusion she felt inside her friend. No one can hurt you as much as someone you love, she thought on her private level. It was so true. She knew how it felt. ~Any memories you shared with me of your dad to that one point are good. I just can't imagine him doing something like that. Especially when you mention he's also someone who dropped everything to be there when they brought you back after Iheolon left you for dead.~

Rett stiffened. *I mentioned that? Pam—*

~Chill. You know I don't go rooting around in here without your permission or cooperation,~ Pam said. ~But Rett, every time you think of your father, every single time, this little niggle of an idea, a memory, or a wishful thought enters your mind, although you never acknowledge it. So I take that as 'mentioning it', yes,~ returned Pam with a trace of defiance.

Rett let her shoulders and posture slump. *Well, I can't deny it. When I was a little kid and had nightmares, I called Dad. He was always there. So I'm not certain if that time I started waking up that it wasn't a wishful thought.* She wriggled her butt into a more comfortable position. *But I was—I still am—so sure. So certain he was there. I can remember his voice, and his scent. Feel his hand on my face. He tried to apologize to me for what he said. But nothing ever happened after that, no follow-through, no contact. I went to telling myself it was a realistic dream.*

~Well, let's not go to *that* particular point in time now. As much as I'd like to know everything, this isn't the right time or place."

Rett chuckled, keeping it soft. *That's my line, isn't it?* Grateful for her companion heading her off to safer—though no less painful—memories, she geared her mind for the sharing she knew Pam would ask for next. *I'm tired of carrying this, Pam. Ari was right. I'm going to have to talk with my father if I'm ever going to let this go, no matter what the outcome.*

~He told you off for no apparent reason?~

I told you, before. Up to the very second, everything was completely normal. Even now I still can't believe it . . .

119

HOUSE, TREETOP PROVINCE, NYORFIAS
TEN YEARS EARLIER

RETT'S FATHER SAT BACK WITH a satisfied sigh. "Next to seeing my girls, this is something I've dreamed about for months. Excellently done, Mahrhys."

Rett had to admit the grilled steelhead had been gorgeously cooked. She was happy her father was in a good mood, because it was now or never, whether people were around or not. It was the third afternoon of her father's leave . . . and she had to meet her transport in just a few short hours.

She clenched and unclenched her hands under the table, waiting for a lull in the small talk between her father, Ariam, and their guests. All her attempts to get him alone the past three days had failed and she had to speak now. She had to try again.

"Dad, can we go outside for a minute?"

Reve glanced toward the window and raised his eyebrows. "It's pouring down rain. Is it something so dire you can't bring it up here?"

If I suggest going to another room, something else is bound to happen. I know it. It's going to have to be here. Gathering all her nerve, taking a deep breath, she spoke. "I've enlisted. Ariam's nearly fourteen. Norlah and Rafe are taking her in to board. I'm getting picked up for Basic in a few hours."

"I'm going when I'm seventeen and a half, too," said Ariam, picking fruit bits out of a roll purchased earlier in town and devouring each plump morsel one by one. Rett knew for sure Ariam wasn't worried about a thing. As far as her sister was concerned, Rett and Reve had already talked about this day two years ago, before he went on active duty.

Wishing she had her sister's lighthearted confidence, Rett watched her father's face, hoping to find the usual approval and support in his gray eyes. Instead, she saw his tanned cheeks slowly turn pale. The lean muscles along his jaw tightened. "You had to bring this up now?"

"I've tried to bring it up c-constantly since you came," she said very softly. "Every time I started to talk to you, we were interrupted."

He didn't say anything, and Rett's fingers twisted even more tightly together. "Please, can we go outside, or into the office, and talk about the arrangements I made for Ariam and the business, Dad?"

Reve's eyes hardened to the sharp temper of well-forged steel. Rett faced him squarely, waiting for his response. Still, he said nothing, made no motion.

Then: "Two years ago I thought you agreed to take care of Ariam and manage this business, Rett." His tone was flat.

"T-two years ago, we agreed that would b-be so until Ariam was older and I was of enlistment age," she said, willing herself not to shake. "Ariam is nearly fourteen, and I'm of age."

"We have an extended internship contract for four years." 121

"Yes." She forced herself to speak calmly and clearly, prayed she wouldn't stammer again or become tongue-tied or forget any of the words of the clause she'd memorized. "However, under the law the terms of employment, 'unless the position is filling an essential community function that cannot be provided for otherwise, contracts were, and are, to be waived without question or penalty for all qualified citizens who choose to enlist in the military.'" She thought she'd pass out before she squeezed the last words out with her breath.

"Well done," said Reve, aligning his knife precisely along the edge of his plate. His face had gone as flat as his voice.

Rett really wanted to take this elsewhere. She was sure her cheeks were hot enough to ignite green wood on contact. She swallowed, not even daring to take a sip of water to ease her dry mouth. "Dad, I—"

Reve cut her short, with a bitter laugh. "Go," he said almost harshly. "Go ahead. Make a fool of yourself. You won't even make it through Basic. You think being a soldier is similar to plinking at pinecones? No backcountry mountain kid will ever be of any use to this war!"

The room, the entire house, had gone dead silent. Rett couldn't even hear the storm that continued raging outside. All she could hear was her pulse and the reverberation of her father's words. Lightheaded with shock and dismay, she forced herself to hold eye contact with her father. She thought she covered all the angles of her departure. She'd made sure her presence wasn't needed; that the business was assured to continue without her or her father, and Ariam would be cared for properly. She had thought now she was ready to do what her worlds needed of her, just as she and Reve had discussed before he went away.

She expected him not to like the short notice. She'd even expected a bit of an argument over some detail or another. She hadn't expected this. Especially in front of outsiders.

Not daring to move, she continued to stare back at him. From beneath the table she felt Ariam's slender hand take hers, clasping tightly in support. Rett tightened her own fingers in appreciation. Maybe Ariam always disappeared when homework or chores needed to be done, but she was always there to back Rett up. Her presence right now made up for every single one of Rett's headaches, annoyance, and extra chores for the past few years.

Say something, Ari. Rett wished her sister were a mindspeaker instead of an empath at that moment. Ariam always knew what to say, and never had any problem saying it.

But other than the tight handclasp, her little sister sat stiffly, her normal bounce and eloquence stifled. The visitors might have been frozen; their faces were blank and no one seemed to be breathing. Only Rett, her father, and Ariam's slightly trembling handclasp betrayed any signs of life.

Rett unstuck her tongue from the roof of her mouth and lowered her voice even more to control the stammer threatening to return in full force. "I might have written you about it earlier, but when you said you were coming, I wanted to t-tell you in person."

"And so you have. I'm sure you made all the proper arrangements. I have no questions." Carefully laying his fork alongside the knife, he lifted his gaze again. "Maybe I'll ask Rafe to hold off on closing up the house for a tenday or so after I go back. Just in case."

She had to blink to make sure that was still her father and not some stranger filling his favorite chair. Of course, they'd disagreed before, both privately and on the job, often to the degree of shouting into each other's faces, nose-to-nose. That was different. This was like stepping on solid-looking rock and having it give way. For nearly eighteen years, her father had given her only his unyielding support and encouragement. In seconds, that was suddenly gone.

Her shock quickly turned to pain, and with it, anger. Despite her hurt and humiliation, she kept her head high. She couldn't control the tears that blurred her eyes, or the clog in her nose, or the ache in her throat. Forcing words out, she heard herself say, "Thanks for your approval and confidence, Dad." She angled her head just enough toward their guests that they would know she was addressing them. "It was very nice meeting all of you. I apologize for any discomfort I caused—I made a mistake bringing this matter up in front of you. I hope you enjoyed your time off." Then she leaned toward Ariam and kissed her. "Take care, Ari. Goodbye."

"Rett—" *You don't have to go yet*— Ariam's lips and eyes conveyed the message as clearly as spoken words.

I do. Rising from her chair, Rett gripped the younger girl's shoulder briefly in farewell. "I'll be in touch," she told Ariam in a low tone.

Then she turned and didn't look back. She didn't want any of them to see her tears, which had burst free as soon as she took her first step away. Grabbing her rain jacket, chaps, and hat, snatching up her already loaded backpack from the spot where it had waited the past two days, she opened the door and closed it with quiet finality behind her.

AURORA BASE, EPNOCE
PRESENT DAY, 0536.02.06 (LOCAL RECKONING)

~So I BET THAT MADE for an awkward moment later when you applied to Special Forces, huh?~

Pam's query broke Rett back fully to the present. She took a breath, slipped off her headband and rubbed at her forehead.

It sure did, Rett thought. *I had no idea that Yidnar was the CO of the 2023rd. The people who came with Dad on his leave were introduced to us only as names. And you know that those not on active duty—no matter their branch— wear plain working grays without any markings.*

~I want the whole story one day. After we take care of this one. From what I gather, you love your dad just as much now as you did then, that's why it hurts you so much. That's why you're still hurting so much about Jaq, as well.~

Rett scratched the side of her neck, and then checked her chrono. *All right. I'll admit that. I just have to figure out what to do about it.*

~You know how much we can hurt the people we love, especially when we're scared,~ said Pam. ~As if hurting them, or discouraging them, can somehow protect them from getting hurt if they go ahead. It sounds stupid, but I think it fits. He thought you'd be safe, at least for another couple of years, until Ariam reached an age where she could stay on her own. It just escalated from there. I think maybe if you had stayed even a couple hours longer, he would've came around.~

I couldn't stay, thought Rett.

~I know. The only way to settle this is to talk to him. Don't wait for him to talk to you. I know how hard it is for you, but you can do it. You probably won't have time before this mission, but hopefully, you will afterward. I'll be here to support you. I hope.~

I don't know why those alien superbeings out there picked me for an ego-merge—or picked you, either—but Pam, even though I do ignore you and get mad at you sometimes, I'm really glad they did it this way, Rett thought honestly.

~I am too,~ said Pam. ~ Even though when I'm home, I worry about how you're doing sometimes. You already know that I write everything down and draw pictures—I've drawn some great pictures of you and F-troop! I wish you could see them!~

I wish I could see you in person, instead of as . . . well, this mostly formless blob of energy who sticks a hand or a foot out at me once in a while.

~Those are the best parts,~ Pam said in a lofty manner.

Rett chuckled aloud. How well she knew Pam's hang-up about her looks! It was hard not to. Hard for either of them to hide a lot of things from the other.

It doesn't matter to me how you look, Pam. You could look like that Coalition officer that almost ate me for lunch back at Complex 412 for all I care. I already know the best part of you.

There was a brief period of blankness from that area of Rett's mind reserved for her visitor. By now, Rett recognized it as Pam trying to keep her emotions to herself.

~Thank you, Rett.~ Pam's thought was muffled and Rett felt the shift as Pam changed the subject.

Rett allowed warm compassion to flow toward her mental companion. She wished she could help. Pam really was lonely and she was going to have to try a lot harder to let her come up for air when they were merged.

~Don't worry about your father right now—just do your job tomorrow. Keep reminding yourself that he's just another infantry officer you've been assigned to assist. Things will work out, you'll see!~

There's one more thing I have to tell you, Pam, Rett thought seriously. *Just in case anything happens and you get yanked out again. I want you to know now—you've been a really good friend. You've put up with more shit from me than anyone, and the amazing thing is, you're still willing to put up with it.*

⁓I've always thought that's what friends are for,⁓ returned Pam.

You're supposed to make sure you get as good as you give out, too.

⁓Well then, that's something we both have to work on, isn't it?⁓

Yes. We'll always be friends. I won't forget you, and I hope you won't forget me.

⁓Better stop right there. You're going to make me cry.⁓

I don't care. Rett swiped at her own eyes. *Damn, I wish I could give you a good hug.*

⁓You just did,⁓ came gently from Pam, with something resembling a mental sniffle.

3.2.5 COMPLEX 117 (REFINERY), ROOFTOP, EPNOCE
0536.02.07 (LOCAL RECKONING)

HEAVING DEBRIS ASIDE WITH A cautious, yet urgent, speed, Rett doubled her efforts upon hearing choking and coughing somewhere in the jumble of smoking rubble.

"Shit!" She ducked as energy beams ricocheted from the smooth quartzite wall, leaving blackened, glossy scorches. She managed to free someone's head and upper body. Quickly she knocked aside a handful of burning embers . . . Jayord. The entire right side of his face was scorched, black in places. The sections recognizable as skin were slick with blood and sweat. She smothered a smoking portion of his hair with her forearm as his exposure to fresh air fueled bits that were smoldering into flame.

"Deities!" She grabbed one of her water containers and dumped it over his face and shoulders, causing him to splutter but at least preventing any more flareups in his hair.

"Talk to me," urged Rett as she freed the rest of him and dragged him into relative safety. She checked quickly for the injuries she couldn't see, dreading the thought of anything burning beneath his clothing. She wasn't carrying *that* much water—well, there was a big, slushy puddle nearby . . . last resort.

"M'fn, g'S'tAr'm," he said and rolled on his side, coughing so hard she was afraid he'd choke in the process. A motion of his blackened hand sent Rett back to the pile. Ariam was under there somewhere.

Another explosion settled the wreckage even more. Rett leaped aside barely in time as a falling support strut and a lethal SMG beam simultaneously converged on her position. Dust billowed with the smoke and Rett jerked her respirator from her belt.

127

Ariam was still alive. The wheezing sounds were proof, and there was no one else under there. Rett grabbed one piece of wreckage after another, hot, burning, didn't matter.

Uncovering a limp hand, she redoubled her effort. An arm. *Broken, two places at least . . . there's a shoulder. Deities, please . . .*

Jayord, still coughing, was back, lending his scorched hands to the task. His sleeves were damp. He must have crawled over to the puddle, or used his own water. She hoped if he did that the water hadn't been too hot, causing more damage than he felt. No, the relative coldness of a droplet hitting the back of her hand reassured her on that matter.

A wide section of pourstone trapped Ariam beneath it. The section extracted a cruel price for the protection it gave: while the wall would not fall lower, supported by roof structure below, it crushed in on Ariam's chest, keeping her from getting a good breath. The smoke and dust only added to the problem. Rett's first effort didn't budge it, not even with Jayord's help.

The sight of flames shooting up from the pile an arm's length away was all the incentive Rett needed. Going flat to her back, she positioned herself at the end of the section, where it was high enough to get her legs into the equation. As when working with any of her platoon, no words were necessary. Jayord was already flat against the roof, ready to slide in and grab Ariam as soon as Rett opened enough space for him. His slim, wiry build would allow him to work in a space far too narrow for her.

Throwing her entire body and will, strength and fear into the task, Rett growled her defiance at the section. Her thigh muscles felt as if they would explode, the joints in her wrists creaked, but her legs, then her arms, began to straighten. As she took the weight of the section of wall, her back ground into every particle beneath her, including a series of cracks that would undoubtedly leave a distinct impression against her skin for a while. She took a second to hope the roof below wouldn't give way, then took the energy she was putting into thinking and applied it to the wall. From her corner, Pam poured over every particle of energy she had into Rett's effort.

The wreckage still above shuddered, and more ash, embers, and dust fell. Rett closed her eyes, closed her mouth, and pushed harder.

"Got'r, S'g!"

She threw herself left and let go. The section collapsed behind her as she snagged Jayord by the shoulder harness with one hand and Ariam with the other. Rett hauled the both of them away from the fresh roar of flame. She made sure the three of them got thoroughly soaked by retreating to safety via the large slushy puddle. In, through, and out again, no time to be nice about it. Rett hauled herself and her comrades, dripping, shivering, and alive, to the nearest cover. First a breath, then a quick look around. Satisfied for the moment, she turned her attention to her wounded.

Jayord's breather unit was beyond salvation, so she gave him hers, since by now he was in hard distress and the smoke and dust was still thick here. Face-burned or not, Jayord's need to breathe was greater than any discomfort the unit would cause.

Now Ariam. She'd lost consciousness when Rett had landed the three of them in the puddle. The younger woman's singed head lolled almost bonelessly, her breath came short between lips gray-blue with cold and lack of oxygen. As Rett touched her now to assess her injuries, Ariam's eyes flew open wide. She tried to take a breath and immediately went into a fit of hacking coughs hard and loud enough to bring enemy attention in their direction.

Cursing silently, Rett went for Ariam's breather unit, which was slightly dented but useable. She slipped it gently in place over her sister's burned, bruised, dirty face. Ariam gasped air into her straining lungs, her eyes streaming from the assault of smoke,

129

dirt, and dust. For a few agonized seconds Ariam's expression was lucid and her gaze locked with Rett's, communicating mortified apology for bringing enemy attention to them.

"I didn't expect you to hold your breath, Ari." Rett touched Ariam's singed cheek gently. "It's okay. We'll get out of this. Breathe.

"Com connect Fang Med!" Rett said to her pcom as she yanked her uniform collar over her nose and mouth. "Med, I need you, have two down over here. We're over near the ventilator shaft cowlings—to your left."

TT-1 in hand, Rett eased away from her wounded and took a fast look with eyes and energy sense over the fan cowlings. The next time her head rose above them, so did her weapon. She took out three pockets of Coalition troopers who were getting uncomfortably close, then ducked down again as SMG fire from two other directions streaked through the spot her head had just occupied.

Returning fire, realizing this was not going to be a safe place very much longer, she felt her belts in vain for a smoker or a flash grenade, reluctant to use anything stronger. There were enough fires burning far too close to even more incendiary materials for her peace of mind.

"Fang Lead," Med said, his voice slightly distorted from energy weapon discharge, "we're hot here. Movement is not a go. Advise me of Bronze Two and Fang Thirty-five's conditions."

"Stand by, Med." Rett abandoned her attempt to return fire and threw herself toward Jayord and Ariam, using her body to shield the pair as another explosion rained more debris among them like hailstones. One big chunk narrowly missed her head, leaving a scrape on her cheekbone. Another thunked into her butt. Those weren't as bad as the ones that were glowing hot or molten blobs of melted glass or rock, which peppered her from boots to hair like a shower of miniature meteorites. *Good thing,* she thought rather sourly, *I'm not entirely vain.* At the same time, the thought of adding what felt like a few thousand impact craters to the topography of dents and scars she already bore didn't thrill her.

Better me than them, she thought with a philosophical shrug, angling her body a little more to the left to deflect another shower of fine particles from Jayord's partially blinded eyes.

The entire building seemed to shudder, and another finger-width stress crack appeared practically under Ariam's head.

One thing for sure, we can't stay here. Rett opened her pcom again. "Stay there, Med—we'll come to you." Pushing herself into a crouch, she again assessed her casualties.

She hadn't found any obvious broken bones on Jayord, although she wasn't going to rule out broken ribs. The head injury slowed him, too. *Nasty.* What she had thought was a burn or soot on the left side of his jawbone was actually a frightful bruise—maybe even a fracture, which compounded the speaking problems he was experiencing. She hoped he still had an eye underneath the scorched flesh on the right side of his face. Burned, bruised, smoke and dust inhalation . . . he was mobile but far from being able to get any distance on his own in a timely manner. Any energy he possessed had been expended in getting Ariam.

Ariam. No longer coughing, but fighting for every breath. Tears streamed from her eyes from the grit and smoke smarting them. The left arm, broken, maybe ribs, although again Rett felt nothing out of place. Right leg definitely fractured.

She treated Jayord and Ariam with what she had in the way of medical supplies, enough to get them where she had to go.

Putting more compression on possible broken ribs or lungs already straining for air left an over-the-shoulder carry for Ariam an unacceptable option. Nor for Jayord, who let his breather unit hang around his neck and was doing his best to give her every impression he was still good to go on his own feet.

131

Far be it from me to tell him otherwise. "Jayord, we're going to move fast, and since you're having a little problem with your eyes right now, I want you to hang onto me."

"Uh." Had Jayord been a stranger to her, she would have never interpreted agreement or cooperation. But his monosyllabic grunt left her no doubt of his agreement, every assurance of his utmost effort. As she guided Jayord into position, Rett glanced over the rooftop once more, trying to decide who was close enough to provide a diversion. She pcom'ed Corporal Pipano.

"Fang leader, confirm diversion—ten seconds—wait for it!" Pip responded. "Team zero-21—Fang team—flash warning for sector five—repeat, flash warning—mark, seven seconds!"

A flash grenade, good. If I had one left I would've used it for this. The device was not lethal, only pyrotechnic, meant to cause a stunning, bright flash that would temporarily blind anyone looking the wrong way—hopefully only Coalition troopers. The flash was intense enough to overload the shielding capabilities of the enemy's targeting devices, rendering them useless.

"Whether you can see or not, keep your eyes closed," she said to her companions. She gathered Ariam into her arms, felt Jayord's breath on her neck and his bony knuckles tight against her back where his hand gripped her harness. She kept her eyes cracked open long enough to see Pip's well-thrown flash grenade drop neatly in front of the several Coalition troopers pinning them down. Then she squeezed her eyes shut just as tightly as she was capable and turned her head aside for good measure.

She didn't have to see what would happen next. Her ears confirmed what previous experience taught her. The troopers couldn't tell one type of grenade from another from looking and didn't wait to find out. As the little missile rolled among them, they scattered. Unfortunately for them, their evasion wasn't quick enough to escape the flash. Even if any managed to close their eyes, their targeters would be useless, and many of them had come to rely on the devices to the extent that they would be seriously handicapped without them.

That lot won't cause any trouble we can't handle for a while. Good old Pip!

She took a moment to double-check her path before letting out the breath that would alert Jayord to her movement. The contact his fingers had with her back remained steady and trusting as she rose from her crouch. Together, they took the opening.

Med waited for them. He was right there to unlock Jayord's blistered hand from Rett's belt and guide him gently to a sitting position. Rett sank to her knees with Ariam. Med deftly traded the breather unit for an oxygen mask.

"Hang on to her a while longer," said Med.

Rett nodded, taking the opportunity to catch her breath and assess the new position. The location, behind one of the big, mirrored solar panels, provided safety as well as a clear view of the fierce rooftop battle. Another member of her unit was already there, struggling to stay alive and conscious. Junior Sergeant H'tenneck had taken a handful of deep SMG burns across his chest and stomach.

Damn Reve! Rett thought, her anger as hot and bright as the plasma discharges from enemy weapons. Even as she automatically followed Med's instructions for those she had brought in she fumed. *He had to jump in on this. Fine . . . because something's going on over there we can't see, and it was obviously serious enough that he felt he had to move on it.*

That wasn't an excuse for failing to clear with her before he deployed the necessary backups, instead of showing up without any notice and opening fire on Coalition positions without checking to see where her people were first. This penetration was *her* responsibility. Colonel Reve should damn well know better than hold back information that important.

She braced Ariam while Med cut the scorched remnants of uniform from her upper body.

Look what happened. H'tenneck got hit avoiding friendly fire! Ariam and Jayord were almost killed when one of the 21st's bubbleheads threw a grenade without getting a clear sector!

"Good thing you didn't throw her over your shoulder," said Med, a motion of his chin holding Rett's position with Ariam. His hands left Ariam's ribcage for his supplies. "She wouldn't have made it here. How'd everyone get wet?"

"Detoured though a puddle half the size of Centerland Lake. Wanted to make sure no one was burning where I couldn't see until we got to shelter."

"Good move," Med said, and bent to his work.

"Com connect CDR21!" Rett opened the pcom to the 21st command channel, almost snarling into the pickup. "Fang leader to 1-21!"

"Fang Lead, this is 2-21, what's up?"

Shit, Rett said to herself as the strong alto voice of SubColonel Nauskova answered. *He would make me talk to his second!*

"Damn it, clear your flaming targets! You people aren't alone up here. We've crossfire patterns going! What's up over there, anyway?"

"Fang leader, we have a supply jumper down and civilians in the trough, sector eight. Coalition's cutting them off. We're hot here—and 1-21's with patrol and cut off with them."

Sector eight? They'd moved fast. *No wonder . . .* she thought almost wearily, glancing toward H'tenneck. When she looked back, she caught Med looking that direction as well, a rare expression of pure worry aging his face. Noticing her glance, Med assumed his familiar sour look.

"2-21, cease all fire into sector eight immediately," Rett said to her pcom. "Fang teams are in the line of fire from your group.

We'll try to clear a corridor for you but we need you stop shooting anywhere but straight ahead until you get a clear from *me*. Do you understand?"

"Understood, Fang Lead, will relay."

Easy enough mistake to make. Rett blew out a breath. *Colonel Reve's not used to working with us.* Damn it, there were no excuses. *We told him about the crossfire—how important it was to stay out of the way. More than once. At every briefing, and even again before we attacked. One communication from him would have made the difference.*

"All right," Med said finally, and at his direction, Rett settled Ariam in a semi-reclining position. His attention went to Jayord.

These three are only the serious ones. There were more—minor and good to go, nevertheless their injuries caused by people from our own side. There is no excuse for this, Rett thought. "Talk to me, Med." She took out her VARs and scanned the area carefully.

"Initial assessment? Jayord will be all right for limited duty inside a tenday, maybe a little longer, but his metabolism is somewhat like yours, so he'll mend quickly. Ariam will be out of action a couple tendays, maybe a month, depends. H'tenneck . . . we'll see. All depending on if we get off this roof anytime soon."

Rett pulled her glance aside and met Med's gaze. He didn't look hopeful and ducked his head as he attended to Jayord.

In the heat of combat, especially this fierce rooftop battle, the only thing on anyone's mind was pushing Coalition troops off before the refinery blew up in their faces. With civilians in the action and a supply jumper down, crew wounded and most likely pinned in place since before the action moved to the roof—she could almost understand the confusion that caused her casualties. Immediate response called for direct action.

Not at the expense of H'tenneck. Or Jayord and Ariam. Not for a stupid mistake that one communication call could have prevented!

135

~Rett!~ Pam's thought was harsh. ~You don't have time for this. Get a grip.~

Taken aback, Rett shook herself. Pam never interfered in combat situations anymore—the fact she did now startled the sergeant. Rett was ready with a hot rejoinder only until she realized her mind had, indeed, started to wander.

Thanks, Pam, but stay out of this!

Pam had already withdrawn, allowing a hint of wounded annoyance to seep from her "place."

Rett's thoughts had taken less than three seconds and she knew what she had to do.

"What's going on?" Med asked.

"Jumper down, crew and civilians in the line of fire over in sector eight."

"I suppose you're going to cause the diversion to get zero-21's patrol in there," Med said testily, leaving Jayord to check on H'tenneck, from there back to Ariam. He slid his short knife from the shoulder harness and started removing the material from the broken leg.

"Do you need me? Do you think H'tenneck will?" Rett crouched on her heels to feather her fingers lightly though the young squadleader's spiky black curls. He was conscious, but so focused on his internal struggle that he was unaware of her. She leaned down and dropped a gentle kiss on his forehead.

Med glanced up. "I asked him before. He's determined to hang on. As far as needing you here . . . of course it would be nice, but I know you have something else in mind."

Rett nodded. "I'm the only one open for this right now."

"N'aptbl alt'rntive wit'civlns, M'd," Jayord said.

"He said—"

"Forget it. I think I understood that. But let's not forget there were civilians involved at Complex 63!" snapped Med. "Or any of the other times—"

"Don't take it personally, Jayord." Rett made her voice very dry, glad to see the grin that flashed on the better side of his blistered face. "Can you see all right from that good eye now that most of the grit's out of it?"

He nodded. Rett picked up H'tenneck's weapon, disabled the bio-safety, and handed it with care into Jayord's bandaged hands. "I need you to cover here for Med and the others."

Jayord made a sound Rett took as an affirmative. He checked the clip and shifted his position to keep watch.

Med shook his head, but didn't protest.

Rett turned her attention back to the battle. Trebor's team was closest to sector eight. "Com connect Fang two! Fang two, this is Fang leader—are you open?"

"Fang leader, movement is not a go. We're hot. Can divert some cover fire, though."

Trebor, I love you, you're right with me as usual, thought Rett. "Hold on, Fang Two. Com connect 2-21."

"2-21 Fang Lead, what's up?"

"1-21 is not holding fire. He's not exempt. Relay him again to hold fire and movement! I want a confirm on that. Divert and assist only on confirm." *All I'll need is my own father to take me down,* she thought. *That'd be rich.*

"Fang Lead, this is 1-21." Colonel Reve's transmission crackled with the static of enemy fire. "Confirm hold fire—come ahead."

Amazing, Rett thought, *his com works just fine.* She activated the link to Trebor. "Fang two—give me confirm on cover fire sector eight!"

"Fang leader, confirm cover fire—go, we're live."

"Keep after H'tenneck," she told Med. "See you later."

Wanting maximum speed and maneuverability only, Rett slung her TT-1 across her back and whipped into action. The sudden onslaught of firing from the small squad with Trebor diverted the Coalition's attention to that direction. She ran hard, skirting or jumping patches of ice, half-melted puddles, or wreckage. At last, she reached the trough that directed meltwater from ice and snow from channels on the roof into the complex's water reservoirs. On the opposite side, she saw the downed jumper, Colonel Reve's patrol, and the Coalition squad keeping them from going anywhere.

Putting the same force into her jump as she did into moving the rubble off Ariam, she cleared the four-length gap of the trough. Land, two more strides, and jump again, her boots aiming for the unsuspecting backs of the Coalition troopers. As she came down, she yelled, finding a second to wonder just how the wordless utterance she intended turned into some nonsensical alien word of Pam's.

Didn't matter. Whatever she had yelled out at the top of her lungs had the desired results. Never expecting a physical assault from the rear, since the trough was at their backs, startled troopers spun about to look. Instead of hitting armored backs and helmets, her feet landed dead center on very breakable targeting goggles and unprotected lower faces. The two she'd slammed rocked backward into several others, and the whole pile of them hit the complex roof.

"1-21—diversion is live! *Move out!*" Rett yelled into her pcom, rolling forward and twisting to her feet. As she rose, her left arm dropped like a felled longcone on the helmet of a crouching trooper, her right elbow rammed savagely into the nose and mouth of another. *More in this pocket than I thought. Not today.* She spun left, slamming another bone and plastic crushing, double-barreled kick to the trooper who tried to cut behind her.

Rett came around to meet another trooper of the squad, who dropped his weapon and drew his knife for close combat. He moved with graceful confidence and she was aware she was the target of his full attention. She blocked a swipe from him with her right hand while backfisting another with her left. Eyes never leaving the trooper with the knife, she took out two more; blocked and ducked another lunge from the knife fighter. It was a rare Coalition trooper who was expert at single combat. Those who were good were sharp, fast, and very adept.

She soon discovered another advantage this individual had—barely leaping aside to avoid being caught behind the knees by it. He had a tail! A tail half again as long as one of his legs and—*ow!*—as flexible and powerful as Unethi tentacles!

"Move your ass, damn it!" Rett shouted in Colonel Reve's direction, ducking a roundhouse kick from the trooper and avoiding the clever follow through by the caudal appendage. She was stunned that one so averagely humanoid in appearance was in possession of a prehensile tail and had a difficult time not letting her curiosity distract her. A burning pain grazing along her upper arm took care of that small problem instantly. Another trooper who'd taken advantage of her distraction managed to score, but she made sure it was the last time he'd wield a knife.

Focused now, Rett settled in to fight; reminding herself she was causing a diversion and had to prolong what she would normally flash through as quickly as possible for all involved. The tailed knife-fighter closed and for a while, she exchanged a series of blocks, punches, and kicks, the drill-like routine of it broken only by the advantage of the trooper's tail.

She managed to keep it from her eyes or from tangling in her legs or arms, but she couldn't avoid the snapping sting of it elsewhere. Several times she had a good opening to simply take the fellow out completely, but she wouldn't be causing much of a diversion if she didn't put on a good enough show for any other troopers in the area to watch, or come and join in hopes of getting a piece of her to take for a souvenir. Most of those already gathered seemed content to hang back and wait, but a few decided to join in the melee already underway. Rett twisted to one side only to get her left knee in the path of a discharge from a stunner. Instantly that leg went numb.

139

An angry shout from the knife-fighter—protesting the close-range firearms discharge—was nevertheless followed instantly with a renewed attack on Rett: a feint to the left and a right side kick that would have broken her numbed left kneecap into a zillion pieces had it connected.

Thankfully it didn't. Pivoting on her good leg, Rett slung the body of the unfortunate shooter into several others nearby, taking them all down.

"Playtime's over," she said, closing distance with the tailed trooper and his knife. The upward block connected so sharply with his forearm he lost his grip on the knife, which flew from his hand and buried itself beneath the upraised arm of yet another assailant. Her blocking hand caught the man's wrist, jerked it toward her, and twisted abruptly. As he doubled forward, tail whisking toward her legs, she jumped up and sent a kick from her good leg directly into his face. He went down without a sound, tail twitching a few times before becoming motionless.

A second time she jumped, turning midair to catch another trooper with a snap kick high into the inside of his left thigh that staggered him right into her hands. Taking the advantage, she slid her fingers beneath one of the flexible armor plates, caught the loose uniform material covering the right leg—the knee of which even now rose in the attempt to catch her in the crotch— and jerked, hard. At the same time her free elbow slammed into his knee.

The trooper crashed hard, on his backside. It didn't stop him from reaching for his sidearm. Before she lost her balance on her numb leg, she went airborne once more, the sledgehammer blow from her good leg connecting with his hand and wrist. A handy chunk of masonry she scooped from the complex roof laid him flat.

Seeing that Reve's people make it into the trough with the wounded from the jumper, Rett didn't waste time playing with those who remained. Taking advantage of the returning feeling to her leg and the realization from these troopers that she was not as disadvantaged as they had thought, she made short work of them.

There's protection from enemy fire down there—it was a good move. They can pull back to a safe area using the trough.

Rett dropped behind a wall to catch a breath and rub furiously at her tingling leg. *Good thing it was a hand stunner—and was my leg, or I'd be dead right now.* "Com connect all Fang team—this is Fang leader, we have zero-21 patrol in trough. Anyone available cover them. Fang two, pass on to 2-21!"

"Fang leader," Trebor answered two seconds later. "Com relay confirmed. We're open and moving. Get 1-21 and the man with him down with the rest—sector's going hot."

What? She took another look. Damn! Reve *was* still on top, and behind him was another figure in the regular grays of Supply—another crewmember from the jumper, guessed Rett. She saw why Colonel Reve wasn't moving yet—another Coalition patrol was moving in quickly. Reve's fire covered for her now, as well as the injured man.

"How flaming nice of you, Colonel," Rett muttered under her breath. She turned quickly, her own stunner in hand, and delivered a solid charge right between the eyes of the tailed knife-fighter.

"That should keep you out of trouble for a while. Are there more like you, I wonder? Deities—I'd love a chance to talk to you on equal terms." She moved closer, extracting the magnetic restraints all Coalition troopers carried from his belt. Applying them quickly to his wrists and ankles, and then activating them, she hoped that would be enough to ensure he'd be taken alive by the Nyorfian forces later on. There were enough species of humanoid already made extinct—or close enough to it—by the Yixolryns.

After swiftly making sure the other unconscious troopers would remain immobilized, and the dead ones were really dead and not about to cause her further trouble, Rett then went after Colonel Reve. Her leg tingled but remained steady under her as she ran toward the officer, who was half-crouched in the doubtful shelter of an exhaust fan cowling, firing at well-covered Coalition troopers

She hit him low and hard, smashing him flat on the complex roof as SMG fire heated the air above their heads. Snarling under her breath, Rett wrapped her fingers around the belts at his waist and rolled with him into the drainage trough. She made sure he was on the bottom when they hit the floor of it and took a perverse satisfaction in hearing the air whoosh from his lungs.

"I've had just about enough of you for one day, damn it. Stay down here until my people move up to cover you! I'm going after that soldier up there."

"Sergeant!"

She spared the officer an icy glare. "What, sir?"

"Be careful," he cautioned after getting a good gulp of air. "You take too many chances—"

She let out a sharp, low whistle of disbelief. "Look, I don't have *time* for this," said Rett, not caring that she was practically spitting in his face. "But later we need to talk. You can yell at me then. Stay here, and think real hard about the next time your people might need to do something. You might remember that you're supposed to com me *first* and make sure my people are clear. I have five minor injuries and three people *down* from your move, Colonel. One of them might die. Just stay put!"

She shook her head in disgust and pulled herself up, rolling flat onto the roof, eyes intent for the last wounded soldier. Rett gasped, a wash of lightheadedness following recognition. Had she been standing, her still-wobbly leg would have no doubt given out on her.

She scrambled forward, finding her voice at last. "Damn you. This is all I need. What in two worlds are *you* doing here?" She pulled him into the shelter of an elevated section before more energy beams scorched their position. "You flaming Zetinorian bubblehead! I should pull your helmet off and stick you back out to draw their fire." She threw herself over him as SMG fire superheated part of the pourstone section, causing it to explode.

"Rett?"

She pushed back the unfamiliar words that again rose, unbidden, to her lips. *Whatever the Easter Bunny is, take it and yourself and back off!* she thought sternly to Pam. Scrambling into somewhat more protected position for the moment, Rett took the time for a more leisurely glance at the wounded soldier beneath the shelter of her body. Her face was a breath away from his.

"Well, now. Where are you going to run to avoid talking to me *this* time, Jaq Pym?" She had her TT-1 in hand a second later, returning fire at another Coalition patrol. "All right," she yelled into the din on the rooftop, "just who put up the sign that said *'Sergeant Killer is behind this wall now'*? Can you give me a few seconds here and pretend I'm still over there?"

For one breath, no longer, there actually was a decrease in unending thunder of SMG discharges.

"Oops. That didn't have the quite the effect I wanted," said Rett when all that happened was the convergence of even more energy beams on her spot.

"You're crazy!" Jaq shouted over the din.

Her head reeled for a few seconds as she caught his familiar scent—and remembered about the weird effects Zetinorian pheromones had on other humanoids. She was unprepared and found herself suddenly struggling between rage, goofy relief at being with him, and desire.

Rage would have to serve her. At least for now.

"Crazy?" Rett snapped off two more shots and dropped back into her former position, her nose less than a fingerwidth from touching his skin. His ruddy face was pale and streaked with soot and bloody lacerations, his left arm sprawled crookedly at his side, and more blood stained that shoulder and the left side of his waist. He'd never looked so beautiful, but she let her anger overcome the other sensations.

With a precise jab from her left forefinger, she hit the quick release strap of the partial helmet many infantry and ground support personnel favored. Nudging the helmet off with her forearm, she took a second to make sure no blood matted his hair before fisting her hand into his unruly locks. She tightened it just hard enough to make sure she had his undivided attention. "Crazy?"

The expression in his eyes tamed from wild to wary as her fingers tightened.

"Crazy. Maybe." She nodded. "Yes. I am. I'm crazy for letting you walk away like that. For letting you believe those lies you told yourself about me. I should have kicked your ass. Then *threw* you on that flaming transport and bid you good riddance. You hurt me, damn it, Jaq Pym. *You* were the one who didn't hold to the conditions you set for yourself in our relationship. You! And there I was, blaming myself that you were so unhappy you had to leave."

Jaq became utterly still as her fingers clenched unmercifully over his sensitive hair. His naturally ruddy coloring deepened to the brown-red of some of the volcanic rock closer to the western coast of Nyorfias. Slowly his expression started to change again. "Rett—"

"Shut up!" she yelled, not wanting to dredge up the terrible memories of events prior to his leaving F-troop. "I don't want to hear it."

"But I need to ap—"

She dared to glance at his face, relieved to see Jaq wasn't wearing the expression she dreaded, that one that had been so cold and righteous. Instead he looked very much like a lost little boy who'd hurt his best friend and wanted to apologize.

Rett didn't want his apologies. She was angry, and she wanted satisfaction for it.

"It's a bit late for apologies." Keeping her hand tightly clenched in his hair so he wouldn't even dare to move, she lifted her upper body again to send a few more shots over the shattered ruin of the elevated section.

"All your effort to build up my trust, to make this bond between us as friends, more than friends. You told me constantly you were willing to let me set the pace of our relationship. That you wouldn't push. That you enjoyed being my friend and being around. You understood and accepted my commitment to *this*— to finishing my job in this war. And overnight you change your mind; you lose any confidence in me, in us. This has *nothing* remotely to do with how I was avoiding you in the beginning. We didn't have that trust between us then." She snarled, showing her teeth in both warning and threat. "Don't even *think* of going there."

145

Jaq, eyes wide, shook his head in movements so miniscule that even Rett, who was used to barely perceptible body language, might have missed it completely had she not been holding onto his hair.

"You couldn't even make an attempt to talk to me. If you put even a quarter of the effort you took to run away from me into communication . . . but no. You *ran*! You know what happened then? *I* took responsibility for it." This time she closed her fist in his hair, putting pressure on the roots. For a moment, she was tempted to give him a good thump against the roof. His wince reminded her that he was injured. The twist her heart gave reminded her, as well, just how much she had missed him. And loved him.

"I—"

"Shut up," Rett said, loosening her hold in his hair only slightly. There was no possible way she was going to allow another second to go by without having her say. "I hope you're happy that I took the blame and guilt for your bruised pride, not only from myself, but from others."

"I'm sor—"

Rett growled. "I told you, it's too late for apologies. I had to tell you how I felt when you were avoiding me and after you left." She sighed and let her hold on his hair soften completely. "But you know what, it doesn't matter any more. This is what matters." Then she closed the distance between her lips and his. Everything she wanted to say, everything she felt for him, everything she wanted for the future, she tried to communicate in that kiss.

Jaq's initial reaction of surprise gave way to a response nearly hotter than the passage of SMG. His good right arm came around her, hand spread flat against her back, bringing her closer. She didn't know if the groan she heard was his, or hers, but it broke her out enough to remember this wasn't exactly a good place for this sort of activity.

146

"How badly are you hurt?" She probed his shoulder, wincing as she felt the hard edges of shattered bone beneath her fingers. The wound in his side was messy but superficial. He'd be mobile if they had to walk, but they didn't. It was a simple matter of moving sideways a length or so and sliding into the bottom of the trough.

Simple, but it won't be easy for him with that shoulder.

~I don't think he's feeling much pain in that location at the moment, Rett,~ said Pam with something that felt suspiciously like a cross between a hiccup from laughing too much and a sentimental sniffle. ~I must say your left leg regained a lot of feeling very quickly. ~

No more comments from you, thought Rett crossly. *Back. Back to your lair. Go away. Later.* "Hurts bad, huh?"

"I don't know—" Jaq's wonderful blue eyes were wide and dazed; his energy aura a maelstrom of conflicting swirls and flashes of color that was beyond Rett's ability to interpret. "What happened to—"

The sound she made would have terrified an entire battalion of Coalition troopers. "I am in love with *you*, Jaq. Never with anyone else." She swallowed whatever he was going to say with another kiss that nearly left him unconscious. She made sure he was paying attention to her before going on. "With you. Remember you asked me once what my problem was, you wanted to help, and I said it was you? That was true. Because I didn't know that was love I was feeling. How to identify it. How to handle it. That maybe I was mistaking what I felt for you as something else. Or something that wasn't coming from me—you being Zetinorian and all."

"But—"

"But what I feel changes nothing. I still can't give you want *you* want—a commitment. Not while this war is still being fought. My original terms stand." She rose on one knee for a fast look over the top of the section. "That is, if you haven't changed your mind entirely."

"I've been *trying* to tell you—"

She covered his mouth with her hand. "Save it. If we don't get to talk later, maybe you can write another one of those wonderful letters. You know, the *'tell everyone I said hi'* sort."

Before he could think about that, she grabbed him and once again slid fast for the depression in the rooftop. This time, she absorbed the impact for them both, but it wasn't enough to keep from jolting the Zetinorian's broken shoulder.

Jaq made a sharp sound of pain, but didn't lose consciousness.

"Sorry. Hang on. Com connect Fang Med!"

Jaq's good hand grabbed her before she moved out. "Wait a second. Where are you going?"

"I've a job to finish. You're safe down here for now. The patrol from the 21st will take care of you. My people have to move. Med will be along in a while."

"I really need to—" Jaq groaned and clutched at his shattered shoulder.

"Stay put?" said Rett, a threatening hand on the stunner in her belt. "On your own or unconscious, choice is yours."

147

His head dropped to the surface in defeat.

"Fang Med, Fang Lead," said Med on the com. "What's up, I'm open."

"Med—I've injured jumper crew and three civilians in the trough with zero-21 patrol, sector eight. They'll be moving toward you, but if you can get in here or send someone else, do it. Some look bad."

The equal blend of ire and desire she was feeling for Jaq (Pam had great fun with the similarity of those words) dissipated instantly as Rett's glance landed on a tall figure coming toward them. *Great. Reve.*

"Shoulder's pretty bad, grazing burn and cut in the side, bruises, lacerations, minor burns elsewhere. A mess but not serious," she told Colonel Reve in answer to his inquiring head motion toward Jaq.

"Fang twenty-eight will hold here," Med said. "On my way."

Good, thought Rett. *Bhayorn made it in to help, so Med won't be leaving the others alone. And if H'tenneck were dead, Med would have told me.* She addressed Colonel Reve. "My medtech will be here shortly. I have to get back up there. Colonel—" Rett sighed, feeling tired all of a sudden. "Sir, if you're going to make any more movements up here, please com me. I'll let you know when you can move the rest of your people up."

* * * * *

JAQ REGARDED THE INFANTRY OFFICER curiously as the older man nodded and watched Sergeant Rett disappear from sight. Then the colonel crouched alongside, opening one of the larger medical packs from the supply jumper.

"You're Zetinorian," said the colonel. It wasn't a question; those sharp gray eyes assessed him anew.

"Jaq Pym."

"Reve." The Nyorfian grinned. "Your species is not as endangered as it seems after all."

"You've seen others?"

The older man pushed back his helmet a bit and swiped a blood-smeared forearm across the side of his face. "Three in the past couple years—one of them just a month or so ago. You make four. We're glad to have you, Citizen. Your people—those we have as well as those still stuck with the Yixolryns—have made some significant differences for us."

"Thanks for what you did up there," said Jaq, not knowing what else to say. "And for covering my butt. How are the others from my team? And the civilians?"

"Alive. Some are bad, but if we can keep the bleeding under control, they'll make it."

As he spoke, the colonel deftly applied a few temporary bandages and some burn spray where it was needed most. Then before Jaq realized it, his position was altered into one more comfortable; the weight of his body off his injured shoulder; his hanging left arm secured in an ingeniously simple twist of his shoulder harness.

"Need anything for the pain, or can you hang in for the moment?"

"I'm fine, sir," said Jaq truthfully. "Thanks again."

"Any time." The colonel's cool gray eyes met Jaq's quizzical glance, then his sandy eyebrows lifted and a small, sideways grin turned up one side of his mouth.

Again, Jaq was slammed by a sensation of familiarity.

"Stay put, sport." Colonel Reve stood and left to help one of his soldiers who called for help in her effort to control a fiercely bleeding wound on another crewmember of the downed supply jumper.

Another body slid down the steep slope of the trough to land with a splash on Jaq's left, cursing all the way. The hissed string of maledictions combined with the startling chill of freezing droplets of water shook Jaq out of the haze of confusion in which Rett had left him.

The cursing ceased at the same moment. "Jaq!"

"Hey, Med."

"Nice to see you. I'll get to you later." Med immediately went past him to the more seriously wounded.

Jaq wasn't sure how long Med was busy and didn't care. He had too much to figure out, and none of it had to do with other Zetinorians. Lifting his good hand to his lips, he fingered the still-tingling surfaces lightly. Those kisses had been . . . Well, she'd never been so intense about it before. He had to admit there was definite extra . . . spice . . . in getting so intense while in the middle of a firefight.

On the other hand, knowing that he had hurt her badly—seeing it in her eyes and hearing it in her voice—cooled his fresh flush of passion into guilty dismay. She was right. He never gave her a chance once Etron entered the picture, even though Etron, after the first time he showed up, didn't actively solicit Rett's attentions until after she had been injured and banned from contact with the Battalion for two tendays. Jaq had allowed jealousy to take control of his reason. His avoidance of Rett and request for transfer had been nothing but an excuse to go off and sulk, pure and simple. All the while trying to justify his actions.

He groaned and covered his eyes with his hand. *I wouldn't blame her if she never wanted to talk to me again. Was I delirious when she said she loved me?* he wondered. *No, you idiot,* he answered himself in the next thought. Her anger and frustration had been stronger because of it. *I never wanted to hurt her. But I did. I stood there and shot her down as surely as if I used a weapon. She loves me anyway.* He shook his head and in the next second, came back to reality with a gasp as careful hands probed his shoulder. "Shit!"

"Try again. It hasn't been all that long for me to accept the possibility you've forgotten my name." Med awarded him his very nastiest glance. "You should have taken the Colonel up on his offer of a painkiller. Would've made my job easier."

"It wasn't hurting this bad then," said Jaq in a mumble. "How bad is it?"

"The shoulder's pretty bad, but you'll survive. I'd say you're looking at least two tendays disability, however, that's not for me to decide. I'm going to give you a painkiller now. It might make you a little sleepy. Try to stay awake because we need to move when I'm done with you."

Jaq nodded.

After administering the drug, Med treated the lesser injuries. By the time that was finished, Jaq was feeling numb and had to concentrate on focusing his vision, because if he didn't, he saw double.

Med eyed him and nodded. "Now I can make an improvement on this rig the Colonel has you in. Say, I didn't know you were with the 21st."

"I'm not." Jaq groaned and broke into a sweat as Med started to work on his right arm and shoulder. Maybe he needed another dose of painkiller. Trembling violently, hoping he could keep down his nausea, Jaq wondered briefly what it would have felt like without any medication at all, then immediately felt guilty again. *Rett's been through worse than this without any pain medication to help.*

"Talk to me, Jaq."

The medtech's reminder pulled him out of the fog in which he'd started to slip. Grateful for the diversion, Jaq didn't disguise his relief for the opening. "I'm still with TRANS, with the sector supply. Coalition interceptors forced our jumper off-course and down before we could make the ground checkpoint. We crashed on the roof, right where they wanted us, I guess. They need supplies too."

"Hmm. And do you know how those other people came to be up here?"

"The civilians? Doing some repairs. They came over to help us when the jumper crashed . . . then we all were pinned down

151

on this roof for a good hour before the real action started. We held them off best we could—" Jaq clenched his teeth as Med tightened the bandage.

"You don't want this shifting around before we get you to a med facility." The medtech rearranged Jaq's arm across his chest and utilized both shoulder harness and utility belt to immobilize it. "You think this hurts now? Wait an hour or so until the shock wears off and things get good and swollen."

"Thanks a lot, Med," said Jaq.

"Sure. Best to know what to expect. Of course after that stupid self-righteous crap you pulled with the Sarge a half-year ago I should let you stew in your own sweat for a while."

Jaq nodded in miserable agreement.

"But you know I can't do that. I'll take more satisfaction out of hurting you badly when you're feeling better." The medtech's talented fingers pressed hard against several points on Jaq's body so remote from his shoulder he wondered why Med bothered. In the next second, Jaq let out a sigh of relief.

"Do you know that officer? Reve? There's something familiar about him, but I know I never met him before. He saved our butts."

"Colonel Reve?" Med gave Jaq a wide grin, something Jaq couldn't ever remember seeing on the medtech's face before. The suddenly approachable, affable-looking sandy-haired stranger said, "Know him? Well, never met him in person before, but I know of him. And maybe you haven't met him before today, but you know both his daughters."

"Huh?"

"He's Rett and Ariam's father," said Med, already returning to the more familiar persona Jaq knew. "And if the roof stays on this complex long enough for us to finish, it's sure going to blow off when the Sarge tells him off! He saved you, your friends and those civilians, yes—but he forgot to tell *her*. Caused problems."

"Rett's *father*—?" Jaq's eyes widened. "*The* Colonel Reve?"

"Nyorfians only use names once, Jaq," the medtech reminded. "So there's only one. There's only one Rett, too. Thank all deities, not even with two planets can we handle more than that."

"I used to hear almost as much about him as about Rett and F-troop."

"Yes, both of them cut from the same tree, as Ariam puts it. The Colonel's already asked me if I or anyone else from F-troop knew you." Some of Med's earlier humor reappeared.

"He did? Why?"

"He thinks he saw the Sarge kissing you while you both were still up on the roof. Apparently, he made a mistake. I explained you were probably having some trouble breathing and she was resuscitating you."

"I *was* having trouble breathing," mumbled Jaq.

3.2.6 COMPLEX 117 (REFINERY), ROOFTOP, EPNOCE
0536.02.07 (LOCAL RECKONING)

"COM CONNECT ALL FANG TEAM! Fang Lead to Fang team, good work, all clear!"

Sergeant Rett set fingers to her lips and the piercing all-clear whistle confirmed the pcom transmission preceding it. F-troop had slammed forward against desperate but determined Coalition forces. Three hard hours later, she was sure they'd still be fighting if not for the fact the enemy on the outer defenses had simply run out of energy as well as ammunition.

SubColonel Nauskova had already—on Rett's go-ahead—started filtering elements of the 21st into positions held by F-troop. *Our job here is finished. We got them in, secured the civilian area—Reve's people can take care of the rest.*

Leaving Trebor and Worren to regroup the platoon, Rett made her way toward Med to check her casualties and those others the patrol from the 21st had brought out from the trough. There were a few more people there than there were earlier—and she felt a rush of anxiety until she realized Med and Bhayorn were treating relatively minor injuries.

~Are you going to leave Jaq hanging like you did for much longer?~

Jaq is the least of my priorities at the moment, Pam, thought Rett, although now that she thought about it, she should have kissed him again. The way his pulse rate and temperature had skyrocketed after his first moment of surprise had been as pow-erful a sensation as taking off in a fightercraft.

~I wonder if he really heard the part where you told him you were in love with him.~

If he didn't hear that, much less get it, thought Rett, *then I'll have some serious re-thinking to do. Like I said, I can't worry about it now.*

"Fang Team, this is Fang two, confirm all clear, pull back as relieved and call in for check-off." Trebor's pcom message, like Rett's, was followed with the whistle for *platoon report!* In case any F-troop member's pcom was damaged, the whistles backed up the transmissions.

"Med?"

He sent Specialist Fiannult on her way with a ferocious frown and an admonition to see him again after they returned to base before turning to the sergeant to give his report. "For F-troop, Trebor, Worren, and Nerrah still haven't cleared with me, but I don't think there's much beyond the usual bumps, grazes, and scrapes, other than that handful who were scorched earlier. Nothing serious there, either," he said in reminder as Rett's expression hardened. "As for those serious, Jayord was lucky, just missed losing that eye. I assured him he'll be his handsome self again in a couple tendays. Ariam is conscious now, and like I said, she'll be good to go in a month or so, with work. H'tenneck—" Med hesitated. "He'll make it, as long as he doesn't shut down. More than likely he won't be cleared back for anything but limited duty."

"We'll worry about that part of it after he's out of danger."

Med agreed. "I have Jayord and Ariam staying on him."

"The others?"

"Jumper crew didn't get off lightly and neither did those two civilians, but they'll make it. Broken bones, a few deep nasty gashes, several serious SMG scores, and handfuls of burns. Go easy on Colonel Reve, Sarge," Med said, dropping his voice. "He should have commed, yes, but from what I heard from several sources, we would've lost all those people if he hadn't moved when he did."

"Medjumper's on the way," said Trebor, joining them. "Everyone else is here, Sarge, Med. Some singed hair and uniform, no other injuries."

"Good," said Med.

Sergeant Rett leaned over H'tenneck, who was aware enough now to recognize her. He managed a tiny shadow of a grin as she smoothed his hair and touched his ebony cheek gently. "I need you. Hang in, okay?"

He made a small sound of assent.

She looked at Ariam, who lay alongside the young squad-leader, the least scorched portion of her head making a light contact with his upper arm. Ariam's return smile was weary and strained. Her psychic focus on H'tenneck helped divert her from her own injuries.

"Semage is going to really kill me for this. We usually try to return what we borrowed in close to the same shape it was to begin with." Rett managed a chuckle.

"He'll get over it," said Ariam, her smile increasing a few degrees. Her voice was rough.

"Deities, Ariam, all those years trying to keep you from breaking any bones, and now look."

This time Ariam managed a rasping laugh. "I'll get over it. But about the virus I'm sure to come down with after you dragging me through a puddle of ice water, I'm not so sure."

The sudden change of expression from Ariam and soft sound of caution from Jayord killed the chuckle growing in Rett's chest and put her instead on wary alert. Someone cleared his throat behind her.

She brushed a reasonably unhurt section of Ariam's face with a gentle kiss. "I'll check back before the medjumper comes." Rett straightened slowly and turned around. "Sir?"

"Can we talk for several minutes, Sergeant?"

"If you have something to say to me, sir, you can say it right here."

It was an echo from the past. From that day long ago when she had tried to get her father aside to tell him she'd enlisted. She could see he remembered those words, too: the quickly masked shock in his eyes didn't hide the fluctuation of energy she read from his body.

She had been prepared to talk with him in a civil manner after the mission—but that was before friendly fire from his unit nearly killed people from hers. Rett didn't back down one fingertip on her attitude. If anything, she hardened her outermost self and prepared for a repeat of the situation all those years ago.

Being around other people never stopped you before, she thought bitterly. *Why get private about it now? Just tell me off in front of my platoon—go right ahead! You were the one who screwed up here, not me.*

"I'd like to commend F-troop for a job well done," said Reve.

Rett sent him a sharp glance. "Thank you, sir. We did our best—despite certain difficulties!" Then in response to her own second thought—and a hard poke in the leg from Ariam—she swung aside, forcing the officer to move with her.

157

* * * * *

REVE CHOSE TO MOVE WITH the platoon sergeant, away from her people, knowing he fully deserved to be the object of her wrath and appreciating, silently, her physical movement to get the two of them aside for a confrontation.

"I apologize for that."

"Damn it, Colonel, you can take your apology and shove it up your ass sideways!"

She spun to face him, every bit as tall as he, so full of tiff her dark eyes burned with threads of molten copper. Deities, this magnificent, furious creature was his daughter—a girl once so shy she could barely make eye contact with a stranger. Despite her outrage, her voice was low and didn't carry.

"What you did saved that jumper crew and those maint-techs, and for that I thank you, since we had no idea what was going on over there. However, sir, if you recall from all the pre-planning meetings we had, this penetration was *my* call, and if movement was needed in a certain sector, I should have been made aware of it."

She made a small gesture toward H'tenneck, Ariam, and Jayord. "My casualties weren't caused by Coalition troops, Colonel Reve. It was interference from *your* unit! Friendly fire. Sergeant H'tenneck caught SMG trying to avoid it. And then some bubbleheaded bomber of yours didn't clear the sector Sergeant Ariam and Specialist Jayord were in!"

"Ariam?" Reve hadn't yet been given the breakdowns, nor yet had the opportunity to check any casualties other than those his patrol had brought in. Had one of those extremely smoke-blackened, burnt soldiers she'd been talking to been his youngest child?

"Yes. *Ariam,* " repeated the sergeant savagely, biting off the end of the word.

"I will make it clear in my report F-troop's injuries were my fault, Sergeant."

It was apparent she had expected more a verbal battle instead of agreement, for her mouth closed, teeth snapped tight around a soundless exhalation. Some of the fire banked in her eyes, but they remained hard and narrow.

"Medjumper is here," called the platoon medtech.

Reve's glance went to the small man, who'd impressed him so much earlier. Deities, anyone he'd encountered from her platoon impressed him. He didn't know what he'd been expecting, honestly—no less than that, for certain, but to witness the way F-troop interacted with their platoon leader, the expressions he glimpsed, the body language he interpreted, told him more than days and weeks of conversation.

The sergeant's frosty tone broke into his thoughts. "If you'll excuse me, sir. I have only a few minutes to visit with my casualties before they leave."

* * * * *

NOT WAITING FOR HIS REPLY, almost wishing he would call her back so she could have the pleasure of ignoring him, Rett turned back toward F-troop's wounded. After taking one step, she checked her motion, feeling Reve so close she didn't need to see his aura. His body heat was enough of a clue.

"Sir?"

"I'd like a moment with them too, if that's all right with you."

It wasn't her place to grant or deny him that sort of permission. The fact he asked her for it brought her up short. She jerked her chin in an approximation of a nod. "By all means."

Giving Reve no further attention, she returned directly to H'tenneck, kneeling to touch his face with gentle firmness. Just enough pressure for him to respond with a faint eye-flutter. "Listen to me. Don't shut down, H'tenneck. Not until Med tells you it's okay." *Sixteen when he hid aboard that Coalition troopshuttle without being detected to bring news from the civilians on Epnoce to Nyorfias. Seventeen when he came to F-troop, his first combat assignment. Barely three years I've known him, feels like a lifetime.*

159

Her throat ached as she studied him, struggling for his life and breath. Her fingers smoothed his damp curly hair with a touch as gentle as a breeze. She dreaded that he would turn to her with that expression on his face, the one that would say he simply couldn't fight any longer. The one that would ask her for a merciful end to his pain.

"H'tenneck." She had to blink back the tears that threatened. She leaned very close, firming her touch. "Can you go on?"

The young man roused himself enough to give his platoon leader an affirmative grunt. He couldn't seem to get breath enough for anything more.

"You're not very loud for someone who doesn't want to die, soldier," snapped Rett in the tone all of them referred to as That Voice. "I can't hear you."

His black eyes shot open. "I can, Sergeant," he said, words faint, but clear.

"Then stay awake. You go out on me, and I'll kick your ass," said Rett, firming the tremor in her voice before it surfaced. "I need you, understand? Don't disappoint me."

"Never, Sarge," whispered H'tenneck, his lips curving up a bit.

"Good." She kissed him softly on the lips, on the temple. "I'll be in to see you as soon as I can. All of us will. All at once. With ale." To pull such a coup over Med had always been a wild thought of his.

A black eyebrow twitched and his smile made more of a curve. "Promise?"

Rett ducked her head so her lips were closer to his ear. "Promise, but you have to be up for it."

"Be waiting." H'tenneck managed a nod.

Rett caressed his cheek, and then straightened. Her glance lifted from H'tenneck to find Med looking a little less worried than he did before.

The medtech patted Rett's shoulder, gesturing for the med-jumper crew to load H'tenneck. "I'm going with him. He'll make it now—just to see if you'll get the platoon past me."

"Oh, we'll get past you even if we have to stun you, tie you up, and lock you in a crate, like the Coalition did back at Complex 412."

Med winced with the reminder. Unlike Ariam, however, he'd been fortunate enough to remain unconscious for the entire ordeal. Rett knew Ariam still had nightmares about it.

"Stay on him, Med."

"I will, Sarge."

She stopped at Ariam's side, and her sister reached up and grabbed her hand, tugging her into a crouch alongside her floater.

"Talk to him, Rett," she pleaded, the rasp of smoke in her voice making it sound breathless. "Don't change your mind about talking to Dad, please? Do it for me? Try to straighten this out! Don't wait. He—" She started to say something else, closed her eyes and changed tracks with a visible effort. "Who knows when we'll see each other again?"

Rett studied Ariam's face, pale and anxious beneath the scorched, bruised skin and the coating of soot, dust, and blood. "Did he say something just now to get you upset like this?"

"No." Ariam swallowed, grimacing with the pain that caused. "As hard as it is, and has been, I can handle you getting hurt, almost dying, getting lost—but I can't take this split between you and Dad anymore." Tears filled her eyes. "I wanted him to make the first move. I tried. He should. But I want it resolved. Even if you have to make the first move. Do it. I want my family back together. Now. Here. Today. *Especially* now we have Valera, Olvero, and Ulorath. *Please.*"

"Shh." Rett smoothed singed wisps of hair back from her sister's forehead, trying not to pay attention to the strands that fragmented or fell away with her touch. Unlike life, hair would grow back.

~Ariam's right,~ Pam said softly. ~You didn't want to wait one more minute to have it out with Jaq. I think it's time to get it out with your dad, while you're both right here.~

Rett ground her teeth together for a moment, then gave in. "All right, Ariam, I'll talk to him. But I can't make any promises about the results."

"Good enough. Just give him a chance. And take yours."

"I love you, Ari." Rett leaned in to kiss her, then straightened. "I'll see you back at the base—hang in there, okay?"

After seeing to Jayord, she spent a moment or so with the others who'd been in the trough, saving Jaq for last. His incredible blue eyes were dreamy from the painkiller and the general letdown of energy now the tension of battle had passed. She poked him in his right arm. "Hey. Bubblehead. Wake up."

He awarded her a drunken sort of smile. "Are you going to kiss me again . . . like you did before?"

161

"No."

It was certainly a tempting thought.

"Oh." He looked down the length of his body toward his toes and succeeded only in crossing his eyes. "Going to yell at me again?"

Rett kept a businesslike tone of voice. "I just wanted to say goodbye. If we don't get to visit before they transfer you to a hospital on the main continent, you can write me, since you're so good at it. I have to go, and they're waiting to load you."

"Rett. Take this, please." With an amazingly coordinated movement from so zoned on painkillers, Jaq pushed a small data storage unit into her hand. "I was wrong. And wrong again for not trying to work things out. These are the letters I really wrote . . . and couldn't send."

She tucked the DSU into a belt pocket without even glancing at it. Then she leaned to kiss his forehead in the same manner she'd bestow on any of her people. "Take care, Jaq. I'll talk to you when I can." She nodded to the medjumper crewmember waiting to load Jaq's floater.

Colonel Reve stood to one side, waiting. She met his gaze, and to Reve's inquiring elevation of eyebrows, Rett motioned with her chin to the spot in which they had stood earlier.

I'm doing this for Ariam, she reminded herself stubbornly.

~How about you're doing this because you said you would. That you were tired of carrying it.~

Shut up, Pam. On the heels of that thought, she managed a sensation of gratefulness for the reminder. And gratitude for Pam's being there to back her up.

For several seconds she stood, as he did, silent, not quite staring, not quite making solid eye contact.

"I admit I made a mistake by not alerting you before I took action," Reve said.

That was unexpected and despite herself, Rett heard her own voice say, "Well, yes, sir, you did. However—" without the slightest help from Pam, who gave every indication of sitting back in her place with a smug expression.

"However nothing, Sergeant. I will expect that to go on record from both our reports. What I did was out of order." His voice was hard. "More people were hurt, and that could have been avoided by one short communication. You're right. There are no excuses. Is that understood, Sergeant?"

"As you will, sir. I'll also add what you did saved those people." Rett immediately resumed her professional attitude. "Was there something else?" *Now he'll zing me for insubordination,* she thought to Pam.

"Yes. I should've done this a long time ago," said Colonel Reve with a sigh.

163

"Sir?" Rett managed to control the surprise in her voice— barely. She still expected him to round in on her for the way she talked back to him. She kept her face still.

"I should have told you I'm proud of you. Told you I love you. Apologized for those terrible, hurtful things I said. When you told me you were enlisting, all that flashed through my mind was a picture of you, dead, with Ariam next to you. I didn't want to lose you—like I lost your mother and Tovadan. Then again, I couldn't expect you to be content staying in Treetop, running the business, but how I wished you would have—so you would be safe . . . and Ariam would be safe with you. At least at that point in time. When the Coalition overran the district a year after Ariam enlisted, I was glad neither of you were there.

"You and Ariam are all I have left. It was wrong of me to be selfish, and think only of how I would feel. Like I'd been since your mother and Tova died." Colonel Reve looked away for a second. "You and Ariam were generous and brave enough to agree to my going, after all. Especially you. Since Tonia and Tova were killed, you just stepped in and picked up the slack. Then I left. Thinking more of my need to run from my pain more than the burden I left you."

"I—"

He held up a dirt and blood-crusted hand. "Let me finish. I admit I overreacted, but it was all I could think of at that moment. So, like today, I did what I had to do, without thinking through, and people were hurt. All I could think of later, after you left, was that you were enough like me to take something thrown in your face and use it. Use it to prove me wrong and make the very best chance for yourself of surviving." Reve's voice was soft and sad.

Again Rett took a breath to say something, but he shook his head. She crossed her arms. She was aware that her position indicated anything but openness, but she didn't know what else to do with her hands.

~Just listen, Rett,~ came gently from Pam. ~He's doing the best he can.~

* * * * *

REVE PUSHED HIMSELF TO CONTINUE. It was hard, with her standing there so still and devoid of emotion, watching him as dispassionately as a raptor would watch a small prey animal.

"I don't blame you for hating me. I've hated a part of myself for this long. I did keep track of you, partially through Ariam, who never gave me personal details, partially through contacts in MainCommand. And partially by . . ."

Serendipity, he almost said. Several years ago, on a day he would never forget, he and the 21st had a stopover at Centerland Base. They were on the flightline, waiting to board a troopjumper that would take them to a new remote location. He remembered clearly the medjumper that had come in so fast and hot it was a miracle it hadn't crashed. The group of medical people already waiting had to scatter to get out of its way.

In that moment, he somehow knew the identity of the casualty. He didn't pause to think about it. Didn't say a word to his second-in-command. He dropped everything and ran, and the 21ˢᵗ went on their mission without him.

But Reve didn't want that to slip out. Not now.

He stopped for a second or two to recover his composure. "I'm sorry I wasn't there for you, all those times when you needed me."

He saw her fingers tighten on her upper arms. Her face remained devoid of expression; her eyes were still, dark mirrors hiding everything she felt. All he saw was the reflection of his own face in them. Did he truly look that old? At this moment, he certainly felt every year. In that moment, Reve could no longer try to hide his emotions from her. His heart ached, full of pain, his love for her, and his regret.

"And I guess that's all I wanted to say." Reve turned to go. He couldn't face the emotionless flatness of her eyes as they coolly rejected him. Had that vulnerable seventeen-year-old seen the same expression from him? Deities, it hurt!

A steely hand caught his arm in a hard grip. He swung back to face her.

"Now that you've had your say, don't you think it's fair to let me have mine?"

He dipped his head once in agreement, and waited in silence. Her fingers would leave bruises where they dug into his flesh, but at least bruises faded with time.

"I can't say I'll ever forget what you did, or how it made me feel. But there's a big difference between hurting and hating, and we were both too logheaded to admit it." She released him and stepped back.

"Damn it, Rett, if it weren't for that very logheadedness, I would've told you this a long time ago, when you visited Ariam before your first combat assignment."

"Why didn't you?"

165

"I started to. But that extremely confident and correct young commando was someone I didn't know, and she froze me."

* * * * *

RETT SHOOK HER HEAD, HALF at Reve and half to Pam, who was thinking *I told you so!* in thoughts sky-high.

"I'm just sorry it ever happened," Reve said. "Any of it."

"I was hurt and tiffed, but I never hated you, Dad."

The startled flash and hopeful warming in his eyes when she said "Dad" erased the remainder of the tension in her body, the emotionless shield she'd been struggling to keep as he spoke.

"As much as I tried to. As much as I tried to forget I had anything to do with you, I couldn't." She managed a small smile. "I kept track of you, too. And I know you came to see me in hospital once, a bit over three years ago, when you thought I wouldn't know about it."

His breath escaped in a whoosh of surprise. "Who told you?"

"No one told me. I knew you were there. Later they told me I must have dreamt it, that I had no visitors outside of Medical staff or Special Forces." She shook her head. "I knew you weren't a dream. I needed you—and you *were* there."

"I couldn't stay. They made me leave."

Reve reached for her and she went to him. He hugged her close, burying his face in her neck.

"I can't begin to tell you how I felt, seeing you like that. Seeing Ariam like she was today was not even remotely close." His voice was choked with remembered horror and emotion. "I was there when they brought in you in off the medjumper. They didn't let me get close until later—ten hours later. They were worried because you had gone so far into deepsleep that they didn't think you'd come out. But then you started waking up—too much."

"I wanted you, that's why. You always came when I had those dreams and made me feel better. You know, those dreams where I couldn't move."

"I would have stayed." Reve's arms tightened. She felt some hot moisture against her skin and a ragged breath. "I would have told you I'm sorry. If I had the power to change anything, it would be that one day. It might have not changed what happened. But—"

She didn't need to see his face, nor even hear his voice. The remembered shock and heartrending pain of his memory was so strong that Rett didn't need her energy sense to scope it.

"You don't have to explain. It's all right, Dad," she whispered. She leaned into him, her head on his shoulder, arms tight around his waist. The familiar scent of him, which she'd known since birth, rose strong in her nostrils. Just as it had back then.

She didn't track how long they stood on the smoking roof of the refinery in silent reunion, but a soft reminder from Trebor in her pcom and a deep breath from Colonel Reve brought her upright. She would have taken a step back, but her father didn't let her go.

"We'll get together back at the Base," Reve said.

"Yes. I'd like that." She offered him a wipe from her utility belt, and he used it on the smears and smudges around her eyes before applying it to his.

"Get some spray on those burns," he said, nodding toward her hands and forearms. "And that cut on your arm needs attention."

"Yes, Dad."

"I'm proud of you. I love you."

"I love you, too." Rett leaned in to kiss him. "You know we have our work cut out for us when we get back to Treetop."

"Yes. I'll look forward to that day." He grinned. "Bringing anyone with you? That young Zetinorian, maybe?"

"Why would you think that?" Rett pulled on her most innocent face.

"Oh, I don't know. Maybe because I can tell the difference between someone in respiratory distress and someone who's being kissed senseless, even from a distance. Well?"

"I'll let you know as soon as I know. I have to go."

Colonel Reve's face became serious once more. "I'll expect a copy of your report, Sergeant."

"Yes, sir. Thank you, sir." Back in Special Forces mode, Rett stepped back and saluted him in her best style. "Colonel Reve, one favor please, sir?"

The tall officer looked inquiring. "What is it, Sergeant?"

"Be careful, sir," she requested. "You take too many chances."

Colonel Reve glared at her, shook his head in disgust, laughed, and then turned to supervise the deployment of his troops.

STRATAGEM
AURORA BASE, EPNOCE
0536.02.37 (LOCAL RECKONING)

"IT SEEMS AS IF I barely started flying, and now I have to stop."
Rett sighed as she stepped outside, her breath instantly
freezing into a cloud of fine ice particles. She'd just come off a
three-day stint of patrol-recon duty with the AirSpacefighters.
For her, it was the last flight duty for the remainder of the winter
season on Aurora.

Winter. She had to chuckle. For many of them who came
from Nyorfias, it had been winter on Epnoce since their arrival.
That was nothing compared to how it was now.

Storms on Aurora continent had forced the pilots of the flight
division to cancel too many missions. Now the fighter wing was
pulling back to the big continent. From there they would fly high
recon and, when the weather was open, support for the troops
on the ground.

She'd miss the men and women of the 114th: Captain Etron,
Colonel Centra, Ash, Briealun, and all the other pilots, crew, and
support people she'd worked with so closely for two hundred and

forty-some days. Just about half a Standard year. A period of time that had seemed at once longer and a lot shorter than it should have been.

"Sergeant!"

She stopped walking and turned partway. Major Yidnar hurried to catch up with her.

"Let's get out of the wind," he said.

She followed him into one of the narrower side paths and into a small cavelike space, one of many created for a shelter against the wind and brutal cold.

~Wonder what's up now, that he's telling you out here and not inside somewhere? I mean, you *were* on your way to report to him.~

You should know by now Major Yidnar has his own way of doing things, Pam. Now hush.

Her commander threw back his hood. "Glad I caught you. A few things have changed during your recon duty. Did you get good maps for us, though?"

"Yes, sir, they should be getting sent up pretty soon. What's up?"

"Transport, Sergeant." Major Yidnar looked very pleased with himself. "You know we've been dealing with unique problems again here on this continent—transport is one."

Definitely. Rett nodded.

"Now there's a solution, at least for the troops who need it the most. Like us. This transport is very fast in snow and ice, very reliable, extremely maneuverable, and totally adapted to Aurora. It's not affected by wind or storm, could never get us lost, and is very easy to maintain. Best of all, it can pass almost completely unnoticed by the enemy."

"Wow. Sounds ideal, sir. What is it?"

He reached into an inner pocket and handed her a DSU. "Report to Transport Area D3, give them this. Easy's already training there. You'll pick up yours and get started; we need all the time we can to get used to this. You've also been requartered—your kit has already been moved. Don't com anyone about this. Just get over there. Now."

"Yes, sir." Rett turned immediately, burning with curiosity. She didn't recall seeing the Major so pleased with himself since he sprung those Section Five Combined Duty forms on her half a year ago that allowed her to cross-train into the AirSpacefighters.

At least, thought Rett to her ego-merge friend, *he's not expecting us to wade through the snow and ice on this campaign.*

~He didn't say what we were getting, either. I'm dying to know. He looked too smug about something.~

He did, admitted Rett, her own curiosity intense. *For him to look so peculiar while ordering me not to com anyone to ask . . .*

~What could it be?~ groaned Pam from inside. ~I guess it isn't snowshoes or skis! Maybe some kind of snowmobile? No. Something that mundane wouldn't make the Major look like the proverbial Terran cat that swallowed the canary.~ Pam added mind-pictures so Rett would get her reference.

Rett chuckled, shrugged, and hunched deeper into her warm jacket, turning up the hood and adjusting her breath muffler as the wind scattered loose snow into her face. *I guess we'll find out,* she thought, turning down the plowed path toward the Transport area.

She found the section the Major indicated and gave her orders to the corporal on duty just inside the shed entrance. He grinned up at her and spoke to the pcom he wore beneath his hat.

"Bring that one you were saving for Sergeant Rett from F-troop."

A soldier soon came toward them, leading a tall, shaggy, antlered beast the same colors as the iridescent snow of Aurora.

~Guess what? It's not a snowmobile!~

"No kidding?" Rett said aloud. She studied the animal with surprise and some misgivings; glanced at the corporal; then back at the animal.

"No kidding, Sergeant," said the corporal.

The luminous violet eyes of the beast returned Rett's scrutiny just as doubtfully.

"Ahh—what is it?" Rett said finally.

"This will be your transport, Sergeant Rett. We call them Ice Beasts. They're native to this part of Aurora."

"Seriously? And we're just hearing about them now?" Rett's incredulous attention returned to the animal.

"Well, you know full environmental studies of Aurora were never completed," the corporal said. "Not to mention the past ten years or so we've been cut off completely from all communication with Nyorfias."

"I guess you're right," she said, but her astonishment was no less. "But not to hear of these even since we arrived on Epnoce? That you've domesticated—"

"Oh, no, they're not domesticated at all," the corporal said, and the other soldier holding the lead rope of the animal was shaking his head vigorously. "They . . . well, it's temporary duty."

"It just worked out," said the soldier with the beast.

"Just worked out," repeated Rett. She'd been raised in a wilderness area; had studied wild animals native to her world, especially to her province. She'd had the chance to observe a pack of snow growtus during the time she'd been shot down and thought they were huge: the adults nearly twice greater in mass than she was.

This creature, however, appeared to weigh perhaps as much as six Nyorfian adults and stood, from claws to shoulder, nearly twice as tall as a growtu. In all her years Rett had never been this close to a live animal this large—unless she counted the big dunos she'd hunted in Treetop. Okay. So it *sort* of looked like a very big dunos.

Pam completely disagreed. ~Not at all like a dunos. A dunos looks like a miniature woolly rhinoceros crossed with a baby moose. Big, yes, but ugly.~

That doesn't help me very much, Rett thought back. *Not even with your visualizations.*

~If you would allow me?~ Pam gave Rett a gentle nudge.

Not now, not with these people watching me, said Rett.

~Come on—let's just try a switch. You've already blown your inscrutable show-no-emotion cover, so a walk around is the next logical thing. I'll be good . . . ~

Rett didn't like it, but she didn't know what else to do. *Just for a minute. As soon as one of them says anything, let me back.*

After a few blinks and a moment of lightheadedness, she was looking at the creature through Pam's alien eyes. Pam was more than familiar with sizing up many animals, especially one domesticated species of large quadrupeds meant as transportation sources.

Was this what it was like for Pam when she thought about things foreign to her Earth friend? Rett couldn't remember the last time she consciously allowed this much shift without action on her own part.

At the shoulder, the beast was level with her eyes, and she was rather tall—just a fingerwidth over two lengths. A short, strong back ended in a powerfully muscled hind end, with a short, furry tail.

That part's like a dunos.

She moved a little closer, glancing up at the man still holding the lines, who nodded encouragingly at her. Crouching, she paid attention to the legs, even reaching out to touch one. The fur was soft and thick, but as Pam made Rett extend her hand and wrap her fingers around the lower foreleg, she felt hard, cabled sinew and muscle beneath the fur.

Here Pam's thoughts really got technical. To Pam, animal legs and the feet attached to them were highly important.

~Rett, of course they are important. How far would you—well, let's not use you—but the average soldier get if his or her toes were broken, arches fallen, and kneecaps popping every other

173

step? You're supposed to rely on this animal for transport, you have to be concerned about his legs and feet.~ Pam interrupted her analysis of the animal long enough to stress that point.

Each limb ended in four-toed, widely spaced, double-clawed paws that seemed capable of gripping any terrain at any speed. The beast's shoulders were well sloped and its chest wide.

~Lots of room for heart and lungs in there. And look, the rear legs are a bit longer than the fronts. With those hindquarters, this thing can probably jump over one of those little moons of yours. Probably fast, too.~

Rett had to admit the animal was beautiful, but it went beyond that in Pam's sight, from merely beautiful to a work of art. She and Pam were equally admiring on this aspect, and enjoyed a rare moment of complete balance. Perhaps one of the few they both were completely aware of as it happened.

The head was small, beautifully shaped, and a pair of three-pronged, blue tinted antlers rose in a proud, graceful arc that swept forward and down at a slight angle. They were almost as long as the length of the creature itself. Its ears were upright, small, thickly furred.

~Big ears just release more heat,~ Pam stuck in. ~Not a good idea when it's always cold.~

She straightened and examined the gear strapped to the animal's body. The beast wore leather straps on its head and a fitted, odd-looking pad of some kind on its back that had more straps that went around the chest and over the shoulders. This gear was all in soft, snow colored material. The intentions of these accessories escaped Rett's perception. Pam straightened her out immediately.

~A hackamore bridle and a saddle,~ Pam informed Rett, secured by a girth and breastplate. ~Bridle for the rider's control, saddle for a more secure seat. Don't know what you will be calling them here, but that's what I call them at home.~

Good deities, Pam, thought Rett, *I didn't understand eighty-five percent of what you thought at me in the past few handfuls of seconds. I understand you approve, the animal is sound and healthy.* Rett didn't really know what else to say, so she added, *Well . . . good. Let me back—*

Blinking and hunching her shoulders a little as the shift was made, Rett gave her attention to the two TRANS people.

"Questions, Sergeant?" asked the corporal.

"I'm supposed to . . . ?"

Pam groaned from her place, giving a mental impression of pulling her hair out with both hands. ~Yes, you're practical, you're quick, but sometimes I think a tree fell on your head when you were a baby.~.

When the corporal laughed, eyes shining in high glee, Rett nearly suspected he was a mindspeaker Talent and "heard" Pam's comment. Then she realized she must have an expression on her own face that was not often displayed to anyone outside her own unit.

I can't be the only one to have looked like this. He probably never saw so many Special Forces people looking dumbfounded— or goofy, as you like to say—in one day, thought Rett sourly. She didn't take offense since the soldier's attitude was friendly, not derisive. All the same, she felt a twinge of chagrin for not keeping control over her reaction.

"Ride him? Yes. Believe me, Sergeant, it's a lot less technical— and a lot more physical—than flying a fighter. Now, I've told you everything I'm allowed, more than that you'll need to learn from the drill captain or the information that'll be released to your Omni later. You'll need instruction, so report to the training area marked for this section—back along the path, turn left, behind Building Four. You'll also be quartered in Building Four—did Major Yidnar mention that? Okay."

The man holding the animal handed the lines to Rett. "Here, take him, Sarge. They don't bite anything except tree bark. I was saving this one *especially* for you," he said. "They don't come any better than this fine fellow!" The man grinned and pounded a friendly fist against the animal's shoulder before leaving with the corporal.

Rett found herself alone with the peculiar snow-colored animal. It turned its small head and blew warm breath, smelling of tree resins, into her face. An intelligent, bold expression glowed from large, beautiful eyes.

~Rett, this is going to be *very* interesting!~

Pam, stop pushing me. I can tell you're all fired up. That was an understatement, since the nebulous aura that defined Pam's presence in Rett's mind glowed with the intensity of a plasma beam. *But—*

Pam wasn't the only impatient one. The beast shoved its muzzle into Rett's shoulder hard enough to push her back a step.

"Hey, you're supposed to be on my side!" Rett protested, and grinned at the animal as it raised its head and *whuffed* in her face again. "Does this mean you like me? Are you supposed to? Do you know I don't have the slightest idea of how we are meant to relate to each other? Aside from a recent memorable experience, I've never had to relate to animals directly. Most of those I studied in the wild were those who hunted other animals or those I hunted—ow! *Hey!*"

She jerked her arm aside as the animal laid back his ears and took a nip at her. "Deities! I thought that soldier just told me you didn't bite."

Inside, Pam was doing an excellent impression of rolling on the ground, clutching her stomach, and laughing her head off. ~Must've been the hunting comment, Rett. Will you please just . . . I suppose it will be easier for you to hear it from someone else. Go to the training area, okay? First, apologize.~

This is an animal, Pam, thought Rett very patiently. *I know you love animals, and think of certain ones as family, but let's not lose perspective here.*

Pam wasn't laughing now. ~After your time observing the growtu pack?~ she reminded pointedly.

That was different.

~Doesn't matter. Animals can be a lot more perceptive than humans give them credit for. They also are capable of associating certain words with bad memories. We don't know anything about this animal, his history, anything. A woman I knew had a mare that had been badly abused by a previous owner. The poor thing would freak out if someone said the word 'Bitch' anywhere within ten feet of her. The Coalition was on Aurora for a long time. Maybe this animal won't understand your apology—but it won't hurt anything. Most of all, it'll remind *you* to go easy until you learn more. Oh, and stop thinking of him as an *it*.~

One hand on the hackamore's headstall, Rett pulled the animal's head around until they both were nose-to-nose. She stared straight into the deep purple eyes, which looked a bit surprised at her action. His ears swiveled forward, as attentive to her as his eyes were.

"Beast, I'm sorry. Believe me, I know how some people in the Coalition can behave, and if they made that word bad for you, I'll try to remember not to use it." Prompted by Pam, she blew her own breath into the Beast's nostrils, felt another warm gust of sweet-scented breath in return. Then she released the headstall to scratch it cautiously high on the shoulder, just behind the withers. The animal appeared to enjoy that.

How did you know to do that?

~It's what I'd do with a horse,~ Pam said with a mental shrug. ~It just seemed like a good idea, from what we both know about animals. They sniff each other, right? We've even watched those cotos creatures giving each other those little teeth rubs on parts of the neck and shoulder. You learned the body language of the growtus quickly enough, that's what you need to learn and do here.~

Rett swallowed down the foolishness she felt.

~Don't be so hard on yourself. This is a novel situation,~ Pam said. ~For both of us, in a way.~

"You can say that again," Rett said, regarding the Beast again. "Okay, Ice Beast, now that I feel like a complete idiot, let's go learn how you work, and how we're supposed to work together."

~I'm going to have fun with this!~ thought Pam, not trying to control her enthusiasm. ~He looks like part elk, part mountain lion—and a lot of horse! I can't wait to see how he moves.~

Try to control yourself, Pam, Rett thought to her interior friend in a dry manner. Then she added, *of course you could help me out if you think you can, okay?*

Pam laughed again, so much that Rett had to laugh with her. The Earth woman's enthusiasm was contagious. Since their merger began, Rett could not recall ever feeling Pam *this* happy or confident.

~If I *think* I can! Well, if there's one thing I'm good at, besides using my imagination—it's teaching beginners how to ride. Been doing that for years.~

The training area was a large arena sheltered from the blowing and drifting snow by a group of long, low outbuildings. Rett saw others from Easy Force already involved in the process of learning to ride and control their newly acquired "transport."

She shook her head slightly, a small smile on her face. *No wonder Major Yidnar wouldn't come right out and tell me. We don't have very many domesticated animals in this system.*

~Those two guys said they weren't domesticated,~ reminded Pam.

Rett waved her free hand impatiently. *Regardless of that, we've never used an animal for riding or transporting things. The only person in F-troop I know who has had experience with livestock is Worren. He was a farmer in Centerland Province.*

She grinned at two people from Sergeant Atira's D-troop who had obviously had enough lessons for one day and were heading back to the quartering shed with their Beasts.

"It's pretty great, Sarge," called one. "Think you're going to like it."

"Hope so," Rett said and started to conclude her conversation with Pam aloud. "And of course where I come from if we need meat we go hunt—Damn!"

Rett almost fell flat when the Beast took a swipe at her again. She avoided getting her arm chomped, but the large teeth managed to close on the material of her sleeve. His ears were flattened again.

"I'm sorry." Deities, maybe Pam was right about the word association thing. She imagined she could feel resentment from him; see it in the reproachful flash of his eyes as they rolled back to focus on her. She stroked the animal's neck, soothing. "I forgot, all right? I'm sorry."

Again feeling rather foolish, Rett continued to the arena, stopping at the fence at Pam's suggestion.

~Let's watch for a while so I can see if this is similar to what I know, okay?~

Rett was more than willing to agree, and she leaned on the dividing wall to observe the drill instructors and pupils.

~On Earth,~ said Pam with some pride, ~we have a long and glorious history of combat astride—using horses.~ She told Rett about horses several times before, but again pictured the animals for her friend. More mind pictures of warhorses and soldiers through the centuries of Earth history followed.

And they armored them? And their riders?

~Yes, the armored guys were called *knights*. They were a . . . sort of elite military group with a special code of conduct, called *chivalry*. They protected the lands and interests of their lord. Of course, later everything changed, and gradually no one rode into battle on a horse any more—or even an elephant, we won't get into those. Now they use tanks and armored vehicles and airplanes and things instead. Better for the horses, I guess . . . but not much changed for soldiers. They still have to go out and get shot at.~

179

You call that a "long and glorious history"? Of slaughtering each other instead of— Rett stopped abruptly and apologized. She knew that Pam's appreciation had not been directed at the bloody wars and battles, rather for the horses and the soldiers who had been made to fight them. *I'm sorry. Your planet's bloody history isn't your fault. Maybe there are just as terrible and unpleasant things in the history of my original people—whoever they were, wherever they came from. But since it's something I've never known, it's hard for me to accept. You've said there's still a chance your people will blast themselves off the face of their own planet because they can't agree to coexist!*

Pam felt the mental turbulence surfacing in her friend. As much as Rett wanted to learn about Earth, there were many things that horrified her. Then there was the matter of that recent comment Rett had made in a mindless fit of tiff, about Earth getting on well with the Yixolryn Coalition.

~Sometimes, I'm sorry I ever told you anything about Earth,~ said Pam with a sigh. ~Let's forget it and get our attention back on the riding.~

Even the Ice Beast was eyeing Rett with concern. He turned his head to blow softly at her.

"Don't be sorry, Pam," said Rett aloud, stroking the shining fur on the Beast's neck. She continued in her thoughts. *You know—aside from a few notable instances where you've called me close-minded and snotty—that I* try *very hard to be open-minded. Of course that doesn't mean I always am. Let's just say I'm culturally limited—and glad of it.* She chuckled a little. *All the same, if we discover we live within a decent space hop of each other—*

~I know, I know—I'll come, you stay. Not a problem. I'm commuting already, why break the pattern?~

Rett let out a breath and gratefully turned her attention back to the riding. *It doesn't look too difficult.*

~It's not, really. The hardest thing is remembering you have a live animal with a full set of senses between your legs and it might respond unpredictably—no matter how well trained it may be. As balanced and quick as you are, you should pick up the basics in no time.~ Pam's mental voice took a turn to the wicked side. ~It's a good thing Jaq isn't going to be back for a tenday or so yet.~

What do you mean by that? Rett demanded, annoyance surfacing. The term of temporary transfer he had chosen to take had ended, and the Zetinorian had, very humbly, elected to return to his former position as F-troop tech advisor. As his commander, she had no problem with that. As his friend and lover, she still had some serious talking to do with him.

He would have been back sooner, but the shoulder injury he'd taken at the refinery last month kept him from Active duty. Epnoce MainCommand thought he'd put the recovery time to better use at the main base. *Why should it matter whether he comes back today or next tenday?*

~You'll know soon enough,~ Pam said cheerfully.

Rett eyed the animal standing alongside her, then the riders in the arena. *If it's something nasty, just remember you feel everything I do.*

~Oh, I know that. This time, though, I'll know what to expect, and just what to do for it.~

You make it sound like menstrual cramps. Rett didn't enjoy that idea. She'd only ever had them once in her life, in the first handful of days of her leave of absence back on Nyorfias. With all the injuries she'd ever sustained, it didn't make much sense to her that something so ordinary could wipe her out, yet it had. *Is that what you're thinking of? I don't see how that might happen. You know I don't get motion sickness, under normal circumstances.*

Pam laughed. ~Don't worry. Let's ride.~

As if to emphasize Pam's suggestion, the Ice Beast impatiently nudged Rett again.

"Okay already!" Rett told them both. "Deities! The things I do for Nyorfias," she mumbled darkly as she led the animal to the gate and the drill captain. Then she smiled. No one in the arena looked as if they were dying. Pam was teasing.

"Trying another new skill, eh, Sergeant Rett?" The drill captain verbally added Rett's name to her Omni's list of active riders. "Okay, grab a handful of the fur and hide on his neck—it won't hurt him. Grab the pad with your other hand. Jump up and swing your right leg over, make sure your toe clears his rump. That's it."

Rett felt some apprehension as she settled herself into the soft leather pad, but Pam's confident enthusiasm was overwhelming any doubts in the commando's mind.

~That's it,~ urged Pam. ~Sit up straight, back on your seat bones . . . yes, like that. Right. Don't be so tense—loosen up a bit. Grip the pad with the insides of your thighs—no! Not that hard, not when he's standing still. Pick up the reins— ~

"Yes, that's right. You've ridden before?" The drill captain sounded surprised.

Watch it, Pam. As far as I know, no one in this system has ridden any sort of animal before, at least not as a means of getting from one place to another. Rett turned a disarming smile on the instructor looking up at her so speculatively. "No—just been over there watching the others for a while. You sure I did it right? What next?"

~Squeeze with your seat a little. Lightly. He should walk right out.~

Rett did this as the drill captain told her the same thing and immediately the animal moved into a smooth walk. At least that was how Pam interpreted it. Rett wasn't so sure; the motion beneath her was new and strange. After a minute or so, she started putting Pam's stream of advice into practice and let herself relax into it.

Pam directed Rett in the use of the hackamore reins, going on about nose pressure instead of bit pressure and delighting in the fact the animal neck reined as well as direct reined and yielded well to leg aides and shifts in weight—

Stop, Pam! I don't understand a single thing you just said! Put it in GTC Standard, will you?

~We're doing just fine. This is one well-balanced and responsive animal, Rett, and if I had anything close to his class at home—I'd have an entire new career as an international dressage rider.~ Pam sighed. ~I bet he's got a trot you can sit to all day long. Let's see how he can really move!~

Pam made Rett shift her weight forward slightly and squeeze harder with her calves. Rett bit back on a startled exclamation as her mount sprang into a ground-eating canter, sending soft snow flying behind them.

~Don't tense up. Relax your hips, plant your ass in the saddle, grip the pad, and go with it. Don't hang on the reins! Use your seat and legs. If you have to grab something, grab the pommel of the saddle, or some of that neck fur. Sit into it or you're gonna fall. Sit up *straighter*. Shoulders back. Center your weight head to seat and flow . . . move with him . . . that's better. Easy as a rocking chair.~

Deities, Pam! You make me wish I had a few of my old training instructors around just so they would give me a break.

~Lose that daylight between your knees and the pad. Your legs are what's going to keep you attached if he needs to swerve or jump.~

Rett closed her legs more securely around the animal's barrel.

~Not as tight as that. Just give me a couple minutes, Rett. You can feel how you're supposed to sit, and notice the difference. Just for a minute or two.~

Okay. Rett was a little more comfortable letting Pam up for this than she had been a short while earlier.

183

~Don't go all the way back. We need to balance, like we did in your fighter that time. Except in a slightly different way.~

By now Rett knew not to ask how she was supposed to do that. She'd learned to believe in Pam's usual: *Just imagine you can. See it happening.*

So she did.

The difference was immediate. Her position astride was more secure; she felt as if her body was a fluid extension of the animal that moved with such effortless power beneath her. Through her seat and legs, she felt the creature's mood, his willingness, the slight shift of his head and flicker of his ear right before her own weight shifted to make a turn.

I think I'm beginning to like this, thought Rett. *This is almost as good as flying. Better, somehow.*

Pam slowly withdrew her physical assistance. ~You're doing great. No, don't tighten up. Keep your weight centered, sit a little deeper, and loosen your hips more.~

"Yes, this is much improved," said a soft mental voice as Pam made Rett sit deeper into the riding pad. "Lighten up on your hands, my muzzle is very sensitive."

PAM?

~Wasn't me!~ came from Pam in a thought of total amazement.~ It was him!~

Rett, shocked, sat back abruptly, and before Pam could warn her, the Ice Beast dropped his hindquarters and slid to a halt. Rett, who'd let her legs loose again, almost flew over his head. As it was, she nearly punctured her jaw on the antlers. After a quick and rather undignified scramble she regained her seat.

"Did you say something?" said Rett.

"Hush—not aloud! Speak to me as you do with Pam."

Rett couldn't breathe. This couldn't be happening.

"That was real nice, Fang Lead, you're a natural! You need more work on those stops, though!" called the drill captain from ringside.

She heard, of course, but at the moment she was unable to respond.

~You can hear me, too?~ asked Pam.

"Of course, both of you. More so now since you've been astride. I have spent time with you two legs and learned your thought patterns, and have had time to mesh with you since we met so that you can interpret my thoughts as well as I do yours."

"Oh, wonderful," Rett muttered. "No wonder you almost bit my arm off, you were in my *head*. Good gods and deities and everything in-between!"

Not for the last time her gaze flew skyward in accusation and demand, her thoughts going to the mysterious aliens who apparently took such amusement in complicating her life lately.

"What do you have against me? I barely got used to having one voice in my head . . . all I need is another!"

185

Pam was having a different reaction. Much to Rett's dismay, Pam was absolutely delighted. ~Intelligent, telepathic animals! This is getting better and better— ~

The Beast turned his head, angling it so the forward sweep of his antlers wouldn't poke Rett. He nuzzled her knee. "You must not tell any other two legs that I communicate in thoughts," the animal said with great seriousness. "My name is H'chan. Do other two legs also carry another entity with them, as you do?"

Before Rett could answer, there was a tap on her thigh.

"Hey, Sarge!"

A smaller Beast had stopped alongside. The diminutive figure astride couldn't be mistaken for anyone but Corporal Carakenne.

"Hi, Cara. Everything okay?"

"Uhm-hmm! Isn't this great?" The visible portions of the small commando's deep brown face glowed with enthusiasm.

"Sure is," agreed Rett. Thank all deities Cara was well over that horrible virus that had kept her out for such a long time. "No problem being so far up?"

"Well, Sarge." Cara's sky-colored eyes twinkled. "At first I thought so, and then I realized his feet are on the ground, so technically, I am too. Unless he sprouts wings, I think it'll be just fine."

"That's a good way to look at it."

"Seems he even tries to keep me from falling—he'll move just enough to put me back straight, or slow up a few strides if I lose my balance. Didn't stop me from eating snow a few times." Cara laughed. Her hands, small even in their heavy gloves, slapped the Beast's neck in rough affection. "I never even *touched* a live animal before. But you know, just after a few minutes, it feels as if I've always been around this one. Like we're synched somehow."

Rett nodded. *Cara's more right than she knows. The damn Beasts can read our minds, who knows what else?*

"Sergeant C'zleni—the drill captain—says they can run with a rider and gear twenty miles an hour for a few hours at a stretch, even though storm. She said the wild herds can move even faster than that over the open tundra between the forests where they shelter and browse."

"Wow." Rett was deeply impressed. So Pam's estimate of the animal's speed and endurance sounded accurate.

"That's not why I stopped though, actually—" Cara added. "The drill captain's been trying to get your attention for some time. Is anything wrong?"

"No." Rett took a furtive, guilty peek over her shoulder toward the drill captain. "She has?"

"Fang Lead! Is something wrong with your com? Move it!" yelled the drill captain through cupped hands. "Now!"

Cara cocked her head in the drill captain's direction and grinned. "Uhm-hmm!"

Rett shook herself, glanced sheepishly at Carakenne, and verbally switched her com to the right frequency for the training area. *I can't believe I forgot to do that.* She signaled the Beast back to his graceful canter. "We'll talk later!" she called over her shoulder, as a result losing her balance and nearly sliding over the animal's rump.

Pam groaned from her corner and sternly told Rett to pay attention.

The drill captain made her perfect those sudden stops, then they worked on sharp changes of direction. Rett learned how to fall off and get right back on again—although that wasn't part of what the drill captain called for.

~I can't help you every minute, Rett,~ was Pam's innocent explanation as Rett landed face first into the snow a fourth time. ~I already told you, until you get a feel for this animal and for riding, you have to watch where you're going.~

I'm just so glad you feel everything I do, Rett's thought growled in reply. *Eat snow, Pam!*

They both heard and felt the Ice Beast's snort of amusement.

187

* * * * *

SOME TIME LATER, RETT AND H'chan came to a halt in front of the drill captain when she called them to report.

"You can call it a day, Fang Lead." Senior Sergeant C'zleni of TRANS pulled down her breath muffler to reveal a wide smile.

"Already?"

"Already? You've been at it for five hours." C'zleni slapped H'chan's neck, a few great, hearty clouts that made Rett protest. "I stopped most of the others after two or three hours, but I couldn't quite make up my mind if you naturally knew what you were doing up there, or really needed extra work. I realize what a stretch this is for most of our people. What I look for on the first day isn't riding talent, though. It's signs of trust and teamwork. I've found that it's best to keep a new rider aboard until I really see a bond starting between them, and it seemed to take you longer to get to that point. "

Rett reached beneath her hood to scratch her left ear. She supposed that was true enough. If only C'zleni knew exactly why that was.

"We'll see how it goes tomorrow. You're going to be feeling this later. I guarantee it. Extra yellowstem at dinner—that can help stave off any cramping. Make sure you go for a walk and do some stretching before turning in tonight." She thumped H'chan on the neck so heartily Rett felt it all the way through her own body.

Feeling what? wondered Rett even as she exclaimed aloud, "Hey! You don't need to bruise him."

"He doesn't mind. You should see how hard they knock each other around in play."

H'chan also sent Rett reassurance that he didn't mind at all and the friendly buffeting was pleasant.

"Specialist H'leelem made you a good match with this one." The drill captain went on to mention several areas she wanted Rett to work on the next day—the same things Pam was constantly correcting.

Then she went over basic care of the animal. "This isn't only your transport, but your partner. Your lives depend on each other. And when you're out there," she gestured to the wilderness at large, "as long as you're with your Beast, your survival chances are quadrupled. More information will be available for download to Omnis later tonight."

When the drill captain had finished, Rett directed the Beast from the arena, exhausted and oddly happy. She rode a short distance farther, slid off, and leaned against the furry, warm side for a long minute. Muscles she had no idea her body possessed protested her movement. She "heard" Pam and the Beast in a purely technical riding discussion that was totally over Rett's head—as well as in it—but before she could focus on their exchange, Pam broke off and H'chan turned his small head to blow at Rett's shoulder.

She scratched his flat, broad cheekbone, needing no prompting from Pam. As the animal raised his antlered head and angled it to expose the underside, it was easy for Rett to guess what he wanted.

She scrubbed her fingertips through the thick fur, feeling the hardness of the jaw beneath, the cabled strength of muscle and sinew. The Beast's upper lip curled and wriggled in delight as his itch was soothed.

"Why haven't we ever heard of Ice Beasts before?" said Rett aloud. "All this time we've had people on Aurora, and not one mention of them."

Why would they have been kept secret?

Rett directed her thought to H'chan. *How did Ice Beasts come to be riding animals? Highly intelligent, telepathic . . . and no one knows? Not even to have reported spotting them in a survey? Were you hiding all this time?*

"Later," the Ice Beast thought in warm and friendly mental tones. "Later we shall discuss your questions. Now it is time for us to eat, and then rest. You did very well, with Pam's help and my own—but we have much, much more to practice."

Recognizing an evasion when she heard one, Rett stopped scratching and sighed. H'chan gave her another push.

"You are now quartered with me. Come." With gentle nudges to her shoulder, the animal guided Rett toward the long, low shed just behind the training area.

The shed was open to air, but protected from snow and stronger winds. It was only slightly warmer than the outside air temperature of almost fifteen degrees under freezing—which they were told was unseasonably warm for this season on Aurora. The huge shed held rows of partitioned areas. Each one was about five by four lengths in perimeter, and had a wide sliding door. Some held Beasts and some were still empty, but empty or occupied, not one door was fully closed.

H'chan nudged Rett toward the far end of the long building, finally stopping in front of a door on the end, near the outside wall. Rett saw her name there and an empty space below it, presumably for the name of her Beast.

"You can read GTC Standard, too? Or have you been in this building before?"

"I scent your belongings," said H'chan.

"You can?"

"Look inside, then," said H'chan with a snort.

"I'm going to go out on a thin branch here and trust you." Rett reached inside her heavy jacket, found a marker. "Just as I am going to guess it won't matter to you how I spell your name." Without waiting for an answer, she went ahead and scribed it in big, bold letters in the empty space.

That look right? she asked Pam. *I'm not noted for my spelling skills.*

~You're asking me? It all looks like hieroglyphics to me. I'm illiterate in GTC Standard, you know. Heck, if something happened and I was the only one in your head, I wouldn't even understand what anyone was saying aloud.~ The fact irritated Pam to no end. No matter how hard she concentrated, or how much Rett let her come forward, she couldn't understand the written form of the language at all, only the translations of it Rett's mind made while reading. ~I recognize the glyphs for your name, that's about it.~

Well, if someone complains, I'll change it. With a chuckle, Rett slid the door completely open and went inside, followed by the Ice Beast.

The bedding was knee deep, consisting of sweet-smelling, needlelike leaves and bits of old bark from the unusual arctic trees native to this cold continent. As Rett had discovered, there were deep clean layers of the stuff in any Auroran forest ditch or depression. Had this material been gathered from one of those places?

The back wall was only a low structure with open space on the other side. The roof formed an overhang down to ground level. Attached to it was a large rack full of twigs and the peculiar peeling bark of the Auroran trees. Next to the rack stood what Rett recognized as a thermal water unit, only this one had an open basin of water sitting on top of it.

~I guess that opening is for antler clearance,~ thought Pam. Otherwise you'd have to have the water and feed racks in the middle of this stall.~

Rett went to investigate the right-hand side of the space, where there was a raised area with a rolled up bedding mat. Rett's kitbag already hung neatly from a peg in the wall above. Shelves and places for other gear, like the riding harness and her weapons, filled a neat, narrow locker below the raised platform.

~Nice stall. This is what I call acclimatizing,~ said Pam.

Rett grinned. *I guess we're already acclimatized. The fact is that going in and out of climate-controlled buildings all the time doesn't do us any good when we're going to be spending so much time outside anyway. This won't be bad at all. At least this time I've everything I need for it.*

~Don't get me wrong, I completely approve! This is great— this place is the Hilton compared to your little ditch out there on the tundra. I love sleeping in the barn, did it lots of times during foaling season—during that long separation we had? Well, long for me, a Standard month or so for you. I'd live out in the barn with my horses permanently if the madman I rented my farm from was less of a . . . well, let's simply let it stand that if I owned the property, that's where I would be.~

Pam quickly diverted Rett, just as H'chan did, by encouraging her to remove the harness from the Beast. Rett hung

191

everything neatly, without prompting, since she was well aware of the advantages of always having her gear in order. In the storage space, she found a coarse-toothed comb and a short, stiff brush and started to groom the animal. She whistled an unfamiliar tune under her breath.

Pam, thought Rett. *I'm glad you helped me out today. I hope you're around tomorrow, too. But right now, this whistling must stop, because any second now you're going to make me sing, because you like to sing when you work sometimes. If I sing, that will set off security alarms, if not earthquakes, from here to the main continent. Besides, I really have to learn to do this on my own.*

~Sorry,~ said Pam, making an effort to contain her still-fired enthusiasm. ~It's hard for me to hold back on something I can do with my eyes closed!~ She withdrew into her corner, but cheerfully.

Rett brushed and curried on her own with less confidence, trying to remember how Pam was making her do it with such experienced ease just a moment ago.

H'chan rolled a reproachful violet eye back at her.

"I'll get the hang of it," Rett said. "Pam isn't with me all the time. Am I brushing too hard?"

"Not hard enough," said H'chan.

~Maybe I should be here all the time, Rett. It seems every time I get yanked out of you, something momentous occurs or you wind up getting into trouble.~

Rett chuckled ruefully. *I was getting in trouble before, whether I was housing a dimwitted alien mindforce or not. It's part of the job.*

She put more pressure into her brushing, trying to get back that cunning wrist action Pam had made her use. By the time she was done, her upper body was aching as much as the bottom parts, but H'chan was sleek and shining, the shaggy, iridescent tips of his fur reflecting all the colors and shifts of light around them, just as the Special Forces uniform did.

I thought I was fit, groaned Rett, *but I can feel I need a lot more work. How many horses did you say you groom in a day?*

~I wouldn't say you were unfit. This is new to you. Riding and grooming use those big muscles of yours in entirely different ways. The only way to improve them is to keep doing this every day. You'll see, two, three days, it'll be second nature.~

H'chan turned and started munching on the twigs and bark in his rack, his pleasure obvious. Rett watched him for a moment, admiring the strong, graceful lines of the animal, the way his muscles rippled easily under his fur as he moved. She felt strangely peaceful and very curious.

"Go and eat whatever it is your people eat," H'chan told her firmly, turning his head to look at her, his jaws working noisily as he chewed his food. "Unless you want to share this? There is enough for us both."

"Thanks, H'chan. I've tried bark and twigs before, and they're a bit too high fiber for me." With a very loud growl from her belly she couldn't deny, Rett reluctantly left the quartering shed. She let her nose take her to the mess building for this end of Aurora Base, now shared by Transport and Supply with the 2023rd Special Forces assault group, Easy Force.

Most of her people were there already, their snow- and cold-reddened faces reflecting the pleased success of the afternoon. Everyone was moving with great care. A few had mild expressions of astonishment. There was Sergeant Ariam at a table near the back, waving for her to come and sit with them. The second-in-command to B-troop sat across from her platoon leader, Sergeant Semage, his wavy red hair unmistakable. At the same table sat others from Easy Force. Before she could make more observations, her hunger again demanded her immediate attention.

Rett nodded agreement to Ariam and wasted no more time collecting a tray and some dinner. She folded a broad green leaf into sections and popped it in her mouth as she walked back, enjoying the juicy, peppery taste. That was one thing she'd noticed about her appetite since coming to this planet—especially to this continent. She felt a real need for a constant supply of vegetables, preferably raw and green. Rett was relieved to note she wasn't the only one. Fortunately, edible leafy green plants were easy and prolific growers even in the indoor habitats of Epnoce.

Her penchant for greens didn't stand in the way of an appetite for other fare, and she noted the sparkle in Ariam's big gray eyes as she set her tray down in the space her sister had saved on her right side.

"Hungry, huh? You'll keep everyone happy with that appetite!"

Rett grinned. Her second, Trebor, on the other side of the open space, obligingly made a bit more room for her. She didn't have to look to sense his approval of the contents of her tray.

"What did you name your Beast?" Ariam asked.

Rett stared at her sister, pausing in the action of lowering her saddle-stiff posterior on the bench next to Trebor. Her legs and seat weren't the only parts of her that ached. As she settled her body, the insides of her thighs and everything between clear up to her neck sent a twinge so fierce she nearly ended up with her face in her plate.

Oof. I get now what you meant before, Pam, Rett thought. The understanding and sympathetic winces from her friends clearly expressed they knew exactly what she had just felt. *From the looks I'm getting, no one from Easy'll be looking for any sexual relationships for a day or so, that's for sure!*

Finally she found a reasonably tolerable position. "What do you mean, what did I—"

"Hush, Rett—" H'chan's soft mental voice was full of warning and mild worry. "Not all of us speak with our riders!"

You'd better back down then. Ariam's an empath, and she can sense Pam.

She felt the Beast had a lot more to say on that matter, but he withdrew anyway. Pam obligingly came forward a bit in hopes of masking the second presence in Rett's head, for which Rett was thankful.

"Well," Ariam said, "didn't you hear the drill captains suggesting we come up with names for them? They're supposed to be our partners, and we're living with them, so calling them by a number a troopjumper or armored rover seems . . . cold."

"And a rover or jumper get named sometimes," someone else said.

"You're right. I named him H'chan." Rett picked up her fork, speared a section of steamed yellowstem and took a bite off one end. "How about you?"

For a brief instant, the happy light faded from Ariam's beautiful eyes. "I'm calling him after Kraym. In some really strange way, he reminds me of him." Ariam's face brightened again as she turned to Semage. "I forgot to ask you, Semage—what did you name yours?"

The husky, freckled B-troop leader's eyes met Rett's, a secret little smile lurking in the brown-green depths. "H'ting," he said.

"Of course," explained H'chan from inside Rett's mind, "like you, he is a pack leader and must communicate with H'ting."

"And you, Trebor?" Rett asked her second.

The lean, hawk faced sergeant grimaced. "I know what I'd *like* to call him. Between landing on my ass a million times and thinking I might have suffered a permanent inability to father children, I have a few good choices. But really, Sarge—I haven't come up with a name yet. Wait'll you hear what Lieutenant Evetez named his, though."

His words extracted snickers from the others at the table and Semage grinned broadly at the lieutenant. "Go ahead—tell her, Evetez!"

The familiar, wicked gleam in Lieutenant Evetez's blue eyes was reinforced by a purely mischievous grin. "MYOTS," he said, snorting back a laugh.

"Myots?" Rett wrinkled her nose.

"M-Y-O-T-S." Evetez spelled it out and started to laugh. "And say it with two syllables, accent on the second. Major Yidnar's Outstanding Transportation Source."

"He just gets worse with each upgrade, don't you agree, Semage?" Rett asked, trying to keep a straight face. "Junior to Senior Lieutenant broke him."

196

"I think he broke a long time before that," said Semage. "I think it happened after you dropped that beetle down the back of his shirt back in training—"

"Semage!" said Rett in protest, but it was too late.

"*Rett* did that? I thought . . . I thought she passed it to Tasheesh, and she did it!" Evetez shook his head.

"Now *this* story I have to hear." Trebor gave Rett's left elbow a slight upward push.

Rett then realized that, aside from a few vegetables, she had yet to get started on her food. She ate the now-cold portion on the fork because Trebor was watching, then took another, but her fierce appetite had fled. Rett picked up the grain rolls, slit them, and started stuffing meat and vegetables inside, making it look casual. She chewed more of the crisp raw greens and another yellowstem for effect as she kept her hands busy. *I'll take these back to H'chan's stall where it is quiet. And cooler . . .*

~You'd better eat them,~ Pam said. ~You might be able to shut me out now, but H'chan's going to be after you, too. You don't want to start this not-eating thing, or eating and throwing up, that you told me about. You know you need twice as much food when it's this cold!~

"Remember the Barrens survival course? Those beetles?" Semage had everyone's attention now.

Munching away on another crisp green, Rett wrapped her sandwiches in a wipe, tucking them deep into her anorak pocket.

Ariam made a face; so did the others in hearing range.

Rett just nodded, chewing industriously. From the size of a thumb to the size of a rover, the beetles were dangerous, attacking anything that cast a shadow and promised moisture and food. Fortunately, they were easy to kill, and while they were edible, the smell when the outer shell was broken dissuaded most from proving that aspect.

"Rett and Evetez developed quite a taste for them, if I recall."

"Yeah," said Rett, picking a green leaf off Ariam's plate, "that was the survival course rule—if something tried to eat you, you eat it first. Remember?" She crunched the leaf suggestively.

"I would think," said Carakenne from her end of the table, "that after that situation in Complex 412, you'd reconsider that rule, Sarge!"

"I wasn't applying that rule to something you'd have a conversation with before it tried to eat you," amended Rett with a laugh, shiver, and roll of her eyes. "Besides, I was sort of disadvantaged at the time."

"Carnivorous intelligent lifeforms aside," someone else said, "out of anything I've eaten on any survival course, animal, fungus, vegetable, or bug, those beetles were the first things to make me gross out."

The sentiment was repeated by anyone within earshot.

Through Rett, Pam took interest to note that despite the faces, comments, and revolted tones of voice in which they were delivered, no one stopped eating.

"Anyway," said Semage, "Evetez brought one back, dead of course, gave it to Rett and she—" Semage had to pause and wipe his eyes with one hand. "She gave it back—you know how well our hero can divert and decoy. Evetez had that stink on him for *days*. Days. I forget how many. He couldn't wash it off. We all were thrown out of the common lounge. We made Evetez sleep outside on the barracks roof for four of those days until he was at least tolerable. In the rain. And it wasn't summer in Centerland."

"Was good for him. Built character. That's why he's the lieutenant we all know and love today." Fixing a calm gaze on Evetez, Rett swiped another green leaf, this one from Trebor's tray, and gave it several loud, unrepentant crunches.

"Tash never denied it!" Evetez glared at Rett.

"She liked you," said Rett, backing up her tone with sweet smile. "If you'll all excuse me—I have to settle some things."

Evetez followed her outside.

"Sergeant!"

"Yes, sir!"

He caught up with her. "Divert and decoy? Like you did with your dinner? Don't even *try* to get out of it. I was watching you every second in there."

Her shoulders fell. "I—"

"What is this with you going off on these episodes of not eating properly? What's wrong? I thought things were going really well lately. We've adapted to the gravity, to those weird shifts of the three moons, right? What is it now?"

She withdrew a hand from her anorak pocket and showed him one of her stuffed rolls. "I *am* going to eat this," she said. "It felt too hot and stuffy in there after being outside all day—"

She didn't resist the grip he took on her arm. She thought about it, but instinct and past experience made her fall into step with him. The grip turned into a companionable linking of arms, and together they walked down the plowed path. Wondering where he was headed, she shortened her stride as he turned into a narrower lane that led to a service door. Against the wall was a snowbank someone had apparently taken time to make into a bench.

Evetez pulled her to sit alongside him, and then leaned back. So did Rett, tipping her face skyward to see the stars and high clouds racing over them.

"Look at that, will you?" Evetez sounded awed. "It's always so cloudy, we never get to see the aurora, much less the stars."

"And Nyorfias." She nodded toward the shining blue-violet disk that looked so small and far away against the backdrop of even more distant stars and the reddish glow from the nebula. Green ribbons and yellow spirals of light shivered and flashed across the opening in the clouds.

Against the building, out of the wind, it was a comfortable little pocket of the night. "Is this better?" he asked finally, turning his attention from the display in the sky to her.

"Yes."

"You're not puking what you manage to eat, are you?"

Rett flushed. Evetez was one of the few who knew she still struggled with eating and keeping her food down when she was really stressed. "No, and I know where you're headed with this. I've been eating, and I eat more than people think I do. Don't you think you'd notice if I wasn't? Like when we first arrived here? And Med checks my weight every couple days now just to be sure."

"I know that. I've still never known you to be put off your food as easily as you've been lately. Maybe I'll just have to request we get extra mushrooms on the menu every day to encourage you. They grow enough of them over on the big continent."

Rett sighed. "Yes. Every Fourthday at the main Base was mushroom day. I never knew there were so many interesting ways to cook them."

Evetez chuckled. "And what else was it that you especially like? Mashed bitternut on grain rolls. Fresh steelhead grilled on a spicebush fire—"

"All right, Lieutenant." Rett laughed as her hunger returned with a rush. She took a healthy bite from one of her rolls. Not mushrooms, but it was good. The meat was savory and had a familiar taste. "Cotos," she said. "Probably from those SMG'd animals one of the patrols found."

"Don't get started," Evetez said. "At least they're not entirely wasted. And we'll bring the wildlife populations back up, you know we will."

Restoring a balanced ecosystem to Epnoce or Nyorfias wasn't going to be as easy as he made it sound, but she nodded anyway, and took another bite. "It's good. Funny, never had one cooked before."

Evetez stretched out his legs. "Do you know how close some of us were to going out to find you then, orders or not?"

"Planning to grab an ice floe and fart your way across the sea? Yes, I heard about that from Med," she said. She wriggled her stiff body and butt around so she could pull her feet up and lean back on him. She chewed another bite thoughtfully. "And I love you all more for it, but I'm glad no one did. I've enough guilt."

"You're not still carrying Zhent around? It's been ten years, Rett."

"I'm carrying them all, Evetez. Everyone. Gerrale. Kraym. C-troop. I could take a few hours listing the names. I'm sure you can, as well. I can never forget them—any of it. I can put it aside, but I can't let it go. I'm so tired," she said. "So very tired of it all. As we all are." She swallowed and shifted her weight onto a lesser-bruised left buttock. "As for Zhent, you tell me how many people you know killed their own squadleader two months into their first assignment."

From Pam came a brief shock, quickly dampened.

"You did what you had to do," Evetez said. "Zhent was being controlled by the enemy. What am I going to do with you, Rett?"

"Hold me up, as usual," she said.

He reached around and took her second roll as she unwrapped it, taking a bite for himself before returning it. For a while they sat, leaning into each other, watching the stars, the aurora, and sharing the silence. Just as hard as Evetez had worked to bring Rett out of her shell, she had worked to teach him to become comfortable in silence, in listening, in being. The only sounds she heard now were the hissing of the wind over the tops of the snowbanks and the granular, sandy sound of blowing snow.

"Speaking of guilt," Evetez said presently, "how did you get that beetle back there anyway?"

Rett chuckled. "Remember? When I thanked you for being so thoughtful, I leaned over, kissed you, and just let that bug go. I didn't know it would take you so long to figure it out. I waited outside for a little while, but nothing happened. So I left."

"I remember you kissing me. You put a lot of effort into it." He laughed softly. "No wonder I never noticed anything else." He leaned his head against hers for a minute.

"You weren't half bad yourself, Lieutenant Evetez, sir," said Rett. "For a bubbleheaded moron."

"Hey, you still love me anyway, and you know it."

She bumped her head into his. "Still full of yourself. I don't know how Carakenne handles it."

"What?"

"Don't play innocent, 'Vetez. Everyone in the 2023rd knows. Even Major Yidnar."

"If you must know, it's going well. But as you also know, there's this little thing called a previous commitment that keeps us in check. Still, I'm hopeful that one day we won't have anything in our way."

"I hope so, too." Rett watched the brief opening in the sky start filling with clouds.

"Say," said Evetez, "there's something else you should know."

She straightened, the shift in his energy and the serious tone prompting her.

"It's Iheolon. He's actually been put in command of all Coalition operations on Aurora now."

Rett knew that from her last briefing, but since Evetez wasn't finished, she just waited for more.

"His cousins are with him. You know—"

"Mott and Shamos. Or Motuk and Sclamuse. I knew that." She was getting impatient now.

"We've had reports that they have some new drugs. Not the same as the ones we found from Avok's stash. But new ones. And that most troopers are going to be carrying them with a long range delivery system. That means if they can identify you, they're going to use it."

Rett's dinner wasn't sitting very well now. She bumped her shoulders into her friend's back and said, "They'd have to have a sharpshooter as fast as Trebor or Ariam to tag me under normal conditions," she said. "Consider me forewarned."

"I wish I could do more than that. Shit, my ass is getting cold now."

Rett had to agree. No matter how well insulated their clothing, sitting still for any length of time on a snowbank was still going to result in a frozen butt. "It's getting late, we should get in."

"And tomorrow's another busy day." Evetez groaned as he stood up. "I don't think I'll ever walk properly again."

"Uuh," grunted Rett as she also came upright. The pain in her inner thigh muscles was incredible. "Tell you what; I'll hold you up if you hold me up."

"Deal," agreed the lieutenant promptly, and linking arms, they limped off together to the quartering shed.

* * * * *

H'CHAN WAS DOZING, LYING DOWN in the deep, fragrant bedding, his muzzle just touching the cushiony material. He flicked an ear toward her and opened one eye as Rett entered.

Rett thought there was no better cure for the sick ache in her belly than a diversion. She'd meant to access the information on the Beasts from the main network. *I can get that tomorrow.* Right now she had so many questions to ask him, questions from herself and Pam. She didn't have to strain any effort to know Pam was ready to pounce on her to elaborate on the memory of Zhent, her first squadleader back from the days she was with C-troop. She wished it hadn't come up. Pam was never going to let that go.

Instead, at the Beast's unspoken invitation, she found her blankets and curled up against his furry, evergreen scented hide. Such a feeling of comfort and security penetrated her that both she and Pam forgot about asking questions. Rett sighed in contentment and fell asleep, for the first time in almost ten years not worried about a thing.

3.3.1 AURORA BASE, EPNOCE
0536.02.40 - 0536.03.02 (LOCAL RECKONING)

PAM HAD BEEN RIGHT. AFTER a few days, Rett's body adapted to the riding, the grooming, and all the new things she asked of it. So, thankfully, did every other body in Easy Force. After a few more days, they started having mounted drills as a unit.

As far as Rett could find out, the new "transport" pleased everyone. The Ice Beasts weren't only an effective method of getting from one place to another, despite terrain or weather. They were quick and agile, responded to the riders' slightest aids; accepted the noises of guns blazing away or explosions without shying or faltering. The animals' smooth gaits allowed the sharpshooters to be just as deadly accurate while astride at a full run. A swipe of a paw or glancing blow from a large body sent many an MP or infantry drill assistant sprawling, and the unexpected assistance in close quarters was marked as another advantage.

Their speed and endurance were astonishing. The Beasts were nomadic, staying in the forests to eat, shelter from storms, or have their young. Their survival depended on being able to cross the long open spaces between the forested areas, avoiding predators or outrunning storms along the way. H'chan assured Rett that her weight and the weight of her gear made a difference, but he wasn't worried.

Rett would be more worried about speed being a factor, but the advantage of using Ice Beasts was in the fact their enemy wouldn't be looking for a herd of animals moving twenty miles an hour. They'd be looking for troop carriers and armored rovers.

-And don't forget,- said Pam, -Ice Beasts are big, furry, warm, and friendly.-

Rett had to give credit to that fact, something she'd never have believed without experiencing it firsthand. Since becoming a mounted unit, there was a positive difference in the normal levels of stress and tension Rett's energy sense was used to sounding.

She shrugged her shoulders to settle her new anorak. She liked their new kit. Everything was designed for riding, the weather, and freedom of movement. A snow-blue inner jumpsuit of thin insulating material went on over a normal set of working grays. The inner suit covered from toes to head and had a piezoelectric heating system, like the ones in their survival shells—that would automatically activate if body temperature dipped to dangerous lows. Over that, an overall and anorak of thick yet lightweight material that had the same color and light refracting qualities of their regular combat uniforms.

Warm mitten-gloves designed for shooting; boots, snow-goggles and a breath muffler, all in the soft pastel shades of portions of Auroran snow, completed the outfit. All the camo paint, tape, and shields for weapons and gear also matched the colors of the snowy landscape and, as usual, would help minimize the readouts on scanners.

"I think we're ready, 'Vetez."

"I think you're right. Which is a good thing, because I said the same thing to Major Yidnar yesterday."

"Goes to show why you're a lieutenant and I'm a sergeant."

He leaned toward her from his seat on MYOTS. "That's a load of shit, Rett. I have it on good authority that your little evasion game is up. In two months, you won't have any excuses that will stop Major Yidnar from handing you new paperwork and rank patches. Everyone will have to get used to calling you *Captain* Rett. You really should have done it in increments—it's going to be a shock going straight up."

Rett's throat already had closed in shock hearing it from him now. She had to admit she'd been warned, but she'd also maintained a childlike hope that dismissing every thought of it from her mind would wipe it from everyone else's, as well. No such luck. She coughed.

"Did you have to ruin a perfectly good day with that?" she demanded.

"How about I ruin it with a spontaneous combat-status inspection? The Major's on his way. Assemble the troop, Sergeant."

"Yes, sir."

In minutes, all of Easy Force was arrayed in the training area, and exactly on time for Major Yidnar's arrival. Rett was rather surprised to see him astride a compact Beast with violet-tinted antlers.

Not a patch on my H'chan, thought Rett with pride as she and her Beast fell into her place behind the battalion commander and the Easy Force leader.

"We look excellent together, my Rett," said H'chan without modesty. "H'vren says his Yidnar is very pleased with us all."

"Could Major Yidnar mindspeak with his Beast?" Rett thought suddenly.

"No."

"What? He is our commander!"

"He does not lead a pack into battle."

"Sometimes he fights with us, but he directs all the packs," argued Rett. "Evetez—can he communicate with his? *Especially* Evetez—who goes with us all the time! Can't he talk to MYOTS?"

"No," H'chan said again.

Rett groaned inwardly. At a signal from Evetez, she rode back to the front of the formation and dismounted to stand alongside H'chan. She and her gear would be checked when Yidnar and Evetez came back this way.

"This isn't a good thing—deities, it's nearly as bad as me not being able to tell anyone about my ego-merge."

She went through the motions automatically when her seniors reached her. For the first time in tendays, Rett felt a stress headache coming on fast. Surely she wasn't the first one to question if the other commanders knew. Did Semage, Tris, or Atira take it for granted Evetez and Major Yidnar knew about the Beasts' ability to mindspeak?

Major Yidnar gave her a nod and moved aside with Evetez.

"Why only the platoon leaders, H'chan?"

The Beast sighed, his warm breath on the exhale causing an immediate frost to collect on Rett's snow goggles. She never moved—she couldn't—not until she was told to dismiss the troop.

"Do you wish Yidnar to speak with H'vren, whom he calls 'Ranger', and Evetez to speak with H'wan—or as he calls him, 'MYOTS'?" The Beast's mental voice came very close to a laugh as he repeated Evetez's name for H'wan.

If Rett hadn't been standing eyes front (to the frost on her goggles) with the perfectly emotionless look demanded for such occasions, she would've been staring wide eyed at H'chan with her mouth open as she understood the significance of his thoughts.

"You each *choose* whether or not to speak to us? Your mind-speech isn't limited at all, is it? If you wanted to speak to, say, to Trebor, or Mordell over in S-troop, as well as me, you could do it."

H'chan flipped his ears. "Do you wish them to speak to us?" he repeated patiently.

"Does that mean I could speak to other Beasts?"

"More questions than a weanling fawn!" Another large gust of moist, warm air streamed from his nostrils, causing another coating of frost to collect on Rett's goggles.

"Sergeant, dismiss the troop."

Finally. "Yes, sir!"

After another minute she savagely scrubbed at the frost on her protective lenses and pulled herself to H'chan's back.

"I'm right, aren't I? You're not as limited as you make yourself out to be."

"Most of us in this group are capable of what you think, but we choose to limit ourselves," countered H'chan. "Then there are those among us less able in mind-speech with species not our own. So no—not all Beasts can talk to just any remote two-leg, or pick up random thoughts from them."

"You're none of you *animals*. You're an intelligent, native species," she thought accusingly to H'chan. "And you're all putting on this act! Why?"

"We *are* animals, my Rett."

"I don't think so. Not as we classify them. And, what you're *not* telling me just took things to a whole new level. I want to know what all the secrecy is about, damn it!"

"Why do you not wish others to find out about your mind-link with Pam?" the Beast suddenly countered. "Why don't you share certain memories or thoughts, with her, with anyone? We both have our reasons. It seems they are very similar."

"So why are your people helping us? How did it happen—you and your buddies just get together, walk off the ranges, and volunteer?"

"Something like that," agreed H'chan. "Shall we ride out and speak?"

"Yes." She directed the Beast to the main gate of the Base so they could be alone.

"We owe the two legs our lives. Our common enemy, those . . . animals from outworld, slaughtered large numbers of my people's packs on these ranges for fur and food, until your people came back and rescued most of us who were left. We are grateful; we also wish to help eradicate those . . . those predatory, barbaric—"

"I know what they are, H'chan. Just spare the adjectives and go on."

"A few, very few, others of your kind know of us—"

Rett sat up very straight, an idea occurring to her and Pam simultaneously. "Those names. Like . . . H'tenneck," she said aloud, echoing Pam's thought. The youngest of her platoon, who'd been wounded so badly at Complex 117.

H'tenneck was Epnoce-born; his parents, like Rett's mother, were eco-biologists. Although H'tenneck's love was technical gadgets, the more complicated the better, he had a peculiar affinity for the wild places, much the same as Rett did. "Is it a coincidence his name sounds like the names you use?"

"I have heard that name," admitted H'chan, reading the direction of Rett's thoughts. "No coincidence. His sire, H'jin's Tennar, and his dam, C'pret's Kytrasian, were two of the first Ice Beast friends."

"Deities."

"H'jin—" there was a great respect when H'chan mentioned that name, "must have named his Tennar's fawns, like some of the others who have known your race a long time."

~The males all get that *hah* sound as a prefix and the females the *sea?~* Pam put in. ~I think I've heard you Beasts make those sounds aloud."

"Yes, that is so. We do not have sound speech like two-legs, but we do use some sounds. I am surprised you noticed this, in my experience, others have not."

~I work with animals on my own planet. People who do work and live closely with animals become really sensitive to the difference in the sounds they make, even if they are close in type.~

"That will be helpful to Rett," said H'chan.

"Wait. Others?" Rett shivered deep, and it wasn't from the cold. Had she ears like the Beast, or a growtu, or any other creature with mobile auditory organs, they'd be pricked as far forward to H'chan as possible. "How long? How many people know? *Humanoid* people? The Trans specialist who picked you out for me is one. And that drill captain we had for the basic riding—C'zleni—she's another, I'll bet anything I own on it."

To her questions H'chan drew a firm line she knew he would not cross. "If you do not wish to know what I will reveal in the order I choose to tell you, then we can go back. I'm getting hungry."

"All right, all right. I'm sorry I interrupted."

"To the others of your people who know, we communicated our desires, and together decided that the best way to serve was this way—as . . . transport, also as guides and in combat. Ice Beasts are very adept at combat. We keep in practice for the mating season."

"Uh-huh." Rett started grinning. "Any significance to one Beast having a bigger set of antlers than another?"

"In our fighting performance or mating rituals?"

"That's it, huh? He with the biggest antlers impresses all the female Beasts. Haven't seen many bigger than yours, H'chan."

"I am very impressive to the does at mating time," H'chan said with pride. "And rarely do our antlers grow larger than the size of my own. We still have to fight before we are chosen by our mates—to ensure only the strongest bloodlines. It is not pleasant, but we are driven into it for survival."

He sounded slightly ashamed then. "We do not try to kill each other, yet in the heat of combat sometimes there are accidents. It is the most barbaric thing we do—"

"I understand," Rett said.

"Anyway," said H'chan, "Ice Beasts, especially the bucks, are capable of communicating with other intelligent species in mind speech. Direct contact is ideal, at least until a link is established. All your communication to other Beasts, and thereby, to their riders, will be handled by me. That is the way we decided." He sounded firm.

"But why only the platoon leaders?" Rett asked. Deities! How often did any of them wish for the ability to mindspeak with each other? What an advantage they would have with such a communication breakthrough.

"We do not wish the matter of our ability known more widely than it is already," H'chan said, his mental voice uncomfortable. "Now that we know more of your people, our thoughts are changing. Still—this is what my people want. Believe me, my Rett," the Beast added, "the others of your pack and the other packs are as bonded as we, but the direct thought communication is held back. That is the only difference. The other bucks would like to communicate with their riders, to other humans in general. But too many would know, and who knows how that will affect all Beasts?"

"I see what you mean, I guess."

"It is the same reason you keep your bonding with Pam a secret," H'chan said. "Very much the same."

"It would make things so much easier if *all* the riders and Beasts could communicate, H'chan," said Rett. "It seems I could pass messages through you to other Beasts, but they won't transmit them to their riders unless they happen to be platoon leaders. Sometimes we have to communicate without using words."

"How did you do so before?" inquired the Beast.

"Want an example?"

"Yes."

"What do you want me to say?"

"Anything."

In about two seconds, the Beast jumped and shied violently, swinging around nervously, trying to detect the source of the low, snarling growl that seemed to surround him.

Rett laughed and scratched his neck reassuringly. "Was only me, H'chan. That meant 'slow down and look sharp' and I would've used it at night anywhere in the woods on Nyorfias or over on the main continent here on Epnoce. We use whistles and bird sounds a lot, too—and I just taught Easy Force this for Aurora—"

211

H'chan almost threw Rett from the riding pad as the blood chilling hunting cry of the Auroran snow growtu rose on the cold air.

"Sounds good, huh?" asked Rett. "I didn't make it very loud. If I did, Easy would be out here by now, looking for the enemy."

"That was the hunting call of the snow growtu," H'chan said, his mental voice angry and his body stiff and tense beneath her legs. "You could have warned me. The growtu is our ancient and sworn enemy!"

"I'm sorry, H'chan."

He ignored her. "The growtu also has other sounds."

"I know all of them, H'chan," Rett said softly, aloud. "Before my people came to Aurora, I came—but in a fighter. I crashed." Sensing the Beast didn't understand, she visualized the scene, felt the large body under her legs shudder.

"I have seen these things flying things, in the sky—and dead in the snow. Go on."

"Somehow I survived, but was injured, cut off from any help. I ran into a pack. They could have killed me and I thought they would. The pack leader attacked me and I fell into a ditch before he made the kill." She was visualizing, with Pam's help adding details, so H'chan could follow. "They could have killed me any time after that, but they didn't. We had . . . an understanding, I guess. Watching them helped me survive. I like to think they helped me until the Free Army lines moved closer inland and I was able to reach them. Some of them actually came with me, turning back after they saw me make contact."

She felt bad for using the growtu sounds. "I'm sorry using the sounds upset or angered you. If it helps, I didn't see any sign of Ice Beasts during that time. I didn't know you even existed. I'm sorry Ice Beasts are prey to the growtus, but that's not going to change the gratitude I feel toward them." She held firm on that.

"Nor will I change how I feel. As long as they hunt my people on these ranges, they will be our enemies—as much as our common enemy."

At least the growtus are an enemy that fights fairly, Rett thought to Pam, trying to keep it from H'chan.

"Warn me well in advance before you use such a voice again," said H'chan, as the violent fire died from his amethyst eyes. He abruptly changed the subject. "Who is your mate?"

"What? I don't have a . . . mate."

"But I could feel you have a bond with a male of your kind. Different from what you feel to the others."

"Yeah," said Rett, slowly. "His name is Jaq Pym. He isn't here, yet." She wondered at the sensitivity of her mindlink with the Beast. *Great,* she thought, again tightly focusing her comment to Pam. *Not only is this animal telepathic, he's a damned empath. All I need is another one of those around me all the time!*

"Then you have, in fact, engaged in mating practices with males of your kind."

"Good gods and deities! Why do you need to know?"

"I know little of two-legs."

She blew out another breath, not knowing whether to laugh or choke. "Okay, yes. I have 'engaged in mating practices'," she said, almost defensively. She hoped this wasn't going in a direction other than having sex by mutual consent, because she definitely wasn't going there. "And 'with my own kind' depends how you classify humanoids. Why is this important, H'chan?"

"I was just wondering if you were a mature adult of your species, or if you've had fawns and a family-pack of your own other than those you fight our common enemy with."

"Oh. Well, you might have asked that straight off, why be so roundabout with it? You know I'm a mature adult, and you already know I have no children, and the rest. What are you really getting at, H'chan?"

213

"I heard—" The Beast turned his head to nuzzle her knee. "Never mind," he said, sending a sense of evasion. Pam noticed it a second before Rett.

~Now that he's been hanging out with two-legs for a while, your Beast is anxious to see what's involved when humans make love.~

Pam's merry laughter brought a smile to Rett's lips, although it was a little confused.

~Who would've known you have a voyeur for a steed? Then again you never figured on having me, either!~

Once Rett understood the voyeur bit, she laughed aloud and slapped H'chan's neck. "You wish. My life's an open book enough as it is, H'chan."

The Beast gave a half-jump and loud snort, clearly miffed.

"I'm sure some of the others, like H'ting, can give you first-hand information," said Rett.

"That is why I asked," said H'chan, his mental tones muffled. "The others said—"

"Keep wondering about it, H'chan," Rett said. "Number one, I don't have a partner here to indulge you, number two, once he gets here, tomorrow as a matter of fact, I'm not going to have time. And, number three, I like my privacy. So just keep dreaming."

She sighed. *Yeah, Rett, keep dreaming.*

She wished H'chan never brought the subject up, because she yearned for Jaq enough as it was. The reminder she'd have to wait for even getting five minutes alone for a quiet long hug, much less enough time for making love, was enough to produce physical pain.

3.3.2 AURORA BASE, EPNOCE
0536.03.07 ~ 0536.03.11 (LOCAL RECKONING)

JAQ PYM ARRIVED AT AURORA Base the next afternoon.

Rett was happy to see him, and F-troop was certainly glad to have him back. His return to F-troop and Easy Force was timed well. Jaq was paired with a Beast, received concentrated, individual instruction, and by the beginning of the tenday, was ready to go with Easy on their first assignment as a mounted unit.

As she'd told H'chan, Rett hadn't five free minutes to spend with him in any other context except as Easy's Combat Team Leader and F-troop's platoon leader. Preparations for the mission, concern about a possible storm front, and potential secondary targets were all on her agenda.

Major Yidnar was troubled by reports of Coalition movements along a remote western section of the pipeline reclaimed by the Free Army, and had sent Lightning and two other assault groups over there to bolster the light infantry battalion guarding it. Easy Force was being sent east, with elements of another infantry division, the 42nd, to secure a middle section. Still another good part of the 2023rd had been sent to another eastern location—the holding area and refinery at the pipeline's end, with the 21st and 3rd Divisions.

The move was a complicated one. If successful, it would drive the Coalition into one small portion of Aurora continent. MainCommand had coordinated simultaneous attacks all over Epnoce. Decoy air and ground units were deployed to keep the Coalition nervous and guessing.

Right before things were finalized, they heard about the two big Yixolryn troopships that had broken through the defenses put up by hardworking Nyorfian and GTC personnel in space. The potential threat there was enormous, especially with the dangerous Epnocian weather that kept lighter fightercraft and jumpers from both sides grounded—but allowed such heavy ships perfect cover for trying a landing. If the Nyorfians on space duty couldn't take out those troopships, and those on the surface couldn't prevent them from landing, there would be extreme complications. So all units going out were told to expect sudden changes in plan; and be prepared for instant redeployment.

As a mounted unit, Easy Force had to organize supplies for Beasts as well as their riders, and remember the Beasts had to carry everything. Rett and the other platoon leaders were extremely grateful for the silent assistance and suggestions from H'chan and the others. Such as altering a route through or near any forested areas would mean they wouldn't have to carry as much food for the Beasts, who could forage from the trees or from those depressions filled with windblown tree castings. The only forested area they would pass through however, were closer to Aurora Base. After that the land was open, rolling in places, but mostly flat.

Rett was busy even as Easy Force started out toward their target area, some ninety miles from the Base. She and the other platoon leaders rode together until after the first rest stop, spending that entire time with their heads over their notepads and Omnis, monitoring the weather, the current situation in space, the progress of the other units headed to various target areas.

At last, the conferencing was over—for a while, anyway. Rett took the opportunity to sidestep H'chan to the left. She twisted her body to try and spot Jaq's position in the group, rising in the pad for a better view. Easy Force didn't ride in organized columns: instead, they kept the same loose formation a normal herd of Ice Beasts would use.

I need to talk to him, if only for a few minutes. I never even had a chance to ask him how his shoulder felt. It had been so badly broken back at Complex 117.

~That mission was quite the circus,~ thought Pam, as usual following Rett's more public thoughts with her own. ~Three good things happened from it, though. You reunited with your father; let Jaq know you loved him; Ariam and Jayord both recovered completely and, thank goodness—H'tenneck made it.

Yes, thought Rett. She sighed. As thankful as she was for his life, she missed H'tenneck. They all did.

"Where is this offspring of Ice Beast friends?" asked H'chan. "You said he was part of your pack, yet no Beast here, or elsewhere on Aurora, claims a rider with that name."

"He was hurt badly on a mission, and is still recovering on the main continent. He won't be coming back for a long time, if ever. At least he's alive and will recover."

"That is good," said H'chan.

She finally spotted her target. "*There* he is." Although he was wearing the same gear as everyone else and one big and tall rider among many, Rett knew exactly when her eyes landed on the Zetinorian. She dropped back to ride alongside him, suddenly wishing she could be a lot closer than that.

"TechAdvisor Jaq Pym."

"What's up, Sergeant?" He pulled down his breath muffler, as did she—the material had a tendency to mute voices with the same effectiveness it insulated.

"I just wanted to say personally that we're all happy you're back." She kept her tone conversational and everyday. It wasn't easy, since if she gave into impulse, she'd be jumping from her riding pad to his and—

An interested snort from H'chan and a mental snicker from Pam quickly cooled part of the heat that had risen in Rett. She loosened her muffler a little more and pulled her outer hood back to let herself ventilate. Clearing her throat, she asked, "And the shoulder, Jaq? Good as new?" She hoped he would attribute the tremble in her voice to riding or cold instead of imagining just how physical it was possible to get while astride.

He obligingly rotated his shoulder for her, moved his arm, and grinned. "Good as new," he said. "I'm happy to be back.

217

I missed all of you." He glanced toward the main group, his lips tightening a little. "Although a few more are absent than I remember."

"The Aurora invasion was rough, and we've had some bad injuries since then."

"I visited with H'tenneck before I left the main continent. He's missing F-troop badly, but at least his parents and two of his brothers got over there to see him. His younger brother is staying with him until he's fit to leave. He asked me to give you this."

He leaned from the riding pad to hand her a pouch that resembled one of the many already in place on her utility or weapons belt. Curious, she accepted the pouch, dropping H'chan's reins (she pretty much just held them without doing anything, anyway) to investigate the contents.

She smiled. "I've always wanted my own, and he gave me his." The pouch went directly into a harness pack with a loving pat. "He devised a gadget that can counter any Coalition maglock frequency," she said in explanation. "Carakenne made her own using this one for a model, but neither of them had much time to make more, much less draw out their designs for replication. Besides, we didn't want to spread the news too widely. These things have come in handy too many times, for various purposes, to let any hints out to the Coalition."

"Is that what he used to get F-troop out of the restraining units back in Circle?"

She stared at him for a moment.

"Forget already I was part of Iheolon's division? The bridge? The rover? You fell asleep on me? It wasn't all that long ago."

"I remember that part—except I didn't know you then. But where were you when F-troop cut loose?"

He shook his head as if she should have figured that out for herself. "Ready to drive a rover, of course. Supposed to have taken a dangerous group of Nyorfian prisoners off for processing.

Except I had to go get something, and when I came back . . . my rover was gone, along with the other one I'd brought around. Imagine that."

"I am so glad we have you, Jaq. We owe you so much."

"That debt never existed, and if it had, has been paid in full several times over. I don't want to discuss that now. What I want to know is, are *you* glad I'm back?"

Rett's gaze turned straight ahead. "Didn't I say that?"

"Not exactly. I'm not sure I remember anything else you might have said to me the last time I saw you, either. Back at Complex 117. The refinery?"

"Yes, the refinery."

"Did you read the letters on the data storage unit I gave you then?"

She had read them—cried over a few of them, actually—but she was going to make him work harder. So she shrugged and said nothing.

"I missed you, Rett, more than anything. More than ever these past few tendays. Did you miss me, even a little?" He was trying so very hard to scope her out, gauge her mood. She pitied him and finally relented.

"Miss you? Not for a minute, Jaq Pym."

Jaq had no reply, but Rett saw the flare of pain and disappointment in his aura.

"No," she reaffirmed, meeting his gaze evenly, "not for a minute. Matter of fact, for the past six months, three tendays, two days and four hours, I've felt empty, alone, and lost without you around—among other things. If the situation had been a little different back at that refinery, I would've done more than kiss you on that damned roof!" She felt the amused approval of H'chan as her fantasies surfaced and her pulse quickened.

"Every time I try to apologize for what I did—"

She made a slashing gesture with her hand. "Jaq. Don't you understand? I don't want your apology. I don't want excuses or explanations. All I want is you. Only you."

The incredible smile that dawned on his face was enough to warm Rett clear down to her toes. "I love you, Rett," he said with simple conviction.

Rett smiled back at him. It took her a while to realize it, to cast aside her own doubts. Now she knew more than ever that what she felt was real, that it went a lot deeper than friendship, that it was something that would last forever. She loved him. She couldn't imagine a future without him.

~So . . . ~ A mental poke from Pam brought her out of the dreamy fog into which she'd slipped for a moment.

What? asked Rett, startled.

~Here is where you get the benefits of my years of reading paperback romance novels—well, the ones I don't throw against the walls. When someone you're in love with says he loves you and looks at you like that, you say it back to him. So—take note of the tone and inflection, and repeat after me: I love you, Jaq.~

Rett rolled her eyes and sighed. *I love you, Jaq.*

~Arrggh! Say it aloud, chicken! And look at him. Right into his eyes.~

Rett cleared her throat again and took a breath. Suddenly Pam's idea didn't seem so silly or frivolous any more. Looking deep into his fathomless blue eyes, she said, voice low, "I love you, Jaq."

Already suffering with repressed desire for him, Rett had to bite her lip as the look he gave her in response to her words practically melted her off the riding pad. Struggling with her composure and cursing the timing, she scrambled for another quick diversion, since stripping off her clothing and jumping into a snowbank was not an option at the moment. Something like that would probably result in her getting Jaq to go along with it anyway.

Will you both stop encouraging me! she snapped at Pam and H'chan, who protested their innocence in unison.

"What did you name your Beast?" asked Rett, changing the track of her thoughts. She wished she could indulge herself; right now she didn't have time for the diversion of intimate, pleasant memories.

Jaq's eyes took on a wicked gleam beneath his snow goggles. "Do you really want to know?"

"I wouldn't have bothered asking otherwise. It can't be any worse than MYOTS," said Rett with a laugh.

"Well, I took one look at a full drill session and came up with a great one," Jaq told her, his voice teasing. "I named him Killer, after you."

Rett made a face and rolled her eyes, but said, "I'll take it as a compliment from you. This is H'chan." She stroked her Beast's neck.

"Curious name. Seems all the platoon leaders came up with similar ones! Let's see, there's Semage with H'ting, Tris from R-troop with H'bris, Sergeant Atira from D-troop with H'sol, and Sergeant Mordell, is that his name? . . . from S-troop, I think his Beast is H'mert. What is it, some kind of secret society for platoon leaders?"

Jaq paused to brush snow off his leg, waiting for her to reply. She wasn't about to comment, especially since she didn't know what to say. *He'll just ask another question in a moment, and then we can move on.*

"I've only seen male Beasts. Where are the females?"

"I guess you didn't have a lot of time to read the 'specs'," said Rett, glad there was a solid point of reference for this answer. It would have been awkward to explain how she knew and no one else did. "From what little we know, apparently the does herd up in the winter season and stay deep in the forests where there's food and shelter from the storms. A few of the younger and older bucks stay with them for extra protection—the does can take care of themselves, really, but most of them have young ones, not only the current season's, but yearlings as well."

"Extra antlers and claws would be handy," said Jaq.

"Unfortunately they're no defense against the Coalition." Rett's tone turned grim. "The Coalition's been hunting the Beasts for food and fur. They slaughtered entire packs before we came to Aurora and managed to make a safe zone for the rest."

"How did they come to be domesticated?"

"They're not. I don't know much more, only that this is an extreme, unusual circumstance, and after the war, any Beast is free to go. I mean, they're free to come and go as it is."

"I've noticed no one seems to lock them up. It's almost as if they want to be around us. It's really strange how they hardly need any direction. And it's funny how each one—"

I'm not going to waste what little time I have left to talk having a conversation about Ice Beasts with Jaq, thought Rett to Pam.

H'chan snorted, but clearly, the track of Jaq's thoughts had been making him a little nervous.

~Divert and decoy,~ suggested Pam with a little smirk. ~Hit him with one of those great big smiles of yours.~

Rett hustled out her best smile, and Jaq, still speaking, stopped mid-word.

"Jaq."

"Yes, Rett?" His voice went low and dark.

She sidestepped H'chan a little closer so she could touch his arm, trying to communicate what she felt for him in that contact. Obliging, H'chan and Killer moved so closely together that they sandwiched their riders' legs between them.

Rett thought she had overheated before, but now she and Jaq were thigh-to-thigh. His arm, the one she had reached out to touch, pressed firmly into her side. No matter how many layers of material were between them, Rett felt the contact as if they were skin-to-skin. She didn't trust herself to speak, much less move. So much for her diversion. All she wanted was to wrap herself around him.

"Well, now," said Jaq in a whisper, "If I may take an example from a certain Nyorfian commando I know—never pass up a strategic advantage." Without further hesitation, he leaned toward her. She met him halfway.

Their snow goggles collided, effectively deflecting the contact they craved. Rett laughed, half amused, half frustrated, but quickly figured out just how much she needed to angle her head to make this work. Jaq also made adjustments, for on the second attempt their lips came together without obstruction. The kiss was short, sweet, light—it was too cold for much of anything else. But the promise of it quenched her raging thirst for him, filling an emptiness that had been within, leaving her satisfied . . . for the moment. She definitely wanted more of that later.

223

Straightening, feeling happier than she had in months, she gave him another smile. "I love you. Only you. What were those names again? Tejaq, Jemrett, Jaquet? I named the moons for them, you know."

For a moment, he looked blank.

"Remember? When we first came to Epnoce, right after you met old Sergeant Wreagor? Mess area?" she prompted. She hoped he remembered that, and not what happened afterward, or they'd be right back to where she never wanted to go again. "Our kids?"

Comprehension dawned on his face. "You *remembered?* You named the moons . . . ?" The last of Jaq's confusion quickly turned into a goofy, silly, pleased grin that made her laugh aloud.

"Well, they're not *officially* named. But I did in my head, and there'll be no changing it." She gave him another smile, not trying to hide her regret. "We'll have to talk about it more later. The present reality calls." She readjusted her hood, pulled up her breath muffler, and signaled H'chan to put some space between them. "We have to move now."

"Be careful."

"Always."

Easy Force moved ahead at a lope. The only sounds now were the soft *sluff* of the Beast's legs moving through the powdery snow, the same sound produced by the wind.

She ran over the plan in her head for the zillionth time. Easy Force was dividing ranks to open a frontal assault as a diversion, allowing a subtle but devastating attack from the sides and rear. F-troop, as usual, would take the point, B- and R-troops flanking. D- and S-troops, with the infantry, were placed in such a manner that their advance would be more of an encirclement than a straight-through penetration.

After a time, Rett signaled her platoon to full alert. They were entering the enemy's territory.

Weapons came off shoulders and out of harness scabbards to rest in ready positions across thighs and riding pads.

"Fang Lead, it's all yours," said Lieutenant Evetez over the pcom. "Easy Lead to Easy Force." The next com was to them all. "Infantry units are in place, we're sitting here with them if you need us. Good luck. Com silence will commence now."

Rett acknowledged. The Beasts slowed to a jog and the three lead units, F-, B- and R-troops, split from the others, spreading out as Rett gave H'chan the message to pass to H'ting and H'bris.

"Just over this ridge," Rett thought to H'chan, just as the he sent "The enemy is ahead, my Rett," in fierce mental tones.

Rett signaled her unit to hold up, and then motioned for Steffi and Mikel to accompany her. The three commandos and their Beasts moved ahead slowly, up the small rise and over the top. The light-reflecting hides of the Beasts and the uniforms of the commandos were virtually invisible against the dark, cloudy sky and snow.

Under Rett's seat and legs, H'chan was tense and quivering. Had she not been connected with him on a more than physical level, she might have guessed the Beast was fearful. He was

224

anything but: his neck was arched and bulging, presenting his antlers. His ears would prick forward and then lie back flat. His lips were partially pulled back—she saw that as he briefly curved his head and neck back to eye her. He was ready for battle, eager for it. "Shall we engage and destroy these . . . predators?" he asked.

Parasites would be my choice. Rett directed her thought to the private level she'd established with Pam since H'chan had come into the loop.

Through a small crack in the imaginary door, Pam indicated she had an entire volume of descriptive adjectives to contribute, but restrained her reply to tight agreement.

The low cluster of buildings at the nape of the shallow hill served once as maintenance huts for this sector of the natural gas pipeline that supplied the northwestern portion of Aurora continent. Four battalions of Coalition troopers guarded this area of the line, hoping to hold on to what they had left of the fuel reserves for their land vehicles. And, hoping to hold out for reinforcements—like those troopships that had been reported enroute to Epnoce.

Although she knew she wouldn't see anything but cloud, Rett glanced skyward. At the last Omni report before they closed down their network access, the homesystem defense had engaged one of the ships in battle and were in pursuit of the second. Directing her attention forward, she studied the target area with her eyes while transferring her VARs from a pocket beneath her anorak to a handier location on the shoulder harness outside of it.

H'chan repeated his question.

"Keep your fur on, H'chan," Rett told him. The raging bloodlust evident in H'chan's normally concise thoughts alarmed her. "We're not to kill everything that moves. Just those who attack us."

H'chan gave an angry snort. "And shall we not wish to kill those who have managed to destroy most of my people's packs on these ranges?"

Rett threw her left leg over H'chan's shoulder and slid from the riding pad. Steffi and Mikel followed suit.

"I didn't say that, I just said we don't kill everything that moves. If someone throws down his, her, or its weapon and is empty-handed, not fighting, we take that person prisoner. We talked about this, remember? Right now you and the others stay here," Rett told H'chan firmly. "We have to get a closer look."

The Beast rolled a reproachful eye at her, but offered no argument.

The snow was loose and well over their knees. Rett and her companions slid carefully down the slight hill, the loose powder allowing them to stay partially hidden beneath it.

Up to her elbows in the cold, loose stuff at the bottom of the rise, she shook her head inwardly. She was glad of three things: their invisibility, the nearness and swiftness of the Ice Beasts, and the fact that if any of them were hit right now, it would most likely be with a full power shot to the head, which of course meant they wouldn't feel it much.

~Lovely outlook,~ interjected Pam.

Have to be practical. We can't really run while up to our necks in snow, loose as it is. Rett lifted her VARs for a detailed scan. On her left, Steffi did likewise, backing up Rett's observations. Mikel kept an alert lookout.

After conferring with Steffi to make sure neither of them missed critical points, Rett gave a last sweep over the area, addressing H'chan. "H'chan, ask H'ting and H'bris if they're in positions, and if Tris and Semage's scans looked good."

"They are ready, my Rett," returned H'chan. "The other pack leaders who look through things say *'all go'.*"

"Good." She said this aloud as well as to her Beast. Then she signaled the others. They half-swam, half-waded up the hill in an excruciatingly slow relay. Each traded a period of non-movement every few lengths for two primary reasons: to keep exertion from elevating body temperature past a certain point; and, while cooling down, providing cover for the two that kept moving.

When they finally reached their Beasts, Rett warned H'chan to tell all the others not to bolt. Then the hunting cry of the snow growtu rose and quavered eerily on the frozen air.

From the direction of the rest of F-troop rose an answering growtu howl, a deeper, male tone: Trebor, answering the affirmative. Soon they were all together again and Rett deployed her people.

Even under heavy cloud, the long nights of the arctic winter never became truly dark. The snowpack reflected too much light for that. The even, gray, twilight quality of the light, however, was an excellent aid, making them invisible against the snow.

"H'chan, double check with Sergeant Atira's Beast—I forget his name—and verify they're in position."

Atira was secondary team leader. Not that Rett doubted Evetez, but since that disaster at Complex 412 when their entire strike team was taken out with gas traps, and with everything currently happening across Epnoce, no one protested a check and recheck.

Rett had to admit having the advantage of telepathic Ice Beasts for an extra verification when pcom communications were suspended worked out just fine. *Thank deities Atira and Mordell are with Evetez,* thought Rett.

"H'sol answers they are, and can be here quickly if we need them beforehand," affirmed H'chan, prancing in place in his lust for battle. "But though there are many at this place, we can take them. The enemy does not expect us, my Rett."

"Apart from a few notable exceptions, they usually don't," she thought. She hitched at her breath muffler. "H'chan, I'm sure you'll get a fight. Just control yourself."

~I'm going,~ Pam put in, settling firmly back in her place. Rett sent her an inward smile of warmth and appreciation, secure in the knowledge that Pam wouldn't interfere without good reason.

H'chan . . . well, he was giving Rett some real concern. He wasn't the only Beast quivering with restraint, tossing his head, pawing the snow, or all but prancing in place. Most of them she saw had their ears laid back tightly, nostrils flared to show the dark red linings. A few curled back their upper lips, exposing teeth. More than one large purple, deep blue, or purple-blue eye bulged and showed a wide white edge. A few loud, ripping snorts broke the silence of the incessant wind and sifting of snow.

She wished her ability to assign an emotional motive to the energy emanations of living things extended past humanoid races, and wished she could consult Ariam to see if her sister's empathic talent could sound the Beasts. *Then again, I'm not sure I want to know what they're feeling now, because whatever it is, we have to move.*

Wondering what had brought on Pam's sudden leak of thought about blowing horns and yelling when she knew damned well they used more subtle, natural signals, Rett settled herself firmly in combat mode, took a deep breath, and gave the signal the others waited for.

* * * * *

As hoped, the Coalition personnel stationed at the pipeline believed a pack of hungry snow growtus surrounded them. Rett saw several troopers come out of a building with weapons ready to deal with the animals.

The Ice Beasts on the attack front leaped into action with their riders, using their own formidable arsenal of antlers and claws. Rett expected that.

As the fight continued, she saw riderless Beasts joining the melee. At first, she thought she had casualties—but a glimpse of a distinguishing mark here, the flash of a rider's ident code on the harness, clued her in that these Beasts were from the flanking units. Instead of waiting as their riders left them, they had joined the battle entirely on their own!

The Ice Beasts were savage, slashing and goring with their antlers, ripping great rents in fallen bodies. Striking with front limbs, kicking with the rear. Their long, double claws easily shredded through heavily insulated uniforms.

The once smooth, clean expanse of iridescent snow, now bloodied and trampled, was littered with enemy dead—and pieces of enemy dead. In the back of Rett's mind, both the commando and Pam were stunned at the extreme violence of the fighting Beasts.

H'chan had personally taken fifteen troopers—he was keeping a very careful count in his own manner—and his antlers were streaked with gore. His mind, in complete link with Rett's, needed no direction. The Beast spun and sprinted after a group running for a vehicle shed, the troopers turning to fire at them as they went. Rett's TT-1 brought down three in three shots, the last two dove for cover, but H'chan was soon upon them.

Rett fired, H'chan charged, head down. He impaled the second trooper on his antlers, lifting his head sharply to drive the long prongs through armor and uniform deep into the flesh. With a twisting jerk of his massively muscled neck, H'chan flung the screaming, mortally wounded trooper off his antlers, sending a spray of red froth back to splatter Rett's face and goggles.

The sergeant cursed and wiped the blood away so she could see. Just in time: three snowsleds burst from the building's entrance, their gunners firing at them. H'chan's large body made forward progress in a graceful, smooth series of agile and complicated movements, his responses fully in tune with her combat sense.

Her weapon blazed, the slugs finding targets in sled pilots, gunners, or snowsled engine cowlings.

Rett had time to be grateful that one of the drawbacks of the Coalition snowsled was the vehicle's immediate inertia in loose powder when the engine was killed. As a result, those usually riding upon them had immediate and unexpected career changes: from soldiers to unguided missiles.

H'chan charged when he had an opening, enthusiasm undaunted and lust to kill as strong now as it was from the start.

I never expected him to be so bloodthirsty, Rett thought in another clear moment. *Not only him—any of them! Is it like this for our entire section of the pipeline?*

She hadn't touched the hackamore reins—except to make a show of holding them—since discovering H'chan was entirely capable of knowing where she intended to go. Not that any of them did much reining while fighting astride. Pam had told her (and Rett discovered for herself) that her legs and body were all that was needed to control such a responsive steed's movements, mindlinked or not.

But right this minute, as H'chan turned on a trooper who very clearly indicated willing surrender, the Beast completely ignored her subtle signals. She shifted her weapon to the right and took the reins up short with her left hand. The pressure she applied to H'chan's muzzle was harsh and abrupt. Her heel dug sharply into his right flank, her weight shifting hard with it. Forced into a spin away from his intended target, H'chan let out an irate snort of protest, too tiffed to send her a clear thought.

"He surrendered!" snarled Rett, her battle of strength and will with her Beast demanding most of her attention. "And *I said,*" she thought, making her mental voice hard, "*we do NOT kill everything that moves.*"

A loose Beast from R troop slammed into the unarmed trooper from the rear. "No!" Rett shouted aloud, but between antler and claw, the humanoid on the ground didn't have a chance.

"Shit! He gave up! Damn it! Someone gives up and disarms— *you don't kill them! They* might do that, but *we* don't! And you'd better flaming remind the rest of them too!" She leaned forward, yelling into his ear for good measure.

H'chan didn't answer, but his disagreement and disapproval were plain. His back tensed and humped. A thought sparked from Pam in a swift warning that the Beast might be tiffed enough to buck.

The moment passed: another target distracted his attention. Deadly targets this time. *Five of them,* noted Rett.

H'chan sprang forward to intercept. As if making up for the trooper Rett made him lose, he thrust and twisted into his next victim with twice as much violence as before.

"Damn it!" exploded Rett as she was again showered with the results. Blinded by the rain of gore, she aborted her own next shot, twisted in the riding pad as an energy beam roared past like a miniature thunderbolt. The smell of singed material that seeped through her breath muffler told her how close that had been.

She swiped at her goggles two seconds too late; the blood had already frozen on them. Snarling curses that went from under her breath to nearly a yell, she scrubbed two rather smeary openings in the frozen residue. "If you have to do that, do it with the wind *behind* us next time! You're going to get *me* killed!"

H'chan huffed, changed leads and direction with the well-oiled smoothness Pam went into raptures over, and increased his speed.

"What?" came from Rett as she snapped a fresh ammo clip to her weapon. "H'chan—" She could feel his surge of rage as the Beast sighted something she couldn't see through her obstructed lenses. Then she heard the first sound she'd ever heard from any Ice Beast besides a snort—a scream of pure fury that was somehow more bloodcurdling then the howl of the snow growtu.

231

She pulled down her stiff breath muffler and smeary goggles to see what had started H'chan. He sped toward a high, wire enclosed pen, where some thirty Ice Beast does, yearlings, and smaller fawns huddled in a tight group.

Rett's jaw hardened and a nauseated churning began in her stomach as she noticed a disturbing sight: a frozen, partially butchered carcass suspended from a frame, and a handful of snow-colored hides stretched out on the fence.

H'chan wasn't slowing down. The fence was getting closer.

"H'chan!" Rett yelled, realizing the Beast's intention. The fence was twice as tall as she was.

~Rett, let me—!~ came from Pam, too late.

The sergeant had already locked down her concentration and the split that Pam's thought had come through closed. Damn it! Pam wasn't the best rider over jumps herself, *especially* not one of this height, which looked twice as big as anything she'd ever seen show jumpers take at puissance events. But at least she knew the form, and imagined it with all her might now, hoping Rett would remember all those mental images she'd shared of riders going over jumps; hoping she would somehow flow into the position Pam was imagining her to assume.

And if not that, Pam hoped the Rett's superb balance and leg strength would at least keep her astride through the takeoff and over the top, because she knew from experience that a crash landing into a jump or through the top of one wasn't fun at all. Besides, this fence was solid metal, not boards or poles or brush, and wasn't going to come apart and reduce the serious injury factor when someone hit it.

Landing . . . ? Pam hoped the snow on the other side of the fence was softer than it looked.~ Keep your head up and don't grab the reins,~ Pam thought. ~I don't think he'll need any help.~

Rett's entire outward focus was on H'chan and the obstacle growing larger and more solid looking with every stride. The Beast's great muscles bunched and tensed under her. Some intuition prompted Rett to lean forward, her legs closing in a viselike grip into the riding pad, both hands tight in his neck fur. Her seat rose naturally as the Beast launched himself toward the top of the nearly three-length high fence.

It was a spectacular jump for H'chan. Rett, however, hit the packed snow of the enclosure with all the grace of a bomb. The breath whistled from her lungs. Her face struck into the snow so hard she would swear the front of her brain smacked the back of the inside of her skull. Great multicolored spots whirled and exploded behind her eyes. Enough presence of mind remained for her to feel grateful she was not wearing snow goggles now, which would have certainly become a permanent part of her face on impact. Then survival instinct kicked in, and she rolled as she realized she had fallen beneath the antlers and claws of panicked does with young fawns to defend.

She heard, rather dimly, H'chan's mental voice ordering the frightened, enclosure-stressed captives to remain still, that the two-leg was not their enemy.

His thoughts were clearer as he directed them at her. "The gate!"

Still trying to reclaim the breath her fall had forced out of her, she rose to her knees. Squinting her stinging eyes, she centered the TT-1's muzzle on the electronic control for the big sliding gate. The box exploded in a gush of yellow flame and cascade of blue sparks. With a metallic screech and the crack of breaking ice, the gate groaned open and she was finally able to drag some air into her lungs.

H'chan, rapping out orders in tones that reminded Rett of Major Yidnar, told the does to run for the safety of the deep forests closer to Aurora Base.

Then something slammed hard against her, forcing Rett to the snow. Several heavy weights pressed her deeper into the stuff and for the second time in minutes, she became breathless. There was snow in her nose, snow in her mouth, and she couldn't get her head up to breathe, because something else just squished it deeper. Rett finally jerked her head up, snorted snow from her nose, and inhaled what she hoped was air.

"Rett!"

H'chan nosed her, pawed snow away, and pushed her onto her back with his muzzle. "My Rett, are you hurt—? The young ones, the yearlings, they were so excited they ran blindly. Rett?" The Beast sniffed her snow-covered face and licked the substance away with vigorous tongue strokes.

"Cut it out!" She pushed his muzzle aside firmly. "Stop. You're going to freeze my face."

She brushed snow from her eyes and scrubbed at the dampness H'chan's licking had left on her skin, hoping to keep it from freezing until she covered her face again. Then she sat up and glared at H'chan.

"Look, there are several very serious issues we're going to discuss *right* now—"

"Are you unhurt?" The Beast interrupted her, his muzzle a finger's width from her nose again, whiskery lips quivering. H'chan's violet eyes were so visibly filled with panicked concern, his telepathic voice so fraught with worry, that Rett found it impossible to stay furious with him.

"I'm fine, H'chan." She gave the muzzle she was going to push aside a reassuring caress instead. Then wrapped her arms around his head and hugged it, resting her forehead carefully in the diamond-shaped hollow below his antlers and between his wide eyes. His warmth felt good against her damp face, and she rubbed her skin on his fur for the comforting contact as much as for the drying effect. "Just fine." She let out a long breath. Later. No sense discussing anything until things calmed down. "Thank you."

Before she released him, he raised his head, the motion easily lifting her upright with it. *You still with me, Pam?* Rett gave H'chan's head a final caress before turning to her harness packs for a clean breath muffler and another set of goggles.

~I haven't experienced a fall like that in years. I'm glad you're younger and fitter than I am,~ returned Pam, her own mental voice reflecting the still-breathless quality of Rett's. ~I thought for sure that impact would have ejected me from one or another of your orifices.~

Rett had to chuckle aloud. "Yeah, me too." Thinking about it another few seconds, she covered her clean breath muffler with a gloved hand and laughed again, harder. *Nice imagery, Pam. Real nice imagery.* This time she had to bury her snow-scraped face into H'chan's neck to stifle her howls. She didn't want them mistaken for some sort of signal.

~Some sort of signal, hahahah!~ Pam's fresh spurt of merriment nearly made Rett choke.

Ow, shit, this hurts! The pain didn't stop Rett from nearly laughing herself unconscious. Her other hand clenched a handful of fur so she wouldn't fall down. *But appropriate.*

"You just never mind." This she directed at H'chan, who had become completely confused. Reaching into her harness pack again, Rett found a wipe and lifted her snow goggles just enough to get the salty moisture leaking from her eyes before it stung into her abraded skin. "I'll explain it some other time. Let's go see how the others are doing."

* * * * *

"ALL CLEANED UP, SARGE," TREBOR said. "You missed the all-clear—I was concerned until I saw you by that enclosure. We're finished here. Tris told me Lieutenant Evetez called in. Major Yidnar recalled him and the backup team—we'll meet them back at Aurora."

"Evetez called in? When?" asked Rett.

"Tris just commed me now, told me Evetez was commed by the Major on tightbeam an hour into the attack. Check your pcom, Sarge. I can understand you missing the whistle, but not Tris's transmission."

"I was dumped hard when H'chan jumped that fence," admitted Rett, reaching beneath her hoods for her headband. "*Really* hard. I'm surprised you didn't hear me fart over the weapons discharges."

"That was you? I sent some people in the opposite direction to make sure a section of the pipeline hadn't exploded."

She laughed, then leaned forward and shook an astonishing amount of snow free from her inner and outer hoods.

"Explains that," observed Trebor with a soft whistle.

"And here I thought my hoods were tight because my head had swelled up. Was almost expecting Med would be after me. Thank all deities!" She addressed her pcom. "Com connect Bronze Lead!"

"Bronze leader, Fang—what's up?"

"Com check. Bronze team all clear?"

"Com check confirmed. We're all-go."

Semage sounded a bit distracted, so Rett ended her transmission and glanced at Trebor. There would be time for discussing details on the way back. "Thanks, Trebor. Any casualties?"

"Theirs, or ours?"

"Theirs first."

"No one reports any survivors, Sarge."

"There were four battalions here, Trebor. *Four*. Over two thousand troops. No survivors? No prisoners?"

"Most of them put up a fight . . ."

For the first time in her memory, Trebor couldn't meet her eyes. He glanced away, and Rett followed his direction to the infantry personnel moving in to take up defense of the newly won territory. The results of battle were never pleasant, but the sight of this unexpected carnage—from Free Army personnel— was creating a stir among the incoming troops.

Rett was going to have to come up with something to tell the garrison commanders. *Can't wait.*

Trebor turned back to her. His avoidance had lasted half a heartbeat, but it was enough to clue her in to his mixed and many-layered feelings on the matter. "I'm afraid we lost control of the Beasts with those who would have been merely wounded or surrendered," he said.

"I noticed. Hard not to."

"I never expected—" Shaking his head, he went on. "They went ballistic at the sight of any Coalition uniform, no matter what the body in it was doing. Even those already dead."

Remembering the partial carcass and the snow-colored hides on the fence, Rett had to validate a great deal of the incredible hatred the Beasts had displayed.

If my family and friends were rounded up and kept in a cage, cut up in front of me for lunch, what would I do? What right did I have to turn H'chan before and yell at him?

The Ice Beasts weren't merely animals to do their bidding. They were allies, with their own rules, their own reasons for doing things, their own way of life to protect. She puffed out a breath. The entire concept of outright slaughter without any attempt to at least communicate and resolve the problem was difficult for her. Because *she* knew the Beasts had the capacity to communicate with whom they chose. She and a limited number of others knew it. To everyone else, they *chose* to appear as much wild animal as the cotos or growtu.

They choose. But to make a choice *not* to communicate? Even if it would have saved their own species? She simply couldn't imagine it.

~Would it have made a difference to the Coalition if they'd tried?~ Pam asked.

Probably not. It hadn't with us. We tried communication, negotiation, everything, and it didn't stop or deter or make any difference to them. We even had the ability to communicate more easily, and on a technical level as well.

Why was it so difficult to try to stand in H'chan's and any other Beast's hide? Rett finally managed by imagining herself back in the purple energy field with the alien officer who had prepared to bleed out and dismember her for his sustenance. He had been fully capable of negotiating and making an alternate choice. She'd offered him a compromise. He had turned it down.

What if they were all like that with us? Then again, what is the difference being hunted, being penned for consumption, or being enslaved?

It was easy then to answer the question she had raised to herself.

I think no matter what, I'd have to make sure that even though they weren't killing anyone now, they wouldn't be around to do it later.

The other side of the issue really rattled Rett: that H'chan had, in fact, *enjoyed* killing his victims; had reveled in the violence of their deaths. Animal or aboriginal species, the Ice Beasts were definitely not humanoid, and she couldn't expect them to think with similar patterns or act with similar behaviors. But like her, they were Nyorfians, and shared this solar system, even making the effort to come forward to defend what they loved and found valuable. She couldn't dictate to them how to behave, no matter how horrifying it was to her.

Goes right back to being culturally limited, I suppose.

But for more than twelve years the Nyorfians—the humanoid ones, she had to remind herself—had strictly adhered to their rules to prevent enemy deaths whenever possible rather than cause them, especially when someone indicated surrender. Now . . .

The various possibilities for complications that were going to arise from this were starting to make her head hurt.

~One isolated incident might bring an inquiry that would likely be dismissed to the novelty of the situation,~ offered Pam. ~If it happens again, though . . . ~

That's the problem, Rett thought back, like Pam keeping her exchange shielded from H'chan.

~You can,~ suggested Pam quietly, ~ask the *Beasts* for compromise.~

"Sarge? Everything all right? Sure you're not injured?"

"No, I was thinking about what happened. Shocked by it myself," Rett said with perfect truth. She blew a hard whistle of frustration between her teeth, causing her breath muffler to balloon away from her face. Frustration for her inability to explain any of the detail to Trebor, bound as she was by the secrecy H'chan had asked her to keep.

"I guess I'm going to have to come up with something to tell the garrison commanders. I don't think something as simple as 'Oops, sorry, the Beasts were carried away' is going to be sufficient."

"For them, or for MainCommand and the Planetary Council," agreed Trebor. "Or to Major Yidnar."

"Or to Major Yidnar," repeated Rett. If there wasn't any way to compromise with the Beasts, there went the concept—and advantage—of his outstanding transportation source.

H'chan, just behind her, stretched his muzzle forward and breathed softly against the back of her neck, his mobile lips tugging ever so lightly on her anorak. She felt the warmth right through every layer of insulating material.

"You are not the only two-leg with concerns over the way we fought today," he said. "We Beasts have discussed the matter among ourselves. Behaving in a likewise manner as our enemy is not acceptable. We do not, after all, seek out and destroy the growtus. If it is agreeable, we will compromise by next time making a greater attempt to restrain ourselves from killing those who do not fight."

Grateful for that much, she continued speaking to Trebor without missing a beat. "What's done is done, and we'll simply have to be sure it doesn't happen again. Now, what about us?"

"Aside from a few scorched uniforms and bruises, F-troop's clean, B-troop called in clean, but you know that. A shoulder graze in R-troop—Corporal Olanzar, I think. She's good to go. No one out of action, no one has reported any Beasts were hit, either."

"That's what I like to hear," said Rett in relief.

Trebor nodded. "That's what all of us like to hear." Then he whistled for *platoon regroup*, his signal echoed by the other two commando platoons.

Rett made sure the fresh defense garrison dispersed into their newly-won position. She didn't want to think about the job the infantry would have clearing up the area. By the time the transition was complete along the entire area of the attack, it was well after new day and almost dawn.

"We sure didn't earn any points with the infantry on this run," muttered Sergeant Tris as Rett joined the strike team.

"Yeah. I tried to explain but . . ." She shook her head. "You go ahead, start back. I need a handful of minutes, I'll catch up." She signaled Trebor the same, then turned H'chan back toward the enclosure that had imprisoned the Ice Beast does and fawns.

Along the way she picked up a few ML-12 powerpacks no one would need any more. From the shift she felt in Pam's energy, her ego-merge friend understood what she planned to do, and approved.

Despite H'chan's assurance there would be cooperation between his people and the humanoids, it was as if he turned off the link between them. The instant it became clear Rett's chosen direction was toward the enclosure so recently liberated of its captives, he planted his feet and refused to move.

She was ready for that. She slid from the riding pad and went forward on foot, leaving him behind. This time, at least she felt a sense of fury, sorrow, and anguish from the Ice Beast.

Rett worked in silence, dragging the frozen hides from the fence; the butchered remains from where they hung. She opened the hut nearby, nearly gagging at the collection of bones, antlers, and offal inside. *They might have left these parts for the growtus and other scavengers, at least.*

~Then again, maybe that was the intention—to lure the growtus in and kill them as well,~ thought Pam. ~We saw how they liked to do that.~

With everything in one place, Rett turned her attention to the ML-12 powerpacks, setting them to overload with a trick Jaq had shown her long ago. She walked back to H'chan, vaulted onto the riding pad, and asked him to catch up with the others.

She never turned back when the explosion went off behind them. She didn't have to look to know there'd be no physical evidence of the site of slaughter and terror but a freshly made patch of slick, black ice, which soon would be covered in snow.

241

3.3.3 UNDETERMINED LOCATION, AURORA CONTINENT, EPNOCE
0536.03.12 (LOCAL RECKONING)

RETT'S PCOM BEEPED SOFTLY A half-hour into their return trip, heralding a communication from outside the usual com band.

She roused herself from the uneasy half-doze into which she'd slipped, grateful for the jolt to her body and brain. "Fang Lead, what's up?" she responded, using the standard query.

"Force One, Fang Lead—everything all-go?"

The full report can definitely wait until we get in, she thought even as she answered Major Yidnar aloud. "Objective secured and all units all-go, sir."

"The others just arrived, loaded up, got another assignment. Complex 55."

"Yes, sir." Complex 55 had been one of the objectives under discussion for the past several days, even halfway into the trip here. She guessed they weren't very worried about the Coalition troopships getting through any more if they were redeploying farther from the Base.

"Fang Lead, that's a day's ride."

"We're able for the trip, Force One. Confirm target area Complex 55." Already calculating ammo inventories in her mind, Rett dismissed any underlying notes in the Major's voice to her own anxiety the new assignment would leave them shorter than she liked.

"Support units will meet you with supplies."

Rett let out a breath of relief that her sensitive pcom picked up loud and clear.

"Infantry is already enroute," Yidnar added. "You'll meet up with them, Fang Lead—good luck."

Rett called Tris and Semage, with their juniors, in for a conference. Then the platoon seconds went off to check supplies while Rett and the other two platoon leaders studied the maps on their Omnis.

~Rett?~

Yeah, Pam. Is this important?

~You bet it is. This isn't right.~

"There is a change in the weather," H'chan put in. "A storm will strike before sun high."

"Midday. Great." Not that the sun rose very high over the horizon at all here this time of year. But the fact that the Beasts had names for distances, relative periods of time, and phases of the moons—even had a name for Nyorfias, calling it "the blue eye"—was just another point to argue against them being the uncivilized animals H'chan claimed them to be.

243

"Storm's a good thing, it'll cover our movement. Unless it's one of those blizzards—in which case it'll cover us instead." Rett's eyes went to the sky anxiously. She itched to link her Omni into the global weather forecasting system. She couldn't tell much: the sky was only slightly lighter with the advent of day than it had been all night long during the battle. Was that a darker smear on the horizon, though?

"Not much snow, but strong wind," said H'chan.

~It's not the storm!~ insisted Pam. ~Listen. I'm not an expert on this stuff, so I have a lot of questions.~

When don't you? Rett rolled her eyes. *But go ahead.* She had to acknowledge that Pam's unique perspective had come in handy more than once.

~Why would Yidnar send you another day's ride farther from Base to a huge complex like 55—and say reinforcements will meet you there and halfway? And why would he contact you, skipping your chain of command—right over Evetez' head? Why didn't he include Tris and Semage, too? And, why would he say

Easy backups were already at the base and loaded? Lieutenant Evetez and the others aren't that far ahead of us are they? What time did Trebor say they were recalled?~

Rett looked at her chrono to check the time. *After we hit. Six hours ago, just after new day.*

~Yeah, and here I was thinking I missed something. If that had been a bomb, you all wouldn't be here right now. ~

Would you say what you mean? Rett demanded.

Pam gave the distinct impression of crossing her arms over her chest. ~Six hours ago, weren't you guys still on com silence?~

Rett remained quiet for a long minute.

~I have no doubt Tris got a com from *someone*, Rett. But *Evetez* should have been the first one to make contact, and he should have commed *you*, not Tris. I don't think Major Yidnar would skip your chain of command unless there was an emergency. And then he would tell you if there was. The Major sounded . . . strange. Stressed. Think about it.~

Rett did and cursed her own oversight. *You're right, Pam—my pcom's not the only thing that jammed up when I fell off H'chan. My common sense must have blown out my ass as well. Damn it, Major Yidnar wasn't even on our command frequency!*

"H'chan, can you reach Ranger—I mean, H'vren?"

The Beast's mental tones were soft and full of worry. "There are no Ice Beasts except these and that pack of does and fawns moving on all of Aurora. I have attempted to contact H'vren—" The Beast's thought paused. "H'vren is not there. I cannot reach any Beast on the Base."

"Not there! Shit!" Rett's spoken reply earned her concerned glances from Tris and Semage. "We need to talk," she said flatly.

They moved apart from the others. Rett told them what bothered her and what H'chan had reported, then verbally adjusted her pcom to the same com band Major Yidnar had used. "Fang Lead to Base—"

244

Semage and Tris exchanged glances. "You know, now that I think about it, I knew something was odd, but we were cleaning up and I just kept thinking about what the Beasts did back there." Tris shook his head. He sounded completely disgusted with himself. "My com was from an outside band, too. And since it *sounded* like Evetez—"

Rett agreed with a nod "So we all fell in the shit on this. Let's not get any deeper in it." She proceeded in an attempt to contact various individuals on different pcom channels and frequencies, staying off the broadrange ones that were shared with other branches.

"I wouldn't say that, exactly," put in Semage. He leaned into H'ting, who like H'bris and H'chan, had followed them aside. "If we kept going, it would be a different story. I mean, if you realized Major Yidnar was in some sort of trouble when he was obviously not mentioning it . . ." He shook his head. "Any contact?"

"Nothing. Signal is going, but there's no one on the other end."

"I'm glad we're finding out now instead of getting back or going on to 55—into something *really* unexpected. I'll see if H'bris can reach anyone," said Tris.

Rett nodded, reminded by H'chan that the R-troop leader's Beast was adept at contacting other human minds remotely without first needing the physical mesh.

"H'ting tried to reach a few Beasts from Easy Force just now," Semage said. "He says their minds are closed—they're not dead. What's going on?"

Rett kept her eyes on Tris, who apparently was deep in conversation with H'bris.

The older man spoke after another minute. "H'bris can't reach any people—although he did manage to touch the Major for a minute. He said the Major's mind was 'too tight'."

"The Major can block any talent less than a Master Adept, he learned how from his time in the GTC Rangers," Semage reminded grimly. "Figures. Of all the times we need him *not* to block something from outside, he does."

"Agreed. H'bris managed to get some impressions before the Major locked him out, though, and . . ." Tris paused, trying to find words. "The situation isn't good. H'bris says most of them are sleeping and unable to be awakened. That says unconscious to me."

Rett cursed again, borrowing several of Trebor's more creative phrases. "Gas traps again?"

"Since it worked for them before, it's likely," Tris said.

"The Coalition's desperate enough to try anything at this point," added Semage.

246

"I'm going back," Rett decided. "I don't like it, either. We're a day from 55 and five hours from Base—and there's a storm coming. You guys can come with me and F-troop, or go ahead to Complex 55—no sense in all of us getting into trouble if nothing's wrong."

"We're all with you, Rett," the R-troop leader said firmly after a quick glance at Semage.

"Are you sure? Think about it. You *know* I make mistakes. We all do. Look at how we let a distraction cause all of us to miss the facts before. If we're wrong about this—" Rett told them softly, "you could be sure Major Yidnar's going to rake us very, very slowly over the hottest fire he could find."

Semage shrugged, trying to make light of it. "Beats freezing to death any day. Let's go."

They turned back to update their units. Rett gritted her teeth together as she saw the black smudge of cloud on the horizon. In that short space of time it had advanced and taken a definite, menacing shape. The towering cloud thrust so high into the sky the top of it actually saw sunlight, which made the parts below even more dark and ominous. Rett didn't remember ever seeing a wall cloud so large from the ground. There wasn't any shelter out here on the open tundra for miles.

"Can you keep your direction and stay as a pack in what's coming?" Rett asked H'chan.

"Of course," said the Beast. "You forget, my Rett, that we Ice Beasts have survived such storms for many seasons."

"I didn't think you'd be moving across the open during one," Rett countered.

"It has been done, although not often. Nevertheless, we can manage. It is rare that one of us gets hit by the flashes."

Rett looked up at the cloud again. Flashes. Deities. Of course, there would be lightning in such a storm. She and Pam simultaneously imagined the antlers of the Beasts, as the tallest objects in the wide-open spaces they'd be crossing, as lightning magnets.

It didn't seem to concern H'chan, who went on to ask, "But what of your protection from the cold?"

"So far so good, but we've yet to see what it can do in a storm like the one coming."

"Then we will make sure our riders are also not in danger from cold. We will stop if anyone is threatened. The strongest and heaviest of us will take outer positions during the worst of the wind. As long as your people can stay astride and keep from becoming separated should a Beast fall from a gust, we will keep you safe."

Leaving H'chan to brief his four-legged troops, Rett turned to hers. Using the penetrating tone referred to as "That Voice", she made sure her words carried clearly to the entire group. "Listen up, people! We're going to get pounded, and soon. Make sure that anything loose is fastened tight! Everyone secure survival packs with extra gear *beneath* outer layers, next to your skin is preferable. Then snug down outer gear as if we're prepping for a jump. Nothing to catch or flap in the wind.

"And I want a line on everyone to their Beast. If any of you get separated from the group, you'll have a better chance of survival with your Beast. Leave enough slack to clear in case the Beast stumbles, and don't attach it to part of the harness, make sure it is around your body on one end, the Beast's on the other. Barrel, base of antlers, or a fixed loop around the neck that won't choke if it's taut, or come off. Do it!" H'chan provided the suggestions for location of the security line; Rett had merely repeated them. "There might be cloud to ground lightning in this storm. Nothing we can do about it, but keep your combat senses alert and—" *and tuned in with your Beast*, she almost added aloud, but stopped herself just in time. Instead, she told H'chan to have the Beasts stay in tune to each rider just as if they were in combat.

She turned her head, seeking a familiar small figure. "Carakenne!"

"Sarge?"

"We're getting a wind that just might toss you clear back to Nyorfias, sport. Knowing how much you hate flying, take extra precautions securing yourself."

"Uhm-hmm, Sarge!"

Bhayorn, followed by his equally burly Beast, promptly volunteered to act as a safety anchor for featherweight Carakenne. After a quick check with H'chan to see if that affected the way he was organizing the Beasts, Rett agreed.

Preparations made, Rett signaled the one hundred and eight teams of commandos and Beasts to ride swiftly in the direction of Aurora Base, ninety miles south. All too soon, the light, stiff wind they'd loped out with turned into a shrieking gale that tore head-on into the group.

Rett had no idea how the Beasts positioned themselves, but she was, through her Beast, aware of the new configuration and the fact that H'chan felt it was his place to be at the forefront of the group for the first onslaught of the storm.

The wind roared with icy fury, trying to separate riders from their mounts. Lightning flashed. Several times Rett felt her skin crawl, or the shorter hairs on her body rise in response to the electricity in the air. Beneath her, H'chan swerved, sped up, or slowed in response. Maybe they didn't need the evasive action, but it was better than waiting to be burnt to a crunch.

The worst of the lightning passed, leaving them to the buffeting gale. After H'chan reassured her no one had been lost from the group—yet—she crouched low and close to H'chan's neck to reduce wind drag and conserve body heat, hoping the others were doing something similar. Soon the snow came, driving with sandblasting force.

Visibility became a term from the past. Rett couldn't even see H'chan's neck, and that was right under her face! She tucked her chin close to her chest and hung on. She became aware of a multitude of whistling sounds that changed in pitch and volume, different from the sound of wind-driven snow and storm. *What was that?*

She raised her head only to feel the wind grab at her body like a fist and H'chan bobble to one side from the sudden drag. Hunching in close and tight again, she realized then what caused the noises.

~The wind through the antlers,~ Pam said at the same time the idea coalesced in Rett's consciousness. ~That makes sense.~

Mystery solved. Rett tuned out most of the sound and closed her eyes. There was nothing else she could do.

Time seemed to stop.

A change in the pressure and sound around her roused Rett from the twilight into which she had slipped. A new Ice Beast voice spoke in her mind.

"My Tris says we must stop," said H'bris. "There is a ridge ahead to break the wind."

The relief from the gale was so sudden Rett almost fell off the riding pad from the sheer effort of holding on against the wind.

She managed to slide off the Beast feet first instead of headfirst, freed her safety line, and after forcing movement into her stiff legs, went to count noses. With the thickness of the storm, the dark day of the arctic winter had turned darker than even the previous night had been. From here and there among the group, she saw the faint glow of well-shielded handlamps.

"We're all here, Sarge," reported Trebor. "How long will we be stopped?"

"Few hours," said Rett. "Until the wind changes. This won't be a windbreak for very long but it'll be long enough for all of us—Beasts included—to get as good a rest we can in the meanwhile. Are you warm enough?"

"Shit, I'm never as warm as I'd prefer to be. But enough so it's not a survival issue."

Rett and the others looked after their Beasts first, removing harness and gear, breaking out the blocks of compressed pine bark and twigs, as essential a part of each rider's kit as his or her own rations. The Beasts ate snow for water. Liquid water on Aurora was the exception rather than the rule. The Beasts in the group at Aurora Base looked upon those ice-free water containers in the quartering shed as a curiosity, something that was more for the riders benefit. H'chan had avoided that corner of his stall altogether.

After the Beasts were munching and comfortable, the commandos brought out their own snacks and water containers from underneath inner jumpsuits, where the stuff stayed reasonably defrosted.

"It's *cold*, Rett!" Jaq stared as she shrugged out of her topmost layers.

"Just noticed that, Jaq?"

"Why are you taking *off* gear?"

"Because it'll be colder once we start moving again," she said.

Jaq, huddled deep in his own clothing, wasn't convinced.

As the Beasts finished eating, they grouped more closely together, digging deep into the snow. Rett watched as they settled in, the riders following to snuggle up close to their furry partners. With the added protection of their survival shells, she knew they'd be comfortable.

~The troops are fed and watered, Sergeant, now how about their leader?~ Pam inquired sternly. ~That pain in your stomach isn't from falling off H'chan—it's from hunger. And don't forget to add extra for this worrying you're doing.~

Rett reached for a ration bar without comment. The ones they carried now tasted good, but were so rich in fat to combat the cold that they left an oily feeling on her tongue. She munched her way through that, half a water bottle, a handful of toasted nuts, and two fruit bars while she and Trebor made a check round of F-troop. She started in on a packet of nuts as she and her second conferred with the other Easy leaders to get a report on the condition of the rest of the group.

"It's amazing," Trebor said as they waded back through the drifts.

"What is, Trebor?" She finished off her water and packed clean snow tightly into the flexible container. She had spares, but habit was habit.

"These animals," said her second.

Rett briefly activated the heating element on her water bottle to melt the snow. She then slid the container beneath her jacket, into a special inner sleeve near the heat of her body. The flexible material of the winter water bottles were more susceptible to damage than their usual ones, but keeping the essential liquid from freezing was more important. "They are amazing," she agreed.

"It's more than that. I mean it's as if they know exactly what to do—as if they can read our minds," he said. "Major Yidnar sure knew what he was doing when he went with this idea, that's for sure. Although, back at the pipeline—" Her second shook his head.

"That was extreme."

"Yeah. But I can't shake it out of my mind. I'm not looking forward to the fallout on that when it comes around."

"Me either, but there's nothing we can do about it right now, and nothing we can do to change what happened," Rett reminded.

"No matter what, you and the other platoon leaders sure lucked out and managed to get the smartest ones in the bunch, especially that H'chan of yours. Although," added Trebor, patting his solid-bodied, still unnamed Beast on the neck, "I wouldn't trade my big guy here!"

Rett smiled as Trebor's Beast raised his muzzle to affectionately *whuff* a breath at her second and tug at his outer hood with furry lips. "I'm sure he wouldn't trade you either. Neither would I, Trebor." She pounded her fist against his arm in appreciation and affection. "We don't need to post a guard. No one is going to think anything'll be moving in a storm like this, even if any readings get through the storm interference."

"And if that happens, even the Coalition would leave those three platoons of insane Nyorfians to the weather," agreed Trebor.

"Get some rest. I'm planning on it."

She found H'chan lying close to Jaq's Killer. She thought she could detect a gleam of calculation in the violet eyes of both animals. Perhaps, though, it was only the soft glow of the handlamp on her shoulder harness.

"Pleased with yourself, H'chan?"

The Ice Beast did not respond, but if Beasts could grin, she'd imagine his would certainly be from ear to ear, since he'd managed to position her close to Jaq for a few hours.

"Don't you even think about that," she thought to him in warning. "This is not the time or place." She pulled her shell from the pack, wrapped it around herself, and settled next to him. "Where is Jaq, anyway?" She leaned against H'chan's warm side.

"Hi, Rett," she heard Jaq say a minute later.

"Mmm," she grunted, pretending she was half-asleep.

He sat close to her, his shell making a thin, zipping sound as it rustled against hers. "You don't mind, do you, H'chan?" asked Jaq in a tone that indicated he didn't expect the animal would understand him.

H'chan turned his head and snorted softly at the man in agreement.

If only you knew, Jaq Pym, thought Rett.

~I wonder if knowing that he has a crowd up here would bother him,~ snickered Pam.

Does it bother you? Rett asked suddenly. *I mean, any time you were with me and I . . .*

~No,~ said Pam. ~It never bothered me.~ And with that, she withdrew into her own thoughts, an evasion Rett recognized instantly, although the sincerity of Pam's thought made it puzzling.

Finally Jaq settled himself, and between the two animals, huddled under the wind-blocking coverings that automatically adjusted to a certain range of heat, it was cozy and warm. The shells were made from the same material as their anoraks on the outside, the inside fused to a skin-thin layer of special fabric. One nearly translucent sheet was capable of keeping the average humanoid body at a safe temperature as long as that body had a pulse.

"That was something, back at the pipeline," Jaq said. "Up until then, since leaving the Coalition . . ." His voice trailed off uncomfortably.

"I understand what you mean, and please, I don't need reminding about what happened last night right this minute.

253

Apparently, we were unprepared to deal with the Ice Beasts' extreme . . . instinctive urges . . . in a pitched battle. But you can be sure that such uncontrolled action will never happen again."

Thankfully, the Zetinorian changed the subject. "Did you eat something?"

"Yes, Jaq, I did." She dug the wrappers from her recycle bag and thrust her hand from beneath her shell, displaying the proof for his inspection without changing the rest of her position.

Jaq didn't comment. She heard him settle more deeply against H'chan. Returning her wrappers to their former location, Rett poked her head into the open so she could see him without the hazy distortion the shell caused. "Something else wrong?" she demanded.

"Yes. You are."

"Me?" She repeated his words of nearly eight months ago back at him. "Me, is it? What did I do?"

His half-smile and rueful little headshake indicated he remembered that very situation. "Nothing yet. That's the problem." He pulled his shell up around his shoulders before shrugging off his anorak. "I mean, earlier you said you loved me, but I need to know if you've forgiven me for being so—"

Rett sighed. "I thought you were over that. I love you and there will never be anyone else isn't enough? What else do you want from me, Jaq? And don't even think of anything physical at the moment, this isn't the time or place."

He adjusted his stretchy hat so it nearly covered his eyes and pulled the hood of the inner suit closely around his face. "And that refinery roof under enemy fire was?"

"That was different."

"Was it? How so?" His voice went deep and soft, like it did before they hit the pipeline.

"Well, yes. It was quite a bit warmer, and we weren't being watched so closely." The heat she'd felt earlier came back all in a rush and she almost stammered.

"Watched? By what? The Beasts? I'm sure they're not the least bit interested."

~Wanna bet?~ came evilly from Pam.

"I am most interested," added H'chan.

Rett gritted her teeth. Pam was one thing. She'd never been aware of Pam as a separate entity in an intimate moment, which had prompted her asking if it bothered her friend. H'chan was another matter entirely. She could just imagine him in her head throughout the entire process, asking questions and making comparisons, why they did that, why they did it one way and not another. The heat she felt now had nothing whatsoever to do with her longing for Jaq.

"I forgive you, Jaq, now go to sleep."

After the resigned mumble he made, she relented and shifted her body, loosening an arm from beneath her shell so she could reach to his face. She drew him close for a lingering, warm kiss, keeping it light, although the contact was enough to bring her body to needy arousal. Barely stifling her groan, she forced that aside and lifted her lips from his. She hoped he'd dismiss her trembling to cold.

So she made a big production out of joining their weather-proof coverings, maximizing warmth for both of them. When they were encased in their filmy cocoon, grainy snow hissing across the thin barrier, she rested her head on his upper arm, once more in control of herself.

~Do you need another prompting?~ asked Pam impatiently. *For what?*

~Awww—jeez! And people think this is the man's problem. It's the *words*, Rett, and how you say them. "I forgive you Jaq now go to sleep" in that tone of voice—grr! You're supposed to be forgiving him, not giving him another punishment. Good grief. You just got back together, now he's all out of sorts again! This time, it is your fault. I should kick *you*. Better yet, I'll tell him myself—and boy oh boy, would I like to get *my* hands on him.~ Pam made a threatening motion as if to suddenly leap from her corner into full control of Rett's body and mind.

All right! All right. Good deities!

Pam gave Rett a mental pat. ~Good girl. Fix this. You'll be glad you did. And you,~ said Pam to H'chan sternly, ~stay out of it, or my imagination will kick the inside of your head so hard your antlers will point back instead of forth.~

"You can do that?" asked H'chan doubtfully.

"You don't want to find out, H'chan, trust me," thought Rett. "Please . . . both of you, stay out of—or stay quiet—in my head for a few moments."

When both her friends withdrew, she focused on Jaq's aura and saw the lingering cloudy shades of sadness and doubt, an edge of wary tension rather than pleasure at her nearness. Rett slipped her hands from her mitten-gloves and wriggled even closer against the Zetinorian. *Careful,* she cautioned herself. Her control was tenuous and no matter how much she pleaded, H'chan would still be delighted to try pushing her past her limits, disregarding what Rett told him about time and place.

"Jaq?"

His voice reflected a hint of the same wariness his aura did. "I'm sleeping."

She lifted her face toward his. "With your eyes open?"

He shifted as if to turn his back to her. *Not this again.* With a sinuous motion she threw her leg over his and straddled his thighs, facing him, her hands gentle on his face. "Jaq. Please don't shut me out again. Will you listen?"

Now his face was every bit as inscrutable as that of Labonne, the school warden at Complex 63. Such coldness from him after the warmth they shared before nearly brought tears to her eyes. *I'm screwing up again. Pam's right. I can't blame anything or anyone but myself this time.*

"What?" He met her eyes but didn't move, not even when she brought her face close.

For a moment her heart froze. Was it too late?

"I forgive you, Jaq," she whispered. "And I hope you can forgive me, too." Keeping her eyes open to watch his reaction, she kissed him, the contact as gentle as a snowflake falling through still air; as sweet as the soothing kisses she would give a child; as simple and uncomplicated as the caring, casual touch one close friend gave another.

His remaining tension softened immediately, his arms held her close. His lips moved against hers in a soft reply, then brushed the exposed skin on her forehead, her nose, her lips. She closed her eyes now, soaking in the warmth he gave as freely as spring rain. He fit her against him as if she were a child and held her in that way she loved. His strong, heavy arms were tight around her, but she never felt trapped or confined within them. She was safe here.

For a time she lost count of, they pressed featherlight kisses here and there on the exposed portions of their faces and necks. When the kisses became stronger, when her breath started to quicken, reality intruded.

"Why not make love right here?" asked Jaq in a husky murmur. "No one to see or hear."

"Any other time," said Rett even as her body heated at the thought, "I would say let's go. But when we do, I don't to be interrupted for anything. I've waited far too long for that."

He cupped her chin and tipped her head back a bit more to look her in the eyes. "You're so tense you're ready to ignite. I thought maybe—"

"Don't say it."

"How long has it been for you, then?"

"Seven and a half months, give or take," said Rett, torn between laughter and tears at his surprise.

"You didn't . . . *seven and a half?*"

"Don't sound so shocked," Rett said crossly. "Before you came along, it was years."

"That was different. But—Etron." Jaq floundered. "I mean . . . You didn't—?"

"I *tried* to tell you. You didn't want to hear anything but what you convinced yourself was true. Are you going to ask me for details now?"

Jaq shifted beneath her until they were both stretched out on their sides between the two Beasts, facing one another. "No. Maybe one day you can tell me, if you wanted to. I don't need to know anything else. All that matters is now." His smile hit her at point-blank range.

All of a sudden it was entirely too warm inside the whisper-thin membranes that sheltered them from the arctic world outside. Pressed against Jaq from breasts to toes, Rett felt him against her as if there hadn't been at least a fingerlength thickness of clothing between them. She wanted his hands on her so badly, to feel the sensual stroking of his fingers on her body, the warm wetness of his tongue. Her fingers clenched over the material covering Jaq's arms and she almost choked on her breath when one of his hands slid languidly from her shoulder to her hip, leaving a trail of fire beneath the material, as warm and real as if his fingers had touched her naked flesh.

She struggled to control her breathing, which had gone ragged as her pulse skyrocketed. His lips touched her forehead, her cheeks. The responses she felt were elsewhere, deep inside where she longed for the most intimate of contact.

This is so unfair, she thought, resenting the fact the Zetinorian didn't display the least bit of the agonizing sexual frustration she did. His Zetinorian pheromones weren't helping matters one bit, either. As tempting as it was, as much as she wanted to, she wasn't about to change her mind about the time and place. Why was he pushing her like this?

258

"Jaq—" Her words ended on a squeak as his mouth closed on hers, not light and gentle this time. The kiss was deliberate, sensuous, probing. He drank down her sharp gasp, and as it turned into a low groan, deepened the kiss, let her feel the weight of his body on hers. Already aroused from her imagination and his proximity, when his tongue swirled around hers every sensation zoomed into one spot. Rett's entire body clenched, then shuddered against him for an endless space of moments. She turned her flushed face away and pressed it tightly into his neck, shivering with aftershocks, trying to get her breath.

"Rett? What just happened?" He rolled back to his side without letting her go. "Was that an earthquake?"

"Damn you, Jaq," she said hoarsely. Damn him, he sounded so amused. If her body wasn't so completely melted from that orgasm she would have punched him.

"I hope there's more of that for later. I mean, for when we have more of an opportunity. I'd like to do a lot more than kiss you for barely a minute."

"You did do more than that," said Rett.

"When?" He didn't quite manage to hold back his chuckle.

Rett rallied herself enough to snarl and make a token attempt at escape, but he didn't relinquish his hold. She didn't really want him to. "When? Ever since you left. Ever since you got back." Her nose was still pressed into the base of his throat. She fought the urge to bite him there, knowing it would start her up all over again. "When we get a later, you'd better be up for it."

"No doubt I will be," said Jaq with a laugh before she could rephrase her statement. He dropped a kiss on her forehead and moved his head so his chin rested on top of her hood. "I can wait," he said comfortably. "Right now I have everything I want right here."

She thanked again, silently, the powers responsible for creating Zetinorians, and Jaq. His aura was right again, the clear blue gradient from almost white to almost black, the middle shades predominant. His long, soft breath of contentment feathered warm air past her face. Letting out her own deep breath, Rett slowly regained control of her body, made sure she was operational, and settled into his comforting embrace.

You were right, Pam. Rett sent a mental smile to her internal companion, both of them for the moment very well satisfied.

"That was mating?" H'chan thought. "I am confused. All the male did was—"

"Never mind," said Rett silently to her Beast. "Just never mind. I'll explain later. Maybe. I'm going to sleep."

Despite the Beast's annoyed snort, she knew H'chan would alert her in plenty of time if anything came up. Jaq was asleep already. A minute or two later, Rett joined him.

* * * * *

H'CHAN ROUSED RETT, WHO IN turn roused Easy right before the wind changed. They were riding again as the once-sheltering rock face became the target of the snow and storm. The going was only slightly easier with the gale at their backs.

H'chan reported the Beasts were fresh and reassured his rider they could go on at full speed.

"Any response from Aurora Base yet?"

"Yes," H'chan's mental voice was sober. "H'vren reports they have been attacked by a large number of enemy two-legs. Something made everyone sleep. H'vren says all the Beasts came awake locked into the quartering shed. Some are injured, a few badly. The rest of Aurora Base is being held prisoner. Some have been killed, ones who did not go to sleep and tried to fight. Maybe a pack in all."

H'chan paused and Rett knew he was exchanging thoughts with yet another Beast back at Aurora. "Atira, for D-troop, tells H'sol to tell me to tell you that they managed to engage them in battle for a while, but were overcome by the same type of bad air was used the last time?"

"Shit. Blazing, flaming shit." Rett's words swept ahead on the wind.

H'chan did not understand, he sounded puzzled. After conferring again with H'sol, he repeated the information, filling in a few points he'd left out earlier. "H'sol says his Atira tells you the enemy threw bad air on the Base from the sky, then fell from the sky in flying things. They waited. When H'sol and the others came back and fought them, they made them sleep with bad air, too."

The exchange was slightly confusing since the Beasts had no thought-terms for technical things, but Rett got the general idea all too clearly. "The storm, of course. Damn it!" The wild Epnocian weather and the unique properties of the planet and its three moon wreaked havoc with communication and scanners even at the best of times. The attack on Aurora Base had been timed with just as much careful attention and precision as the Free Army attacks on outlying positions.

261

There was only one Yixolryn Coalition commander Rett knew who paid attention to details like that.

Iheolon.

* * * * *

A FEW HOURS OF HARD riding with the wind at their backs and Rett felt almost as stiff with cold as that time her fighter crashed into Aurora a month or so ago. Tris and Semage, through their Beasts, suggested another stop.

"How close are we, H'chan?"

"Close. Maybe only a quarter pack range—"

"Twenty miles," said Rett and agreed to the stop. They had to, of course—they all needed the break and a chance to warm up. Rett told Semage and Tris of her new suspicions, they in turn told her what their Beasts had verified.

Iheolon.

And he was waiting for them to get back in, no guess as to why.

Uneasy, Rett prowled impatiently the entire time they were stopped, going to each member of F-troop, making sure they were well and good to go with her own eyes. The bite of the wind finally forced her back to the shelter of H'chan's furry body.

"H'sol is angry! They are all angry—" H'chan's mental voice sounded shocked. Rett, alarmed, noticed a general uneasiness among all the Ice Beasts. "The enemy kills," continued H'chan, his thoughts a snarl now, "those they have made defenseless." His normal concise patterns were too turbulent to follow.

"What—who?" thought Rett in panic. "What's going on?"

"H'sol's Atira is too angry and upset to think in a way H'sol can relay. I will speak with H'vren." H'chan paused, his mental tones calming a bit, but still heated. "Two of Atira's pack and four others, three of his Yidnar's officers—H'vren tells me the enemy made them examples. Others are hurt. Several Beasts have been killed for food."

Rett felt sick. She had a good idea what had happened now. It only deepened her determination to return to the Base and use any means possible to make the mission a success.

"H'chan, I think it's time you and your friends decided to talk to all of us." Her gloved fingers tightened in the fur of his neck. "*It's the only way.* We have to explain to our people about Iheolon and his division—and how we knew about it. We *must* set up something with the people back at Aurora. H'chan—please! Please. I'm begging you."

She felt the Beast's deep sigh.

"They'll kill everyone. He's wanted to from the beginning. Iheolon hates the Special Forces, hates Nyorfians—hates *me*. Iheolon," she said, scrambling for something that would really hit home with the Beasts, "is one who takes pleasure in killing even when no one has harmed him or anything he cares for. It is the killing and pain for its own sake—not for food, revenge, or defense—that gives him pleasure. He doesn't care if his victims are animal, human, male, or female—even those from his own Coalition."

H'chan's head jerked up slightly, his ears pricking toward her.

"This barbarian has hurt you so deeply as well?"

"*That doesn't matter.* The people back at the base matter, the others on this planet. Right now, we're the only ones who can stop him. But we *must* be able to communicate, undetected."

~If you can't trust Nyorfian commandos to keep a secret, H'chan,~ thought Pam, echoing Rett's entreaty and adding staunch support, ~there's not much chance. Ice Beast lives depend on this, too!~

"I will speak to the others on this matter." H'chan's mind became closed to Rett, who thought she would freeze solid in suspense during the endless minute before the miracle happened. The energies of the one hundred and five people around her phasing from shock, surprise, and sudden understanding created in her mind's eye a pulsating effect of color as mysteriously beautiful as the aurora for which this continent was named.

Tears in her eyes, Rett hugged H'chan's head to her in gratitude. Now Easy would understand the unmitigated violence of their four-legged allies at the pipeline. Now they could comprehend the strange, evasive, almost telepathic behavior of the platoon leaders, the similar sounding names those senior sergeants used for their Beasts.

"I know you didn't want to—thank you."

H'chan nibbled with his lips gently along her shoulder, a gesture Rett had seen Beasts exchange between each other. "I have always been among those who desired to extend our contact with your people. But the will of the many governs such a decision."

"Please thank them for us."

"Such is not needed. I have made sure all Beasts have informed their riders of the situation we will face."

263

"Thanks." Rett fished for a wipe and managed to get it beneath her snow goggles without letting too many snow particles fill the open space. The wind was horrid. As much as she hated it, the killing, shrieking gusts would be their best cover in what was to come.

"Sarge." Trebor, followed by his Beast, moved to stand next to her. Even in the gloom and swirl of snow, Rett could see his tawny eyes shining behind his snow goggles. "Turns out the big guy had his own name after all," he said, and introduced H'poll. The next words he spoke were serious. "We don't have enough ammo to take on a division, Sarge." H'poll stood stolidly alongside H'chan, sheltering the two humanoids from the wind.

"Four battalions at the pipeline, Trebor," she reminded. "We'll simply have the Beasts be more selective this time. As for us, we've had tough odds before. We'll do this. We have to."

"Yes," he said after a moment. "So it's Iheolon, is it? We won't waste time speculating on what will get his attention."

She heard the undertone in his deep voice and her hands left H'chan to grip her second-in-command's shoulders. "I'm sorry, Trebor. There is no other acceptable alternative right now. Although we'll hope for one, once we can make contact with others at the base."

"I know. Sergeant Tris will take the Easy Force, and I'll take command of F-troop if you run the diversion, Sarge. But it had better be *temporary*."

Rett didn't say anything. Instead, she hugged him, glad of his loyalty, his foresight, his understanding, and his love.

3.3.4 2023ʳᵈ CO'S OFFICE, AURORA BASE, EPNOCE
0536.03.12 (LOCAL RECKONING)

Major Yidnar, commander of the 2023ʳᵈ Special Forces, sat quietly. *No sense in struggling,* he thought. A struggle would be exactly what his enemies wanted; it would feed their power, give them another excuse to perform another act of murder or barbaric cruelty.

He managed to dampen the fury from his eyes, remaining cool and calm. Inwardly he felt nothing even close to calm, especially after witnessing the savage mutilation and killing of two commandos from Sergeant Atira's D-troop; his longtime second, Captain Mahrhys, and three GIs. A pair of TRANS personnel died trying to prevent the enemy from killing several Ice Beasts. Iheolon had made sure they lived long enough to see the Beasts slaughtered and prepared for cooking.

Two other officers, including Evetez, and a handful of non-officers had been brutalized, as far as he knew, they'd been left in the snow where they'd fallen, or pinned between rovers and buildings, left to die slowly from loss of blood or, eventually, freeze to death, whatever came first. He had no idea if they yet lived.

His muscles burned with energy begging to be released. Had he been free to move, he'd do his best to make sure not a single enemy trooper in this room, or their commander, would live out the next minutes. He again forced down his desire to fight his restraints, quelled his intent to kill . . . hoped for a miracle to present itself. Someone from Easy Force's main strike team, Rett or Tris or Semage, anyone, would eventually realize there was something seriously wrong.

At least he hoped so. Rett had sounded preoccupied, and he wondered what event so momentous occurred at the pipeline to distract her. He'd tried to give her enough cues to rouse her suspicions, short of openly declaring Commander Iheolon and his division had taken over Aurora Base. He doubted he'd get another chance.

Yidnar wasn't worried about getting himself killed with that sort of direct warning, but he was worried it would prematurely ruin anyone else's chance to survive this. As long as the commander who led the ingenious attack on Aurora Base kept his attention focused on Yidnar in hopes of him bringing in Sergeant Rett, the others would have a better chance.

Of course, catching Rett wasn't Iheolon's only goal. The half-Yixolryn took the installation in hopes of holding out long enough for the Coalition troopship that still evaded Nyorfian pursuit to land. The prospect of gaining his long-coveted prize, however, added to Iheolon's incentive the same way oxygen caused smoldering embers to burst into flames.

Yidnar shifted his stare to two Yixolryns who conversed with Iheolon. He barely recognized them. The last time he'd seen Motuk and Sclamuse, they'd looked as humanoid as any Nyorfian: two sleeper agents who'd been on Nyorfias for decades. They'd fooled everyone, managed to do a lot of damage, caused a lot of casualties. As commanders of the 52nd, known then as Colonel Mott and Major Shamos, they had come very close to turning the tide of the war back to the Coalition's favor.

Had Rett's unit not escaped after that ambush at the Wide River Gap, had Jaq Pym not made it easier for them to make that escape successful, the enemy agents would have succeeded.

Motuk's heavy, gray-skinned face turned toward Yidnar, as if feeling his stare.

I owe you, Yidnar thought. *You and Sclamuse. If I had the choice to kill anyone in this room first, I'd start with you two.*

A minute later, Iheolon sent them both from the office. Yidnar had overheard or lip-read enough to know they were being sent to question others. Sclamuse awarded Yidnar a sneer as he passed.

* * * * *

IHEOLON REGARDED THE SPECIAL FORCES officer with grudging respect and growing impatience. Now that he had the Base, whether that troopship made it or not he fully intended to put an end to the Nyorfian Special Forces. Those few he killed earlier were meaningless, enough to show these Nyorfians he meant what he said. The real business would start with Sergeant Killer.

Look at this one, so cool you would think his ass was parked on a snowbank outside instead of indoors. Although it seemed the Nyorfians on Aurora didn't believe in heating the interiors of their buildings much higher than it took to keep their water from freezing.

Maybe I should strip his lower half and plant him in the snow. We'll see if he can remain so impassive when we thaw selected portions of him later.

Iheolon considered the prospect as he glanced idly from the window, where he could see the outline of that long-legged lieutenant who'd led a futile—yet admirable—assault against them. *That one won't think so fast on his feet again, if he's even still alive.* He'd all but crushed those long legs, left the Nyorfian snarling impotently with the still-running vehicle grinding him into the building. Even if the lieutenant lived to get medical attention, they wouldn't save much.

Iheolon lifted a set of Nyorfian VARs to get a closer look, had there actually been movement from him?

How long would it take with this one? he wondered, laying down the VARs to regard the major. On the other hand, might he provide motivation to force Killer's submission? No, the lot of them would let each other die first. He learned that a long time ago. Then again, he'd heard a rumor Avok had found a weakness, although no one seemed to know what it was, and Avok was dead now. He dismissed her memory with a wave of his hand, as if chasing off the annoying insects the native mainlanders called stingflies.

Avok had been greedy and ambitious, and although he couldn't deny she was a masterful officer and highly efficient, she had come up through the ranks on her back more than from work or deed. Her only interest, besides entertaining herself in amazingly varied and perverse ways—even to him—had been becoming as powerful as the Leader himself. Perhaps she had intended to take over that position, as if that would ever happen for a female. The best news he'd had in years was that she'd been killed, the stupid bitch.

On the other hand, the Coalition ill-afforded the loss of Commander Frgerrizolont. Dietary and personal habits aside, the creature had been a brilliant scientist, yet completely unsuited for a command position. Iheolon had advised against it vehemently, almost more forcefully than he had at giving up his longtime officers to other purposes. They had hated him, true, but they had given him their loyalty and obedience.

But did the Leader listen to him any more? By breaking those officers out of Iheolon's command and scattering them, sending them to positions as isolated commanders of glorified prisoner of war camps like those Epnocian complexes, the Leader had weakened, not strengthened, the Yixolryn presence on this icy planet.

One by one, they had been killed. Now they would be bereft of the clever devices that talented genius Frgerrizolont had spun out as effortlessly as the average trooper passed farts. Sure, Iheolon had Sclamuse now, but Sclamuse's talents, although strong, were minor in comparison. Unless it came to drugs and biological weapons.

He had an attire array of Sclamuse's latest carefully refined, filtered drugs just waiting to be tested on the all-too-resistant Sergeant Killer. Several promising devices, too. Motuk had come up with some splendid concepts. This time, his cousins would assist in their application.

Iheolon swallowed as the possibilities caused him to salivate. Imagined the expression of surprise Killer wouldn't be able not to show at seeing her former commanders in their natural Yixolryn state. Motuk and Sclamuse were both anxious for some payback, too.

He would hear Killer's screams for mercy yet. He had no doubt.

Once I bring these insufferably arrogant Nyorfians to their knees and keep them there, the Leader will pay attention to my advice, thought Iheolon grimly.

Then there's a certain Zetinorian I also need to have a few words with—we'll have to make sure he's taken alive. Along with Killer's pretty little sister . . . who will be useless for anything but genetic material once we get through with her.

The anticipation brought a pleasant tightening to his loins. Then, aware of the dark blue stare fixed on him so coolly, he imagined a degree of contempt had entered the major's impassive mien, as if the man could read his mind. Iheolon sent a brief glance to one of the guards, who slammed the side of a metal-shod fist into the juncture of the major's shoulder and neck with such force the Nyorfian officer and the chair he was secured to went tumbling over sideways.

"I've not yet heard word of your task force's defeat or capture, Major," said Iheolon, steepling his fingers and watching closely as the troopers brought him upright once more.

Of course, aside from an already swelling lump on his neck and a bloody nose—he couldn't have obtained *that* from falling sideways—the Nyorfian looked no more ruffled than if hit with a passing breeze. Iheolon's glare moved to the other guard, who'd looked pleased with himself until that exact moment.

He enjoyed watching the color drain from the idiot's face. "You know that causing damage above the shoulders is not your prerogative. Was it an accident?"

"Ye—" The trooper glanced down at his chest, where a double handful of gleaming metal needles had penetrated his armor clear through to the skin beneath. Before he could gasp, he was dead.

Paying no further attention to the body, Iheolon laid his weapon down, well pleased by the results. The device was no larger than the average marker and supposedly capable of sending those slender, poisoned spines through armor much heavier than that lightweight beam-deflecting stuff his troopers wore. He'd have to try one on a Nyorfian Spacemarine or one of those intolerable GTC Rangers—now that would be something.

Then again, mused the commander, *this one has also been a Ranger.* He felt the same way toward that corps as he did toward the Nyorfians, most especially the branch led by this same man. Iheolon's attention returned to the Special Forces officer's face, which was set in the exact same expression it was before.

Getting up, Iheolon came around to lean against the front of the desk. "Something should have happened by now."

Yidnar raised one eyebrow. "There is a storm out there, you know," he returned coolly. "You barely got through yourself. My people are good, but they're not superhuman."

Iheolon dismissed that with a wave of his hand. "Could it be, perhaps, they are disobeying your orders, and returning here?" He leaned his upper body across the gap so his face was barely a fingertip away from the Nyorfian's. "No matter—either way, I'll have them, too, and that Sergeant Killer of yours. I might even let you watch each other die. I'll let you know. I haven't quite made up my mind. I may put her into storage for later. Unless, of course, she is killed outright by my troopers first. I'll think about it as I take care of business with the Zetinorian and the pretty empath."

* * * * *

Yidnar kept his face impassive, but it cost him effort beyond any he'd ever had to exert.

Iheolon reached behind him for something on the desk, and passed the Coalition version of an Omni from one hand to the other. "Of course, Killer must die . . . eventually. First, I think it will be interesting to see if she's as resilient as she was three years ago, especially now that I've made improvements to my devices. Would you like to see more of that, to pass the time?"

Yidnar didn't allow his face to change one molecule. He didn't even blink. Iheolon would show him or not without a response, and Yidnar didn't want to offer any sign of encouragement. Iheolon had taken great pleasure in presenting excerpts from what he called *"a most entertaining tenday with your Sergeant Killer."* Despite being made to actually *see* and hear the repulsive, sickening horror of it, more than he ever wanted to, Yidnar had to take intense satisfaction and fierce pride in the sergeant. She hadn't given Iheolon and those under him any satisfaction for their efforts.

Sounds had come from her body, of course . . . the nause-ating sounds of joints being pulled from their sockets; of muscle and tendon ripping like cloth . . . other sounds, each worse than the last. Only the changes in her breathing marked those events. Sometimes there was a cough, grunt, or gasp, a sound of strain, but those were acceptable. She had made no others.

271

He shook the horrors away from his thoughts, keeping only the fact that it had been Iheolon's failure to force an outcry of pain from her that had plunged the half-Yixolryn into his maniacal obsession. Iheolon's single-minded need to bend Rett to his will had even constantly led the Leader of the Yixolryn Coalition's invasion force to reassign Iheolon elsewhere if the commander's current location was anywhere near even a rumor of Special Forces operations.

However, as the Coalition was running out of troops and places to go, it was inevitable Rett and Iheolon would someday end up in the same geographic location. The possibility of getting his hands on her again had driven the enemy officer's takeover of the Base, more so than the prospect of opening a landing area for a troopshuttle from outsystem.

I wish you could hear me, Rett, Yidnar thought. *I know you're headed back here. I wouldn't expect any other response from you. Do you know you're up against an entire division, no less Commander Iheolon's elite?*

A tentative, gentle touch in the Major's mind almost caused him to lose control of his face. He nearly slammed up his shields again—something had probed him earlier—but hesitated. Something was familiar. Carefully he opened to it.

"Yidnar," the mental voice said, "it is I, H'vren, whom you call Ranger. What you have just thought, H'chan's Rett already knows."

"Ranger?" thought Yidnar. "I knew Ice Beasts were smart, but—good gods and deities, all this time—a native intelligent lifeform!"

"You must put aside your surprise and questions for now," said Ranger. "You must concentrate so they do not suspect. It was H'bris whom you felt try to contact you earlier, he who carries Tris. You also must not speak of this to any except your own people," added the Beast. "Only Beasts who have Pack Leaders as riders are supposed to communicate with each other, however in this situation we have made exception. They all know what took place here."

Shoving his desire to instantly process and analyze this new development with the Ice Beasts was painful. Taking the time for it, however, was out of the question. Yidnar swallowed, making it look casual, keeping his face still and his gaze cool as he scrutinized the enemy commander.

Iheolon, idly flipping the Omni in his right hand, leaned forward a bit more and dipped a fingertip in the blood yet streaming from Yidnar's nose.

Was he . . . No. Yes.

It took a good moment to push back the incredulity that threatened to raise Yidnar's eyebrows as Iheolon proceeded to smear the blood around Yidnar's face, in designs that had sharp angles as well as swirling curves.

Clueless, and planning to remain that way for the moment, Yidnar realized the good thing was that Iheolon's creative yen took a good deal of the commander's attention. The half-Yixolryn's heavy features and small dark eyes were completely absorbed in the task of redecorating his face. So, despite the commander's proximity, Yidnar felt safe enough to divert his inner self into a conversation with Ranger.

"Ranger—I mean, H'vren—our only chance is with Rett. Iheolon has the base, but he wants her so badly he'll do anything to get her. Rett can provide the distraction to get the others in. Are they with her?"

"All three packs are together. Yes."

"It's risky—but it's the only chance. She can't let herself get caught before the others have had a chance to infiltrate."

Risky, that's an understatement, Yidnar thought to himself. *If she's the primary decoy, her chances of coming through this alive are next to nothing. She probably knows that. It won't stop her.*

"H'chan's Rett says she understands what you want her to do. They have already considered this plan."

"Where are they?"

"They are very close, if not for the blowing snow, within sight of the main gate. She says, through H'chan, to remind you she is good at . . ." H'vren paused for several seconds. "Howling loudly and making the enemy chase her."

"We call it divert and decoy," thought Yidnar, managing to keep a rueful chuckle in his thoughts.

The com crackled into life a few minutes later, just as Iheolon straightened up to admire whatever he'd done to Yidnar's face.

"Fang leader to Base—"

Commander Iheolon looked expectantly at Yidnar, nodding to a trooper who stood by the audio pickup. "Answer her," advised the enemy officer. "I know you wouldn't want to cause more unnecessary deaths."

As if it might stop him from warning Rett, another trooper shoved his weapon into Yidnar's temple.

Iheolon is *desperate.* The threat of the weapon at his head didn't bother him in the least. If he suspected Rett didn't already know the situation, he'd be warning her and anyone with her now, weapon or not, but since H'vren had spoken to him telepathically the plan changed.

You didn't count on Ice Beasts, Commander, Yidnar thought with a grim inward smile. *Neither did I.*

"Fang Lead to Base."

Keeping his eyes fixed on Iheolon's and his expression unchanged, Yidnar spoke. "Fang Lead, this is Force One," said Yidnar. "What's up? What's your position?"

"I don't know, sir," complained Rett in reply.

"Where are the others?"

"I don't know, sir," she said again, with the perfect touch of freezing cold, exhausted self-pity in her tone.

If I didn't know any better, I'd say that wasn't Rett at all, thought Yidnar in private astonishment.

"We became separated when this storm hit—" A note of peevish accusation crept in. "Why didn't you give us the met updates? As far as I know, the others are still headed for the target area—or headed in a hundred different directions. When the storm started it seemed all these damned animals went crazy."

Her voice trailed off a little and after the space of a few breaths, she continued. "This stupid beast I'm riding keeps taking his own way—nothing I do could slow him up or get him to change direction—so I figured he must be hungry and heading to his warm corner in the shed." A sigh followed this, a cold, shivering kind of sigh. "How'm I reading? I haven't a clue to where I am. Everything looks the same . . ."

Is that really Rett? Or is someone imitating her voice? He'd never heard her sound like that; if he hadn't known it was for show he'd swear she was sincere. *Not the right time to mull it over,* he reminded himself.

Ignoring the weapon, the itching of the blood drying on his face, and inwardly cursing the pain in his neck, he managed to turn his head enough to note the signal direction and strength readouts on the com panel. "You're not even a half mile away, Fang Lead—heading looks good. Keep the wind at your back and come on in. We'll worry about the others after you get here."

"Yes, sir," said Rett.

"Fang Lead—"

The gun pressed harder into Yidnar's temple.

"When you get in, we'll have a private discussion about dis-obeying my orders."

"Yes, sir," she said in a subdued voice tinged with embarrassment.

"Force One, out."

"Very good, Major." The satisfaction on Iheolon's face made Yidnar's gorge rise. "Have details bring in those that are still alive, and hide those who are dead, animal and humanoid alike," the commander directed one of his retinue. "I want nothing to seem out of place."

Keeping his outward composure, Yidnar pushed his nausea down beneath a deep, bitter regret. *Luck be with you, sport.*

"H'chan's Rett says—thank you, Major Yidnar, sir." H'vren's relay to Yidnar reflected the gravity of the man's thoughts and the absolute seriousness of Sergeant Rett's reply.

3.3.5 UNKNOWN LOCATION, AURORA CONTINENT, EPNOCE
0536.03.12 (LOCAL RECKONING)

GOOD JOB AS USUAL, PAM, Rett complimented her ego-merge partner.

~I hope Iheolon bought that~, returned Pam.

"He did," H'chan thought to them after a minute. "Yidnar was suspicious it was not you speaking at all, my Rett."

~He's more right than he knows,~ Pam commented.

"H'chan says Iheolon went for it," Rett told the other platoon leaders and their juniors. "I'll go ahead, make a big noisy fuss. You know what to do from there."

"Between you and the storm, everything should be covered well enough," nodded Semage. He caught her, pulled her close for a hard hug. "Take care."

"Leave some for us," said Tris when Semage let her go. His strong hand closed over her shoulder briefly.

She nodded. "I'll try."

Rett turned toward H'chan only to find Ariam blocking her path. Her sister's gray eyes were wide and frightened behind her snow goggles.

"I don't like this, Rett. I don't like this one bit." Ariam's voice was tight and pitched higher than normal. "One or two others of us should go with you. I have a horrible feeling—"

Rett laid a finger on Ariam's breath muffler, right over the spot her lips were. "I'll be okay." She slid her other arm around Ariam and pulled her close, taking her to H'chan's side, where Rett reached into one of H'chan's harness packs. "Take this, Ari. H'tenneck sent it with Jaq for me, but I won't be stopping long enough to put it to use if anyone needs it. You remember how to use it? Carakenne has one, too."

Ariam transferred the maglock breaker to a deep pocket of her anorak. "Thanks, Rett. I still think you shouldn't go alone—"

Rett squeezed Ariam into silence by folding her into a hard embrace. "Ariam. For any of us, live or die, this is it. Just like at the Gap bridge, just like Circle. I love you."

Ariam had to clear her throat before she choked out, "Love you."

Rett touched her forehead to Ariam's before turning away. H'chan followed her as Rett made her way through F-troop, distributing most of her remaining ordnance with her encouragement to each of them, same as she tried to do before every fight. She'd be running and looking to make noise more than taking aim at specific targets, and they didn't have ammunition to waste. She finally checked H'chan's harness and started to pull herself onto the riding pad.

"Sarge!" Corporal Carakenne waded through the loose drifts, hanging on to her Beast's riding pad for balance. "I guess I should've ridden over," she offered breathlessly. "Anyway, take these. These are the regular ones, here's a handful of flash grenades, these are smokers, and here's a few frags. Then there's this little number . . . made it myself, and I only have one other. Uhm, you might want to save this one for something really special . . . three seconds, and make sure you're way back, down flat if you can manage. This thing can take out half Aurora Base in the right spot, so make sure you're nowhere near fuel storage or any of the ammo lockers."

Rett eyed the small device doubtfully, but her reservation wasn't for Carakenne's claim of the explosive's force. "Are you sure it's stable? I need to make a diversion, not have it go off at the wrong moment and obliterate the Base."

"I've been falling off H'yaris with it on my belt for a few tendays," said Carakenne. "Anyway, may help. You wanted to make noise . . . these are all I have ready made." She nodded at the last device. "Besides, depending on the route you take, you may get a chance to throw that at something interesting, like the ship they came in on."

"Good enough for me," said Rett as she stuck the various devices in belt pockets and shoulder harness. Thanks, Carakenne." She smiled her appreciation at the small woman who'd become an invaluable member of her unit and a precious friend. Like all of them. She took a quick glance around at everyone she could see. "The others at Aurora are waiting for us. Let's not disappoint them."

Before she could mount H'chan, Jaq Pym caught her arm, pulled her against him, and kissed her with sudden passion. "Be careful, Rett," he said, and then pulled up her breath muffler and outer hood. "I love you."

"Only you, Jaq." She pulled herself into the riding pad and turned H'chan away, her deep feeling of unease growing as she nudged him into a lope. *Ariam feels disaster,* she thought. *I mean, this isn't going to be shit-simple, but it should work. What do you think, Pam?*

"Pam is gone," H'chan announced at the exact moment Rett realized this for herself.

"Gone . . ." repeated Rett in a whisper. "Always before I get . . ."

She closed her eyes. A deep rush of fear and nausea swept her from toes to hair. *I wish I didn't figure this out just now . . .*

"H'chan, if something happens and I fall, you get away as far and fast as you can." In her mind she saw the snow-colored hides stretched out on the fence. Deities! "Maybe I should go in alone, grab a sled or a snow rover."

He cut her short. "No! You must not think such thoughts!" he thought fiercely, his mental voice angry and upset. His forward motion halted. "We will be successful! I will not leave you—as I have chosen to ally with your people, I choose to stay with you! No matter what."

Her throat closed and she threw her arms around his shaggy neck, hugging him hard, sucking in deep, comforting breaths of his evergreen-scented hide. She loved him every bit as much as she loved her human friends, and wanted him to know that.

"And I love you, my Rett," he returned, his inner voice muffled.

"Come on." Rett again asked the Beast for a lope and they continued toward Aurora Base. Her focus tightened on the two thousand people at Aurora Base, Ice Beast and humanoid alike, who needed help.

And they were going to get it.

3.3.6 AURORA BASE, EPNOCE
0536.03.12 (LOCAL RECKONING)

THE GALE WINDS DIMINISHED—TEMPORARILY—TO A stiff breeze as Rett and H'chan loped toward the open gates of the compound. Rett eyed the gatehouses—no sign of the usual guard detail.

"There's probably some inside each gatehouse," she thought to H'chan. "Just be ready, because if they are, as soon as we go between the gates they'll be out. H'chan—this time you don't have to hold back. Someone gets in your way, take them out."

H'chan snorted in agreement. Rett felt his back muscles tense under her as he trotted slowly through the gates. She was covered head to toe and made sure the ident strip on H'chan's harness was covered. Under those circumstances, not being stopped and asked to identify herself—before getting within a length of the gates—would have been enough warning in itself that something was seriously wrong. That was, if she hadn't already been expecting something like this.

Sure enough, as soon as H'chan's rear paws were completely inside the compound, a group of Coalition troopers rushed from inside and behind the gatehouses, trying to surround them. Pretending surprise, Rett let out a startled yell, wheeled H'chan clear of the ambush, and used her hand stunner to best effect, hitting hands, lower parts of faces, throats, legs, and places unprotected by armor. The low-powered shots were enough to cause weapons to drop, aims to be thrown off, troopers to start choking, lose balance. Enough for general chaos, since almost every one that fell took down a neighbor.

H'chan did battle with his usual enthusiasm, but this time remembered to throw his victims in a manner that kept Rett's vision free from obstruction. From astride, Rett was able to get her legs into action, too. She had a moment's thought that to a few troopers it must have seemed as if the Ice Beast had six legs instead of four.

Rett hurled her weapon into one trooper's face with enough force to crack the targeters, in the next second slamming her foot beneath the jaw of the one behind him. Nudging H'chan close, she leaned far from the pad and scooped up his ML-12 and powerpack. The troopers remaining on the ground scattered for cover, but not before she dropped a handful and a half more. The thunderous reverberations were obviously unexpected—*what, they were expecting to take me without a shot being fired?*

Troopers without helmets or outer gear appeared in windows and doorways, just as quickly dropping from sight as Rett picked them off as easily as she and Ariam had used to clean tree branches of pinecones without chipping stem or bark in the process.

"Bubblehead didn't recharge this thing lately," she yelled in disgust as the powerunit bleeped at her. A nearby trooper heard her shout and the telltale sound, and leaped toward her and H'chan, calling his comrades to follow. Rett discovered the ML-12 made a nicely balanced club when turned backward, and with H'chan's forward leap, swung underhanded toward his face just as hard as she could. It caught him under the right ear with a crack so loud it echoed from the buildings around him.

"Just like that game Pam told me they play on horses," she said, watching the trooper sail away to land with a splatter against several others, taking them all down. "Whacking a ball with sticks. Baseball? Or was it hockey . . . ?" She raised her voice again. She felt stupid for yelling. But he yelling kept the attention on her, where it belonged. "Ah, shit! I'm out of ammo! I think we better start running—"

Her improvised bat caught another trooper with a shattering wallop that spun that hapless individual into a crumpled blot on the snow. Leaning forward, digging her heels into H'chan's sides to get his attention, Rett shouted, "Go! Go, go, go!" The Beast shot forward, flattening into the ground-eating strides of his gallop, which soon gave way to the incredible bounding leaps of his utmost speed.

From between buildings, snowbanks, and paths, Coalition troopers on snowsleds gunned their machines out of hiding and followed in hot pursuit. Rett whistled in surprise as more swerved out of concealment ahead. Reaching for a flash grenade, she activated it and dropped it neatly in front of one group that came a little too close. Tossed a frag into another shed where she heard more sled engines starting up.

"This is what I call extreme, even for Iheolon," she mumbled. She could have been taken down any number of times already and concluded this was a final effort to take her alive. She shivered suddenly, remembering what Evetez had told her about the drugs. For sure, some of these troopers coming after her might have weapons that could deliver . . .

"Not today," she said grimly, and tossed a smoke grenade into a group of sleds arrowing toward them. "Yeah!" She whooped when, over the expected sounds of crashing and curses, came the retching, coughing, and gagging of humanoids in alimentary distress. She'd come into possession of one of the "enhanced" smokers Ariam had devised, the recipe of course enthusiastically embraced by Carakenne and other chemical-demolitions personnel in Easy Force. A quickly dissipating, non-toxic, yet highly effective additive in the smoker guaranteed any humanoid, and most of the known alien species of the Coalition, would lose their lunch in the initial burst of smoke before they could think twice about it.

Good thing the wind was in their favor and that H'chan's forward motion never halted. He swerved and jumped over sleds and ran as if all the snow growtus in Aurora were chasing him. She could see the east perimeter of the base now.

They'll start shooting soon, thought Rett, keeping her profile low and her weight centered just behind the Beast's shoulders to allow him the greatest freedom of movement. *We'll be in the open and they won't have to worry about hitting each other.*

3.3.7 AURORA BASE, EPNOCE
0536.03.12 (LOCAL RECKONING)

"Stay sharp, H'tan." Ariam slid from the riding pad and stayed close to the snowbank.

F-, B-, and R-troops had quietly infiltrated the captive Base and before long, with very little noise or fuss, large amounts of Coalition troopers began to die. Normally, Ariam was tuned to her comrades and not so much to her enemies on this level, but she was wide open for this situation and couldn't help but feel the various fluctuations in emotional energies, and the blank spots that opened when nothing more was generating them.

She crept up to the quartering shed. No guards. They probably figured they didn't need to guard a bunch of dumb animals. Ariam unlocked the door, slid it back just enough to slip inside, leaving H'tan to keep watch outside. Satisfied no troopers were within she rushed to the occupied stalls to release the restive Beasts inside. There were some injured, but they'd have to wait.

"Remember to keep it quiet!" Ariam told the able-bodied Beasts before sliding the door wider. Battle-ready, the animals disappeared into the storm without a sound.

A nudge and nip to her jacket sleeve made Ariam turn, ready to admonish her Beast, but it wasn't H'tan who had prodded her so anxiously. It was MYOTS, the distinguishing triple-swirl of fur dead center between his eyes making the identification easy.

"Evetez?" breathed Ariam hopefully, looking past the Easy Force leader's Beast and expecting to see the lieutenant.

"H'wan says his Evetez needs your help," H'tan informed her. "He is very badly hurt."

Ariam changed direction instantly, following the Beast. H'tan kept several paces behind Ariam.

H'wan led them without incident to a spot where a patrol rover sat parked near a building. *Not parked*, noted Ariam as she

283

eased closer. *It looks as if it crashed into the wall.* It was as close as possible to that point the H'wan tried to get, even wedging his large body between the rover and the wall. Eyes rolling white, Evetez's Beast clawed at the snow in agitation. High-pitched snorts and squeals rippled from his nostrils and muzzle. Ariam didn't need her empathic talent to feel the horrible, helpless frustration and panic the animal broadcasted.

"Move back, H'wan, let me past."

In his mindless need to reach Evetez, the Beast aimed a powerful kick at Ariam that she barely ducked.

"Ask him to move back, H'tan! *Make* him move!"

H'tan's nostrils jetted steam and a whistling snort. When H'wan didn't yield, Ariam's Beast stretched his neck forward and closed his teeth in H'wan's rump.

Ariam rushed forward as soon as H'wan backed off, sliding to her knees to go beneath the front of the vehicle. In the shadow of the rover, against the wall, lay Evetez. He wasn't wearing an outer layer; his arms were outstretched, over his head, mag-restraints on his wrists. His hands looked frozen. The bottom half of him was black with frozen blood. Ariam didn't have to look closely to know his legs were crushed. His face was white, lips blue and bloodless with more than cold. The snow showed no sign of melting where it contacted his skin.

"No." Ariam closed her teeth on a soft moan. She didn't want to think of the terrible agony he'd been in, or how long he'd endured it before . . . *But wait a minute!* H'wan would not have made such a frantic scene if Evetez were dead. *Would he?*

"No, my Ariam," H'tan said. "H'wan would be upset if his Evetez was dead, but not like this. The two-leg still lives, but only just."

"Lieutenant." She pulled down her breath muffler, leaned close to his face, close enough to kiss him if she was so inclined. She held her breath and waited for the ultrasensitive skin around her lips and nose to provide the physical evidence she sought. She almost greeted the soft rush of air she felt from him with a shout. He *was* still alive, but for how much longer? "Lieutenant!"

To her amazement his ice-whitened eyelashes moved. A harsh sound escaped from between his stiff lips.

"It's Ariam," she said softly, digging into her belt pockets for painkiller, for a stimulant, for her shell. Then she hesitated and took a deep breath. "Lieutenant, it looks bad . . . can you hold on for a medtech? Or—"

"That you, Rett?" His lips barely moved, but she understood.

"No, it's Ariam." She wriggled her left hand from its glove and laid it flat against his neck, warming the spot as well as letting him feel her familiar empathic mind touch. "It doesn't look good, Evetez," she told him frankly. "Can you hold on? Or do you want mercy?"

"No . . ." His head moved so slightly she thought she imagined it. "I'll wait."

Without further hesitation, she pressed the injector with the painkiller against the spot she'd warmed with her hand.

"Rett?" This time she actually heard him.

"Ariam," she said again, patiently. "It's Ariam. Rett's running a diversion—as usual."

Thanking all deities for them, she withdrew the maglock breakers Rett had given her. Evetez's manacles opened and fell into the snow. She brought the lieutenant's arms in closer to his body and another huge rush of gratitude filled her—his limbs were stiff, but not frozen solid. His agonized grimace filled her with hope. A snap of her wrist unleashed the gossamer folds of the survival shell.

"Ariam."

"Yes."

"Knew the rest of you would come . . ."

"Your eyelashes are frozen together. Don't try to force them open. Relax."

"Watch out . . . for Iheolon. After you, too. And Jaq."

285

"I hope I run into him. I have something I personally want to give him," said Ariam with such fierce intent Evetez actually managed to show a bit of teeth.

"Others, too. Motuk. The other one . . ."

"Shh," said Ariam, although a twin surge of utter hatred and cold fear ran through her at the same time. *Of course they'd be with Iheolon.* "We'll get them. Don't worry. I'll warn the others. Hush for now."

She finished wrapping the shell around his hips and upper body, and the sensors in the inner lining, which responded to the body temperature of person it contacted, immediately began to heat up. She figuring Evetez's legs were better left chilled to slow any more blood loss. "This will probably hurt, Lieutenant, but it can't be helped."

Deities, how many times? How many times had she said that over the years now? How many times had she heard it?

Wrapping her arms around the lieutenant's upper body, she scrambled backward until they were clear of the rover. With both Beasts guarding her, she wasn't worried about anything except a stray weapon discharge. Once in the open, she inserted her body beneath Evetez's now-unconscious one and stood, balancing him across her shoulders. She sent H'wan to locate the nearest medtech and followed H'tan toward the closest safe shelter with her burden.

Happily, the nearest medtech and shelter were in the same place. Guarded by three GIs too injured to travel but well enough to defend the position, R-troop's medtech had set up an aid station just at the end of the next row of buildings. Ariam left Evetez in his capable care and returned to the mission.

3.3.8 SOMEWHERE EAST OF AURORA BASE, EPNOCE
0536.06.02 (LOCAL RECKONING)

H'CHAN AND RETT KEPT RUNNING. They'd put a comfortable gap between their pursuit for a little while, when H'chan had leaped the east gate of the Base. It was a jump Rett stuck with and wished Pam saw—but now the enemy sleds were gaining on them. SMG shots were searing into the snow, making it hiss and steam just to freeze again in seconds. Rett also heard the sounds of more conventional firearms—not just the usual SMGs and smaller sidearms. She cursed roundly and started H'chan on a zigzagging course in an attempt to evade the slugs as well as the energy weapons' fire.

Weird! Maybe not so strange after all, she thought more clearly, *they have no supplies coming in any more—they have to fall back to what they took from us—at least what wasn't locked down.*

And the stun settings use less power, they can get off more shots . . . that's why I used them before myself.

Carakenne's grenades helped keep them warily back in addition to making a sizeable difference in the size of the pack in pursuit.

H'chan tried to keep his incredible sprint going strong. His breathing labored now, and she felt the strain in the great muscles beneath her legs. Rett wished she could give him more somehow. She imagined she could; she strove to pour her physical strength through her body into his.

H'chan responded, flattening himself and extending his stride even more. Then something smacked into her with the force of a meteorite, shoving her forward onto H'chan's neck, nearly throwing the Beast off balance. She clung to his neck, his fur, the harness.

H'chan's stride slowed as she struggled to stay astride. "No— keep going!" she hissed into his ear. "GO! Even if I fall, don't stop!"

Left hand tight in the Beast's fur, she straightened herself, settling deep into the riding pad, teeth clenched tight in pain. She closed her eyes and fought to lock down physical control of her body while allowing her combat instincts to guide the Beast.

As if sensing she was out of explosives, the troopers on the sleds came closer. H'chan was tiring rapidly, his strides rough, causing the shattered bones in her shoulder to grate against each other with every step. Then the Beast lurched, stumbled, and went down. Thrown forward, she landed hard on her wounded shoulder in the powdery snow. Even though the surface was soft, the shock of it took her breath away.

Snowsleds came to long, sliding stops all around them, throwing up huge wakes of snow. The wind swirled the loose particles into a blinding vortex, making sight impossible for several minutes.

H'chan's familiar light touch in her mind was gone. Her heart ached in agony over not knowing if the Beast was dead or unconscious, but she didn't have time to worry about him now, or even glance around for a clue. She hoped that if he were yet alive, by keeping the attention on herself he'd have a chance to stay that way.

Taking advantage of the flying, glittering particles of ice that blocked her view as much as confused the targeters of the enemy, she rolled to her feet, her TT-1 braced against her left hip, her left hand on the trigger. At this close range, her last fifteen rounds did the work of twenty as some of her slugs passed completely through sled pilots and lodged in the gunners who rode behind.

The surviving troopers scrambled for cover behind their sleds and she made the most of the opportunity to open distance between them.

Five of them left, she thought as she hurtled through the snow, looking for a likely place to make a stand.

Five of them. They had guns and solid cover; she had a knife and a lot of loose snow. To take them on would mean getting close and physical. The droning whine of another snowsled engine was growing louder, too. *Make that seven.* She added two more since the sleds generally always had a pilot and a gunner.

She gulped in a breath, realizing she was out of options. *No place to go. You have to turn and fight, make a stand here. Live or die, you have to finish this.*

"Oh, shit," she muttered. "Maybe an offensive is going to have to wait a minute." She sprinted for the doubtful shelter of a depression in the otherwise flat surfaces as some of the troopers hastily tried to activate a big caliber automatic on one of the sleds. A few others lifted sidearms. She risked a glance back in time to see one emit a puff of white vapor. At once, the air seemed filled with high-pitched *vipps* and she felt several stinging impacts with something before remembering about Carakenne's thermal grenade.

Still moving, she slammed her knife back into its sheath, unclipped the tiny bomb, activated the three-second delay, and threw it. She aimed for a spot behind the troopers and hoped she was far enough away. Then she jumped for the depression.

* * * * *

H'CHAN GROANED AND LIFTED HIS head from the snow. He felt terrible. Nothing had ever made him feel this way before. He had to get up: it wasn't safe to be so vulnerable to predators. He managed to get his legs under himself and with heavy, deep groans, lurched upright, head down, swaying slightly, dazed and confused. He vaguely wondered why he wasn't able to put weight down on his left rear paw.

Stumbling, uncertain on three legs, H'chan moved, not knowing where he was headed, only that he had to go somewhere . . . yes, the forest. He had to get away from this open flatland, into a wooded area, there he could find other Beasts, find the shy spotted plants that hid beneath the snow and grew among the interwoven roots of the big trees. These plants were never eaten as food, they were instead used to dull pain, prevent infection, and accelerate healing.

Ten strides, thirty, fifty. His steps came easier, but his brain remained fogged. Then he halted abruptly and stared with dull incomprehension at the slick sheet of ice where there had once been swirling white powder. And what were those?

Enemy two-legs and their running things!

He turned his aching head toward the place the ice was nearly black in spots, where curls of smoke still rose from some of the wrecked sleds and bodies. Stumbling forward, the Beast hoped for a better look, hoped to understand where he was and what happened. He skirted the edge of the ice. His claws would allow him to cross it safely, but it didn't belong here and besides, he wasn't steady on his feet even with the good, familiar footing of powdery snow beneath them.

Then he saw the hump in the snow a distance away from all the other lumps and broken bits of machine. He remembered. Hot panic wiped the pain and fog from his mind and body as he bolted toward his fallen rider.

"Rett! My Rett—" He used a front paw to brush an accumulation of drifted snow from her twisted body, touching his muzzle to the frozen blood on her hood, her shoulder, her back. Like a branch from a tree, a large jagged fragment of something stuck up from one of the scorched, bloody places on her back. Her blood was all over the snow, although most of it was hidden beneath the loose powder that had already drifted to cover it.

The smell of it upset him more violently than any other blood scent he remembered. Only when the breaths whistled harsh from his throat did he realize he'd started to run away. He came to a halt, for a long moment frozen in place, trembling, fighting to overcome instinct and replace it with reason.

Returning to her side, H'chan carefully nosed her again. "Rett."

The Beast received no answer or response of any kind. He made every sound he was capable of making; pushed at her face with his muzzle, tugged at her hood gently with his lips and teeth. The absolute limpness of her body and the blank emptiness of her mind sent fresh panic through him. She lived. This he knew. But for how much longer?

He spun and paced the length of the site of violence, trying to decide what to do. His head hurt, sending a thought any distance was not a possibility. He tried to, straining until his legs almost buckled under him again.

He had to help her! How? Had he the power of humanoid speech, he would activate her communication device. That was impossible. As she had explained to him once, the device activated to her own sounds. So, even if he had the ability to speak, it would not be her voice he used. The device was worthless to him.

He wondered if he could lift her with his antlers, the way Beasts sometimes lifted and carried piles of branches and twigs they gathered when one or more of them couldn't come to the source; or the way some carried a fawn when it was sick or injured.

291

It was only then he noticed there was something wrong with that idea. Because no matter how much he rolled his eyes, or angled his head, he couldn't see his right antler at all. It was gone. It explained why his head hurt so much, but it only increased his agitation.

Then there was the matter of his injured foot. He lifted it, twisted his head around to sniff at it, started to lick the icy blood and packed snow from between what was left of his claws. Instinct warned him to leave it alone; cleaning it now would start it bleeding again.

What was he to do? Stay here and keep her warm, and hope the other two legs came looking for them? Maybe. No, doing so would do nothing for the blood still seeping from her body.

Resolutely, H'chan turned and started for the base. After a few stumbling steps, he didn't have to concentrate on balancing himself—missing an antler didn't help matters—and holding his injured paw off the ground. A few more steps and he broke into a lope.

3.3.9 AURORA BASE, EPNOCE
0536.03.12 (LOCAL RECKONING)

"R-TROOP JUST CALLED IN. SIX confirmed dead, one serious, ten minor but good to go, and two unaccounted for. That's all units from our Battalion checked in, sir," said Semage to Major Yidnar. "We've not yet accounted for eighteen total of our personnel. Six were out there." He nodded toward the scene they faced.

Six. And one of them had been from B-troop.

Rimms. His third-up, who'd been with him the longest of anyone. Semage had no idea of the units the others might have belonged to.

As the wind puffed smoke in his face, he grimaced at the heavy reek of it and turned so his face was downwind, pulling up his breath muffler. Beside him, Major Yidnar tightened his hood and pulled up the collar of the anorak he'd so hastily grabbed once he'd been freed. The Major had taken time to arm himself, but didn't stop to put on the rest of his outer gear. Semage slid his hands beneath his double hoods and slipped off the thick, stretchy hat he wore beneath them, handing it to his commander without a word.

"Thanks."

"I'm glad you remembered to wear gloves."

Semage felt awkward in his present position as temporary adjutant to the battalion commander, but with many of the other 2023rd officers killed—before and during the battle—and others wounded, and everyone else busy with other things, well, it was a matter of right place, right time. Everything was out of sorts; everyone was doing the best they could.

The oily smoke, billowing like a living black mist on the fitful leftovers of storm winds, came from the remains of the ship upon which Iheolon had attempted to escape.

"We got off lightly. It might have been worse. Too bad we didn't catch Iheolon and Motuk, but at least they're no longer a problem." As true as the words were, Semage hated saying them; they sounded so banal in the aftermath, in this reality they stood in. The larger scope of their success meant everything to Nyorfias and Epnoce. Yet, at the same time, on a personal level, it seemed somehow so meaningless.

So he remained silent, like the officer alongside, eyes assessing the inferno on the field, ears listening to the reports on several handfuls of channels covered by the broadrange command frequency of his pcom. Only long practice allowed them both to filter the welter of messages while continuing with matters in their immediate vicinity, a talent honed to a reflex similar to the one used to chase away an annoying insect.

The infiltration had started easily, but by the time they had worked toward the offices and command centers of the Base's different units, the silent invasion had escalated into an all-out battle. The closer any Free Army unit had been to a command center, the better the Coalition troops guarding them. B-troop and a handful of infantry had stormed the 2023rd's offices, encountering Iheolon's more elite troopers. Fortunately, thought Semage, by that time they'd found enough ordnance and able-bodied personnel to even the odds.

Semage knew that at least a third of the 2023rd stationed at Aurora had been casualties, two- and four-legged alike. He didn't know how many infantry personnel were killed or seriously injured, but it had to be nearly as many. He shifted his stance to ease the new set of SMG burns that scored the outside part of his left thigh and made sure the camo tape he'd slapped over the scorched rents in his clothing was still tight.

The dead still lay where they had fallen since those living were still being assisted, the missing still being sought. The fighting had been fiercest along this path, where Semage and Yidnar now stood. It had ended out there where a firestorm still raged.

"If it hadn't been for the Ice Beasts . . ." Semage's voice trailed off.

Major Yidnar's gloved hand closed firmly over his left shoulder, firmly enough that Semage felt the distinct impression of every long, blunt-tipped finger.

"One of our more fortunate alliances. But tell me, you mentioned Motuk and Iheolon were seen going for the shuttle—but not Sclamuse."

Semage inwardly berated himself for the oversight. "We caught him—rather, a few GIs caught him. I did confirm that with my own eyes. He's confined and under as heavy a guard as we can spare right now."

Yidnar nodded. "Now we—" His statement was checked as a message came over the general channel shared by all military personnel. In a voice steady yet tinged with exhaustion and emotion, the infantry officer who was commander of Aurora Base confirmed the installation was now secure, and commended the whole of Aurora Base, those fallen as well as those alive. He then went on with some updates and requests for reports.

"Iheolon left him for dead, too," Semage told Yidnar quietly even as they listened. "Good thing no one bothered to double-check or take a second shot. Tris's medtech said the Colonel's left arm was gone completely, and he'll need major reconstruction of his shoulder before he can get fitted for a prosthesis."

Yidnar puffed out a breath. "Deities. Damn Iheolon. I suppose it's a good thing he's dead. Had we taken him alive—"

"*I* would have killed him and taken the consequences from MainCommand and the Planetary Council. Damned if I would let a disease like that simply get locked away to wait for some GTC trial. Like Sclamuse, damn it all. He's lucky one of F-troop didn't find him first. Or me. I'd—" The words burst from Semage's mouth like vomit, hot and acidic. He was shocked he had allowed them to escape in such a manner, but felt not in the least apologetic for them.

"You're not alone in your sentiment."

"Rimms was out there."

* * * * *

Major Yidnar glanced over, but Semage stared straight ahead. The younger man was calm once more, yet the flash of anger and raw grief in his voice didn't go unnoticed.

"Rimms was with you a long time." Yidnar had no clue to the identity of any of the mixed group who'd given everything to keep Iheolon from taking his escape.

"Not as long as Mahrhys was with you, sir." Semage's swallow was audible.

Yidnar again squeezed Semage's shoulder. The losses had been heavy for them all. He closed his eyes briefly only to see again the demise of the Coalition troopshuttle that had brought Iheolon's division. As it had the first time, the action unfolded in that strange, slow motion of dreams.

The lumbering Coalition troop shuttle straining to gain altitude at head-height above the pourstone. A half-platoon's worth of mixed Special Forces and infantry, distinguished only by the properties of the uniforms, close, too close to backwash of blast and emissions, but undeterred by them. A GI taking aim with a shoulder mounted missile launcher, someone in a snow-colored Special Forces uniform acting as backup. The small arms fire from the others may have caused minor damage to the big ship, but it was the true trajectory of the missile that sped right up the atmospheric engine's giant intake vent that brought it down . . . .

295

Debris had barely missed Semage and Yidnar, even as far away as they'd been. The concussion had blown them back a good ten lengths. Both of them were singed. If not for the thickness of their anoraks and leg coverings, both would more than likely be covered with cuts. Where the material wasn't scorched, it looked as if it had been slashed with a million tiny knives.

Maybe when this mess was sorted out they would even resolve what the GI's name had been, who anyone else, besides Rimms, in that indomitable group had been. The explosion had engulfed them all, flattened that end of the Base. It would burn for hours yet, and they would allow it to burn itself out. Only when personnel checked in, unit commanders reported those present and those missing, and the results checked against bodies from elsewhere still complete enough to be identified, would any casualties from the airfield be determined.

"Has anyone heard from Rett?" Yidnar asked finally. "H'vren tells me he can reach to H'chan, but H'chan can't respond. H'vren can't get enough of a link to determine what happened to him."

"H'ting said the same thing. Her pcom's off, sir. None of us has picked up a return signal. And trust me, sir; I think every single one of us has tried more than once." Semage eyed him. "You'd better get inside, Major, and finish gearing up if you're going to stay out here."

"Won't be much use to anyone if I freeze myself," Yidnar agreed. He spun away from the site of the smoldering ship and strode back toward his control center. Semage followed. Everywhere they passed, everywhere they looked, the complement of Aurora Base was outdoors, pulling their snowy fortress together again.

"Where's Sergeant Ariam? She's indicated nothing amiss?"

"Yes, sir, she has. Several times."

Yidnar shot the B-troop leader a glare. "And?"

Semage kept his voice level. "At each of those times, sir, we had more immediate priorities."

The Major nodded, accepting that as well as the fresh pain in the younger man's hazel eyes.

"Since we had yet to completely secure the Base, I kept Ariam's information quiet. This is the first open moment we had since we infiltrated." Semage gestured. "She's there, sir, with Med Shenyver."

"Sergeant Ariam!"

Yidnar's tone prompted her immediate response. As she drew close, he took one good look at the portion of her face visible through the snow goggles. Yidnar felt his stomach drop. The hopelessness in Ariam's tear-filled eyes modulated into concern and alarm as she drew nearer.

"Med!" Ariam's sharp summons was no less peremptory than Yidnar's had been.

Med Shenyver glanced up, stared at him, and started to rise. "Major—?"

Yidnar had forgotten about the blood all over his face: Iheolon's artwork, now dried. Along with an accumulation of greasy soot, it was the only thing between his skin and the frigid air. The notice from the medtech and the B-troop second only added to Semage's reminder that he finish gearing up before he became frostbitten and was added to the casualties.

"No, Shenyver, I'm all right."

Shenyver gave him a second, more assessing, glance before nodding. She then returned her attention to the pretreatment of her casualties and those helping to get them moved indoors.

"Sir," insisted Ariam, "let me check—"

He intercepted the B-troop second's hand, gripping it firmly. "Ariam, I'm all right. But I need to know about Rett." He needed to know and dreaded her answer.

"I don't know where she is—that way, somewhere, not anywhere close. I haven't had time to focus completely—" Her words were clear, voice steady despite the harsh sorrow visible in her eyes. Duty kept her anchored and steady, but for Ariam, her duty now was a cruel diversion, not a kind one.

"You have time now. Is she dead?"

Ariam closed her eyes for a moment. "It won't be long."

A transmission over the Easy Force command channel, which the three of them monitored, alerted them.

"Razor Lead, this is Fang Two, we're picking up a heat source and ident signal bearing east, about five miles out. It was moving, but it just stopped. It's H'chan, sir—"

Although Sergeant Tris was currently acting Easy Force commander, Yidnar cued his pcom instantly and interrupted Trebor's report. "How long ago, Fang Two?"

"Less than a minute." Trebor, as Yidnar had come to expect, didn't sound surprised.

"We've several snow rovers idling, Force One," put in Sergeant Tris over the com. "We can be there in about eight minutes. Permission to send—"

"Yes. Fang Two, designate a team and pick me up on your way out, and get your medtech if you have to drag him by the hair," Yidnar said. "Razor Lead, you're in charge of any Special Forces concerns on this Base until we get back. Bronze and Dart Leads will assist."

"Understood. Keep us informed."

"Major," said Sergeant Semage, "take Ariam with you."

It would be better for Ariam to go. Easier for her to deal with the worst in a more open setting, better for them both if they managed to reach Rett while any life remained in her. Yidnar was going to ask the B-troop leader, but Semage had also need of his second-in-command and her unique abilities and skills.

"This is a family emergency, in more ways than one," Semage went on, and Yidnar knew the younger man had been having the same thoughts.

Combined with the emotion she already generated, visibly and temporally, the dazed surprise and gratitude from Ariam was like a break of clear sunlight from heavy cloud.

"Come on." Yidnar took a firm handful of Ariam's outer garment, nodding his thanks to Semage.

"I'll have Medical ready and get a vet med and transport organized to follow you out in case we need one for H'chan," Semage called after them. "And I'll make sure someone's on Jaq Pym."

Yidnar nodded again, already a handful of lengths away, making more pcom transmissions as he went.

3.3.10 **Unspecified location**

RETT CAUGHT A BREATH AND blinked. One moment she'd been certain she had died. And here she was in the snow. Unable to move. Staring up at H'chan and a stranger in Coalition winter garb.

No, not a stranger. She blinked and the features, uncovered in the bitter cold, sharpened. The face was heavy, the flare of the jawbone and gray hue of the skin marked him as Yixolryn. She'd never even imagined seeing him again, as a humanoid or in his natural form. But she knew who he was.

Colonel Mott. No, she reminded herself, not Mott. Motuk Iheolon. The sleeper agent.

He stared down at her with a growing expression of contempt and triumph.

"Now I have you," he said softly, voice rich with victory and much deeper than before. "After all my trouble and all this time—now I have you."

What's going on? Vaguely, she wondered why she felt no pain, why she didn't feel cold. She couldn't move, although nothing restricted her. "What happened, H'chan?" she thought to the Beast, not daring to test her voice.

He didn't respond. Those beautiful amethyst eyes looked at her with no interest or expression whatsoever—the eyes of an animal without wit and intelligence, the eyes of a mere beast of burden.

What's happening? thought Rett wildly as the humanoid continued to change before her. She'd heard of alien shapeshifters but had never encountered one; at least not one she knew was a shapeshifter. Nor had she ever heard of such beings among the Yixolryn Coalition. There were rumors of the device created by

Sclamuse Iheolon that altered DNA and outward appearance somewhat, but not in her wildest dreams did she imagine such a change would take place in moments. Not like this.

Real fear squeezed her guts.

"What's happening? You're out of the Game. You belong to me now, Knight-Protector. And I have long awaited this victory, however small!" The being's voice had deepened into the bass ranges. It laughed again, cruelly.

The transformation became complete before Rett's bewildered, apprehensive eyes. Bending over her, gloating, was a tall, powerful creature. Eyes as bright as meteors flamed from a face without feature or distinction, a nebulous darkness rather than skin and bones. It was clad in black metallic armor that seemed to crackle and spark with electricity.

"H'chan!" thought Rett, reaching desperately for something familiar.

H'chan, too, had changed. In the place of the Ice Beast, there stood a huge winged creature. It gave a harsh scream, its sable wings snapped open and closed with the sound of thunder.

"W-what's going on? Who are you?" Rett's hoarse voice cracked. She forced it steady. "Who are you?" she repeated.

The alien laughed again and straightened, fully three lengths tall. The wind whipped a black cloak from massive, armored shoulders. The blazing eyes bored right through her, and even if she wanted to, Rett couldn't look away.

"I am known in this Game as Xonomer. I am your final destiny. Pheasyce, the weak neophyte Guardian of this world, has failed to maintain their precious Balance. You've played well, as I have said, but you are mine now. I control you. I own your mind and thoughts and soon, very soon, I will own the whole of you."

His words and voice pressed into her powerless body like boulders. "You will beg me to take your soul. Soon, Knight, very soon, you will play the Game *against* that upstart opponent of mine and deliver the killing blow."

At first, she didn't get the reference to night. It had been day-light—such as daylight was this time of year on Aurora. Before she could think about it any more, Xonomer leaned toward her.

"Yes, of course your culture has no reference. No matter, you are no longer a key Player, defender of Balance, for the upstart neophyte. You are now my new key Player, and it's time to end this match."

"I don't understand," Rett forced the words from stiff lips. "What do you mean, a game?" She was scared, from her hair to her toenails, totally and utterly scared. Was she dead, or dreaming?

"You are not dead, or dreaming," said the being who called itself Xonomer. "Your two little worlds and the others controlled by my kin are all merely pieces, matches, or moves in our Game. The true battle is between us." A black gauntlet crashed into the being's armored chest. "We are the ones to whom your people refer with such naïve offhandedness as 'gods' and 'deities'."

Good g— Rett stopped herself before completing her often-used exclamation. The being looming over her, reeking of evil, could in no way be construed as "good". She caught a breath and a sudden rush of insight. *A game! Why is it so familiar . . . a game! All those times, all those situations I've been in that make no logical sense . . . forget those—there have been things about this entire war that defy classification.*

"I see you are beginning to understand me now."

"You call this a *game?*" Her voice was no more than a disbelieving whisper that grew stronger as it went on. "Over twelve years. Hundreds of thousands of lives." A deep, flaming anger consumed her and she wished her eyes were weapons capable of burning out that pair of meteor bright, alien orbs holding her in such helpless thrall. "Our population, reduced over half—and this is a *game to you?*"

She was so tiffed her voice clogged in her throat. Then the cold, cruel laughter of the being crushed her anger back into fear.

"That's why you pathetic, short-lived creatures of flesh exist. There are plenty of lives, enough to waste, more are born." The alien sounded bored. It sounded like Avok. "Avok, yes, a useful and interesting creature, while she lasted. Unfortunately, she was loyal only to herself, to her own vision, and not to the goal. Your Trebor did me a service, killing her. But come, we must be off. Enough time was spent on this move."

The being picked her up with one hand as easily as she could pick up her kitbag, and mounted the monstrous space-black bird-creature that had once been H'chan.

Only it wasn't a creature. Whatever it was launched into flight, a dizzy rush of speed and light nearly causing her to black out.

What am I going to do now? This can't be real. I'm not even on Aurora any more, much less on Epnoce. Or am I? Those look like stars going past . . . It has to be a bad dream. I was hit in the head pretty hard with something . . . I must be . . .

"Do you think you are dreaming because you feel no pain?" A great, nasty laugh rang out, crashing over the thunder of their passage through space. "I took the pain away because I needed your undivided attention. Here then, have it back."

The instant return of pain took her breath and sight. She struggled for control. She had to stay on top of this . . . whatever it was. But how could she stay on top of something that knew her thoughts almost before they surfaced into her consciousness?

Desperate, she considered giving in to the pain. At least if she was unconscious she wouldn't have to listen or think.

At once, her body was numb again. Xonomer laughed down at her. "There is nothing you can hide from me. No escape. No matter how much pain you feel or do not feel, you will not become unconscious, nor sleep, nor will you die, unless I wish it," it taunted.

Now it sounds like Iheolon. Out will come the devices and drugs to make sure I stay awake to feel everything.

Xonomer's amusement peaked. "Unlike my former key Player, the one you know as Iheolon, I have no need of such artificial aides."

"Iheolon . . . is dead?"

"Does it matter? I have no further use for him so he is no longer in the Game." A black-gloved hand waved in dismissal. "I must admit disappointment over the lost opportunity for a rematch between the two of you. I did so enjoy those of the past."

Rett bared her teeth, scrambling to redirect and blank out her mind. Physical pain she could handle, and she'd made her hearing selective when she wanted to. But while she could deter a moderate probe from an empath, she'd never been trained to block a direct attack. None of them had been given that type of training, except perhaps for the Major during his time with the GTC Rangers.

But . . . maybe if I imagine I can—

No. The alien was there, preventing her, mocking her, ripping her to shreds.

Don't give in, don't give up! No fear, no pain—it can't hurt you!

The alien's mocking words and cruel laughter promptly shattered what fragile barriers she'd attempted to construct. "Oh, do not stop," Xonomer told her. "Do go on. Your thoughts amuse me, and I will enjoy the taming all the more now that you are mine!"

An armored limb crushed Rett against the hardness of the metal surrounding the alien form. They hurtled forward, stars and planets, even galaxies, rushed past in a blur.

I'm flaming tired of providing amusement to the likes of you. Rett rallied herself, found some power in her numbed limbs. She closed her eyes and struggled with desperate savageness. Xonomer's arm crushed her, making her feel as if her body from hips to shoulders had been flattened entirely. The crushing tentacles of Avok's Unethi guard, Wik, was a baby's grip compared

303

to this. Rett opened her mouth, but no sound emerged, not even a gasp. The pain returned, more intense than ever, blinding her mind, burning. It filled her entire being with a frozen fire and her ears rang with hateful, triumphant laughter as her body, unable to fight Xonomer, went limp, powerless.

An instant later Rett became aware they were no longer madly careering through the universe. Instead, she was lying flat, on a cold, hard surface. There was a powerful presence of voices. The unseen chorus repeated her every thought, reverberating and echoing them maddeningly, continuously.

She tried to move, failed. The ugly specters rose, ghosts from the nightmares that would never leave her. Biting back a sound that would have emerged as a whimper, Rett fought to control both her mind and body. Her heart raced so swiftly she felt as if it would explode from her chest. She was exhausted and afraid. It would be so easy just to give up—

" . . . so easy to give up!" mocked the voices.

"I won't!" she yelled and the voices screamed it back at her in a sarcastic echo. "I never give up!"

" . . . never give up! Never give up . . ."

Xonomer was next to her. She didn't get an impression of male or femaleness from it once it no longer looked like the part Yixolryn agent she had once known as Colonel Mott. She didn't have a doubt that it could appear as whatever it wanted her to perceive. *I'm not going to look with my eyes, then.* She squeezed them closed before the terrible glowing eyes could burn through her. A breeze—or was it the alien's breath?—fanned icy and hot against her face. The jeering voices became taunts, the crude remarks of Coalition troopers she couldn't see.

It's not real. This isn't real. It's hallucination. I just have to wait it out . . .

"Oh, it's real all right, Sarge." The voices became one voice, female. A familiar voice, but so full of hate and anger Rett thought she was mistaken in identifying it.

"You? Make a mistake with a voice? Impossible."

Rett gasped in disbelief. "Gerrale!" She opened her eyes and wished she hadn't.

Junior Sergeant Gerrale stood nearby, soaking wet from rain and the puddle of floodwater in which Rett had last seen her. Water and blood made dark streaks on the squadleader's features, matted her hair. More dripped from her body. The other side of her head was burned and blistered, scorched black from the point-blank stunner shot that had been delivered by Rett's own hand.

Gerrale moved closer, droplets of water and blood falling over Rett like rain. "No, you never make mistakes. Except with me." Looking down with accusation and rage, Gerrale said through bloody lips, "I didn't want to die."

The scene at the Wide River Gap bridge, in the dark, thick dampness, flashed back in the clarity of daylight. Gerrale's broken body, Med's bitter resignation and failure, Rett's doubts, insecurities, agony for those already dead. Gerrale had asked for her, and she had come to give her mercy. As Rett asked her for confirmation, if she was sure this was her choice, things changed. Instead of calm acceptance and encouragement this time, the dying commando's face contorted in denial and horror as Rett pulled her close and squeezed the trigger anyway.

"You killed me!" Gerrale's harsh, hating scream tore through Rett's guts like a frag grenade. "Just like you killed the others! Oh, I forgot. You don't make mistakes, so you must have planned it. I know why—so you could be a hero!"

"That's not true. I—"

"You did! Oh, yes! From the start. Starting with me. So you wouldn't feel useless and like the failure you are. To prove yourself to your father! And damn anyone who stood in your way!" screamed Gerrale. "Well, you bought your Freedom Star and your father with our blood. We were stupid enough to think we could follow you through anything. Was it worth it?"

305

But my father had nothing to do with my enlistment or my choices. I never mentioned my father or what happened to anyone until—

Gerrale sneered. "You didn't have to. It wasn't a secret. We might not have figured Ariam for your sister, but *everyone* knew Colonel Reve was your father. We just never mentioned it because you didn't."

"Gerrale's right."

Now Kraym was there, standing next to Gerrale. Her former co-second's melted corrective lenses hung askew over blind eyes; over roasted, blistered skin split open to reveal horrible purple-red flesh and scorched bone beneath. As he spoke the motion of blackened gums and singed teeth was visible through the gaping opening where his left cheek used to be. Shreds of muscle and skin over his shattered ribcage barely hid the struggling flutter of his lungs.

"Kraym," she whispered, her voice and body trembling. No wonder he shut down. No wonder Med was unable to save him. Tears blurred them both into more horribly distorted images. "Kraym. I wasn't there—"

"Too flaming right you weren't there," he snarled and bloody froth sprayed over her from his cheekless, lipless face. "Then it might've been you, as it should have been, instead of me."

"I was ordered to go on leave," Rett gasped, forcing her protest through numbed lips. He'd wanted her to go, thought it was a great idea!

"You would have been there if you'd taken your leave of absences regularly instead of ignoring them. You never think ahead. Never thought of what you did affecting anyone else in the long run." Kraym snorted with contempt, spraying more horrible fluid and bits of burnt skin into Rett's face.

Guilt hammered hard, drove sharper than azurium-alloyed metal through her head and heart, stung more painfully than the incandescent kiss of an energy beam grazing her skin.

"You killed me, too."

It was Zhent. Her first squadleader, from C-troop, her first assignment after training. "You didn't have to hit me that hard. You just wanted to make sure I'd never wake up to tell my side."

"Your side? You ambushed and attacked *me*. You were leaving me for the Coalition to pick up!"

Rett squeezed her eyes closed as the memory flared strong.

"You knew I was being controlled, you could have pulled that punch. You just wanted to be squadleader."

She shook her head. "That's not true, I never—"

A host of other dead soldiers joined Kraym and Gerrale, everyone she knew or had seen killed. From past to present they came: infantry, AirSpacefighters, civilians; young, old, and in-between. They were all there, accusing, seeking revenge; declaring themselves casualties not of the war, but of Rett's selfish, log-headed pride.

"It's not true! I did my best for—"

"For yourself. Always for yourself."

Through her increasing weight of guilt and self-doubt threaded icy-hot, mocking, triumphant laughter. A huge, hazy shadow was imposed over the ghosts of the dead: that of an armored alien, his unseen visage oozing victory, glorying in the ease of her defeat.

"NO! Damn you!" Rett shouted, putting all her futile energy at physical movement into focusing on what she believed was the truth. She wasn't going to deny the fact that her Basic training might have been fueled by the anger and hurt she'd felt toward her father. All that had changed by the time she joined Special Forces. All she had ever wanted was to do her part to keep her homeworlds free. To keep what had happened to her family from happening to others. And once the threat of the Coalition had ended, all she wanted was to go quietly home.

Rett managed to close her eyes, shutting out the faces, willing the hating voices to cease. "It's not real! None of this is real . . ."

"It's just a bad dream, *kelani*, wake up," she heard someone say in that tone he used with such love. Jaq's voice. It sounded so beautiful she felt fresh tears come to her eyes. She opened them and through the swimming haze saw his familiar wild hair, the light reflecting from it until it wreathed his head and face in flame.

"Rett. Are you with me?"

What would he accuse her of? Was he now going to throw their reconciliation into her face? She didn't want to hear it. *No. Go away. Let me keep my memories of you as they were most recently.* Closing her eyes again, she felt more tears well up, spill over.

Gentle fingers touched her face. "Wake up, everything's going to be all right."

Was it possible? she wondered, needing to hope. Maybe they were still napping in each other's arms, wedged cozy and warm between H'chan and H'tero, whom Jaq called Killer. *Maybe this is the nightmare.*

She opened her eyes. No, they weren't outdoors, but Jaq was there, his face close, loving, full of concern.

"Jaq! I—"

More words silenced as his lips met hers. Those few stolen moments on the ride and during the rest stop came back in a rush. Her entire being yearned for him as strongly now as it had before, and her eager response came from relief as much as desire. She soon realized the frosty chill pulsating through her was not her usual reaction to Jaq's kisses, the dark aura enveloping her was not the familiar one she associated with the Zetinorian. Another illusion, another trick!

"No," she said, trying to turn her face aside. Her body refused to obey. "Jaq, stop. I can't move," she whispered, panic stabbing her deeper than any physical wound.

"Easy, *kelani*," whispered Jaq.

His hands soothed her face and head with the delicacy that never failed to amaze and delight her. Now his touch brought reassurance. His incredible sapphire eyes were dark with love and concern. The smile he gave her made her forget she couldn't move, and as his lips met hers again, liquid fire coursed through her veins, making her immobile body throb with a sweet ache. The warmth was delicious after the marrow deep ice. This was Jaq's kiss, his lips, his face—

The aura was still wrong, and as much as she wanted Jaq, trusted him, it had to stop.

"Jaq," gasped Rett, between his kisses, torn again between giving in to him and the discomfort from her inability to reciprocate. "Jaq, I can't move—stop."

He pulled back a little, a furrow deepening in his forehead. With a deep sigh he said, "You were badly hurt, *kelani*."

That's what they said before.

There had been another time she regained consciousness in a Nyorfian hospital, unable to move anything but her eyes and lips. Except for those few semiconscious moments when she was sure her father had been present, she had been among strangers. Even after she had become fully awake, there were no familiar faces or voices to reassure her. Only an endless stream of well-meaning medical staffers that kept evasively telling her she'd been badly hurt.

"You're safe . . . You've been badly hurt . . . We have to keep you immobile until . . . Don't try to move . . ."

The time before that . . . several months into her first combat assignment. When she'd been set up and ambushed by Sergeant Zhent, who'd all but paralyzed her with a point-blank stun in the spine.

All but. She'd still ended up killing him . . .

Her breath caught. "I can't go through this again." The words came on a low moan of despair. Fresh tears rose to make her vision swim. "I can't . . . I can't, Jaq—"

"Easy." The voice was his. Warm, soothing and gentle. His powerful blue eyes drew her in. Rett slowly relaxed. Jaq was here now. Her salvation now as he was three years before, before she even knew him. The unknown Coalition trooper who gave her the chance for life or a more dignified death . . . the man who loved her and taught her to love again.

"I'm glad you're here," she whispered.

"Only for a minute. I have to go."

Her heart jolted painfully in her chest. "Why? What happened?"

"Oh—well, everything went all right with the Base and all," he said quickly. "We took it back. There were some losses, but that happens. I have to go. I couldn't leave without saying goodbye. I'll come and visit at least once a year. They're waiting for me." He leaned close and kissed her again. "Goodbye, Rett."

"Jaq, what are . . . ? Losses? Who? Leaving?" She couldn't breathe. Her voice squeaked from her throat. "You've just returned. Where?"

"Well, since you're paralyzed, I got another job—" His voice faded as he moved away from her.

Paralyzed! What? "Jaq! Deities! But . . ." His leaving upset her more than his admission of her physical state. Rett struggled, in vain, to make her body move, to turn her head to see him go.

"Look, I'll send you a nice long letter. My transport is leaving. Good-bye, Rett."

The one breath she managed to jerk into her lungs left her with a gasp of disbelief and shock. The terror of inertia paled beside her sensation of loss. A great wide gulf of loneliness, once closed, yawned open again and she was falling . . .

3.3.11 UNSPECIFIED LOCATION EAST OF AURORA BASE, EPNOCE
0536.03.12 (LOCAL RECKONING)

"There."

Ariam tried to pierce the blowing snow with her eyesight. She had to clench her fists not to reach out and snatch the VARs from Major Yidnar's hands. Instead, she pulled up her breath muffler and adjusted her goggles, and was the first one out of the rover and running—wading, rather—through the wind-combed powder toward a hump in the otherwise flat expanse.

"Be careful, Sergeant," warned the voice of the vet med on the general com band. "He might—"

The hump of snow exploded and Ariam jumped back barely in time to avoid the swipe of a deadly antler. Swaying on his feet, head lowered, steam jetting from his nostrils, H'chan prepared to charge.

"H'tan!" Ariam again appealed to her Beast, glad they were still in telepathic contact. "Help me!" She lunged forward, getting to H'chan's shoulder where it was harder for him to reach her with his antler or a kick. "H'chan, it's me, it's Ariam. We're here to help." She projected her meaning to him as strongly as she could.

"H'chan says his Rett needs help," said H'tan in her mind.

"I know. Where is she? How far?" She leaned against the H'chan as he stood spraddle-legged, trying to calm the shuddering that racked his body. For the first time she saw the bloody stump on his head where another proud antler used to be. The middle tine on the remaining one was broken. His fur was streaked with blood and she knew some of it had to be Rett's.

"Rear paw is shot up pretty badly, too."

This time the voice was at her side, and it was Major Yidnar's. He took H'chan's drooping head in his hands and from the expression on his face, Ariam knew he was communicating through H'vren.

The vet-med and the three F-troopers who'd come to help him took over the wounded Beast.

Ariam pointed along the path the Beast had come, one almost completely erased by the blowing snow. "We need to go this way." She'd learned the Beasts traveled in perfectly straight lines through the open spaces. She hoped that was true for Beasts with wounded paws and head injuries, because that was all they had.

Because she wasn't getting anything from Rett any more. With that thought, the barely flickering light that was her sister's constant connection in her mind was gone.

3.3.12 **Unspecified location**

THE HUNTING CRY OF THE snow growtu roused her. Opening her eyes, Rett noticed she was in a part of the Auroran forest she recognized. She wasn't lying down, rather, she was upright, her arms over her head somewhere, most of her weight on them, her back against a tree. The brutish, heavy-featured faced of Commander Iheolon swam before her eyes.

"What?" To Rett's shock, her disbelieving word came right out.

"Killer." Iheolon smiled.

Whenever Rett had faced Iheolon in the past, she'd always experienced a fleeting moment where she wondered how the wide, ridged skull with its flaring jawbones had passed through a humanoid birth canal. Just as quickly, she would tell herself that she couldn't begin to imagine Iheolon had at all ever been an infant, much less one that had been born of woman. This flash would bring her humor; her humor would be channeled into the strength she needed to endure whatever terrible reality would follow. The partial grin she would allow to flash at him in an offhand gesture of indifferent contempt would drive part of the reason from the deep-set black eyes of the half Yixolryn.

This time, however, Rett only felt shock and confusion. Wasn't he supposed to be dead? Or at least out of the picture? For that matter, what was she doing here?

From the pleased expression growing on the features of the enemy officer, what she felt was entirely visible on her face just as clearly as it had been expressed in her voice.

Iheolon, still smiling, lifted a hand, pushed the flat of it against her forehead. Against the back of her head, she felt the rough caress of the peculiar, peeling tree bark of the common

Auroran evergreen. In her nostrils was the unique yet oh-so familiar resiny fragrance and the shocking, tissue-shrinking cold of the Auroran air.

"They don't eat carrion, you know. So you have to be alive when they come. We'll give them some fresh incentive," he said.

Give whom what? And why?

A knife was in his hand. Hers, clean and free of camo tape. A squeeze of his hand extended the full length of the blade and the flash of light off the brushed metal nearly blinded her. His hand on her forehead moved to her chin, angling her head up sharply. A sharp line of heat was drawn across her throat. Iheolon's breath was hot on her face as he peered close to examine his work. "A bit deeper than I thought. No matter. I'll be watching. Don't disappoint me."

He let her go and turned away, leaving her alone.

"What in two worlds?" No words came, only an ugly, spluttering sound from somewhere below her chin. Instead of being unable to breathe, the air her lungs demanded she inhale and expel sucked and gurgled from the opening across her throat. The sound of it sickened her. She tried to move, she had sensation in every part of her body, but her muscles from the nape of her neck down refused to respond.

Why am I back here, and why this? This never happened. What is Iheolon doing here? Another, more horrifying thought rose. *What if I never left in the first place, and what I think happened after I crashed—was only a dream? What if this is the reality?*

The growtu pack broke from the trees, the giant form of the silver pack leader coming straight for her.

The growtu's heavy body smashed into her helpless one, throwing her so hard against the tree her arms were jerked from their sockets. His teeth closed on her flightsuit, rending it open with three mighty shakes of his powerful head and shoulders. His fangs slashed at her, opening the flesh across her ribs, ripping into her belly.

The shock of the first attack left her breathless. Then the rest of the pack joined in, snarling, slashing, rending and ripping at her with ferocious intensity. Unable to vocalize her pain, voluntarily or not, she could only endure it.

Then all was silent. The growtus were gone, leaving her hanging by her wrists, struggling to suck in air from the hole in her windpipe, staring down at the remains of her torn body. Watching the steam rise from her guts strewn on the blood-soaked snow.

I guess I didn't taste very good, she thought, but her attempt to humor herself out of a bad situation fell flat. *Why did they leave me?* Tears leaked slowly from her eyes and burned acid on her face.

"Rett."

Evetez. She knew his voice. She lacked the energy to respond, to raise her head, to move her lips.

"Good deities," said another familiar and loved voice: Semage. Shock made his normal tone crack into the ranges of a young boy.

Why did you come? You came for nothing . . . Iheolon will be back!

Strong fingers gently tilted her face toward the source of the voice. "Oh, Rett," Evetez whispered. Those mischievous blue eyes filled with tears of compassion. "I'll here. I'll help."

"Deities, 'Vetez, don't make her wait." Semage came into her range of vision. The expression of horror and sorrow on the faces of both her longtime friends sent fresh waves of pain through her mangled body.

Just go, Rett's mind cried to them. As much as she now craved relief from her torment, she didn't want it at the expense of her friends. *Iheolon used me to trap you . . . just go now!*

Evetez lifted his sidearm into her range of vision and the touch of his fingers on her face became a caress. "Rett?"

She knew her eyes gave him an answer as clear as words, no matter how the rest of her begged him to leave, as quickly as possible. Danger was coming. She would die soon enough, they shouldn't waste what little time they had to escape waiting for Iheolon's trap to close. *Go. Go now. Please* — Again, she tried to make words come from her mouth, but the knife had taken her voice.

Then before anything else could happen, the crackle and thunder of SMG weapons shattered the stillness of the snowy forest.

"No!" The scream only had volume in her imagination. The fingers so gently cradling her head stiffened for a heartbeat. Abruptly her head, unsupported, dropped toward her chest, giving her an unrestricted, grisly view of the ground around her feet strewn with the contents of her lower body.

316

Into Rett's line of vision fell Evetez. From where he lay in the stinking pile of her entrails, he stared up at her and she watched the light slowly fade from his eyes.

"The other one is dead, too, Killer."

The thud she heard—that unmistakable sound of a heavy boot slamming into an inert body—brought another sharp cry of protest from her very center, which exhaled as a gagging noise. Semage's headless body was again brutally kicked into her sight, which soon mercifully blurred with fresh tears.

As much as Rett knew her friends had come of their own will, she couldn't turn aside her guilt, her grief, the horrible knowledge that because of their love for her, others would suffer. Ariam, Carakenne, how many other lovers and friends? A terrible spasm shook her. *I killed them, as surely as if I fired the shots that did it.* More tears came, crystallized on her cheeks. Hideous gasping, sucking sounds emerged from her throat.

The cold, gloved fingers of Iheolon's hand dug roughly into her face as he lifted it for his inspection. Contempt and satisfaction oozed from every pore. The Coalition officer laughed aloud in triumph. "And I have it all recorded . . . it could have used some screaming on your part, but—well, I'll dub that in later, from your sister, perhaps. I promise you I will enjoy her screams."

"*No—*" Her breath failed her, not even a gasp escaping this time. The darkness beckoned, promising an unending, unfeeling safety she didn't have the strength to refuse.

There will be no coming back from there, part of her mind warned.

Come back . . . for what. Why. Nothing left. I have nothing left. Even as she cried this out in the emptiness of her thoughts, she knew she was wrong. But she was so tired . . . she needed to sleep.

I'll let you sleep for a few minutes. But not there . . . not there.

I can't go anywhere else. Ears still burning with Iheolon's laughter, Rett closed her eyes and let herself go.

3.3.13 Unspecified location

"RETT."

I can't do this again I can't

"Rett." The voice came again, commanding, insistent. She tried to ignore it, ignore the growing brightness and warmth the voice led her toward. She was desperate to sink back into the void from which she was so inexorably pulled. As cold and empty as it had been, there wasn't any pain, physical or otherwise.

The voice wouldn't allow it. It gripped her and refused to let go. She was too tired to fight it.

No! *I can't do this again I can't go there go away leave me alone I don't want to come back*

"Come on, Sergeant! Come up. *Now.*"

She hated him, hated him for being impossible to disobey, for the power of his voice and the compulsion of his aura. Damn it, why couldn't he just leave her alone? Let her stay where it was safe for a while? Pain flooded her, crashing into her with the actinic brightness of multiple lightning strikes.

She opened her eyes, narrowing them against the light. Less than a second's assessment told her she still lacked control over her limbs.

"That's it. Stay with me, Rett."

Yes, *he* was there, same as last time. There to yank her into reality and keep her there no matter what. Her throat closed with the recollection of that long-ago episode, when Medical had kept her even more immobilized that Iheolon had.

No! I can't stay here. I can't do this again!

"Easy, sport. Breathe."

She wanted it to be him. She needed to believe it was him. Deities, she needed to trust someone.

She forced words from her numb lips. "Major, I can't move. No one will tell me why." She struggled to move her eyes enough to see his face. Panic rose strong—even that much motion was now denied her. She could only stare straight at the ceiling.

You have your voice. So she did, and but what good was that going to do her?

"Apparently you were caught in an explosion. Med's concerned about your spine, there's a bruise the size and shape of the Rift Canyon right in the middle of your back. You've also some bad internal injuries. Took a sliver of debris in the kidney. Have a hole in your lung. Also took a handful of slugs, some SMG. Tore up your shoulder pretty badly. Concussion." He moved into her view, dark blue eyes level and calm. "It won't be for long," he promised. "It's not the same as it was three years ago. You didn't have Med Rhozev back then. He's on top of things, and he says as soon as most of the swelling goes down he'll re-assess. I'm going to be right here. You won't be alone."

She let out a shaky breath of relief. "What happened?"

"You're safe now. We're here. You've been raving, and no wonder. At least three of those new drug darts of Iheolon's hit you out there."

She had to think for a moment. Right before she'd thrown the grenade . . . those stings she'd felt. Was that what they were? "Three of them—?"

"Yes. Shh." Yidnar's firm, callused finger gently stroked her jaw. "Just relax. From what we've been hearing from you, you've had some wild hallucinations."

"It wasn't real . . . ?" Hope rose.

"Not a bit of it."

It wasn't real. Her relief was so sudden and strong she couldn't stop the tears it brought. They filled her eyes, overflowed the hollows they were in, spilled down the sides of her face, into her hair, her ears. Her nose started to clog. Part of her felt a slight chagrin at displaying her reaction so openly. Another part remembered

319

that it was perfectly acceptable, she only had to restrain her feelings around those not Special Forces, hide them completely from an enemy.

Then again, I showed them to Iheolon . . .

"He's still alive—?"

"Iheolon and Motuk tried to escape on their shuttle. They didn't get far. Sclamuse was captured."

"But I saw—" *The Major said it wasn't real,* she reminded herself. *He should know.* Major Yidnar, after all, had managed to see most of his personnel through at least a portion of every stage of their training, knew their weaknesses and strengths, their likes and dislikes, to the last fraction. Told them each personally that they had to let go, and there was nothing wrong with it. Encouraged it at every opportunity, whether they needed to grieve, to laugh, to feel loved or to feel anger, or simply find an outlet for frustration or a reason to celebrate. Their tight discipline made it all the more necessary and important.

His presence now was soothing and supportive, and she was so tired . . . Maybe now she could rest.

"Easy Force? The Base . . . ?"

"You're talking to me, aren't you?" A small grin reassured her that something, at least, had gone according to plan.

"F-troop . . . ?"

"Battered but not broken. A few will be down for a while. You're the most serious casualty from F-troop, sport. We'll tell you all about it later."

She needed to know more. "Evetez and Semage are all right?"

He gave in with a patient nod. "Yes."

"And Jaq didn't leave?"

"What made you think that? It's all any handful of us can do to peel him off the door to this room." He smiled a little. "No more talking now," he added firmly.

She closed her eyes, exhausted.

"Why didn't you tell her the truth?" said the deep baritone of Sergeant Trebor.

Startled by the odd note in her second's tone, she struggled to open her eyelids again, but the crusty, gummy residue of sweat and sickness glued them shut.

"She's too far gone to know the difference," said Yidnar.

Confusion and disbelief froze the breath in her chest. For a long, painful moment hurt and doubt rose, and with the effectiveness of chemical foam on a fire it quenched the warm hope she'd gripped.

Damn it, he lied! Why? What did he mean? What did Trebor mean?

Blind and motionless, stinging with betrayal, aching with anger, Rett sought the darkness this time, wished it back. She was going in and damned if she was going to let herself get hurt any more.

I've taken enough for them. I've given everything. All they can do is lie to me. He lied to me!

A tiny spot of brightness burned through her closed eyes. Through the feelings of hurt and doubt, a voice that should have been familiar yet was not reminded Rett that the Major would never lie to her. With her last breath, or his own, he'd never lie to her, to any of them.

This is not real. *None of this is real.*

She hesitated before plunging into the safety of the shadows. For a moment, she closed her mind to the creeping, nagging possibility that maybe it was true, that everything from Gerrale's accusations to Major Yidnar's lie was the truth; really the way things stood . . . the actual events instead of delusionary inventions.

The doubt and guilt grew anyway, matching her effort to force it back and reason against it. The mocking voices filtered into her ears, into her brain. And she remembered.

NO!

This time, she fought the nothingness into which she'd nearly leaped. Dug in hard with her fingers to stop her momentum. Refused the safety darkness offered—it was a trap, one without hope, from which there would be no escape. Perhaps it offered safety, painlessness, but it also meant giving up herself, her will, her soul.

"NO!" She yelled it with everything she had. "No! This isn't right! This is only Xonomer!"

Her surroundings came back into focus. She forced herself into a sitting position, preparing to fight, gearing her mind for combat. She could move now. She could think—she closed her mind to the sarcastic, mocking chorus.

* * * * *

THE ALIEN ENIGMA WAS FURIOUS that she saw through his deceptions so quickly, yet was pleased her fighting spirit was still intact. But something was wrong with his plan, and his fury swelled. *What is this? Where does her sudden surge of strength come from?*

Snarling, the alien dredged more memories with which to feed her doubts and fears, her despair and aloneness. She was still weak and it was easy enough to crush her into seeking out what he offered her.

* * * * *

THE ILLUSIONS CAME, EACH MORE horrible and twisted than the one before. Helpless again to move, to fight, she tried to control the sobs choking her throat. Only incredulity lent strength to her defiance this time. How dare he use her mother, her brother? As in the incident with the Major, there were things Rett knew that were certain and unchangeable.

Nevertheless, it sure had seemed real . . . too real. Tonia's agonized face, Tovadan's thin, twisted body, burning as Iheolon watched and laughed. The others who'd been on that shuttlecraft, as well, finding the ultimate mercy of being blown to the base elements their bodies were composed of only after Iheolon and the others who'd boarded their craft had nothing left alive to sport with.

That didn't happen!

How do you know it didn't happen? No one knows what happened. All they knew was that the shuttlecraft was attacked, exploded, and there were no survivors.

I know that they didn't suffer. Her conviction shook as the vision loomed again, detailed and graphic.

You know only what you forced yourself to believe. Don't dare admit you had no doubts!

I don't—!

Her mother started to scream. Tovadan's charcoal dark eyes were terrorized, his wiry arms outstretched to her for help. *"Rett! Help me!"*

The muscles knotted in her frozen limbs. "That didn't happen!" *Don't think of it. Think of something else. Think of F-troop—*

"No," she moaned, realizing her mistake the instant the thought left her. Instead of the living, the ghosts of the dead returned to taunt her. The hate and scorn in the voices she loved as much as her own family were too much to bear.

You love them, Pam had said.

Yes. Unconditionally, she had answered.

"I even asked Major Yidnar about it. He told me that people who fight with and for the people they love have more power than any technology in the universe," said Jaq.

Nothing was right.

She had no idea where to turn, what to think.

Brief, bright snatches of reason surfaced in Rett's turbulent mind from somewhere deep inside. A fragile, brilliant light grew, warring with the insidious strength of darkness. A faint mental voice, the same as before, familiar yet unidentified, spoke to her deepest mind with forceful desperation: *You loved and love them all. You must believe in your love. Don't let it go. The only truth . . .*

* * * * *

"THERE IS NO TRUTH!" XONOMER slammed his own thought atop the growing clarity. He tried to find the source. The woman's mind offered no clues, no faces to attach to the voice, no memory of a physical entity. He tunneled savagely through her mind, seeking to destroy the foundation of that deep thread of hope. Failing to find something, anything, the alien maneuvered quickly to nullify it or turn it to his own purpose before she could focus and allow the lambency to increase and destroy everything he so carefully arranged this far.

324

* * * * *

THE LIGHT BURNED HER, PAINFUL and intense. Again, the darkness promised refuge, promised to hide her safe this time from the probing intensity of the beam. The light was nothing more than yet another enemy weapon zeroing in, intent on her destruction; another weird energy field that would return her to unmoving helplessness. Her skin prickled as the field grew, came closer.

Back off! Back off now, before it's too late!

But it was so beautiful. Deadly beautiful. As scintillating like opalescent flashes of light off the snowy surfaces of Epnoce. Writhing and twisting against the surrounding darkness with auroral streaks and ribbons of living, pulsating color. So what if every hair on her body stood on end, every nerve hummed as if she was about to be struck by lightning? She had to touch it, to see if something so beautiful was real. She reached, forcing her arm to move bit by agonizing bit. Stretched her arm and fingers as far as possible.

Take it, Rett—you must take it. The elusive voice encouraged her.

Burning pain, physical and mental, slammed her back.

No, she screamed in incoherent denial as the control only just returning to her slipped out of her grasp. *I have to take it, I'm so close . . . !*

Already the thread of brightness dimmed. It flickered and guttered, its flame about to go out. She again reached for it despite the assault of doubts telling her the light, bright or dimmed, meant death. As her straining fingers neared the thread, it burst into pure crystal brilliance, startling a gasp of awe from her. The hand and arm nearest it burst into flame, her gasp of awe became a harsh shout of pain. Her body twisted in agony, but she didn't pull back. After the ugliness and horror, she wasn't going to pull away from something so vibrant and beautiful . . . and most especially because Xonomer wanted her to!

If this is death, then so be it! she thought, closing her flaming fingers over the fiery pulse of a million suns.

The pain was more than she'd ever experienced. She tried to fight it, but it came too suddenly, too strongly. A tortured scream ripped from the very core of her being. Her own agonized groans beat into her soul. When relief came suddenly, like a windbreak against a blizzard gale, she captured a few gulping, sobbing breaths of air into her straining lungs.

"Come to me. Let it go. There will be no more pain, no more deceptions. You will be immortal and powerful. You will love me, be first among my Players. Let it go, let me take it for you."

"No." Her word emerged as more whimper than rejection.

The molten eyes of Xonomer held her helplessly and again, she was besieged with terrorized agony. Instead of letting go of the thread, she gripped it even tighter, fusing it to her hand, her fingers, making it part of her. Even as Xonomer's assault escalated and Rett's resistance wavered, part of her knew she would never let it go.

Her other defenses buckled, cracked, crumbled. Xonomer's dark hand closed around her mind, the cruel fingers digging deeper than ever before. Panic rose as Rett realized Xonomer had only been toying with her until now.

"Yes, I have yet to begin," he said. "I grow weary of the persuasive approach. Experience now what it will be for you for all eternity if you continue to resist."

He had absolute control of her thoughts. A blizzard of events; every awful thing that had ever happened to her, every deeply repressed memory, was methodically and ruthlessly uprooted and brought to life. For what seemed an eternity she was made to re-experience them all, the incidents made more horrible by the entity's obvious enjoyment. Her social awkwardness as a child and into young adulthood. The deaths of her mother and brother, of friends and people she knew from Treetop who'd gone to fight before she became of age. Her concern over disappointing her father . . . and that horrible scene right before she left . . . twisted beyond her wildest nightmares.

The ghosts of earlier returned, all the soldiers from the time Rett first saw combat, joined with a horde of Coalition officers and troopers in assaulting her with her own insecurities and doubts, her thoughts and concerns, and what she considered personal failures to others.

He dragged out every emotion, every reaction she'd felt yet never displayed. The situation didn't matter. The Rett she was forced to become again didn't try to hide or turn what she felt. This Rett showed everyone exactly what she experienced, every fear, level of pain, every doubt, every revulsion, or terror.

And once more she was a prisoner of Iheolon. More realistically than ever before, she experienced those times over again, in graphic, visible detail. No blindfold left what happened to tactile interpretation or imagination this time. No matter where she looked, whether her eyes were opened or closed, she watched her own body receive the torture and abuse; experienced anew the full range of physical sensations. The taste of blood. The smells of sweat, fear, and rape. The white-hot burns or stabs of different thicknesses of metal sliding between skin and muscle. The sounds of blows against flesh, breaking bones . . . the different noises as they were crushed or struck. The almost clothlike tearing sound sinew and muscle forced past limits could make.

Avok's long, sharp nails tore slowly through her flesh, carving words, designs, the sound of it and her pleasure bringing sickness up to choke Rett. The crude words and cruder actions of Iheolon and his officers, acting out their experiments or ideas upon her body in a hideous parody of a group of scientists performing scholarly research. This time she saw with her own eyes the skin being peeled from her legs, the pulse of her exposed veins, and every involuntary twitch of ropy pinkish-red muscle as layers were carefully parted to expose what lay beneath almost to the bone.

This time she had no control, no hope of respite or rescue. This time, the woman she was forced to witness and become again didn't retain a stoic silence marked only by changes in her breathing. Her screams and retching cries deafened her ears, horrified her by the very fact she allowed them to emerge in front of her enemies—another failure!

"This will mean more than suspension!" thundered a twisted image of Major Yidnar, whose features were fused with those of Iheolon and the lumpy alien commander who invented Iheolon's devices. "This means expulsion! But first—we'll have lunch!"

And joined by the pack of mutant growtus who resembled the big gray beetles of the Barrens, the entire crowd dove upon her helpless, tortured form to feast, ripping into her living flesh with teeth, claws, nails, anything. Just when she thought it had to stop, that they had to run out of body parts, there seemed to be an unending supply of her, enough for all, enough for more.

For an eternity it continued. Over and over again, each time, her enemies were stronger and Rett weaker.

Exhausted past her limits, sobbing, she didn't resist the next relief from the humiliation and pain in the dark embrace of Xonomer. His voice was deep, resonant, and gentle. No longer was it mocking and cold. He held her as gently as if she'd been as fragile as a snowflake.

"You want it to end."

She couldn't answer. Her body shook with such violence the words stuck in her throat, froze in her thoughts.

"Let go of the light. It will stop. Come to me," he whispered, the voice as low and seductive as a lover's. "Be one with me. There will be no pain, no fear. No one could ever hurt you again. All you have to do is let go of the light. It's causing all your pain; can you not feel it burning?"

The flesh was blistering on her bones; the bones themselves conducting searing agony to every fingerlength of her body. Still she held on. Every breath Rett took seemed forced from her quivering soul. The thread of lucent energy she held clenched, fused in her fist, was dulled, but the living heat of it stabbed straight into her heart.

The chorus of echoes screamed and gibbered in the distance, growing louder.

"The thread brings them. The light attracts them just as light and heat attract insects. There will be no end to it this time. You must let it go."

She coughed violently and a sharp ache deep in her side made her gasp. This pain was different. Somewhere she found the energy to think: *this is real.*

"It's holding you here, binding you fast. They will come and tear you apart for eternity. Wouldn't you rather go there?"

Mountains and forest beckoned, a familiar backdrop of the Treetop ranges she'd known since birth. The dark line of peaks stood sharp and clear against a starry night sky. Cadie's Peak punctuated the familiar horizon, its starlit glacier nearly bright as one of Epnoce's moons against the dark rock and deep, safe, secret shadows under the trees.

The sight tore a low moan of longing from her.

"We can get lost there, no one will find us. No pain, no memories, no dreams. Let it go," the alluring voice cajoled.

Home. The lure was intense. *I want to go home.* Her quivering body leaned toward it.

The pain in her side increased; a pulsing, throbbing ache that ebbed and flowed with every beat of her heart, every breath. *This pain is real.* She tore her eyes from the Treetop mountains and closed them tightly, focusing on that different pain, focusing on the thread she gripped.

"Come, we'll go there. Let me take you home."

Dragging her eyelids open, she stared into the alien's blazing eyes. The snarl of the snow growtu twisted her lips, a growl rose from her aching chest.

"Never." She amazed herself at the calm tone of her voice. "You may control my body. You may control my mind. But you'll never possess my soul!"

Her words distorted into another helpless scream of pain. This time, she held onto it, digging her burning hands into the brightening thread of hope she refused to release. "Concentrate on the pain!" she shouted at herself, trying to shut out the echoes around her.

Pain wasn't her enemy. Pain was good. Pain meant she was alive . . . *remember those times you thought you were dead, but it just hurt too much?* If she was alive, she had a chance! *Block him out! Focus.* "Concentrate!"

3.3.14 MEDICAL SECTION, AURORA BASE, EPNOCE
0536.03.19 (LOCAL RECKONING)

MED BARELY TURNED HIS SHOUT of triumph into his habitual sour expression just as his patient opened her eyes and focused them on him. He didn't expect the violent recoil; the instant redirection of any energy she had into a defensive mode. He figured she would be too groggy and in too much pain to do anything but mumble a curse, give him a glance, add that quizzical sideways grin he came to expect some semblance of, no matter what.

" 's up?" she'd ask. He anticipated what she would want to know: *"Everyone okay? Any casualties?"* and the usual answer: *"Theirs first, or ours?"* Then, just how many seconds he'd take to fill her in before her eyes rolled right back in her head again and she went to sleep—a real, healing sleep this time. Not a semi-coma fraught with hallucinations.

At least that was what he'd hoped for.

This surge of fighting energy and an animal sound of threat from her throat, primal and savage, was the last thing he expected.

"No pithy comments this time, Sarge?"

"Back off."

"Take it easy, Sarge, it's just me. Same as ever."

Her mouth twisted into a snarl of repulsion. "Stop trying to delude me."

"Threaten? Yes," said Med, not trying to hide any silly, relieved amusement he felt. "Delusion, no. Not my game. You know that."

"Take your flaming Game and ram it up your ass sideways. I'll never give in."

No, that she wouldn't. "You know, Sarge, I'm glad to see you too. I'm happy you're awake—you have no idea how happy I am. But shut up, all right? I've had just about all I could handle with you this time around."

Med passed a weary hand over his eyes. Okay, unusual wakeup aside, he was still elated beyond belief she'd pulled through whatever nightmare she'd been experiencing and coming back to reality. Ariam would be thrilled, not to mention just about everyone else on Aurora Base. He reached for his Omni and accessed a detailed report from the biomonitor on his patient's left arm.

For a long, long five days, going on six right now, Rhozev had fought the battle of his life to keep her alive. He refused to let this negative waking reaction bother him much. Deities, what could he expect from someone who flatlined at least six times in the first thirty hours after they picked her up, and twice more after that? Not to mention the lung going out on her, thank all deities she'd been unconscious—she never would have tolerated the tracheal airway had she been more aware.

Then there'd been surgery, with her nearly waking up at one point. That would have been a disaster, compounded by her condition and inability to handle anything stronger than the one variety of anesthetic that didn't cause her any complications or hangover effects. He would have had to resort to something stronger and deal with the aftereffects later. The surgery was followed by another flatline an hour into recovery.

Med was most grateful for his timing: he'd removed the tubes snaking into her windpipe, up her nose, down her throat, and everywhere else at new day, just six hours ago. The other medical personnel argued against it. However, Med knew Rett's fears and limitations. Had she awakened and discovered herself so arrayed, the shock and panic would've killed her quicker than a shot in the head.

He blew out a soft breath, getting his mind back on track. Of course she was disoriented. She just needed a few minutes to get herself together. So, ready to indulge her, Med continued to smother the happy grin that wanted to burst out all over the place and waited for her to realize she *was* awake now. Once she got

331

a hold on herself, made the inevitable dry, quirky comment or comeback to his words, he'd consider giving in to the fatigue he felt creeping through his veins like a disease. Deities, he needed to sleep. Anywhere. On a countertop. Under her bed. On a shelf in a supply cabinet.

He shook back the tempting thoughts, blinked the glaze that had come over his vision, and gave his attention back to his patient. "Believe it or not you actually had me—" He stopped short as his glance went back to hers. "Sarge?"

Of course he'd seen her look dangerous before, but this was extreme, and directed at him. Rabid, raw fury and defiance blazed through lids slitted against the glare of the overhead lighting. Her teeth were bared; nostrils flared wide. And in the flat dark slits between her long, sooty lashes, he saw death.

His.

"Shit!"

He threw himself back even as her strong left arm moved with the blinding speed she was noted for, the velocity of her motion making an audible swishing sound in the air. Her long reach snagged him before he cleared her range, her fingers closing around his throat like docking clamps to a starship.

Maybe tighter than that, he managed to think as those long digits dug in, forcing a gagging sound from his mouth.

His body lifted abruptly, causing instant vertigo that he didn't have to worry about for more than a second, because after that everything went gray anyway. The blood that couldn't circulate between his head and body roared in his ears. Faster than he would have thought possible, the strength melted from his muscles, the grayness of his vision faded to black. So this was death . . . he expected it, of course. He was a doctor after all, and understood death even as he tried to fight it off whenever possible.

Yet, surprise lingered strong. He never expected his death from her hand.

The pressure released. Feeling exploded into him with his first sobbing gulp of air. Med sagged to his knees, doubled over, coughing violently, nearly retching. The taste of blood and phlegm brought the acid from his stomach.

No time to waste on this! Drawing firmly on physical and mental training that he had to complete the same as anyone else in Special Forces, he redirected, rerouted, forced his thoughts clear. He didn't know what to expect, but when his head rose, his body was geared for defense.

Who stepped in? Who's keeping her from finishing me? He blinked the sweat from his eyes and sucked in a breath of surprise.

Ariam. Ariam was facing off with an upright and snarling Rett, who obviously didn't recognize her own sister . . . or cared not to. The deadly intent in the platoon leader's eyes hadn't changed one bit. If anything, it had intensified.

333

Deities, it would have been bad enough if she had killed me. But if Ariam holds back because she's afraid of hurting her more than she is already, and she kills Ariam by mistake and wakes up to it later—

The very idea horrified him. He tried to shout out, to bring some sense to this silent, wordless battle. In the next second, he realized his concern for Ariam was needless. She came back at Rett in the same manner she would to anyone else intent on causing harm. Ariam's beautiful face was as cold, pale, and hard as ice; her gray eyes lethally flat. She fought an enemy, not a sister.

His warning to her turned to protest, but too late, he found his voice. "Ariam, no!" Med cringed and winced as Ariam went directly for the sergeant's partially healed hip and shoulder, that deep contusion over her back; the wound over the kidney. Ariam's blows slammed home without mercy. Rett staggered, losing control over her entire right side. Her assault turned instantly to defense; defense turned into a personal struggle to remain on her feet.

Ariam took advantage of it without hesitation.

"Ariam—!" Med groaned as Ariam's right foot connected with Rett's ribcage. That was too close to the damaged lung for Med's peace of mind. Her left foot followed instantly, smashing hard behind Rett's left knee as the taller woman twisted, trying to keep her right side from taking any more damage. While coming back from its arc, the left foot again drove mercilessly for the leg, and a blur of motion from Ariam's right leg ended in a meaty thud against the side of Rett's neck. Med's hands clenched in his hair. "Deities!"

With a hoarse sound of pain, Rett fell back across the bed, her body twisting so it landed on her left side. The reflex was a trained one to avoid falling on her critically injured side and causing herself to black out. Before Rett could turn again to shield her injuries and bring her good side back into the fight, Ariam, possessed of the same lighting reflexes as her sister, was on her.

Med covered his eyes as Ariam's weight came down on Rett's injured right side with every ounce of force the younger woman could produce. The low, agonized groan from Rett was echoed by his own voice. *In less than fifteen seconds, five days of surgery and reconstruction go right out the window,* thought Med. He pulled his hands from his face, sweating in the effort to contain the overflow of sensation to his sensitive talent. Rett's level of pain threatened his own reason; nearly swamped his control of it. But Ariam needed his help, too. If they couldn't get the sergeant under control, there'd be three of them—maybe more—in dire need of medical care!

As he moved in to assist, he saw that Ariam had the situation well in hand, at least for the moment. The maddened, revived body of her sister lay shuddering between her knees. Rett's right side was incapable of movement now; her left limbs locked tight in Ariam's capable hold.

"Get help, Med." Ariam lifted her face as he came near. Her eyes were still flat, her voice, despite its breathlessness, matter-of-fact. "If she decides she's not finished, I'm not going to be able to hold her for long. Get help."

✳ ✳ ✳ ✳ ✳

THE LIGHT THREATENED TO BLIND Rett even through her closed eyelids. The pain was localized and very real. There were no mocking echoes. There was no burning ice, no freezing flames. No darkness. Her sister's voice was real, as was Med's reassuring Ariam to hang on.

She shivered, panted, lay drenched in her own sweat and Ariam's. Her eyes focused, adjusted to the familiar overbright illumination of a hospital facility. She twisted her head to find a pair of worried, yet steady, gray eyes locking gazes with her.

"Back down, Rett!"

Her sister. Ariam's bone-snapping hold did not yield even as Rett forced herself to remain motionless. *Is it Ariam? Is it?*

Ariam yelled a fingerwidth from Rett's face. "Damn you, Rett—don't try anything else! You've already tried to kill Med. I'll break both your arms if I have to. I'll start by cracking your shoulder and collarbone again, so help me!"

Ariam tightened her pressure to emphasize her words, jammed her knee into the partially healed wound in Rett's right side, forcing another grunt of pain from her.

"Maybe I'll just crunch these ribs and open up this hole in your lung again too. Damn it, Rett! If Med doesn't ground you for a year from *this*—I'll give him good reason to! Back down!"

Rett blinked, once, twice, moving her eyes as much as she could to notice the familiar hospital look of the room, the hospital smells. The familiar odor of her blood, her sweat; the scent of Ariam. Letting her head drop, she concentrated on the well-known pains of wounds in parts of her body. Her right side was one unending agony from heel to head. Every breath hurt. There was also the threatening, bone-cracking pressure from Ariam's hold. The force increased, producing a burning, ripping sensation as the strain pulled at her shoulders.

Rett couldn't fight any longer, there was nothing left, no energy, no breath. As she had with the growtus, she figured that if she had to give up, it might as well be to something Nyorfian, something familiar and natural. What better than Ariam, real or illusionary? She didn't have the will to fight back the deep-rooted love she had for her outspoken, impetuous, and irritating baby sister, the same one who was also so unswervingly loyal, trustworthy, and wiser than anyone so young had a right to be.

I'd give my life for her in an instant, why not my surrender?

Rett released the tension in her muscles, let out a shivering breath, and yielded. "Ari?" She cleared her throat and tried again, pushing the words past the sobs that wanted to overcome them. "Ari, is it really you? Or is it Xonomer in another disguise?"

*   *   *   *   *

ARIAM GAVE THE LIMP BODY beneath hers a rough shake. "No, it's not me, it's the fucking Leader of the Yixolryn Coalition!" she said harshly, shaking Rett again, closing her ears to the deep whimper of pain she caused. "Wake up, Rett. Wake *up*."

A sob answered, bringing hot tears to Ariam's eyes in response.

"It's me. Ariam. It is, truly." Her voice broke on the last word. Still, she kept her punishing hold strong, her tone resolute. The tension had gone out of Rett, there was no fight left. She hardly breathed. Her entire body quivered and trembled. The emotions tumbling from her were so jumbled and chaotic Ariam couldn't make sense of them.

What will it be next? If she thinks I'm not me, then what? Will she fight me again?

Then Rett's body, already limp, seemed to collapse, boneless. Ariam released most of her punishing hold, let down part of her mental guard, and was nearly overcome by the terrified uncertainty that gripped her sister. Tears and sweat streaked down Rett's face; the brown color of her skin was faded to a muddy gray.

"I can't be sure—" whispered Rett, panting for breath. Her body, still below Ariam's knees, shuddered. "I can't be sure. I can't trust him! Deities help me be sure!"

Ariam moved to one side carefully and gathered her shaking, shivering sister close. She snagged the rumpled covering from the floor, tucked it lovingly around Rett's quivering frame, and wrapped her arms around her.

"Shh." Pressing her cheek against her sister's matted dark hair, she said nothing else. She just held Rett, gently rocked her, and hummed softly. She filled her mind with the tranquil blue-green-brown of the Treetop forests in summer, the cool sweet wind off Cadie's Peak, the constant soft voice of the river. Soothing thoughts. Beloved familiarity. Just as Rett used to do for her.

Rett was always there for me. No matter what. It's my turn now to mother her. Oh, Rett, what happened? What happened during those drugged nightmares to make you act this way? Ariam hugged her sister close, her throat tight, silent tears sliding down her cheeks to mingle with those slowly drying on Rett's face.

Med burst into the room, followed closely by Major Yidnar, Jaq, and Trebor. Ariam halted them with an abrupt gesture, asking them to come no farther but to stand by.

The Major motioned for the others to leave. Jaq stood rebellious for few seconds, his platinum central crest nearly rising straight up in preparation to challenge his right to be there. He reluctantly gave way to Ariam's pleading glance, Trebor's insistent tug, and Yidnar's lowering eyebrows.

Ariam watched her commander as he silently came near and sank into a crouch, just within reach of his long arm from the bed. Her mouth opened to speak, but the Major held a finger to his lips and shook his head, lips forming the words without sound.

337

Wait, let's see if my presence now causes any trouble. His rugged face showed his intense concern, yet the position of his thick, eloquent eyebrows revealed his equally intense curiosity.

Her attention returned to Rett, who was apparently unaware of anything beyond the solid reality of her half-healed injuries, fresh bruises, and Ariam's presence.

"What happened, Ari?" Rett's words caught roughly between the back of her throat and her lips. "Did the decoy work? Anyone hurt?"

"The Base is recovered. The decoy worked brilliantly, between you and the last of the storm. There was some intense fighting once they realized what was happening. No one came out of this without something to show for it. There were fatalities, yes, lots of casualties."

"How many?"

"Many, but less than there would have been otherwise. Please don't worry about that now." Ariam kissed her temple, her fingers stroking Rett's face gently.

"How did you rescue me from Xonomer?"

"It wasn't easy," said Ariam after a long pause.

"Then it's not over."

"No, the war isn't over, if that's what you mean." Ariam hugged Rett a little tighter. "We almost lost you."

"What happened to Xonomer? And H'chan—he turned into this big, black, bird thing—"

"That's gone for now," murmured Ariam. She hid her confusion and curiosity, although it burned in her so much she wanted to scream out her questions, demand answers. She hadn't one idea in two worlds what her sister was talking about. All she knew was that that overload of drugged darts that hit Rett complicated an already critical condition of physical wounds and sent her into a nightmare of which she had yet to emerge.

For all Ariam could guess and from what she felt, the experiences Rett had been having were all too horribly real. Even in a

semi-comatose state, Rett's reactions to the slightest hints of pres-
ences or mentioning of names—especially Jaq's, Major Yidnar's,
Evetez's, and a frantic H'chan—had been negative and violent.

"All gone for now," repeated Ariam softly. "Rest."

"It wasn't a dream . . . ?"

"No," agreed Ariam. "It was not a dream, Rett."

"Was I dead?"

"Almost." Ariam smoothed the short, dark hair with her fingers. "You almost died a handful of times." She turned her shiver
into a swallow, for a second going straight back to that awful ten
minutes of the pickup. Rett had been clinically dead when they
found her.

*If the weather hadn't been so cold . . . If Med hadn't been
along . . .*

If onlys waste time. Ariam bared her teeth in the effort to shift
her thoughts.

"Whoever this Xonomer is—we didn't see him—he certainly
almost killed you, and even used some of us against you, H'chan
included."

Rett raised her head. Hungry and haunted, her gaze raked over
Ariam. "I saw Mother and Tovadan, burned, hurt, tortured—"

Ariam hugged her tighter. "*That* was hallucination." Her
conviction on that matter was strong.

"Zhent, Gerrale . . . Kraym, others—they told me I caused
them to die. I killed them, Ari . . ." Her voice broke.

"Oh, no," whispered Ariam, pressing her cheek to Rett's.
"No. That's not true and you know it. *Tell* me you know it!"

Rett hesitated. Her pause took far too long for Ariam's liking
and her fingers tightened painfully. Rett hissed, tried to squirm
away in protest.

"*No,*" Ariam said with the strength of her physical grip.
"*Feel* this! I can't speak for Zhent, because I didn't know him.
From what I heard, you did what you had to do. His death was
sealed when the Coalition put those implants in his head. They

were designed to kill him when they had no further use for him. Remember? However, Gerrale and Kraym and the others, they loved you, as strong and real as this, as I do! They died in combat, for Nyorfias, for our way of life; they took complete responsibility for their lives with the oath we all took. Do you understand?"

"But I saw—"

"I don't deny you saw anything or anyone, Rett. But you were under drug influence and you know as well as I, maybe better than I do, that things get twisted."

Another long pause followed, but since empathic Ariam felt her sister's doubts begin to fade in face of blunt fact, she traded her infliction of physical pain for support. When Rett's tension relaxed, she cradled her sister with loving gentleness. Her fingers returned to glide in a soothing manner along her face and head.

"Semage is fine. Evetez never came near you at all. He was injured." At Rett's startled reaction she hastened to add, "I heard you say their names, that's how I know."

"Iheolon?"

Ariam gasped, turning it into a cough.

"He killed them . . . 'Vetez and 'Mage both. I saw them both dead. Hallucination or not, it was very real to me. I need to know the *truth*. All of it, not excerpts." Rett's breathless, tired voice took a hard edge of strength.

"Iheolon injured Evetez, yes. Both his legs were crushed, he was burned, he's frostbitten, and he'll be off Active, but the doctors and medtechs are fixing him more every day and expect he'll make a good recovery. Even Med says he will, although it will take a long time. I am *not* going into detail, not now. So don't push me.

"I *will* tell you that he's right down the hall, driving everyone crazy. He's threatened to come in here a few times, once he can muster the Tickle Patrol complete with parental units and Safkas' great-grandmother—from Complex 63." She let bright humor lighten her voice as she went on. "And of course this will happen as soon as he figures how to move with the top half of him bandaged and grafted, and with both legs immobilized from toes to hips."

"Deities."

"You should know how that feels." Ariam could have bitten her tongue in half for saying that.

"At least he's one to make the best of it," whispered Rett. "I think I would die if I had to . . ."

"Don't go back there, Rett." Ariam soothed her with fingers, voice, and mind. "And as for the others, you weren't even conscious when they came to see you. The Major, Jaq—"

"Jaq?" Rett clutched at Ariam's body. "He didn't leave?"

"Jaq? Leave you? He was only that stupid once. Even then, his heart was yours. Deities, Rett."

341

"Why can't he see me?"

"I'm trying to explain that. I guess the drugs really twisted things for you. You reacted so badly to him, to anyone else even coming through the corridor, that Med kept everyone away. Any kind of sound, general com communication, even normal conversation. Med had all coms to this room closed off. After that, no one except for Med or me came past that door over there until just before. We even left our headbands behind."

The tension returned to Rett's body. "H'chan?"

"He was hurt pretty badly—and now he's very sick. Ever since you came back to Base, he was screaming your name on a range the entire galactic quadrant couldn't possibly miss."

"I don't hear him." Rett was frightened, her breaths coming short and sharp again. "I can't hear him—"

"Shh. The vet-meds had to keep him sedated. H'chan was so worked up about you he was injuring himself more, getting sicker." Ariam kept her voice matter of fact. "He's sleeping now. Kraym—I mean, H'tan—is with him. So is Zharré."

Rett's nose wrinkled and Ariam hastened to explain. "We found a young girl with the Coalition troops here, a sled pilot. Twelve years old. Kyarta. Not trusted with weapons and enslaved to one of Iheolon's unit commanders."

Rett's mouth opened a little and a furrow appeared between her brows. It was so like her, thought Ariam, to feel a sudden surge of protectiveness for someone she never met. "She shows a talent for healing and a great affinity with the Ice Beasts. She's in the shed with H'chan, hasn't left his side since he was brought in."

"Poor kid . . . Kyarta? But . . . Kyarta was destroyed two hundred years ago . . ."

Ariam was glad to talk, and Rett was soaking it up. "Apparently she was in stasis all this time and her memories only go back half a year or so. It's a good thing the Ice Beasts talk with her because she can hardly speak Standard."

"Jaq—"

"Major Yidnar's had Jaq talk to her a few times. She's taken quite a shine to Trebor. They have the same eyes. Those openers of H'tenneck's came in handy more than once . . . first time for Evetez, and then to remove the devices the Coalition had on her neck and limbs."

Ariam shivered and tried to disguise it by shifting her position a little. They'd found more devices like them in Yidnar's office, a set undoubtedly earmarked for Rett once Iheolon had her. Semage had promptly taken those off and tossed the lot into the already burning portion of the Base, where the Coalition troopjumper had crashed.

Some people had questioned his action, saying the devices and such should be studied. Sergeant Tris, acting for Major Yidnar, had answered those who did so without words, his expression stating clearly that as far as he was concerned, Semage had the right of it.

The infantry colonel who commanded Aurora Base unexpectedly backed them up and ordered anything Coalition, from dead troopers to snowsleds, to be incinerated in the inferno that consumed their ship and the portion of the landing field. Later, after things were sorted out and the fire confined to a smaller area, still burning hot but much cleaner, they had ceremoniously sent those humans and Beasts fallen in battle with the last of the flames.

"Did Med leave?"

"Actually . . . yes, for a half hour." Ariam shook her head. "He's been with you night and day; I think that half-hour was the longest he spent out of this room."

"And I hurt him . . . I almost killed—"

"Hush. Hush. That's over, it didn't happen. He's fine; you know how tough he is. Did him some good, more than likely, shaking him up like that. Deities know we've all felt like it from time to time."

"I almost killed you, Ariam! I thought you were Xonomer trying to trick me. I was going to kill you—"

"But you didn't. I kicked your ass, remember?"

"No, you didn't." Now that grumble was more like the Rett Ariam knew. "You kicked me everywhere else, but not my ass." One dark eye cracked open and tried to glare at her. "That's the only part of me not hurting."

Ariam smiled and kissed her gently. "Now you really must sleep."

But the horrible shuddering convulsed Rett into just as tight a knot as before. "I can't, Ari. He'll get me if I let go and sleep. I can't!"

"You can. I'm here. He can't get past me," said Ariam fiercely. "I'll kick *his* ass, then rip him to shreds."

On the wings of that thought, she silently released the catches on her weapons and utility belts, shifting a bit to pull them away from her body. She felt Major Yidnar's ready hand take them from her. "There, that's better," she whispered, as if her

343

only thought was to make the both of them more comfortable. Pressing her cheek against her sister's hair, she said, "I'll keep watch—you sleep."

* * * * *

AN HOUR LATER, ARIAM OPENED her eyes as movement from Major Yidnar's direction caught her attention. He rose and stood for a moment, flexing the stiffness from his knees. Just past him, Ariam noticed Carakenne peeking around the edge of the doorframe, her sky-colored eyes dark with anxiety, her teeth worrying her bottom lip. Since Evetez was in the regular annex at the opposite end of the hall, Ariam couldn't count Carakenne's seeing him or any of the other wounded as the small woman's excuse to be there.

Would Rett react to her the way she had toward the others? Ariam waited one minute, two. Rett had reacted in seconds earlier with the others. Cara's presence didn't seem to provoke a response at all.

Major Yidnar sank again into his crouch before turning his head toward Carakenne. Ariam saw him signal the small woman to drop her weapons and utility belts and join him.

He wants to talk to me, see if Rett will be all right with Cara if I leave the room for a few minutes, guessed Ariam. She sent a little smile to Carakenne as the small soldier crouched on her heels alongside the Major.

After another long five minutes and no change from Rett, Ariam indicated agreement when the Major silently informed her that he wanted to talk and Carakenne was going to take the watch.

Ariam shifted, and Rett opened sleepy eyes, mumbling a protest.

"I need to go out for a few minutes," whispered Ariam, smoothing her sister's hair. "I'll be back. You won't be alone. Cara's here. All right?"

Rett closed her eyes again, that action and the limpness of her body enough of an indicator she wasn't going to argue. Once Carakenne was settled in place, Rett's head on her small, sturdy shoulder, Ariam saw Rett give her demolition squad leader a brief glance and a tiny grin of greeting before closing her eyes again with a weary sigh.

In the hall outside, Jaq Pym waited with Sergeant Trebor. Ariam didn't have to strain any talent to know every nerve and muscle he possessed was stretched to the maximum with anxiety. His telltale hair and the darkness of his eyes were physical clues. She slid her arm through his as the Major indicated they should all move a little farther down the corridor.

"It seems we're all under more stress from this situation than we've been from anything else, and that bothers me. It just doesn't seem normal, or natural. Anyone else feel that way?"

Ariam let go of Jaq and hugged her arms across her chest. "I do. It's almost as if everything stopped since then. As if the entire planet is holding its breath . . . or that the Base is in a bubble, separate from everything else. It's weird, and all that might mean is that I haven't had much sleep lately, either." She tried a laugh, but chillbumps prickled her skin.

"We need to know more."

* * * * *

JAQ STOOD WITH THE GROUP, feeling frustrated and left out. He felt the wrongness, too. His sensitive hair—not only on his head and spine, but also all over his body—was twitching in so many different directions he felt as if insects crawled over his skin.

His attention wandered back along the corridor to Rett's door. Why couldn't he go in there? Why had she responded so badly to him—when he hadn't even been in physical sight of her since they brought her in? He'd heard her talking with Ariam. Rett thought he left her. Left her! As if he'd be so selfish and stupid again.

He should be the one in there now, not Carakenne. He should be the one holding Rett, offering reassurance, comfort, and protection. Weird bubble around the Base or not, nothing would be right until he was with her. He ground his teeth together.

But what if she never recovers? What if she always reacts badly whenever you get within range of her perceptions?

Jaq's guts twisted. Where had that thought come from? From him? Fine then. If he thought it, he had to answer it.

I can't live without her. Of that, he had no doubt.

"Jaq. Jaq Pym. *Jaq.*"

The fresh grip on his arm, tightening to the point of acute pain, finally registered. He turned his attention toward the 2023rd's commander. "Sir?"

"Have *you* ever heard of something called Xonomer?"

Jaq blinked. "As what? A title? An entity?"

"In the Coalition, on Zetinor Prime, from any other source or language, have you heard that term, 'Xonomer'?"

"No, sir. It might be different if it was in another language. A lot of my memories before the Coalition are gone—or still pretty garbled. It might have been something I connected to as a child. If I come up with any connections, or remember anything, I'll let you know."

"What we need is something to calm the Sarge down," said Trebor.

"Deities, if I thought it would work I'd bring Shannai and Olvero and some of those kids from Complex 63 in here . . . I had some wild thoughts about that," said Major Yidnar. "Another wild thought involved sending Rett and Evetez, maybe a few others, to Complex 63 for recovery, since it would help settle them to have the kids around."

"They're good ideas, sir," Ariam said warmly. "But I think not for right now."

346

Yidnar nodded. "Agreed. I can't begin to think of bringing those kids here with Rett so totally out of herself there's no telling what would happen."

Med, on one of his innumerable forays between the main patient annex and Rett's isolated room, stopped in the middle of the group. He looked tired and strained, and absently fingered the purpling marks on his neck as he eyed them. His baleful glare settled on Ariam.

Jaq jerked his full attention to the medtech only because Ariam edged away and bumped against him.

He felt the shiver vibrate through Ariam's slender body into his. They'd all been under tremendous strain, but Ariam . . . he couldn't imagine what it was truly like for her. She seemed a reservoir of bottomless fortitude and strength, her effectiveness only increasing with the need of others around her. But, more than once, she'd broken down weeping in his arms, or in Semage's, turning to them for reassurance and support.

If there was anything he wished Rett would learn from her sister, it was to let others support her. How to let her worries and troubles out instead of holding them back; how to ask for help, and then take it when it was offered.

Right now, through the contact of his body with Ariam's, Jaq felt his crest rising partially in defense as Med continued to stare down the B-troop second. As protective of Ariam as he would be of a blood-sister, Jaq slid his hand to her back, moved so he stood alongside and slightly ahead of her instead of behind her, and studied the medtech's tired, drawn face, wondering what it was that had Med target the B-troop second. The medtech and Ariam had worked side-by-side for the past six days in complete accord, what suddenly came between them now?

"Are you all right, Med?"

Med didn't seem to hear Jaq, but Trebor had also noticed something amiss. The older man took a stance on Ariam's right, a half step in front of her.

347

"Med? Is something wrong? Can we help?" Trebor's deep baritone seemed to break the medtech out of whatever trance into which he'd slipped.

Jaq saw Med scowl around the group with impartial malevolence, more of his usual fashion, which brought a puff of relief from Trebor. He felt no lessening of the tension from Ariam's muscles.

"Tired. Tired." Med blinked and shook his head. He stomped off down the hall to Rett's room.

"I think we can agree this situation needs to be resolved," said Major Yidnar. Jaq noted that he, too, looked puzzled. The major's glance followed Med down the hall for a moment before returning to the group. "Which brings us back to Rett."

Jaq's sensitive nape itched. He was sure he wouldn't like what the Major was going to say next.

"What we believe to be drug-induced hallucination was— is—very real to her. I've seen Rett, and many others, through drug trauma before, back in training."

There was a general reaction of discomfort among them. Jaq had observed the commandos were careful never to speak about certain aspects of their training at all around those who didn't undergo it themselves.

"And, while Rett had some adverse reactions that still stand as GTC records—none of them were quite like this. Once she was conscious, she was always completely aware what was real and what was not."

"That was a long time ago, sir," reminded Trebor softly.

Yidnar shook his head. "No matter. The point is I think this is beyond a drug reaction, Sergeant Trebor. At least any that I've seen. I try to be involved with that phase of training as much as my schedule allows. Over the years I've seen many of reaction by the 2023rd's people during that phase—with just as many variations. But nothing that hangs on like this."

"Is it possible that three years ago, Iheolon gave her some drugs that might have changed the way she handles anything now? Especially the drugs he had in those darts?" Trebor wondered.

"I doubt that," said Jaq. "He used more technology than drugs. With Rett, it didn't take much for him to see he was risking far more than he was willing to lose. Iheolon was very aware of her intolerance and he wanted to keep her alive as long as possible. What drugs he did use were variations of those she could handle without adverse effects." His voice was flat. "The adverse effects she experienced came from living and technological sources, not chemical ones."

"Can we consider what Rett has and is experiencing *is* real?" Major Yidnar glanced around at his group.

Jaq jumped on the new approach. "My people—my original people, the Zetinorians," he corrected himself, "have a belief in supernatural phenomena."

He earned three skeptical glances, but skepticism was soon replaced with what he interpreted as a troubled readiness to try anything.

"Since it has a lot of misunderstanding attached, let me define what I call supernatural," he offered. "Inexplicable, intangible paranormal activity."

"From an alien source?" Major Yidnar's eyes narrowed.

"Maybe. Define alien. Think about it. Ariam, did you scope anything tangible from Rett, or in general, other than . . . feeling weird?"

Ariam shook her head. "Not another mindforce, if that's what you mean," she said honestly. "Then again Rett's so chaotic, it's hard to filter through what's on top. That might only mean I'm not strong enough to feel another mindforce—or that it might be able to hide itself. Whatever it is, Rett's convinced it's real, every bit of it. And that's what counts."

* * * * *

"IT's LIFE AND DEATH TO Rett," agreed Major Yidnar. He didn't think his heart had ever felt heavier. It was indeed a matter of life and death, and there was a sensitive subject to broach while he had the opportunity. "Ariam." With a motion of his head, he indicated he wanted to speak with her alone.

The expression in her eyes as she stepped away from the group told him that Ariam knew exactly what was on his mind. Still she asked, "Sir?"

He gave her credit for the composure and stillness of the rest of her features. The tremble in her body, however, she couldn't hide.

Placing a hand on the young woman's shoulder in support, Major Yidnar spoke bluntly. He couldn't phrase it any other way. "Med is beginning to suspect the drugs have caused permanent damage to her mind. Of course that may not be so, and we hope it isn't—but you know Rett wouldn't want to live that way, as a danger to herself and most importantly to her point of view, a danger or burden to others. That's on her file, in her own words and voice."

"Yes, sir," she said softly.

"If it comes to that—we can't find any outside influence, and Rett grows worse, or shows no sign of recovery, and Med finalizes the diagnosis . . . and you make the decision," Yidnar paused only slightly, "I will take responsibility for her mercy, since Lieutenant Evetez is disabled."

She bit her lower lip and ducked her head a moment, then met his gaze resolutely. "Thank you, sir. I know that's what Rett would want. That's what I would want for her if things were worse, if they were hopeless. But I'm *not* giving up, and neither is she." Ariam's tone turned fierce. "Med might feel she's damaged and won't recover, but *my* abilities tell me Med is wrong. He's *wrong*."

Which might explain Ariam's reaction to him earlier, thought Yidnar, having noticed Ariam shrink into Jaq when the medtech had come among them.

"It might be completely emotional on my part, sir. But we have to take every chance to see if this will change! Rett would want that, too, Major, you know she doesn't give up on chance. She doesn't give up on much of anything—she would have died years ago, if that was the case."

"Yes. I know. You were also strong in your conviction when she was lost on Aurora. I *do* trust your feelings."

"Thank you, sir." She swallowed and glanced toward the others down the corridor. "But then again, there's Jaq. The Zetinorian compulsion to take one's own life when a lifemate dies is part of who he is. It's his right, but . . . I don't want to lose him either." She shrugged, helpless to explain exactly what she meant. "He's putting on a good front right now. But it might fly to nothing in the face of reality." Ariam scrubbed her hands along her arms as if feeling a chill.

"We'll hope things don't go that way. But I had a duty to say what I did, and it's better said now than later."

"Understood, sir, and I appreciate it."

"As far as Jaq . . . as far as any of it goes, we won't give up without a fight. You're not the only one who would hate to lose Jaq along with Rett." He squeezed her arm briefly.

"Thank you, sir."

They turned back to the others.

"We need to find out more. Whatever Xonomer is, whoever it is, or whatever it means, has Rett so terrorized it's heartbreaking. I want some answers."

Their pcoms crackled into life. "Emergency—in Medical, Post Four!" Carakenne sounded harsh and frantic. Her words ended on a grunt.

3.3.15 MEDICAL SECTION, AURORA BASE, EPNOCE
0536.03.19 (LOCAL RECKONING)

THE PLATOON LEADER WAS ON her feet and in a fighting stance, her hoarse denials incoherent, directed at empty space. Yidnar reached her first. *"Sergeant!"*

At his touch and word she swung toward him on an instant offensive. There was not a single shred of recognition in her blazing eyes. All that was written there was that he was the enemy. She was going to kill him. She very nearly did, since his surprise was almost complete. Yet while his mind still screamed a denial, his body reacted, deflecting the lethal intent of her opening blow, turning Rett's strength and force against her with the next. She'd had to leave the ground completely to get her good left leg into play, as her right side wouldn't support her. Intending to take her off her feet altogether, he went after the left ankle and hip, hit them with sharp, stunning blows even as he deflected the killing impact of her foot.

She was already weakened and hurting from her fight with Ariam, so as she stumbled, Yidnar hit hard and fast where he knew she'd feel the most pain. Rett crashed to the floor with him on top.

His troubles weren't over. For someone in her condition, especially after what he heard happened earlier, she should be unconscious. It wasn't in her nature to quit, but this—this went beyond that. Maybe she was unable to stand upright to do it, but fight she could, and did, with the slick, amazing strength of a just-hooked giant northern steelhead. Having battled those great migratory fish before, Yidnar couldn't help the comparison.

However, he took no pleasure from this battle. Whatever drove Rett had to give out. He feared it would at the expense of her life.

He had the advantage right now and pressed his offense, forcing her to expend even more effort in the attempt to evade a locking hold from him. From where was she pulling her energy? *This has to stop, and I mean right now!*

"A little help here—!"

It took all of them to subdue her. Even then she didn't quit or make it easier. Snarling, twisting, she fought back with a fearsome power. Finally, everyone got a hold she couldn't break, and they wrestled her back to the bed. Yidnar fell across her upper body, pinning the injured right arm between them. Jaq sprawled across her hips and thighs, most of her left arm trapped by his thick arms; her left wrist gripped in both his large hands. Ariam and Trebor each were wrapped around a leg, like bugs clinging to blades of grass. Still Rett struggled and growled, her breaths whistling harsh from her straining lungs.

"I knew she was always abnormally strong," gasped Yidnar, blinking a trickle of blood away from his eye, "but when did she get *this* strong?"

Ariam and Trebor both made sounds that might have been amused disbelief.

"All her life," Ariam got out.

"Good gods and deities, we're lucky she's wounded and tired," Trebor said. "We may have needed a lot more help otherwise. A lot more. Maybe full charge from a stunner besides."

This was someone who was tired? Yidnar thought incredulously.

"How do you think the Coalition came up with that nickname?" Trebor coughed in the careful manner of someone whose ribs had stopped an armored vehicle. "You've sparred with her, but you've never seen the Sarge pull out everything she has, or in actual hand-to-hand combat, have you, sir?"

"Not until now," he said, troubled and awed at what he had helped to create. He'd been indirectly involved in her training, read all the reports, knew she held back her abnormal strength despite her TIs encouraging her not to. But he never expected this. In this light, the realization of the tremendous self-control she exerted in training exercises—even during those times she lost some of it—was mind-boggling.

"She has to be restrained." Med, now on his feet, pressed his right hand to his bruised side and swiped blood from his nose and a cut lip with his left. "And I didn't want to do this, but I have to quiet her down a bit. She'll kill herself or one of us if she's allowed to continue like this! Five days of surgery and recon-struction—right out the window." He turned to a workcounter, grumbling under his breath.

Yidnar hoped not, although the amount of fresh blood that stained Rett's exposed skin and her thigh-length hospital shirt wasn't encouraging. And that was only from the portions of shirt visible through the commando bodies pinning her down. Even now he felt a growing circle of sticky warmth beneath his chest where their bodies touched, one that her every straining gasp for air caused to spread.

"No, Med, we *can't*!" Ariam sounded choked. "We can't do that to her. She's frightened enough."

Yidnar glanced at the chilling, deadly flare burning in the space-dark eyes below him. *Scared? Not at the moment. She's just waiting for her chance to start up again.*

"Restraining her might push her right over the edge. Just everyone get out and let me talk to her again—"

"No, Ariam. I'm sorry." Med was firm. "And I don't want a protest from any others of you."

Yidnar guessed Med was referring to Jaq, who made a sound as if he was going to speak. He didn't dare turn his head to find out, not with Rett's gaze shifting and alert for any opportunity to escape.

"I'm not backing down this time." The medtech had a tone unyielding as azurium hull plating. "She's dangerous like this. To herself as well as the rest of us."

"But—"

"Sergeant Ariam." Major Yidnar adjusted his hold so he could angle his head enough to meet Ariam's gaze and keep Rett in his peripheral vision. "Med Rhozev has a valid point. No argument." His eyes held hers until she acknowledged.

Then he dared a quick glance over his shoulder toward Carakenne, who struggled to sit up, her small dark face clouded and dazed. "Are you all right? What happened?" Yidnar managed to bring his breathing under control. Then his full attention was diverted back to Rett, who stiffened and struggled afresh under them. There was a different quality to her movements now, and the eyes that had been so lethal before were turning wide with terror.

"No." It was a whimper. "Med, no—"

Glancing aside, Yidnar followed the direction of her glance. Med, holding a mask in his hand. *At least she recognizes him!*

Knowing where much of her terror came from, Yidnar could only sympathize, but this was Rhozev's venue. He called the moves, knew what was best. The major's trust in the medtech still didn't ease the guilty ache in his heart as the sergeant's distress elevated with every forward step the medtech took.

"No." The sergeant's hard, tense body trembled as much in dread as it did fighting the restraining holds they had on her. "No! Please. Why are you helping *them*? Med, you don't understand. Don't—"

"Easy, Sergeant. You've had this anesthetic before—it's the only stuff I can use on you when you need surgery." Med calmly came closer. "I'm not going to give you enough to put you out completely; I don't want you that far gone. I *am* going to slow you way down."

"No!" Rett strained for freedom. "Can't you *see!* You're helping them—helping Xonomer! Deities, Med, please!"

Major Yidnar cursed and the others scrambled to re-secure their holds as one desperate lunge actually moved the entire

355

tangled knot of them half a fingerlength to the left. The sergeant's movements became more frantic as Med brought his free hand to her face.

"You can't do this. I can't fight him if you do this. I need to move, I need to think—don't, *mnph*!"

Rhozev's hand clamped over her mouth and nose, muffling her protests, cutting off her air supply. Yidnar knew this routine. It would only be for a few seconds, and then the medtech would switch hands, putting the mask in place so she would be forced to take a huge, deep lungful of the anesthetic.

Rett gathered herself for one last attempt even as her eyes started to unfocus. The major again shifted, slamming his forearm between her face and his as she blindly tried to ram him with her head.

356 A grim Med switched and held the mask over her nose and mouth. Rett's struggles weakened, her muffled protests faded. The force and strength she displayed melted like snow beneath them, leaving her limp. Only a convulsive, shallow shudder quivered through her body every few seconds. For a long space of moments no one dared let go or loosen their grips. Yidnar thought he heard a sob from Ariam.

Med put the anesthetic aside and swiped sweat from his narrow face. "Ease off the right, but watch her left side," the medtech told them without tone or energy. "I need to see what got torn up—again—over here."

Ariam stayed where she was. Yidnar, having the most control in his position, moved only enough to allow Med access to Rett's right. Jaq slid to his knees alongside the bed, gently extracting Rett's left arm from the tangle in which he'd locked it. His blue eyes were dark, his wild hair as wilted as Rett's body now was. Yidnar had one heartbreaking look at the Zetinorian's ravaged visage before Jaq dropped his forehead to the limb in his hands, lips moving soundlessly.

Trebor unlocked his arms and legs from his quarter, rolled off, got to his feet, and went to Carakenne.

Yidnar's gaze followed him there, to the spot the small woman had remained half-sitting, half-splattered on the floor, bewildered, dazed. Hunkering alongside, the F-troop second checked her condition, with a firm touch and soft word bringing the corporal back into the present. She shuddered and blinked, her eyes clearing. Only then did Trebor help her rise.

"Carakenne?" Yidnar found his voice as Med finished his examination of Rett. When the medtech asked him to move, he repositioned his body so his weight was off the semiconscious sergeant. He remained seated on the bed, ready to flatten her again if he had to, praying he wouldn't.

"Good to go, sir, it's nothing much."

Med looked up briefly, snorted, and returned his attention to Rett. With the same precise care he would use to immobilize an injured patient for transportation, the medtech began at her head and worked his way around without a word.

Yidnar kept the sigh in his thoughts. "Trebor, will you clarify that—and be more specific?"

"Broken wrist, dislocated shoulder, bruises, bump on the forehead—enough to shock her but I don't think she's concussed."

For a moment it sounded as if he'd add his own comment, but he lapsed into silence. Without further ado or warning, he took an experienced hold of Carakenne and set her shoulder right with a *pop!* that sounded much too loud in the heavy silence of the room. Cara, still dazed from her experience, was too surprised to do much of anything but inhale so sharply it made her choke. The sounds of the procedure brought a tiny, reflexive movement and a distressed mumble from Rett.

"Tell us what happened if you can." Yidnar tried to tell himself this wasn't some lame attempt to turn his mind from what they were doing to Rett. But after the keen disappointment he felt when Trebor said Cara needed a minute, Yidnar knew he couldn't deny it was.

He knew firsthand Rett's greatest personal fear was of being immobilized and helpless, unable to control or direct her own body. What happened now had to bring every single one of the nightmares she'd experienced during her life—imaginary or real—to the surface with brutal clarity.

Here he was, allowing it to happen again; assisting in making it happen. As much as it made his stomach turn, there was no acceptable alternative. Not at the moment. Through the contact his body maintained with hers, he felt her muscles clenching in intermittent shudders, her breaths wheezing in short, fast, shallow gasps.

Cara, who'd been leaning into Trebor until her head cleared, straightened, let out a soft sigh, and poked her shoulder gingerly. "It happened so fast, sir. I think she tried to warn me. She started going on about a Xonomer. Whatever that is, it's big, black, evil, and seems to be able to invade her mind at will, and make her powerless to move or think for herself."

Cara's dark complexion had a sickly, grayish cast, as if covered with fine dust. Yidnar guessed it was more than the pain she felt from her arm. She was shivering against Trebor, her sky-colored eyes going unfocused and frightened again.

"Did you see anything, Carakenne?"

"No." She shook herself and blew out a hard breath. "But I felt cold." Her voice quivered, producing the same reaction in him, in anyone listening. "Cold. *Really* cold. Colder than outside. The air was almost alive. Moving. But there was no wind. No unusual scent."

She stopped, took a breath, and backed up her story to the beginning. "I was sitting there, and she was leaning on me, just still and quiet. She knew it was me, and that Ariam had gone out, but she was fine with that."

Yidnar nodded. He'd seen that himself.

"Well, after a while, she asked me how I was, said the grenades I gave her really had come in handy, small stuff, almost random. That was fine. She seemed to doze off again. Then, around the same time I got cold, she started to shake. Then she told me to move out of the way, it—Xonomer—was going to attack me. When I didn't move instantly, she just picked me up in one hand and threw me over here. Then Med came in and she yelled at him, too—he didn't listen, either. She got up for him, tackled him flat as if he was walking right into an SMG shot. There may have been something, but I wiped wall with my head and had so many flashes and bangs going on I can't be sure it wasn't just me." Carakenne shook her head. "But I can't explain the cold, that was creepy. She's scared out of her skin, sir, and so am I," finished Carakenne honestly.

His face still and set, Med finished securing the sweat-drenched, shuddering body of Sergeant Rett and gestured for Carakenne to come to him. Yidnar stood up, stood still a few moments, unclenching his taut muscles and nerves. Then he took a step nearer to Jaq, his hand closing gently on the Zetinorian's shoulder. "Get up, Jaq."

As if in a dream, the big man obeyed. Ariam immediately slid into the vacant space. Yidnar had one brief glimpse of her tearstreaked face before she averted it from him and everyone else in the room.

"Carakenne'll be all right, Med?" asked Yidnar after clearing his throat. Was the air thick in here or was it just him?

"She'll be all right. Some muscle trauma aggravated in the shoulder—" here he shot a disapproving glance at Trebor, "but the break in her wrist is minor, so is the bump on the head." Med busied himself setting Cara to rights.

Yidnar's attention returned to Rett.

Her eyes were partially open now. She looked at him with recognition and dizzy confusion. "What . . . ?" Her voice was slurred and thick from the gas Med used.

Her muscles from the neck downward stood out in stark relief as she forced her body to move. When it met the resistance of the restraints, her shallow, rapid breathing became more ragged.

"Why?"

"We had to, Rett," Yidnar said.

"No!" She nearly choked as she gasped out words and tried to take in air at the same time. "Y-you d-don't understand. They're g-gone now . . . but they'll be back . . . Xonomer will be back! You c-c-can't leave me like this!"

"You almost killed Med—twice," he said evenly. "Once earlier and just now. And Carakenne." *And me*, he added silently. Had he been one split-second slower when she turned on him, he would have died. It was closer than he liked to admit.

"Sir, I admit . . . the first time I saw Med I . . . tried to hurt him . . . I d-d-didn't know . . . it was really him." Rett's effort to vocalize through the haze of the drug and her rising panic was painfully evident. "But this time . . . C-c-carakenne and Med were . . . about to be attacked—"

"You tried your best to kill the rest of us too," said Yidnar.

"I-I-I . . . d-did? But I d-didn't see—"

"There was no one else here but Med, Carakenne, and us. No one. You attacked us with intent to kill."

Her perplexity was heartbreaking. Her jaw clenched, her eyes closed tightly for a moment. A deep sound of anguish came from low in her throat and when her eyes opened again, they pleaded for denial. "I d-did?"

"Yes."

"I-is th-that why . . ."

"Yes, for that and for the fact you are hurting yourself. No. Not another word. Get yourself together, Sergeant. Breathe. Calm down."

He tried to make himself continue to meet her expression of baffled distress—but he just couldn't. He couldn't remember another time in his life where he felt so horrible giving orders. "I'm truly sorry, sport," he added gently. "Until we find out what's happening to you, this is how it has to be."

He abruptly turned toward Med, who now stood staring at the displays on the monitors.

"Luckily she didn't rip up as much as I thought. Just surface area. I'm still worried about that lung, and her heart, and after that little . . . episode . . . I thought all that repair work we did the past five days was shot to shit," said Med. He crossed his arms over his chest, fingers tight around his upper arms. Meeting Yidnar's eyes, he dropped his tone to one the commandos used when they wanted only the person next to them to hear what they had to say. "That drug is completely gone from her system. It has been for two days."

"Yes, so . . . ?"

Med swallowed, glanced toward Rett, and shook his head slightly. "Two days clear, Major. I'm willing to grant a certain amount of this current behavior to disorientation, to stress, to her metabolism—which has gone off the steep end—taking the energy it usually puts toward healing her into fighting us. You and Ariam didn't help matters at all."

"We did what we had to do, Rhozev. Just as you did."

"I know that." Med leaned his head wearily against the housing of the unit he'd been staring at. "If this behavior doesn't stop soon, Major, I don't think there's anything else I could do for her. That whiff of gas she got is already wearing off, as you can see, and she's fairly immobilized, but far from calmed down. If she goes off again, she'll kill herself with the stress."

Rhozev's left hand clutched at the material over his chest, near the heart, his knuckles nearly white with the tightness of his grip. Yidnar felt a growing alarm, fearing more for the medtech at that moment than he did for Rett.

"Rhozev, you should take a break."

"I can't. You know I can't. At the same time I almost can't stand to be in range of her," he whispered as if admitting a deep failing. "She's in so much pain it's overloading me."

"Can that be affecting her behavior?"

"It's possible. People can get violent and . . . delirious in extreme pain, but I know Rett, so do you. I feel safe in saying this is not a pain-related reaction we're seeing." He closed his eyes for a moment before continuing. "I can use more of the anesthetic; all it does is slow her down. It doesn't stop her from thinking, from feeling anything. It won't, unless I give her enough to put her out completely."

Med took a breath, for once not looking sour. His sharp features were drawn, near despair as he indicated a monitor. "She can't take much more. If she doesn't go into cardiac arrest, *again*, if she doesn't have an aneurysm or a stroke of some sort . . . In her condition, I can't even afford to block or sedate her more than I just did.

"I'm not even sure if what I just did isn't going to make things worse. If she's to stay secured like that," he jerked his head toward her, "for very long, she's going to crack. That is if she hasn't cracked already."

"Do you truly feel she's mentally damaged? You weren't too sure earlier."

"I don't know what to believe. All I know is she must stay conscious. We can't let her shut down, and that will be her next attempt, to put herself in deepsleep as a means of escape. If she loses consciousness again I don't think we'll get anything we recognize back. If she comes out of it at all."

"I agree we can't leave her like she is for much longer," said Yidnar. "*Something* has to be done. But I'm out of ideas."

"I'm running another batch of tests," said Med wearily. "These will take about ten minutes. I'll have a better idea of—"

He stopped, and turned aside. "Of next steps. Maybe you should call in her father. Whichever way this goes . . . I'm sure Colonel Reve will want to be here if it's possible."

* * * * *

KNEELING NEXT TO RETT'S BED, trying to soothe her sister, Ariam couldn't hear what Med was saying. However, her capability of lip reading was acute. It was a skill the Special Forces encouraged in all their personnel. Rett and Ariam had the advantage of having developed proficiency in it as children. She felt more blood drain from her face.

It's not mental damage, it's not, Ariam thought, more than tiffed, not bothering to stop the fresh tears coming to her eyes. Rett's terror and distress were overwhelming. Ariam needed a buffer to absorb some of the excess emotional energy she was trying to dampen in her sister. Someone natural at it, like Kraym had been; someone like Semage, who was learning. Her hand shook as it smoothed Rett's hair. *Rett isn't cracked. She isn't!*

Med was right about calling in Colonel Reve. Ariam couldn't deny that, especially with the 21st Division so near. She'd been keeping Reve informed and he'd wonder at the sudden lack of communication between them. No doubt he would show up on his own, taking the break in the Ariam's regular updates as his cue.

Dad steadied her out of more than one nightmare, maybe he can help again . . . and if not, I'll need him to be here.

* * * * *

UNTIL NOW, RETT HAD BEGUN to feel safe with her friends and the return to reality. Then Xonomer's voice, with his cruel, mocking laughter, had informed her of her foolishness in relying on them to protect her. Just to prove his point that even an alert commando guard was ineffective, he'd lashed out at Carakenne with his icy, burning hand.

363

Rett was sorry Carakenne hadn't taken her warning. She tried to warn her, expecting the corporal to react without question as if she'd warned her out of the path of a weapon discharge. Carakenne hadn't moved, so Rett had to force her aside so Xonomer's blow didn't crush the small woman. Then he'd directed a surge of deadly energy at Med, who also refused to move.

"Now look what that got you," said Xonomer. "Always trying to help, even when it's not wanted. Look what it got you."

Until now, Rett had been able to fight Xonomer a little—until now!

"Your *friends* did this to you. You're helpless. Immobilized. Tied down and partially anesthetized. Your *friends*. The friends you tried your best to kill," said the alien.

"You made them appear as—" She stopped her own damning words even as he cut her short.

"So you see—I own you. You admit I control your perceptions. Do you think I'd let you go, even for one moment?" The alien laughed. "Don't you see now you can only surrender to me? I already control you," he repeated. "*Nothing* here has happened without my control. Nothing. I control even the moods and perceptions of your friends. I turn them against you. Erode their trust. Reinforce their doubts. All that rapport you've built up over years I can change in the blink of eye. Or did you forget so quickly what happened when you first came to this planet? If I choose to exert my power over them even more strongly than I did before, do you still think you can convince them against me?"

Her recently awakened sense of reality and control wavered. She gritted her teeth until her jaw ached, his words flaying her mind like the fangs of a predator rending flesh from a carcass.

All the while, his triumphant laugher rang in her ears, loud and hurting.

There had to be way. There must be a way out. He had to have a weakness.

He does. You can take him. You only need to look deep, Rett.

That voice again! It came and went so quickly she thought she imagined it. She might as well have. Rett knew damned well she wasn't going to defeat this entity, and she was deluding herself to imagine it.

"At last you're beginning to see reason."

She snarled at the alien standing on the right side of her bed. "I d-didn't say I would make it easy for you, either." She glanced around. Why weren't the others going to do anything now that Xonomer was right here, close enough to touch?

Major Yidnar and Med didn't see him. They were busy pretending to look at the computers. She knew it was her fate they discussed. Rett turned her head to the left to see if Ariam, Carakenne, Jaq, and Trebor were going to do something. Her stomach clenched as she realized they couldn't hear or see Xonomer.

All they had seen was her speaking to empty space.

"But—he's right here." She sounded demented even to her own ears. "C-c-can't you s-s . . ." Hearing the dreaded stammer of her youth come back strong as it had just moments before, Rett closed her mouth.

"Look at them. Look at yourself in their eyes. Poor, broken Rett. She's gone quite mad. Broken one time too many. They will have to make choices shortly. You should know that now, even if they give you mercy, you'll be mine. You can give yourself to me willingly, or let me take you by default—making them suffer in the meanwhile over the decisions. After all you have seen about yourself, will you remain that selfish? Your sister, your lover, your friends, the longer they have to look at you, see you in your insanity, the worse it will be for them."

"You're wrong," whispered Rett, but she wasn't so sure now.

"Look at them," ordered Xonomer. "Look at them carefully. Resignation and pity. They will feel nothing but relief when you're gone, I can assure you. It is easier to explain the hero of Nyorfias died from her wounds rather than admit she went as a raving lunatic. Look at them."

Unable to resist the strength of the alien's compulsion, she obeyed. Rett saw Ariam, her face tear-streaked, strained, but loving, filled with shared pain and compassion. Jaq, confused, struggling between hope and despair, his love for her so deep and strong that nothing could force Rett to deny that no matter what happened to her, his love would remain. Trebor, Carakenne . . . whatever else they felt through their surface helplessness overall was, again, loyalty and love. Even with her eyes closed, she saw the truth in their auras, auras that surrounded her so strongly that she didn't need to pull her exhausted concentration on them to interpret their meaning.

366

No pity. Only their burning desire to help any way they could, written in orange battle tension shot through with empathic greens. The love and loyalty, like the fathomless blue of Jaq's eyes. The muddy colors of fear and uncertainty battled with the clearer ones, but Rett had seen enough.

She felt her tension and fear ebb as she stopped resisting the alien's urge to look at them and gazed of her own free will, filling herself with what she saw. The hideous constriction in her chest eased. Ariam, responding to the change immediately, offered an encouraging smile, her fingers tightening over Rett's left hand.

"Maybe you can influence *how* we see things," Rett said, turning back to face the terrible presence. "But you can't dictate what they feel for me, or what I feel for them. Do you see resignation and pity for me in their eyes? Maybe you're the one having delusions now."

A crack appeared in Xonomer's confidence. It was fleeting, but enough for her to taste the entity's doubt. Her chance, the edge she'd been searching for.

"You won't control me again," she said.

The alien laughed horribly. "How short your memory is. I never let go of you. I will never let you go. If I cannot have you completely, if you will not submit, I'll keep what parts of you I do have. Your friends are loyal, yes, but they will still be convinced of your mental instability."

The entity's mental fist tightened around her mind, sapping her newfound strength and will. Ariam's hands, however, had found and fortified the thread of hope Rett had never released, her unabated energy feeding the opalescent light within it, enriching Rett's confidence.

"Rett, Rett, whatever it is, fight it," Ariam whispered. "Let me help you. We'll fight it together."

Her sister's voice was a lifeline; her presence and physical contact firming the defensive mental barriers Rett tried to hold against Xonomer's encroaching claim of darkness. Heartening her. Bolstering her bruised courage. Allowing her to start taking back control, bit-by-bit.

The meteor eyes suddenly swirled with fury. "What is the source of your resistance?"

"Forget it," snarled Rett at the alien. "You don't have a chance in two worlds now."

* * * * *

A PAIN CUT THROUGH ARIAM as Rett spoke with empty air again. The action gave strength to Med's dire guess to Rett's state of sanity. The shiver of reaction from Jaq, Carakenne, and Trebor added weight to her nagging doubts.

No, I have to believe I'm right! I know I am!

Wishing for Semage, needing the support he was so capable of giving, Ariam tightened her physical and mental contact with her sister, her eyes never left Rett's face. Something was going on inside her sister . . . a lot more definite that a mere weird feeling. It came from just beyond the edges of her empathic perception.

367

She was starting to sense something else now, too—from outside, beyond the room. But she couldn't focus on that right now, or she'd lose what little connection she'd managed to make with Rett.

"Jaq, I need help. Will you help me?"

"What do you want me to do?" He turned to her, his desperation to do something, anything, sharp and clear.

Ariam gauged the Zetinorian's current level of emotional stability. He wasn't exactly the buffer she needed, but he certainly could provide her with the amplification she wanted. He didn't pull back when she rested her hand on the pulse in his throat for a moment. Jaq was upset, desperate, but he was well in control, nothing chaotic about him. As soon as he had a definite task to perform, he would settle even more. She dampened her dry lips with her tongue.

Before she tried to explain, Trebor, ever quick, anticipated Ariam's request.

"She needs to boost off you, Jaq. She used to do this with Kraym, sometimes with H'tenneck and Nerrah. All you need to do is give her your hands and don't resist if you feel her . . . uhm, *pulling*, as Nerrah described it. Here, like so—"

In another second, Jaq's big, warm hands were wrapped lightly around Ariam's neck, his thumbs at the base of her skull, his longest fingers just over the pulse points in her throat. "Are you sure about this, Ariam?" Jaq asked nervously. "I can kill you in a second. What if . . . the thing affecting Rett tries to get at me?"

"I put my life in your hands before, Jaq. My trust in you hasn't changed since then," she said calmly, leaning into his grasp.

"That's great, Ariam, but I'm still not sure about this."

"Relax. If I see you making any wrong moves, I'll stop it." Trebor sounded encouraging and calm, but left no doubt he'd stop it instantly, in whatever manner he saw fit. "Carakenne will watch, as well. We have to help the Sarge."

Ariam let herself go. The difference was immediate, also the sensation of *otherness*.

Whatever it is, it's certainly not Pam . . . it's not coming from inside Rett. Ariam cast around, puzzled, since she distinctly felt Pam's familiar mindforce. *Distant . . . but present, watching— but from the outside this time . . .* She acknowledged Pam's wispy presence briefly and continued her search, freezing onto the strange, weird sensations she'd picked up earlier. Unable to locate the source, she backtracked, hoping to find a stronger trail to follow outward. *Something evil. Alien . . .*

Yes. Tagging the source as the alien filled her with a fierce satisfaction. She deftly pulled more psychic energy from Jaq, broadening her range, redefining the sensations she absorbed as she edged closer to Rett's consciousness. She reached for her usual entry.

369

"Ow!" Her soft gasp was a shout of astonishment in her mind as she came up sudden and solid against a wall. It hurt and surprised her as much as if she'd run into it physically. Confused, more than a little frightened, Ariam moved her other hand to Rett's temple, making a stronger contact, pushing every ounce of her awareness in a desperate penetration to breach her sister's sudden mental shields of steel-azurium toughness.

Where did she get these? Rett never learned to shield on more than a basic level! None of us did, except the Major . . .

Pam. Somehow she learned it from Pam. At any other time, I would say it was a good thing, but not now! Oh, deities, Rett, this is the wrong time to block me!

"Let me in, Rett," whispered Ariam, her hand sliding through the dampness of Rett's slick hair to rest over her sister's forehead gently. "Let me pass. I need to track down what's attacking you, to feel what's happening!"

Jerking her head aside, Rett continued looking at empty space, growling her defiance at something only she could see.

From somewhere behind her came a sharp breath of frustration. Not Jaq, who had entered a near trance of his own accord. Trebor.

Ariam turned her head slightly, Jaq's hands moving with her. "Trebor," she said softly. More tears jumped to blur her vision at the naked agony in his golden eyes. The practical, quick-minded former professor of structural engineering, his composure usually as solid as the hard planes and angles of his face, finally showed a crack.

"Damn it," he snarled, "I need to vent *something*. I've had it with six years of some unknown cosmic whatsis having it in for her, for some reason or another. Six years of it, Ariam! I've been trying to find some pattern, some structure to it. It has none, but it's still there—"

His frustration was mirrored in Carakenne's bitten lips. The small woman slid her uninjured arm around his waist in and for support. Her pale eyebrows puckered in deep thought.

"Trebor, you can't give up," Ariam said. "*She's* not, that's why she's fighting it so hard. There *is* something unusual going on. I can feel it now. I think Jaq is right about supernatural phenomena. You have to believe in Rett. We all must. In who and what we know her to be."

"I do," said Trebor. "We do. Always have. I didn't stay with her all these years because I had doubts about her, Ariam. But seeing her like this—knowing what she's been through—doesn't make keeping the faith any easier."

"Not too much worth having is ever easy," Jaq said softly, his voice dreamlike. "I forgot that once, not too long ago."

"Sergeant Ariam," breathed Carakenne, "can you really feel something?"

Ariam didn't answer. She didn't have to. Cara's hopefulness was like oxygen to a dying flame, kindling the fire in Trebor's golden eyes again; firming the contact of Jaq's fingers on Ariam's skin.

With hope came faith, like sunlight on morning fog, burning away the miasma of doubt. Ariam's nerve endings tingled and she put everything she had into pouring their strength into Rett.

* * * * *

WARMTH BEGAN TO PENETRATE RETT. Filtered and focused through Ariam's hands came new strength and a warm fullness. Like before, the lifeline of light and hope against the darkness.

Her friends, her sister, might not believe what Rett saw, but they believed in *her*.

"Your sister? Don't you know she cares nothing for you? For twenty-five years, you were there for her, every minute, ready to drop anything, give anything for her, even your life. All she ever did was take. Take, and leave you to pick up after her. Her thoughts even now are only to finish this quickly so she could be with the man she loves. She resents you for keeping her from him all this time, you know. He resents that your actions gave him more responsibility and work than he ever wanted. That relationship is doomed. But never fear. Your sister will seek another, as she ever had. She will comfort your Zetinorian. She's very intimate with him, even right now, right here."

"Damn you and the way you keep twisting things. You're wrong!"

"Am I? She knew you were out there wounded, dying. She knew it for a long time. Both of them did, your other best friend and your sister. They did nothing; *she* did nothing. Made no move to help you when you most needed her."

"*No!*" Rett's heart flamed with a challenging denial that rivaled Xonomer's meteoric gaze and cleared her head of the last effects of Med's gas. "You're not going to get me with that. With any of it. I know Ariam, as sister and soldier. As soldiers, we have to draw a line. Mission operations supersede anything personal. We all had our jobs to do. Mine was to run a diversion. Theirs

371

was to secure the base. After they did that, took care of what needed immediate attention afterward—*then* they could take the time to look for me. It happened exactly as it should have."

"Yet you altered your mission operations to go to your sister's rescue," Xonomer pointed out.

"I made sure my absence would be compensated for," returned Rett coldly. "It was a different situation entirely." That was one incident during the entire Wide River and Circle campaign for which she refused any guilt. "And you're wrong. She's always been there for me, every bit as much as I've been there for her. You've picked the wrong subject this time."

"Then we shall see if you are willing to repeat what you were ready to do in the past. I will give you her life, leave her unharmed, in exchange for your surrender."

The tendrils of lethal energy rose around him, preparing to carry out his threat.

Rett twisted violently in the straps holding her down. "Ariam, get out of here. Leave me alone. I don't want you to get hurt. Jaq! *Jaq*—let go of her and *wake up*! Get her out of here!"

Jaq pulled his hands from their contact with Ariam as if burned, his half-lidded eyes going wide.

"I'm not leaving you, Rett," said Ariam with maddening calm and that logheaded expression Rett knew all too well. "Not this time."

"Jaq, Trebor, please! Get Ariam out of here. He'll kill her!" Rett pleaded, begged. "Cara!"

The two men hesitated, exchanging glances.

"Damn it! *I'm not crazy*. Look at me. Jaq, please." She locked her gaze with his, putting everything she could into her eyes and face, begging him. "Jaq. *Please*. I'm not crazy. Even if I am, what harm could it do to take Ariam outside the room? Please. I'm asking you to protect Ariam and yourselves! Carakenne, remember what happened before? You felt something, I *know* you did!" Rett choked, her voice broke. "I can't fight him if he kills her!"

"Your precautions are useless," Xonomer said. "I can have your sister as easily as I have you."

"Rett, calm down," pleaded Ariam.

"I think she's right, Ariam. Come on."

Ariam angrily shook Jaq's hand from her shoulder. "Right or wrong—I'm not leaving her! Rett, take it easy!"

Rett, frustrated, savagely fought the straps holding her prisoner.

"Damn it, Rett, let me in, I feel—"

"Ariam, *go—there's no time.*"

"I'm not leaving you."

"He'll kill you. Just like he tried to kill Carakenne and Med. He'll kill all of you to get to me. Trust me!" Tears blurred Rett's eyes, clogged her nose. "When in our lives have I ever t-t-told you something that w-wasn't true?"

"Never, Rett. But live or die, I'm not leaving!"

With a harsh cry of frustration, Rett made a desperate lunge against her restraints. The pain nearly blacked her out, but she was sure something had loosened. She had to keep trying.

"You are getting tiresome. I grow bored. Let me remind you of what I promised for eternity if you continue to defy me," said Xonomer, and the helpless, horrible, body wracking agony returned to crush Rett and her defenses. "Your sister will be only the first to die!"

"Not Ariam—!" Rett screamed as the cruel, lethal power of the alien being trembled in check for a final moment. When he unclenched his right fist, she knew it would unleash with the force of a lightning strike, as it had earlier. Only this time she was sure the force would be far stronger than the bursts directed at Med or Carakenne.

The entity reached for Rett with the left hand, as if about to bestow a caress. She expected the pain this time, but expectation made no difference . . . except to give her vocal response to it more purpose and direction. "Ariam if you won't leave—*move out of the way!*"

* * * * *

FRIGHTENED BY THE SUDDENNESS OF the change, prompted by the searing urgency in Rett's hoarse voice, Ariam straightened and took an uncertain step back, another to the right. On the bed, Rett convulsed; the snap her body made against the restraint coinciding with a gagging exhalation. Before Ariam could return to her sister, her hair came loose from the tight braid and tuck she wore it and crackled into a nimbus around her head. The shorter hairs all over her body snapped and prickled between her skin and uniform.

"What in two—" Instinct made her sidestep again, and she had time to feel a blazing cold that went to her very bones before *something* exploded in the very spot she'd been kneeling. The force of it lifted her off her feet, sent her slamming into Jaq's large, hard frame, sent Trebor and Carakenne stumbling back as well. Ariam was sure she'd caught a glimpse of Carakenne strung out horizontally from Trebor's belt.

Filled with surprise and pain, she thought: *Rett was right, that would have killed me if I didn't move—but what was it?*

"Are you all right?" gasped Jaq.

Ariam didn't answer. She staggered to her feet.

"*That* didn't come from the Sarge." Carakenne unclenched the fingers of her right hand from Trebor's belt.

Ariam met the smaller woman's gaze, then glanced toward Med and Major Yidnar. They couldn't have missed that. Ariam took some satisfaction at the thunderstruck expression on Yidnar's face.

"I think that's exactly what's happened before," Cara went on with a nod. "After she threw me out of the way and went after Med."

"What in two worlds was it?" Trebor asked.

"That's what I want to know. Damn it, let me go!" Ariam shrugged off Jaq's supporting hand, ignoring the pain in her chest. Deities, she'd only experienced that sort of concussive force before from explosives. But there had been no sound, no flash.

She resumed her place next to her sister as Rett's long frame strained and convulsed in helpless torture. A silent scream of pain thickened Rett's brown throat, a sound finally forced out as a gasped: "No . . . I . . . never . . . will!"

"Something really strange is going on," Trebor said uneasily.

For the first time since she'd known him, Ariam heard a tremor of outright fear in the older man's deep voice.

"This is what I meant by supernatural," said Jaq. "There *is* something in here. I feel it now."

Ariam glanced up as Med approached, drawn to the bedside by the incredible pain Rett was experiencing. His body froze into stillness mid-step, his expression wavering, altering. If she hadn't seen the unnaturalness of it, she might have let his words upset her.

"There's nothing else I can do, Ariam. It's not going to stop. There's nothing more I can do for her."

Whatever it is has taken over Med. It has probably influenced our moods all along . . .

"Thanks for trying, Med," said Ariam, allowing her natural reaction to such an announcement surface. She ducked her face, thinking fast, pulling up every defense she was capable of. "Did the Major com my father?"

"He did. Colonel Reve was already enroute."

"I think I'd like to be alone with her for a while before . . . before Dad gets here and the Major comes back in. Jaq can stay."

* * * * *

"No, Ariam. Get out of here!" Rett might have shouted into a vacuum for all the volume her voice gained. Xonomer, however, heard her perfectly.

Laughter blasted from the alien entity. He made sure Rett knew exactly how much of a hold he had on Med at the moment, even causing the medtech to reach for the anesthetic mask again, reconsider, and pick up an injector instead. With deliberate motions, Med fitted a dark amber vial inside the dispensing chamber.

"She's too dangerous, Ariam. I'm going to sedate her again first. I'll use this; she won't develop adverse effects for a few hours, and . . . well, by then it shouldn't be an issue. But at least you and your father will be able to talk to her . . . not like with the gas," said Med, his lips forming the words that Rett heard Xonomer speak.

"Don't do this to Med. Hurt me if you must, but don't do this to him." As much as she pretended not to notice Med's softer, gentler side, Rett knew her medtech better than even Rhozev thought she did. "He'll never get over it. Let him go."

"Then come with me. Let go of the thread. Let it all go. Your friends already think you have lost the ability to reason. I have made certain that one," Xonomer said, indicating Med, "is sure of it. At least for now he is sure of it. As you say, when it is too late he will realize his error."

"Damn you, let him *go*."

"Very well, then, for the moment he's served my purpose." Confident, the alien laughed again and Med staggered, released from his moment of possession.

"Come with me now. They will deal with the empty husk that is left. Or do you want your sister to experience this? To live through everything you've been through? I can assure you, as empathetic as she is, she cannot even begin to imagine the scope of it. She is strong in her own way, but in your place she would shatter like thin ice. And for eternity you will hear her screams in the part of your mind I will allow you to keep."

"You leave her and anyone else out of this!"

* * * * *

ARIAM REACHED FOR HER SISTER again. "Rett." But try as she might, she couldn't get past a barrier of force that suddenly sprang up between them. The field was so charged with energy Ariam recoiled a length simply from touching a fingertip to it.

Visible, writhing bands of force wrapped around Rett's body. The soon became so bright it was a miracle that somehow Rett and the bed were not in flames.

"This isn't hallucination!" yelled Ariam as the energy repulsed her yet again. "Something psychic's going on—something alien!"

"I feel it too," said the Major, shuddering and blinking hard as if awakening from a dream. Strain and concern dug long, deep slashes in his face.

"Do you feel the cold?" whispered Carakenne. "That's what I felt before—"

Words were ripped from Rett's straining throat. "I . . . won't . . . let . . . you . . ."

Med cried out and clamped both hands to his head, his fingers tight in his sandy hair. The injector he'd picked up fell to the floor and rolled away as the planet beneath them seemed to pitch and yaw in segments, like an entire raft of logs shooting a rapids.

Earthquake? No—it was generated from nearby, within this room. As she fought for balance, Ariam saw Rett's head move sharply aside; felt the rushing movement of air; heard the sound of impact. She was on her feet as bright blood splattered over her and those closest to her.

"Look!" Ariam gestured to the blood coming from Rett's nose, her mouth; splattered on their uniforms. "You saw—damn it, Med, you can see it! We all just felt—whatever that was, and it wasn't an earthquake. Is this the product of a hallucination?" Ariam demanded. "Is it? Rett's being attacked, damn it—and we're not helping *her*, we've been helping whatever's attacking her!"

"But from what, Ariam?" Bewildered, Med swayed where he stood, only Major Yidnar's hand on his arm keeping him upright. "From what? Us? Empty space? Cold air?"

Ariam shot him a look of scorn. "You can't always see the germs that cause disease with your eyes can you, Med? But I suppose I should give you a break, since it's had a hold on you almost as long as Rett's been awake—and it had you completely under its control just a minute ago."

"What did!" shouted Med in tiffed agitation. "What are you talking about? Can someone tell me what's happening?"

Major Yidnar leaned over and scooped up the fallen injector, handing it to Med without a word. The medtech stared at it, the faint color remaining in his pale face draining completely.

"I wasn't going to give her this, was I? Tell me I wasn't. Was I?" He sounded sick.

"Nhoz Palen."

Ariam spun to face Jaq. His voice sounded strange speaking the alien language—was that his own? She'd only ever heard the endearment, *kelani*, from him before.

Sick horror was growing in his emotional aura, his voice, taking over his face. "I don't know why I remember this now. But I do. I know this thing. Xonomer," he finished in a near whisper. "The Ravener. The Black King. It's not the first time. Everywhere the Yixolryns have been, every world that fell to them, all that I know of, anyway . . . all have a name for this being. Some called it a god. To others it was just a force of evil—or motivation. How did I miss making this connection sooner?" The horror in his eyes gave way to anger, darkening them into the dangerous blue-black of a storm cloud.

Ariam didn't doubt that Jaq, too, had been under its influence at times. Maybe all of them had. It didn't matter now. Now it had a name, it was real, and she was ready to fight with her sister. Whatever it took.

"Jaq, you can see it now?"

But now Jaq seemed locked in place, his expression as frozen as his body.

"I'll take that as a yes. Pip!" Ariam motioned to the older commando who had taken up a station just outside the door. *Probably escorted Dad here,* she managed to think. "Knife. Now!" She lifted her hand and caught his blade by the hilt as, without hesitation, he drew it from the scabbard and tossed it toward her. "Thanks, Pip. Wait out there but stand clear of the door, and if Colonel Reve is out there with you right now, keep him out of here."

"Agreed," said Trebor. "You and whoever is with you secure that hall and hold it. No one comes near the room until we say so. It's bad enough this thing is after Ariam."

Pip's silver eyebrows lift in puzzlement, but he turned away with a nod.

Ariam turned back to her sister, extending the compressed blade with a *snick*. The azurium-steel alloy passed through the medical restraints like an SMG discharge through snow. Sure, she could have unfastened them in a normal manner. But she wanted to make sure they were out of commission in case this Nhoz Palen Ravener Dark Entity Xonomer alien thing convinced anyone else Rett needed to be immobilized.

"Major, Med—Jaq can see it now, too. Unless you think *he's* hallucinating. I think *we* were the only ones seeing things that weren't there. Go. I'll stay with Rett and take my chances if you can't." Ariam flung this at the others and returned her full attention to her sister. "Fight, Rett, fight! You're free now. I'll help you. It can't beat you. Use the mind-place! Get behind that door you made, remember? Come on, get behind it and fight this thing! It can't hurt me. Think, Rett! It's had plenty of opportunity, enough time to kill all of us! It's blowing a lot of flash and smoke, trying to trick you into something. *Think*, Rett. Fight it!"

* * * * *

"This Nhoz Palen, Jaq, what can you tell us?" Yidnar asked.

Not taking his eyes from the empty space near the top right hand side of Rett's bed, the Zetinorian shuddered from top to bottom. Then he spoke as if in a dream, his Standard more accented than ever, the words falling into a soft cadence that was more song than spoken word.

"Arneaut Holm was a great warrior, but over many years of battle after battle he had forgotten how to dream, how to imagine how things might be, or how things once were. He lived only for battle, lived only to drive the enemies of Zetinor Prime back from where they came. He lived from moment, to moment, one battle to the next. He fought alone, as he dared not form attachment or friendship to someone who might be killed. He needed no distraction, no deterrent to his purpose.

"Thus the one defensive weapon he needed lay unused and forgotten, its once-bright edge rusted and dull from long years of neglect and disuse. The wise ones despaired, knowing the true nature of the battle to come. And then, with the help of a creature of legend—a companion and steed capable of great magic—and a *Prenzzirhim* sent by the One, Arneaut Holm's weapon was honed, made bright and ready.

"Nhoz Palen did not suspect. Nor did the dark one have any defense against this weapon. Yet the warrior Arneaut Holm did not recognize his advantage for what it was. When the challenge came from the evil deity, he spurned his new weapon as useless to a soldier. And thus he also turned away the companionship and alliance so freely offered not only by the steed of magic and the *Prenzzirhim*, but of the other defenders of Zetinor Prime.

"*'Reconsider. No one fights a god alone'* urged the wise ones, but Arneaut Holm, who was proud and strong, said *'I do. I want no one else to get hurt'*. In this matter the great warrior had made a fatal error."

Jaq stopped speaking, blinking hard as if awakening.

"Please continue, Jaq. What happened to Arneaut Holm? He died?"

"After the battle, his mind was gone. Many years later, his body died. His final battle was in the shadow realm. His dreams and imagination. His own mind. It was that weapon he rejected—he'd been given gifts to make it strong, but . . . he tried to fight instead the only way he knew how. And . . . he failed."

"And what's this . . . *Prenzzirhim?*" Trebor wanted to know.

"Uhm . . . there isn't a term for it in Standard. A divine assistant." Jaq paused and thought some more. "A spiritual guide."

"Like an ego-merge?" breathed Carakenne.

Major Yidnar's had taken one long step toward the Zetinorian, but then Carakenne's remark froze him. *An ego-merge?* he thought. *Rett? Is it possible? It would explain so much.* "And what is *Nhoz Palen*, Jaq?"

"A god, agent, or force of destruction. A Ravener, as we would—as we used to say—on Zetinor Prime. The elemental force of evil. Darkness. Corruption, disorder, defilement . . . on that it preys and draws strength. It's what rules over the Yixolryn Coalition.

"This is the first information that's made sense all day," remarked Trebor. "And makes the pattern that was eluding me. I can see it now."

"If this entity defeats Rett, Nyorfias will fall. And here we've been, not helping at all."

"It's not exactly like any of us knew—" Before Yidnar could complete his statement, the temperature in the room plummeted. All the humidity in the air seemed to dissipate. He saw that Ariam and Jaq were not the only ones with wild hair. Carakenne's long locks came loose, and as if they were alive, wrapped around her face, covered her eyes. It got into her mouth, trapping her hands and fingers to her head and face when she tried to push it away, gagging her when she tried to speak.

Electricity snapped between Trebor and Jaq, a torrent of neon blue sparks that rivaled the amazing shade of the Zetinorian's eyes.

"Flaming shit!" Ariam dropped her borrowed knife, which glowed molten hot. The blade clattered to the floor and shot away as if jet-propelled toward Carakenne's boots.

"Carakenne!" Yidnar snapped in warning.

Bound and blinded by her own hands and hair, only his warning and the small woman's intensified ability to rely on senses other than sight allowed her to move aside before it impaled her through the foot.

Jaq's mouth opened, but no sound emerged. His hands went to his throat, eyes huge and dark in sudden terror.

"Major!" came a hoarse yell from Rett's direction. "Jaq's tiffed him—damn it, get him *out*—mmff!"

Her voice cut off as if an invisible hand smothered her mouth and nose just as Med's had before. Yidnar, already in motion, glanced over to see Rett's body arc in a convulsion so hard it was a miracle her spine didn't snaps.

From the empty space by Rett's bed, a spark leapt, became a streak of dark lightning, and snapped toward the Zetinorian.

Ignoring the shocks that prickled and pulsed through him, Yidnar snatched Jaq, jerked him against his body, and twisted the both of them aside and down to the floor as the blast thundered past overhead. The snaps of static both of them had experienced on contact with each other was nothing compared to the energy surrounding the bolt. He wondered if he had uniform left on his back. He didn't have to guess about the likelihood of blisters, already he felt them forming.

Ariam was just going on before about how this thing couldn't hurt her, he thought, following through his move by returning to an upright position, bringing Jaq with him. The maneuver brought them both to the recessed area surrounding the door leading into the corridor. He kept his body between Jaq and anything behind them, hoping if he failed to get him out of the path of another shot like that the barrier of his flesh and bones might do some good—although he doubted it. Deities, they both would end up as carbonized scorch marks on the wall and floor with another one.

"You have to get out of here."

Jaq frowned. "I can't leave. And—uh, I think your hair's on fire, sir. It's smoking."

"Let me know when you see flames. You said we weren't helping Rett—what can we do?"

"Trust her," he said simply. "Believe in her. I don't think we can do anything else."

"If this thing kills you, Jaq, Rett's not going to have any hope left."

"I'm needed right here. I left her once; stopped believing in her once—never again," Jaq said, his voice strong, gaze level.

"There's a good chance this . . . creature . . . had something to do with that."

"That may be, sir. However, I believe we all have free will, and even if we're influenced by outside factors, we have to own the choices we make. It's time I did."

Yidnar couldn't argue with that. He released his hold on the Zetinorian and moved aside. "Just—try to stay alive then."

"I will, sir."

Things were quiet in the room behind them. Had that malignant lightning bolt caused a wider angle of damage than he thought? But no, as Yidnar moved back it seemed no time had passed at all. *It's almost as if we have to be within a certain range. We don't exist to whatever it is unless we're right there . . . it has to be connected to that that distorted time feeling I just had a few seconds ago.*

Rett mentioned a game. Xonomer made his move. He's waiting for ours. That is, if it is for us to decide . . .

"Sir?" asked Trebor as Yidnar stepped closer to the main part of the room. Everyone was still there, as they were before, looking a bit confused, singed and windblown, but otherwise wary, ready.

Yidnar swallowed, shivered. All his experiences offworld and on, and he'd never experienced this sense of distortion, of unreal reality. *As if time stopped.*

The blend of plea and ultimatum from Ariam caught his attention. Apparently, all her efforts to touch her sister were still being repulsed. Rett, free of restraints, still dazed from the second blow that had cut off her warning, was attempting to get up, a fierce Ariam glancing around the room as if daring anything to interfere with the process. She was urging Rett's virtually motion-less progress in equal measure.

"Get up, Rett. Get up. Come on, you can do it."

"I c-can't d-do it, Ari . . . I t-t-tried . . . I just c-can't."

He'd never heard a voice so emotionless, so lifeless, so terribly exhausted, so much so that his knees nearly buckled in response to it. To actually witness Rett at the absolute bottom of her seem-ingly inexhaustible endurance and vitality was shocking.

"You must," said Ariam harshly. "Try *harder.*"

An intense urge to turn on Ariam and tell her to leave Rett alone almost overcame him. But then came a voice inside his head, one much different from H'vren's. The new thoughts tore through his impulse, shredding it.

Like that will help? Screw that! Don't listen to that shit! Wake UP, Major—you bubblehead! You've been given an edge. USE IT! Or I'm going to kick your ass!

The voice was abruptly gone, replaced by yet another mind-touch, swift, fleeting, delicate compared to the one previous. Yet the source behind it was so enormous and incomprehensibly vast he reeled from the contact.

"Major!" Trebor said sharply.

384

Yidnar shook his full attention back to his surroundings and glanced to the F-troop second. The pain digging into his upper arms came from Trebor's sinewy fingers; the hard yellow light in the other man's eyes burned right through the confusion that had frozen his limbs.

"If I didn't know any better, sir, I'd say you went completely out of your body for a second."

"Maybe I did." Yidnar cleared his throat, wondering if his face and eyes betrayed his inner astonishment.

"What happened?"

"Hindsight," he said. "I really wish Jaq had that memory a lot sooner, but . . ."

"*If onlys* waste time," said Ariam.

Yidnar nodded. He pushed down the turbulence in his mind, sifting through the information from whatever—or whomever—had so briefly linked with his mind.

385

"Major?"

"Never mind. We all have to help Rett."

3.3.16 MEDICAL SECTION, AURORA BASE, EPNOCE
0536.03.20 (LOCAL RECKONING)

"But how can we help?" Carakenne had knotted her hair, retrieved Pip's knife, and held it readily in her left hand. Her eyes searched in vain for some target, her augmented senses of hearing and smell detected nothing. There was something in the room with them, she knew it for certain, a huge region of bitter, burning, living cold. She saw that everyone felt it now.

She wished for her Omni, a few other handy devices she'd made, anything that would give her information she could work with, ponder over, apply to the empirical data her eyes and body experienced. Somehow she could take all that and make this into something they could understand, could fight. They established it was alien, and had a mind. Therefore, what produced energy had to have some sort of mass, some composition. Even air had mass. Cold simply didn't *happen*.

In addition, there was emotional energy being generated. She couldn't visualize it like her platoon leader could, or sense it like Sergeant Ariam. She didn't have sensitive hair like a Zetinorian. But she felt it as much as any other humanoid felt strong emotions. That alone told Carakenne the user of the energy, or the source itself, had to be defined as something more than *alien*. Anything foreign could be considered alien, whether machine, thinking being, or inert matter. Emotional energy—at least the emotional energy she and the others had experienced—was not caused by something constructed. Therefore, the source was alive. Maybe not in the sense she knew it, but a thinking being.

Not even thought is made of nothing, since thoughts have energy that can be measured—that's fact. And this . . . Thing . . . has to be drawing energy from somewhere, which means we have to find out what source or sources it uses, and remove, block, or jam it somehow.

But what if the Thing is drawing energy from the entire universe? Can it truly be what some races define as a deity—a for real one, and not just a term of convenience like the one we use for psi-powerful alien beings—as we believe them to be?

How do you stop that without destroying everything as it exists now?

She forgot to breathe for a moment, faced by the overwhelming enormity of such an idea. Then Carakenne dismissed this with a shake of her head, refusing to rise to the convoluted challenge, as intriguing as it was. She didn't have time to get lost in speculative thought. She had tangible evidence all around her, and that required direct action.

"Before we get lost on all sorts of cultural tangents, let's nail down facts," she said.

Everyone in the room—except the Sarge—turned to look at her.

Still not comfortable with being a center of attention, especially with Major Yidnar himself regarding her so intently, Carakenne swallowed and took a deep breath,

"The facts," she repeated. "Fact, there is *something* in this room with us. And it has a mind. Therefore, we're dealing with a living being. Maybe it doesn't have a physical form like we do, but it's definitely sentient." She took three steps forward, turned, paced back. "It has psi. It's very powerful. Apparently, it's telekinetic, telepathic, and empathic. It's after the Sarge. It will threaten any of us to get to her, but it doesn't really care about us otherwise—or else we'd be dead already. It had any number of chances to kill us. We all know that." She paced the three steps again. "So, how do we fight it?"

* * * * *

"You're right, Carakenne. It is some*thing*, and it has a very powerful mind." Yidnar growled under his breath, some of the contact he'd had starting to make sense. "We were being manipulated by whatever it is. Ariam was right—as usual—whatever it is almost had Rhozev all the way. Shit, it just about had me, too."

He went to the medtech swiftly, grasping Rhozev's upper arms with a painful, harsh grip. "Listen, we were being influenced by an alien mind, shake it off! Just knowing what it is can help you resist it. Look at me, don't think, just look at me."

Med dropped the injector he stared at and shuddered as if someone had poured a tankful of ice water over him. His eyes widened as he stared into Yidnar's face.

"You know what's in your heart, Rhozev. That's the only truth. Rett is badly hurt, tired, and afraid, but she is in full possession of her senses! Believe it!"

"I can feel that now," said Med, using the toe of his boot to loft the injector into a far corner of the room. "I can also feel you're going to cripple me if you squeeze any harder."

The familiar disagreeable facade was in place. Med was back. With a sigh of relief, Yidnar let him go.

"The fighting part is up to Rett," Yidnar told them, channeling his frustration into positive strength and faith. "She can't lose as long as she resists. If she chooses to give up, back down, that's it. If she feels as if we have lost confidence and abandoned her, she just might give up. She doesn't have enough of her own energy any more . . . it has to come from us."

"That's it!" said Carakenne to no one in particular, but her voice startled him. "If it's pulling energy from anything that puts it out—that'll cut off part of its source . . . but how to make sure what we want to give the Sarge gets where we want it?"

Trebor swallowed. "Do you really think Nyorfias will be next, like Jaq said—?"

"Do you really want to find out?" interrupted Yidnar evenly.

"I'm glad we can do something I understand very well," said Trebor. A fierce grin bared his teeth. "Support and back up." He swatted the Zetinorian's arm. "Just as you did with Ariam, Jaq, except you concentrate on Rett."

"All right," said Yidnar. "Carakenne, this is how we support Rett. It might not be completely scientific, but it will work."

Carakenne retracted the extension of the knife blade and tucked the unsheathed weapon carefully into her boot. "Uhm-hmm!"

"Rhozev?" asked Yidnar.

"When I can think for myself, you know I rarely let go of hope," returned Med grimly. "But when we're done with this, I'm grounding her from active duty for a year."

Yidnar turned to Ariam. Her eyes were still filled with tears, but now the moisture merely intensified the luminous shine of love and determination from them. She met his glance steadily, smiling when his lips said without sound: *"I understand about Rett's ego-merge."*

The vast alien mind had clarified it. Not only that, but he was sure the first voice in his head had been Rett's "spirit guide", and it had definitely been female.

"I'm glad you understand, sir," Ariam said aloud. "It'll make the entire situation easier to discuss with you . . . maybe tomorrow. Right now we need to get busy." She turned back to her sister. "Rett, damn it! Get *up*, now!"

The shift in the emotional energy around him was so strong, Yidnar wondered if this was what it felt like to be an empath. He saw Rett lift her head, push her upper body off the floor. So she felt it, too. Hope rose strong in him. Between Ariam's verbal encouragement and the wave of fresh support coming from himself and the others, Rett actually made it to her knees.

Yidnar shivered; heard Jaq suck in a quick breath, saw Ariam turn her head suddenly. Before anyone could react an invisible force hit Rett again, snapping her head back as it caught her

389

under the chin. Yidnar moved then—but he went after Ariam, who started toward her sister. He managed to snag her belt and yank her out of the way as Rett's body rocketed past them. Rett's impact with the outer wall was uncontrolled and so hard she actually stuck to it for several seconds before oozing to the floor with a deep groan, leaving several long smears of blood on the wall to mark her descent.

* * * * *

THE REINFORCEMENT FROM HER FRIENDS that, seconds ago, had felt so encouraging, faded as Rett's body clearly reminded her of the overwhelming reality of her present condition. She wasn't sure if it was blood or brain matter leaking from her ears and nose. Her tongue was raw, and she felt a vague surprise it was still whole and attached. A few teeth were loose, several chipped, one cracked. The wobbling sensations gave her the shivers—she hated it when she lost teeth. Didn't matter how they could be fixed so no one knew the difference. The taste and feeling of broken teeth made her nauseous; the sensation of having them about to fall out was somehow more irksome than taking SMG through a muscle.

Not even the distraction of tooth discomfort kept the rest of her body from joining the current protest for long. Her entire right side burned. Her breaths wheezed asthmatically as lungs labored for oxygen. She was sure her nose was broken and, loose teeth or not, the way her jaw felt she wasn't going to be chewing anything with enthusiasm even if she lived long enough to feel hungry. Each uneven, painful beat of her heart only increased her agony.

I can't do it . . .

Again too weary to hold up her head, she let it fall against the wall with a *thunk*. The smooth surface jumped and undulated beneath her skin as her pulse throbbed. The extra motion added to her nausea.

I can't.

* * * * *

FORGETTING HERSELF IN THE FACE of Rett's fragile resistance and bodily peril, Ariam moved to help her, but Yidnar held her back again. "No, Ariam—" he said fiercely. "We can't touch her. We must *not* interfere physically."

"I know but she's taken so much already. I —"

He shook her, fingers digging in her arms. "Think! It would be exactly what this Xonomer would want—to kill the first one of us who comes past a certain point. *Especially* you, since Rett would be completely demoralized by your death."

"I'm not leaving!" cried Ariam, jerking her arms from his grip. "Not even with your order. I accept the consequences, but I stand *here*." Her gray eyes blazed.

"I would expect nothing less from you, Ariam," he said. "I'm not asking, or ordering, you to go. Rett needs you, needs to know you're here—we all do, since you are our link to her. But it's her battle, live or die."

Torn, Ariam's glance went from him to her sister and back again, no longer defiant, asking for direction.

"Rett doesn't have her, ahh, helper any more?"

"No, sir. But I sure wish she did."

"We're going to make up for that. Now that we're aware of Xonomer, it will ignore us as if we don't exist—as long as we don't interfere directly. It's more powerful than we can imagine, but it's not omnipotent, it has limitations, too. Just concentrate on support—concentrate with everything positive you have! As you always do. It got her this far. Don't stop now!"

* * * * *

"ARE YOU READY TO CEASE this nonsense? Accept my terms, come with me, and I will allow them all to live."

As slaves to the Coalition! shouted a dim, familiar voice as if from a great distance away.

391

Pam? Rett tried to clear the ever-expanding supernovae from her head. Now she was really imagining things. Pam wasn't inside her any more. *I can't. I just c—*

Don't say it! Don't think it! Imagine you can! Remember what Ariam said!

And open yourself to the help your friends are willing you to have. You won't fight alone. Not this time.

That last thought wasn't Pam's. It was Rett's.

She peeled her face from the wall. On one side of her was Xonomer, standing in the glamour of a cool, painless alternative to her exhaustion and pain, the offering a lure of limitless strength. Usefulness. A guarantee that something like this would never again happen to her people. All she had to do was nod to him. The war would end; people would be able to get on with their lives. Children would live to see adulthood, live to see their children, those after them. Wasn't that worth her allegiance to him?

On the other side was the hazy brightness of an unknown future. Where death or peril could snatch the people she loved from her at any time. But weren't their fragile lives even more precious because of the uncertainty? Wasn't that what kept them strong as much as it made them weak?

The growing confident, supportive feelings from her friends cleared the fog of confusion induced by pain. More assurance seeped into her battered mind and body. She lifted an arm to swipe at the blood trickling from her nose, her mouth.

What was it Ariam said before? What? She had to remember, it was important. What?

" . . . *use the mind place! The door—*"

The mind place—Pam's place. The corner in her mind Rett had always saved for Pam.

As if in a dream she heard Jaq speak. The words echoed in her brain, distilled the story to a bottom line. *Refused to dream of past or present until he forgot how . . . was given assistance, recovered the ability, but failed to—failed to use it in his final battle.*

That was me, to whatever extent. Until Pam came and reminded me . . .

The final battle had been inside Arneaut Holm's mind, and he failed, because he didn't recognize the weapons Xonomer could not fight. Because he rejected what he'd been given, what was offered freely and without reservation.

Arneaut Holm was an idiot, she thought, swallowing. *Was I that bad? No. I know I wasn't. Wait . . . where are the voices? Why isn't he reading my thoughts now?*

Whether she lived through it or died, the dark entity could be defeated.

"Of course." Rett closed her eyes, letting her body go limp, taking the energy she had left to look deep inside herself. Her consciousness had slipped into Pam's place, and Xonomer could not go there.

393

Only it wasn't Pam's place. Pam had just taken temporary residence there. Traces of her ego-merge friend remained, forest green-blue, earthy brown. Some sharp and vivid shared memories in a bright spray of every color imaginable were left here. Everywhere Rett looked, her own memories. Every direction she turned, the patterns and colors of them hung, like art at an exhibit. Some were still hiding in the shadows at the very edges of the space. Others, within the area, were dark, painful; some bittersweet; some bright and happy. Still more were simple and ordinary. They all waited for Rett to remember them.

"I grow weary of waiting!"

She pulled part of her attention outward. Xonomer was gathering another one of those terrible dark bolts and here she was, still physically vulnerable and pasted to the wall like a target on a firing range. But her mind was safe. She didn't know how she knew that, only that she did. As long as she stood here, she could take anything the alien could give. She took a step deeper into that corner, and gasped. Here was the vault of the pure bright energy of her own hopes and dreams, dreams she dared to have again since her ego-merge with Pam; since meeting Jaq.

My place. The source of the opalescent thread she still held in a mental grip she knew not even death would break. It had been within her all the time. *This is the soul I refuse to let him take— that I refused to let any of them take.* Now that all her nightmares had been uprooted and exposed, she could see all along that in trying to protect it, she'd only been blocking herself—from herself. She raised her mental hands, examining the thread, pulsing and glowing with every possible tone and shade, the brightness of it growing as she watched. It was a soft brightness, shimmering like sunlight under running water. It wasn't blinding and painful, as it had appeared before. That contrast had to result because of the darkness from which she'd emerged.

He can't take it unless I choose to let go. That's why all the persuasion, the demands, the threats not quite carried through. Of all the horrible things Xonomer can do, he can't take away my soul or will, unless I give it to him.

"No chance. Let's get this put away." She took the thread in both her hands, squeezing it hard, watching it press into her skin, slide into her flesh and bones. Back where it belonged. The lambency warmed her with the gentle heat of spring, dispelling the lingering ice and darkness from her body and heart.

My place. It was safe, familiar. Rett used to come here all the time. Here she would stand again, and see this through, no matter what happened on the outside.

This is why Pam and I were merged. The superparanormal aliens the Nyorfians referred to as gods and deities, the ones fighting Xonomer, wanted to give her an edge—a secret weapon—a fighting chance!

Xonomer would never think I would be hiding someone in my mind. Someone helping me to re-learn how to use my imagination.

Someone making me use my mind in ways I never would have remotely thought possible. This place is part of me, yet at the same time, I can remove parts of myself completely from it . . . like so. Just like when Pam was here. And then with H'chan, deities, we were on so many different levels it's a wonder I didn't get lost—or get motion sickness jumping from one to the other.

A soft, short sound escaped her. A laugh.

All that was more than companionship—it was training. For this.

Training for the fight that would decide the outcome of this long war—the aliens' game!

Now Rett was ready. She understood, not everything, but close enough. Pushing herself off the floor, she faced the entity the others could not see, the energy of purpose firing her tired limbs. Fully diverting the pains in her body into ready energy, mental and physical, she controlled her breathing, straightened to her full height.

Rett dug deep into the armor of her haven, refurbished and reinforced so recently by Pam. She turned the door into a shield, and took up the weapon of love and support emanating from her companions. She took a step away from the wall, seeking contact with the meteoric gaze of the alien enigma.

"What's this?" A trace of surprise came through Xonomer's contemptuous query. The dark energy he held ready to release swirled around him as he hesitated.

"My answer," Rett said.

This time, she didn't even blink as the alien lightning engulfed her again. It broke around her as a river current broke around a rock.

Rett laughed. "You can do better than this. Come on. Where are those great illusions? Where are the voices?" She made a *come-get-me* gesture. "Come on, Xonomer, you can't miss!"

The terrible, lethal energies gathered. Rett imagined her shield expanded, strengthened, became strong enough to protect those beyond her. Beyond pain, calm now, she met the enigma's assault. Deep in her soul she was surprised how easy it was, after all. Despite the lingering touch of Xonomer's hand in her mind, she was in control. As long as she held on and made her stand, she had a chance.

Rett took another long step forward, this one bringing her, as if the floor beneath her had shifted, to stand directly in front of the being.

She didn't miss the split-second of hesitation from the alien presence and grinned, a predatory display of threat rather than expression of amusement. "You're not so sure of yourself, are you," she snarled into his face. "Is it that you can't control my mind anymore? Is it possible you're not as omnipotent as you want me to think you are?

The meteoric eyes whirled with fury . . . and fear.

Rett jumped on the opening, threw a wedge into that crack in the same manner she would use to split a big log. Forget trying to hurt the alien physically—it would be a waste of time. But she could undermine Xonomer's confidence, play off doubts; use the same methods the entity used against her. With every tap she would give the wedge, no matter how insignificant it seemed, the small crack would lengthen, deepen, and finally split right down the middle, until that black armor that hid the essence of the entity fell apart, leaving the true nature of the being exposed. Visible. Vulnerable.

"You're making the same mistakes Iheolon and the other in the Coalition did. It all makes sense. Why they're so driven. Why they're so blind. Why they're so damned full of themselves. The total control and manipulation of the people who fight for them, bound by fear and threats and bribes. The control reinforced with devices and chemicals."

Very aware the threat of mental and physical injury remained as real as ever, she pulled hard on her reserves, strengthened her mental defense, convinced herself that despite her injuries and exhaustion, she was as strong and fast as ever.

When his armored hand struck toward her again, she intercepted the blow with her uninjured left hand and arm, altering the direction of the force with the ease of long experience. Instead of moving back, she moved forward again, forcing him to take a step away.

"I understand now why they took so long with the games and torture instead of killing me and getting it over with. You weren't about to let me die, were you? If I died without showing weakness or giving in to you or one of your agents, you wouldn't get anything—except someone else to take my place. Just as I must have replaced whoever was before me. There was one before me, wasn't there? One or a hundred others, I don't know. I can guess that they died before you had a chance to play with them, to force them to submit to you, as you tried so hard with me. Is that it?"

397

She clearly saw the shift from the being she faced; the overbearing, condescending assurance gave way to anger now that the odds were turning in her favor. It was all so familiar. For most of her adult life she'd seen the same pattern from her enemies, and it all made sense.

She thanked all good deities for it now. This powerful being, fully capable of the destruction it threatened, was blinded and bound by its own vision, unable to see beyond it. Just like the Yixolryn Coalition.

"Iheolon, Avok, the Leader, a few others, they all had their escape routes planned in case they had to face off someone who wasn't tied down and half dead, too. It doesn't make much sense that someone who thinks nothing of causing a war makes such an issue out of avoiding confrontation. I can't even grant the Yixolryns and their allies the grace of . . . for lack of a better term, humanoid failing. It's been your failure all along. Your errors they repeated. Your belief that your way was the only way, even if it didn't work after repeated attempts. You're a bigger failure than I am!"

Oh—Xonomer didn't like that! That telling blow against the wedge she had driven widened the breach in the alien's armor.

"Don't know what I mean? Let me detail."

She took another step forward. He retreated. "Mistake number one," she told him smoothly, "the most important. You allowed me to become fully conscious in this room, among my friends. You had your players make similar blunders often. You've never learned from it." Rett shook her head. "What is it with you, that you think having my people around to witness my, ah, demise, makes things better for you?"

3.3.17 Unknown location

THAT'S IT, RETT, DON'T BACK down. You own him now. From her place in a formless, misty fog, Pam willed with all her heart and soul for her friend to continue.

Rett stood tall, a Nyorfian commando, all fire and steel, wearing her attitude as if it was her uniform. Her friends saw that. It was clear to Pam that they looked past the grim reality of the blood and sweat-streaked limbs, the stains on the thigh-length hospital shirt. That didn't matter. As Pam did, they saw Sergeant Rett geared for combat. They stood ready to back her with everything they had.

"I must send you back," said the voice that resounded of windchimes and rain. "There is danger for you here if she fails. It is yet possible she might."

The gentle words opened a cold pit in Pam's belly. At least where she imagined her belly to be, since she didn't have a physical form here . . . wherever here was.

"No, please, not yet. A few more minutes. You can't get rid of me until I know how this ends—this part of it," she corrected herself hastily, since the being Pheasyce had already gently informed her there was never a true ending of anything. Pam didn't want to get into a deep philosophical discussion with a godlike entity. Not now. Even if time, as anyone mortal knew it, didn't exist in this not-place.

"I mean, of course you can," Pam amended, "and I can't stop you, but—"

"You *are* the one stopping me, Pamela."

"Oh. Right. Free will and all that." Pam wrinkled her nose. "For that matter, I don't recall anyone asking me if I wanted to get involved in the first place. Please, Pheasyce, Rett's my friend. Closer than that. It's all your fault, you know. You put me in her. Talk about free will—I don't remember anyone asking me if I wanted to take the magical mystery tour to god knows what galaxy and get stuck inside someone in the middle of a war."

"Perhaps not with words. But you *were* asked, with opportunity to refuse."

Pam wrinkled her nose. "I just woke up in—"

"Before that. Before you slept, I asked, and you opened your mind and accepted. You could have changed your mind at any moment, the merger would have ceased."

Pam swallowed. She honestly couldn't tag a moment when it felt like she had been issued an invitation to step into another consciousness, to share the life of a stranger. Then again, she couldn't come up with any moment when she wished it never happened or wished herself back home, either.

The shimmering being that was Pheasyce started to say something, but Pam pushed ahead.

"I'm not going back without knowing what happened, good or bad. It was awful enough not knowing what was going on for an entire year." *I kind of get I won't be coming back.*

She didn't dare say it aloud, but knew Pheasyce understood. The enigma made no response in support or denial of her thought.

"I want to see this through. There's too much in my life that I start and never finish. Please. I'll take the chance of something going wrong if she fails. I *choose* to."

"Then you must *not* speak directly to any of them again," Pheasyce said. "Your last attempt very nearly revealed your presence to my opponent. Xonomer's ignorance of your existence and role in this entire stratagem is still important to maintain."

The entity chimed sternly at her. "Not to mention what you did almost broke the Rules of direct interference. Had you tried that direct of a contact with Rett, or with Ariam, or anyone physically nearer to Xonomer, it would have."

"But you spoke to Yidnar, too."

"It is *my* Game. My battle, my test for proving a worthy Guardian of Balance. Not yours. Xonomer's penalty for striking physical blows granted me certain countermeasures. *Your* last impulsive action, however, brought me a warning from the Arbitrator—if you dare do that again, all that was gained is forfeit."

"I'm sorry. Will I get to say goodbye at least? If it all turns out?"

"Pamela." A hint of impatience made Pheasyce's windchime voice sound a little off-key.

"I'll be good," Pam promised meekly.

"No matter what."

She swallowed past the painful ache in her throat and let out the breath she was holding. "No matter what."

3.3.18 MEDICAL SECTION, AURORA BASE, EPNOCE
0536.03.20 (LOCAL RECKONING)

RETT'S WORDS TO XONAMER WERE having every bit of an effect as physical strikes. "You don't know very much about us. Too bad you have to learn now from a humanoid. Someone whose very existence to you, under normal circumstances, is no more than that of a spore of common mold to me."

"Mistake number two," continued Rett, "is resorting to physical violence. You should have kept up with the illusions and voices. The visions. The dead playing off my guilt and doubt. Yes, I made mistakes. I could have done things differently, better, maybe even prevented people from being killed. Using the people I love . . . and loved, that hurt. That almost had me, right from the start." She flinched at the painful memories of those twisted images. "That almost had me. Then you changed tactics. Stupid move."

He backed up, she closed the gap. His hand extended, to ward her off or attack her she had no idea, but it hardly mattered now. She wasn't afraid of pain. Pain meant she was alive. Being alive meant there was hope. She never gave up on hope. She'd come close to it, but close didn't count.

"Mistake number three—the biggest one—overlooking this place I've held back in my mind. Because it is . . . *imaginary*. Imagine that. The specialist of illusion can't see something created by someone else's imagination. You could have had me right in the beginning and avoided all this. Better yet, you could have made this move a year ago; I didn't have much of an imagination then. My ability to control different parts of my mind and the way I think were nothing compared to what they are now, either."

A darkly glowing whirl of energy started forming around his outstretched hand.

"Go right ahead. Yes, you can kill me, hurt me, wipe out my mind and my memories and leave me a shell. But no matter what you do to me, you lose, because you can't get what you want unless I hand it to you willingly. And that's not going to happen."

"And you care nothing for the others?"

Rett's dry laugh came out as more of a sharp exhale. "I wouldn't be here staring at that black hole you have for a face if I didn't. Don't even *try* to use threats to them any more. If you want a fight, it's going to have to be on my terms now. With the shape I'm in, we might even be evenly matched."

The entity drew back.

The others could see him, now. Of that she had no doubt, since they moved out of the way as the towering figure backed closer to where they stood. Their confidence flared, and she gratefully absorbed the energy they were willing her to receive.

When she continued her relentless advance and the alien took yet another step to avoid her, her friends' positive feelings intensified.

"Let's get back to the first mistake. The important one. Twelve years may not be a very long time for you." She almost felt pity for the entity. "Maybe it's just an hour or so in your Game, a day? Maybe that short of a time wasn't long enough for you to make specific observations and act on them, instead of applying generic tactics that might have worked elsewhere."

Xonomer's fiery eyes seemed to falter; seemed to smother under her gaze. He stepped back again.

"I don't think I've ever had such a long, one-sided conversation before in my life, but you know what? That's fine, because I'm really too tired to do anything else, and it's working. You see, unlike you, I'm adaptable. I can change to meet the conditions of my environment, instead of making my environment change for me."

There was am ambiance around her that seemed to increase with each forward movement. She noticed it, but was so focused on Xonomer she didn't have time to worry about danger from any direction but straight ahead. The glow didn't hinder her, instead it helped her to fully concentrate and focus on the mental support and sheer love her friends were willing her to receive from them. She pressed on, inexorably, a joyful confidence in her advance, her eye contact never breaking or allowing the alien's to break.

"I'm going to give you the bottom line. Just in case anything else I said was confusing to you."

Xonomer retreated before her, his form fully solidified. Confusion, shock, and a tension of uncertain fear exuded from the being.

"Until you can learn to love," Rett said, "love anything, anyone, with something beyond physical sense, love so much it hurts—you can only exist. Empty. Cold. Forever alone."

The alien, cornered, could not move without trying to get past Rett. Armored back against the wall, it was cornered. With every one of her words, the meteor-bright eyes flickered, dimmed. The once fearsome entity panicked like a small animal in the talons of a hunting raptor.

Now Rett knew how to end this, and end it she would. She was tired, and she wanted to go home. To get back to her life.

She almost felt sorry for Xonomer. Almost. But the creature had made its own choices, just as she made hers.

Her voice remained clear and steady, but it now held a cutting edge as keen as the azurium-alloyed steel of her knife. The words came, unbidden, from the energy surrounding her, but they were good words, and she said them aloud willingly.

"This ends here. The Balance is maintained. This game goes to Nyorfias, Xonomer. You have no more power here."

There was a loud noise, a bright flash of light, a second of icy heat. The alien vanished.

No longer able to stand, Rett collapsed.

3.3.19 MEDICAL SECTION, AURORA BASE, EPNOCE
0536.03.20 (LOCAL RECKONING)

"WHAT JUST HAPPENED?"

Trebor's voice broke Rett from the near blackout that had claimed her. The room came back into focus. She shifted, got a knee under herself, and started reaching toward the wall for support in preparation to stand. But a silvery energy formed in the space that Xonomer had last stood.

Tendrils reached from the softly glowing form, lifted her to her feet.

"Well done, my daughter."

The voice was familiar and unfamiliar. It was neither male nor female. The sound was as silvery and ethereal as the lambent cloud from which the voice came. Like the wind through icicle-laden branches.

The energy field in which she stood washed over her, as refreshing as standing in the mist from a waterfall after a hard day's work. Rett stared at the nebulous shape taking form in front of her. She saw the wall right through it. Yet the tendrils that were still touching her felt solid and real.

She couldn't say this being's presence made an opposite statement from that of Xonomer—not at all. She imagined Xonomer's opposite would be just as bad . . . in an opposite sort of way . . . so what did that mean?

She shook her head. *I'm just not cut out to think that deeply. Even if I could, I can't do it now.*

The chiming of the alien voice was like laughter. "You are correct in assuming I am not Xonomer's opposite. I am neither Light nor Dark, neither daylight nor night. I am the Guardian of this solar system and everything in it. My task is to protect the Balance between Light and Darkness upon which all life in the universe depends, letting neither dominate the other. You have nothing to fear from holding back information of the merger I made for you with the being named Pam. The choice is yours."

"You can do that? About the ego-merge?" Rett supposed no one would argue if an entity such as the one before her changed some archaic rule concerning an event so rare it had only happened four times—on record—in five hundred years.

"Yes," said the being. "It was my rule from the start, part of the long-term strategy for the moment just passed. Thus I kept the right to alter it when it was no longer needed. No one will ever know except those who know already, unless you wish to tell others."

"Only Ariam and H'chan know—"

"The being Yidnar I have also allowed to know of this."

"Major Yidnar?"

"Worry not," said the being, something resembling a smile impressing itself on her. "He has known only since Xonomer struck you physically. Physical contact with Players is not allowed. Xonomer's error gave me an extra countermove to compensate. The first part of that move was finding and releasing a memory in the Zetinorian. After he told the story of Arneaut Holm, I then communicated with Yidnar, focusing in him the thought of how he and the others might support you against my opponent. Do you understand why this was necessary?"

She nodded. "Arneaut Holm . . . was real?"

"Yes. He existed not so long ago in mortal time. Like you for Nyorfias, he was a key Player in Zetinor Prime's final battle. He fought bravely, but he failed. The Zetinorian resistance lasted a little longer after his defeat, but it was already too late."

"Were you there—?"

"No," said the entity gravely. "My responsibility encompasses this solar system only."

"Zetinor Prime, Kyarta, and all those other places taken by the Coalition . . . for Xonomer."

"Yes. Know that Xonomer was merely one manifestation of the Dark. The struggle for balance goes on between Chaos and Order, between Dark and Light, continually. My people can do nothing but try to maintain it, letting neither the light nor the dark, the good or evil, chaos or order rule completely."

Rett closed her eyes for a second, the concepts so far over her she struggled to put it in terms to which she better understood.

"Think of it as an ecosystem," said the entity. "Or, perhaps, an aberration in weather patterns. Too much sunlight, not enough rain. Too much rain . . . days and days of cloud."

The concept that had escaped Rett before clarified. The opposite of Xonomer would be as good as Xonomer was evil, but too blindingly bright with its own goodness and need for order than it would stifle creativity and passion with every bit as much force as Xonomer's darkness of chaotic disorder. The reference to ecosystems made perfect sense to her.

407

The gentle lambency of the entity remained visible right through her eyelids, and she nodded, smiling a little. Then she became serious once more. "What about Jaq?"

"Jaq Pym and other survivors of Xonomer's victories are proof that not all that is bright is quenched when darkness takes over. Perhaps he can add his unique stamp to my Nyorfian children, as so many others from other worlds have done, including your mother."

"Maybe he will." *And what about Pam?* she asked in her thoughts. *What happened to her?*

"The others cannot hear when I speak directly to you," responded the presence, reassuring her. "Pam." Something like a laugh of sheer amazement came from the entity. "Pamela was loaned to me by the Guardians of her world. Even now I remain unsure if it was with enthusiasm or desperation. I was . . . apprehensive when presented with their choice. But it turned out to be the right one."

Rett found herself smiling despite her concern. "I take it you've had a conversation with her."

"She has been near this entire time, she is near you now, yet in no form you can discern. Her concern has been only for you since I broke the merger." Easily sensing Rett's next questions, the alien continued. "I know nothing of her world that I did not learn from her mind, and her Guardians set parameters on her participation far beyond the limits set in the Game. Since I had no control over circumstances you encountered, nor control over results of those circumstances, there were times when the merger had to be broken. But she accomplished what I hoped she would—she opened the door you had closed on your soul, gave you back your dreams and hopes. The extra training your interactions gave your mind was a fortunate extra. More than that I am not permitted to explain. Pam knows all that took place since I took her from you and H'chan. But soon I will send her back to her physical form and home, to the Guardians who protect her and her own universe."

"Pam's has people —has Guardians?"

"All solar systems with sentient life forms have Guardians, just as all face constant battle with Light and Dark."

"Constant?" Rett didn't want to hear that.

"The battles do not always take the form they did here, child. Just as this battle newly won wasn't always a military one. I strived since the beginning—since bringing your people to this solar system—to keep this from happening, I could not. However, all of you, all living things on Nyorfias and Epnoce, managed to help me overcome Xonomer in the end. I could not have done this alone."

"And Pam's world? Is that why she told me it was—"

"I can't answer that."

"You said she's with you, can I see her?" Rett pushed her awareness forward, trying to find Pam's familiar energy somewhere in the being's circle of ambiance.

"I'm afraid that isn't possible. Already her world's Guardians are drawing her back. But know her love is with you."

Rett swallowed, her throat hurting. She drew a circle over her heart with her longest finger, her vision blurring, the words catching in her throat. *I love you for always. Be safe, be happy.*

"Pam wishes the same to you. And sends her love."

"What are you?" Rett asked after sound found its way back to her lips. "Besides a Guardian of Balance? I suppose I'm not to say 'good gods and deities' now that I know better? I mean, we all know your people—if they can be called that—aren't really gods, but it was easier to say than 'superparanormal alien' . . ." Rett sniffed, then tried to laugh and pushed a hand through her hair, tugged the ends. She was quite sure this was all real, every weird bit of it.

"It doesn't matter what you call me, or us. But we are not omnipotent beings. Simply Guardians. Constrained by Rules. I do my best to protect and nurture. I regard you all as my children."

"Will you give me your name . . . if you have one?" Rett was sure Xonomer had mentioned a name, but she couldn't remember it.

"I do have a name. I give it freely. Pheasyce."

"Please, Pheasyce," whispered Rett, "I need to know one more thing—" The horrible visions of Gerrale, Kraym and the others, were too strong to erase.

Pheasyce drifted close. "Daughter, you know in your heart the truth. Xonomer twisted your memories to his own purposes. Be reassured."

A soft beam of light stretched forth to touch her face, became something tangible, real, solid. For several endless seconds Rett stood, supported only by the being's radiant hand, her entire body, mind, and soul flooded with Pheasyce's presence.

"I am sorry, my daughter, my warrior, for your suffering and pain." A lambent finger brushed tears from her face. "So many times I longed to offer comfort. Even now, I would heal you fully if it were permitted. What had to be, was. What will be, will be."

"It's not a problem," she heard herself say.

"And I, for the sake of Nyorfias, may have need of your services again. You are still my key Player. Your role ends only when your physical form ceases to live."

Rett tried to swallow. "I'll do my best."

"I know you will. As ever you have, never holding back."

The alien entity drifted back, passing each in that room, sending a finger of silvery energy to touch every one of them. "I am Pheasyce. I am not a god. I am a Guardian. I protect the Balance of this solar system, with the assistance of my people, my Players—of you. You will not consciously remember me unless we must directly interact together again."

410

Rett didn't have to look at the others to see the wonder and understanding suddenly dawn from the others in the room with her as Pheasyce's aura spread to touch them all.

Like the leaves of plants to sunlight, like roots to rich soil and water, the energies of Rett and those she loved stretched toward the soft radiance and soaked it in.

The soft ambiance disappeared, and Rett's right knee buckled. Thankfully, Jaq reached her before she fell. She was grateful for the supporting pressure of his strong arms, despite the extra aches they caused.

"Rett. What *happened!* Are you . . . all right, by the One, that sounds so trivial!"

She leaned into his solid body, trusting him to support her. Tipping her head back just a bit, she said, "I feel sick. And . . . I'm really tired."

"You've a gift for understatement, Sergeant." Major Yidnar was at Jaq's left elbow.

"You're a mess, Rett. But you're the most beautiful mess I've ever seen."

"Now I know for sure you love me." She laughed, but not very hard or loud, it hurt too much. "Just please—watch the right side okay?"

"I'm not even going to make an attempt to figure out what happened in here today," said Carakenne. "I'm just glad we lived through it."

"And what really counts," Ariam said, moving to join Rett and Jaq, including both in a very careful embrace, "is that Rett is here, alive, herself, and going to be all right."

"As long as you don't hit me again, Ari," Rett said wryly.

She then met Yidnar's midnight blue gaze, asking the question in silence, ready to give him an apology. She could have trusted him with her secret any time. She knew it, right down to her toes. Was he angry, maybe insulted, at her holding back?

"No, sport. Secret weapons should stay that way. You did the right thing."

His smile cleared her mind of worry and she smiled back and let her head settle on Jaq's shoulder, too tired to hold it up any more.

Major Yidnar's Omni bleeped softly, the triple-chirp of a priority signal. Rett's head came up. *Now what?*

He looked at his device, snorted a soft breath from his nose and turned away from them, headed for the outer door.

"Wonder what's up?" Trebor muttered.

Rett was more than ready to get back in bed, but she couldn't move. She watched the Major as he stepped into the corridor and looked down the hall. He beckoned to someone with one hand, motioning for them to come ahead, into her room, before accessing his message.

Rett squinted at the doorway. Her energy sense was completely tapped out, her vision was blurred, and both her eyes were swelling closed fast. But she recognized the familiar shape there. "Dad?"

"Rett. I'm surprised to see you standing, I was told—"

"I'm not standing, Dad. I'm being held up. There's a difference."

Med said, "Bed. Now. Soon."

"I think I need to sit and breathe for a while first. But I'm having some trouble moving."

"May I?" Jaq gently scooped Rett in his arms.

Then it seemed that there were twenty pairs of arms helping to settle her into a comfortable semi-upright position. She lost count, as the flurry of activity made her dizzy.

Something scraped across the floor. She heard Trebor say "Here, sir," and guessed he moved a chair, since her father sat down close and then leaned forward to drop a light and tender kiss on the least bruised portion of her face.

"I was told to expect the worst," he said, reaching for her hand. "I'm so glad to see that isn't the case."

"It came close," Ariam said softly.

Rett left her hand curled in her father's. Ariam stood alongside him, her hand on Reve's shoulder. Rett smiled, feeling the singularity between the three of them the same way she used to feel it between Ariam and Tovadan.

With a shallow little sigh, her attention returned to the Major's, curious about his message. He still stood in the doorway, sideways to them, staring at his Omni. He wiped a finger across the display as if smudges or smears distorted the text he read.

When he glanced toward the room at large again, all the lines of worry and fatigue were lifted from his features. He looked very much like the younger officer who'd come to Treetop for a short break and some fishing, over ten long years before.

"Just got a note from MainCommand," he said, his glance going from face to face in the room, finally settling on Rett. He took a breath, and then cued his pcom to open as many frequencies as the device was capable of covering. When he spoke again, his voice came from everywhere there was a communication panel.

"Couple of announcements," he said calmly after the routine identification. "All personnel can start using the wireless networks again immediately." Again, his gaze went around the room. "And, the Yixolryn Coalition has chosen to withdraw, no conditions, no questions. They will not return to any GTC sector. The war is over. We will transition into a clean-up and stand-down phase at new day."

For a few seconds no one moved, spoke, even breathed. Rett was the first to react. She disengaged her hand from her father's, and painfully reached for the blanket that partially covered her legs. Then she lay back against the supporting cushions and pulled the covering right up to her battered nose. She closed her eyes. She couldn't see much anyway.

413

"Wait," Med protested, "I need—"

"Med. You put one finger on me, one finger, and I'm going to do something violent. I'm tired. As a matter of fact, I'm *beyond* tired. I don't feel well—at all. Would you *please* just leave me alone to sleep for a couple hours? I'm not bleeding . . . well, not to death, anyway. Leave me alone for a while." She flexed her left hand, hoping her got her meaning.

"Whatever you want, Rett," agreed Med hastily, stepping away, one hand going to his neck in a protective reflex.

"Truly? Then what I really want is for you to get some sleep while you're waiting. I'm messed up enough without needed to worry about you being tired enough to make some stupid mistake that can complicate matters."

Med hesitated, and it was easy for Rett to guess he was making a huge effort to hold back a comment. "Agreed."

"*Thank* you. And then," she said, feeling magnanimous, "as soon as you take care of my teeth—you know how I hate broken teeth—you know all that other stuff you're always threatening and tiffing about that I need done? Well, you can go ahead and get started, as long as you're going to be messing about inside me anyway." She cracked one eye open and managed to focus long enough on him to see him turn very pale.

"What?" His voice came out as a whisper of disbelief.

Figure that out, Rett thought to herself in disgust, *some people just can't handle what they've been asking for.*

She felt a sleepy nudge to her mind from a half-awake H'chan, and sent gentle reassurance and a feeling of love to the Beast—her friend. *Sleep now,* thought Rett. *We'll talk later.*

"Move over," said Jaq, nudging her through the blanket.

She pulled down the covering just enough to expose her eyes. "Are you stupid or something? Go away and come back in three or four months. I might be up for it then."

"Forget it," said Jaq. "I'm not letting you out of my sight, or reach, until . . . well, let's just not put a time limit on it." He deftly moved her the necessary distance and inserted himself under her blanket, on the left, of course.

"Dad—Med!" Rett protested.

"He's not exactly a cute five-year-old, but . . . he'll do as a pacifier well enough," said Med.

"Don't look at me," said Colonel Reve. "Not that you can," he added.

Too tired to argue, Rett sighed. "Fine, do what you want. Just don't wake me up."

"Heads up, Jaq. At least try to get this on her face for a bit. That way, when she wakes up from her nap, she won't think she's gone blind."

That sound was a gelpack smacking into Jaq's ready hand. A gelpack was a good idea, but what she wanted was for everyone to go away. Starting with Med.

"Med—" said Rett in warning.

"I'm leaving, seems I have a *lot* of stuff to get scheduled."

"He's right, you know. Now settle back."

Rett settled in the comforting circle of his arm, more than ready to let someone else take over.

"Now, if the rest of you don't mind—" said Jaq.

"Not in the least," said Trebor.

"Wait a minute, Carakenne," said Rett.

"Sarge?"

"Sorry about throwing you before."

"No problem, Sarge. Now I know there was a good reason. I'm all right."

"Remember, back before the drop on Complex 412, when you asked me what I was going to do after the war?"

"You weren't too sure."

"*Now* I am." Rett nestled a little closer to Jaq. Being closer hurt, but she didn't care.

"What's that, Sarge?" asked Carakenne softly.

"I'm going home," Rett said.

415

EPILOGUE
FARM, HUNTERDON COUNTY, NJ USA EARTH
CURRENT ERA

THE LONG NYORFIAN WAR WAS over.

This wasn't the reason Pam woke up with tears in her eyes as her alarm buzzed.

Of course she was happy. Her Nyorfian friends weren't going to be obliterated or made into slaves or taken apart for their genetic material or tortured. She should be dancing a jig for them, but instead was lying here feeling all sorry for herself.

At least, thought Pam, *I don't have to imagine how it really began and how it all ended. I'll just always wish we got to say good-bye. Directly.*

"Jeez. Just get over it."

She sat up and swiped her eyes on the sleeve of her sweatshirt. No one else would ever believe it. Her best friend was even starting to think she was nuts. Well, now she knew it was over, it was time to stop obsessing. Well, that was once she got everything else written down while it was still fresh in her mind. She didn't want to forget any of it.

There was one happy discovery from that time both brief and endless she had spent in the "not a place" from which Pheasyce had allowed her to observe. Everything she'd been writing—all the parts she'd imagined from the point of view of people other than Rett just to fill in the gaps—had been laced with truth. Pheasyce had admitted to influencing her even while she wasn't merged with Rett.

Pam hadn't dared ask why that concession had been made, but she was grateful for it.

But there'd be no more of that. Pheasyce had been quite clear that the Guardians of Earth didn't want to have their attention diverted any more. As if, with everything going on in the world and the Guardians struggling to balance a power play on two fronts, Pam was worthy of their attention. She had to chuckle.

She reached for her glasses. The digital clock display read five-thirty. Sunday morning. Time to get up, make coffee, take care of the horses. There were no holidays or weekends when one took care of livestock.

417

But first, she pulled her sketchbook close, found her mechanical pencil, and started to sketch H'chan the Ice Beast. The soft graphite point flowed around the powerful curve of his haunches, the proud crest of his neck, the long, forward sweep of antler. His head was high, and he looked wary and surprised. Of course, because the figure that flowed onto the page next to him, in bulky winter gear, was Rett.

One hand on the hackamore's headstall, Rett pulled the animal's head around until they both were nose-to-nose. She stared straight into the deep purple eyes, which looked a bit surprised at her action. His ears swiveled forward, as attentive to her as his eyes were. "Beast, I'm sorry. Believe me, I know how some people in the Coalition can behave, and if they made that word bad for you, I'll try to remember not to use it."

She'd scan it into the computer later to fancy it up, but for now, it would do. She started flipping through the sketchbook, the familiar faces not as carefully rendered as she would have liked, but she'd know them anywhere. At least now she could take the time to make better ones.

Then she stared out the window to the brightening world on the other side of the glass.

It really is all about balance, isn't it? Night and day. Dry and wet. Hot and cold. Too much good and too much evil.

She traded her sketchbook for her laptop, checked her email, looked at the weather report and headlines. *If we all don't do something here, we might end up like one of those worlds the Coalition took over.*

I know there are aliens out there. Good guys and bad guts. And they don't have British accents. Pam chuckled and finished getting ready for work. As much as she wished for some improbably Scotty to beam her up and into a better life, or a better place, there wasn't any place better than what she had now.

But she'd stay wide open for any possibilities.

MEDICAL SECTION, AURORA BASE, EPNOCE
0536.03.26 (LOCAL RECKONING)

"I SWEAR," RETT SAID, GLARING at the ceiling. "I'm so bored I'm going to start breaking things."

She would have liked to add some dramatic impact to her statement: a deep sigh, a fist pound, or better yet, thumping the upper half of her body into the bed. Truth be told, she was far too sore to make any movement that wasn't absolutely necessary. Glaring at the ceiling was painful enough.

Not being able to move very much made the prospect of boredom all the more agonizing.

"You've been fully awake for how long? Four hours?"

With care, Rett turned her head to see her sister, arms crossed, standing in the doorway.

"You don't want to break your teeth, Med Rhozev just fixed them. So stop grinding them together," said the B-troop second.

Rett relaxed her jaw and checked her teeth with her tongue—thank all deities they were fine. After what she put him through, if something as petty as boredom cracked or knocked one of her teeth out of place, Med would be sure to let her suffer with it as long as possible out of spite.

Six days. Six days of nothing but sleep—four of those in an induced deepsleep healing mode—and she still hurt from toes to hair, a deep breath caused aches across her entire midsection, and her vision was fuzzy.

"Be careful what you wish for, too." said Ariam. "Easy Force is going to be bombarding you with busywork from every possible direction as soon as you can sit up and work on an Omni and notepad."

419

Busywork. The bane—and salvation—of any soldier laid up and still capable of reading and scribing. Endless reports, forms, checklists, filing. At least she'd be in good company. The Easy Force leader, Lieutenant Evetez, and a few handfuls of other casualties slated to be discharged from critical care would likely be doing them with her.

"Med said I'll get moved in with Evetez and the others, too," said Rett. "I'll bet Semage is glad to have you back on duty."

"He is, especially since he no longer has Corporal Rimms as third-up." Ariam moved deeper into the room, bringing the scent of cold and tree resins. So she'd been out with her Ice Beast, H'tan.

Rett winced at Ariam's reminder of Rimms. She still hadn't fully wrapped her head around the losses suffered by her own platoon, much less the rest of Easy Force, in the battle for Aurora Base. *And here I was just moments ago feeling bored and sorry for myself.*

"I'm sorry," Rett said.

"You've no reason in two worlds to be sorry." Ariam started loosening her outerwear and Rett felt stupidly grateful this visit would be more than an in-and-out. "This past tenday has been strange for all of us. Despite being in reasonable proximity to each other, some of us might as well have been worlds apart. Don't worry, you're not the only one."

"Still, I've no reason to be so cranky," insisted Rett. "H'chan is sleeping, or I'd have been chatting with him."

"What about Pam?" Ariam asked gently.

Rett swallowed a sudden, sharp ache in her throat and shook her head in shallow motions.

"You think she'll be back?"

"It's over. Done. It's not as if she died, though."

"I think in a way it is, for you."

No fooling Ariam. Rett kept her sigh inside.

Ariam shrugged her anorak off and discarded it carelessly on the floor. Sitting on the edge of Rett's bed, she touched her fingertips lightly over Rett's heart. "As with our other loved ones, she'll always be with you, part of you, in here. Every time you pause for a moment and think, 'what would Pam have to say about this?' Don't push those thoughts away. I know you'll try."

Maybe Ariam was right. But right now, Rett didn't want to think about the alien friend she'd never see—well, *be* with—again. She knew the ego-merge was never meant to be permanent.

She never expected the shocking emptiness that followed. It hadn't been so bad while Jaq was next to her, but he'd gone off on a mission.

Thinking about all those she'd never see or talk to again only added to her pain inside and out. She wasn't ready to process any of that. Time to change the subject. "How about you, Ari? Are you doing all right?"

"I'm well, now that I've caught up on some sleep." Her sister leaned over for a careful hug. "It's easy to forget you don't have the full story of what happened with us while you were running that diversion, much less what's happened between then and now." She pushed a strand of golden hair back into the braid and tuck that kept her locks tight against her head. "Has Trebor given you any reports yet?"

"No. I've been completely out of it." Rett picked at her blanket. "I know he was in here talking to Jaq while I was waking up. That little Kyarta girl that was found during the battle was with him. Next thing I know, Jaq was telling me they had a mission."

"Jaq, too?" Ariam's pale eyebrows pulled together over her nose. "I know he's been translating for her, but her Standard's really improved since she's been with us."

"He's part of my platoon, isn't he? And who else is there who knows better what they might have to deal with in a Coalition bunker. I don't mind he went—Med told me Jaq hardly stepped out of this room since . . . well . . . since . . ." Rett started twisting off a broken piece of fingernail and sent a longing glance towards a window. Thick snowflakes swirled in a blinding eddy on the other side of the clear material, but she would a hundred times rather be out there than stuck in a hospital bed. *The smells,* she thought. *The smells, the sounds.* Not only from immediately around her, but from everywhere. The smell of disinfectant and cleaning solutions and sterility as well as the more organic ones.

"Did you expect Jaq to leave you? After everything that happened?"

Rett slanted a half-grin at her sister. "I guess not. I told him he doesn't have to sit in here and watch me sleep anymore. He said he'd never get tired of watching me: asleep, awake, didn't matter."

"That's our Jaq." Ariam smiled. Her fingers closed over the hand Rett was destroying. "Stop that."

Rett fought the petulant impulse to pull her hand free and continue worrying the broken nail. Instead she took a breath and

421

opened her mind to the calming influences her empathic sister was projecting. She focused on the familiar contrast of Ariam's paler fingers intertwined with her darker brown ones.

"The girl's name is Zharré," Ariam said. "She's quite an incredible child. She was a great help to the vet-meds, also kept H'chan calmed down. And if it hadn't been for her giving me an energy boost before I came back up, I never would have been able to take you in that fight."

"About that." Rett winced. "I'm sorry."

"It was nice to whip your ass for once."

"Barely."

"Uh-uh. I flattened you fair and square."

"I had to be half-dead for you to do it."

"I'm just glad that that's over with. Don't ever, *ever* do that to me again. Ever."

"Not planning on it."

"Trebor and Nerrah offered to adopt Zharré, by the way. I'll have to content myself as an honorary auntie. You are, too. I insist. This is Trebor and Nerrah's first child, after all."

Rett couldn't help a grin. "All right. Wow. I sleep for a few days and suddenly I have a niece? I have been out of it."

"Yes."

"I *hate* being out of it."

"I know. Don't worry, it won't be for long now that Med's let you up for some air." Ariam patted Rett's left knee gently. "So what do you think is going on?"

"I know some of it, but only because Jaq gave me a short version before he left. Before that I was too groggy to comprehend anything, but whatever they told Jaq put his energy on high alert. I came straight awake so fast from that, Med and a crash team came in."

"Rett—that's not funny." Ariam's smile faded and some of the color left her face.

"I'm sorry." Instantly Rett felt guilty. It was easy for her to forget that Ariam had been there while Med was fighting—more than once—to get her heart going. "I didn't mean it to be funny. It's just what happened. You expect me not to react when I see people's energy go into danger modes? It's kind of automatic."

"I'll give you that. But thank all deities you didn't need Med. So what is it then, causing this excitement?"

"There were some rumors of a hidden cache of a couple thousand troops in deepsleep on Aurora, as you know—and don't interrupt, Ari, or else I won't finish before Med comes in and chases you out for getting me worked up." Rett saw the questions rising to her sister's lips and held up a warning hand. "The kid—I mean, Zharré—thinks it might be the place she was revived. One of the Coalition troopers who surrendered had an idea where it is. Zharré also thinks there are children there in stasis, not adult troopers."

Ariam gasped. "Children!"

"Can you imagine? A thousand or more children. If they're all alive and can be revived safely . . ."

"That would be so wonderful, to welcome all those young lives after so much death." Ariam's gray eyes lit up like stars, a soft smile on her lips as she gazed off into the distance for a moment.

So many families had lost daughters, sons, brothers, sisters. Those children would have no trouble finding welcoming homes if they couldn't be returned to any still-existing homeworlds or family.

Rett huffed out a breath. "So the Major sent F-troop out to investigate. Since Jaq's part of F-troop, he went, too."

"And here you are, bored and alone."

Rett made a face.

"Try not to worry, Rett. I know it's hard to be left behind and out of things. Trust me, I do. Or did you forget that I was bedridden for a long time when I was a kid?"

"I'll never forget. My turn . . . again . . . I guess."

"Your turn again." Ariam made a face, then cheered up. "At least this time, I don't have to take over for you. And you can think about something other than going back to fighting."

"Going home." Rett would never get tired of saying it.

"Well, last I heard, That Old Tree is waiting. I found someone who can give Jaq some tree-climbing lessons while you're recovering, too. By the time you get home, he'll be ready. You would, after all, want to carry on the family tradition."

"What?" Rett rubbed her forehead, wondering if she completely missed something.

"The kids of your own you want to get started on? You still think I don't know Dad and Mother conceived their firstborn—you—in That Old Tree?"

Rett laughed. It hurt her face, ribs, and back, but at the same time, it felt good. "Now *that's* something to think about."

~oOo~

Here ends the main story arc of Journey to Nyorfias... but for extra reading, check out the novella *Carakenne*, which takes place during a mission described in JTN2 *Gravity*, and find out about the young Kyarta girl mentioned at the end of *Stratagem*, in her very own words, in the supplemental novella *Kyarta Girl*, which overlaps the ending of JTN3 *Stratagem*.

AFTERWORD

T HANKS FOR READING STRATAGEM, JOURNEY to Nyorfias Book 3. I hope you feel as if you came along for the journey. Pam was disappointed, too, that it just came to an end . . . just like that. She woke up, it was time to go and feed the horses, start her workday. It still bothered her she'd never "see" any of those people again, those people close to Rett and the few who were aware of her own existence as a unique entity, like Ariam and H'chan.

Whether the events in these stories were events that actually happened during their merge, or simply what Pam imagined, will only remain known to Pam. Pam is a character in all of this, too, and I had to project what this journey was like for her as a real person. She hasn't talked to me very much after the ego-merge ended, but she's indicated that she wouldn't mind finding out more about Rett from an early age and, of course, what happened after she left.

Thankfully, as the author and creator of the characters and Nyorfian universe, I can tell you that there are more adventures to be had. And yes, going back into Rett's past as well as forward!

For now, I'm sure you want to at least know what went down after Rett's last words. (Not that they were her *last* last words, mind you, but that they were the last words in the story).

Lives for the postwar Nyorfians might be peaceful for now, but we can't say it goes back to normal. The Nyorfian and Epnocian ecosystems have taken big hits from the war. Many of the citizens have changed, whether or not they served with the military, or were in or out of occupied territories. The battles they must fight now are to fix the issues they can and adapt to the situations that cannot be fixed, at least not in the short term.

Immediately following the story, *Stratagem* . . .

- Special Forces and other military units on Epnoce go on a few clean up missions on Aurora and the Epnocian main continent, rooting out small pockets of Coalition troops who missed or chose to ignore the fact the war was declared over. Able troops are redeployed to help get Epnocian residents back to sustainable operations. Gradually all who want to return to Nyorfias are shuttled back to Nyorfias. One BIG DISCOVERY during all this: a hidden bunker on Aurora hiding a huge underground facility full of cryogenic deep-sleep pods. This has significant impact on the upcoming future volume . . .

- When Aurora continent is secured, the Ice Beasts are all let go, returned to "the wild." Since only a few people know of their sentience, that's pretty much it. Some partners had the chance to say goodbye. Rett and H'chan never did—Rett was sent to Epnoce MainCommand for her recovery and H'chan stayed at Aurora until his injuries had healed, then he was released and went to rejoin his family-pack.

- After almost four months of recuperation, several surgeries, and rehab, Rett finally gets to go home, with Jaq.

- Ariam returns to Treetop also and helps them get started on the plan to clean up and replant the area, then goes to live with Semage.

- Semage and the people of Nyorfias's East Coast, the earliest parts of the continent to fall under Coalition occupation, have a long, long, struggle on their hands to get their environment cleaned up and rebuild their lives.

- Semage is determined as soon as possible to get back to schooling and follow his prewar career path in marine biology; his dream to be assigned his own ocean research vessel and spend long periods out at sea.

- Ariam turns her career path to counseling and is retested as an Adept level empath.

- Evetez also has a long recovery from his terrible injuries. He and Carakenne eventually commit to a relationship. Evetez goes back to the family business, but with the postwar cleanup a major effort all up and down the Wide River, things have changed.

- Carakenne decides to stay with MainCommand as a tech-ware developer but works out of the SeaCorps base at South Point.

427

- Trebor and Nerrah make their union official and officially adopt the young Kyarta girl found enslaved to the Coalition during the attack of Aurora Base.

- Trebor's prewar occupation as a teacher of structural engineering turns to hands-on work as a contractor and builder, since rebuilding is needed almost everywhere.

- Nerrah is an artist, and returns to creating astonishingly beautiful things which attract intense interest from various visiting GTC support personnel. Offworld sales help the Nyorfian system get a lot of needed resources to help in their postwar cleanup.

- H'tenneck remains on Epnoce and, a surprise to many (but not so much to Rett), gets involved with wildlife. He still likes to tinker, but he doesn't want to do it for a living.

- Most of the surviving F-troop personnel try to go back to their previous homes and ways of life. Some are able to adapt back to peacetime right away. Others have issues.

- Nyorfias, having no wars or permanent military structure prior to the war, is fairly unprepared to handle many of the problems of the veterans. The GTC support personnel do their best to help them get counseling and resources in place to help in whatever manner is needed.

- Major Yidnar spends some time personally visiting the families of those fallen in battle and those who were injured badly enough to be sent home. After a period of extremely active postwar service on various levels, and making sure the people who had been under his command were being taken care of if they needed help, he eventually returns to Circle and picks up his law practice.

- Valera, Ulorath, and Olvero remain at their farming complex. Valera's Master Adept status is made a matter of public record. It becomes known that Olvero is also a powerful Talent and special trainers are sent to help him learn to live with his rare gifts.

- Shannai and the other kids try to get their lives back to normal.

- Labonne gets with Safkas's mom and becomes the best dad ever as far as Safkas is concerned, and since he's so good with kids, stays involved with the school system of Complex 63.

- Etron and Briealun stay together and continue to do what they do best: fly.

- Many former Coalition soldiers ask to remain on Nyorfias.

- The GTC stays insystem to assist recovery and oversee the retreat and/or expulsion of Coalition remnants.

- Pam goes on, writing about her experience, drawing pictures, and exploring other writing adventures. She gives up talking about Nyorfias to her friends: to them it will always just be a story she was working on. She eventually leaves full time work on the farm and, since she's good with computers, gets a scary new job in an office.

If you want more, stay tuned to my blog or facebook page for information about upcoming releases. A prequel and a sequel are both in the works!

Stay tuned . . . this might be THE END of Pam and Rett's journey together, but there are still tales to tell.
Stories that happen before . . . and stories that happen after.
Check in at Terry Roy's blog or Facebook page for updates.

https://teryvisions.wordpress.com/
https://www.facebook.com/Teryvisions/

429

Liked this story? Hated it? Your opinion matters—a lot! Please consider leaving a review at your place of purchase. Or, you can drop me a line: terzap@gmail.com

GLOSSARY

By no means complete, this glossary should at least help with the pronunciation of some Nyorfian names and definitions of a few Nyorfian terms, places, etc. It's very informal. Please remember that even though Pam was in Rett's head and experiencing people, places, and things, she was also illiterate in GTC Standard. Any Nyorfians or GTC citizens reading this (if you learned to read English, anyway) might want to be a little forgiving if she was extremely creative with the spelling.

If I forgot anything, suggestions are always welcome for additions. You can email me at tmroy@zapstone.com. For news of the full supplemental, *THE NYORFIAS FILES - A Compleat Guide* (and yes, the spelling is deliberate on Compleat), stay tuned to my blog http://tmroy.teryvisions.com.

* * * * *

PEOPLE . . .

Ariam
AR·ee·ahm

F-troop's co-second. Ariam is an empath of moderate ability; sometimes mildly clairvoyant. ("Moderate" is the official designation, however, Ariam's Talent is definitely due for reassessment.) Certified in demolition and chemicals as well as a sharpshooter. In Gravity JTN2, she opts to leave F-troop to become B-troop's second-in-command.

Arneaut Holm
Arne-ought Hoom

A legendary Zetinorian who was the Key Player for Balance in Zetinor Prime's battle against Xonomer and the Yixolryn Coalition.

Asherle
ASH-er-leh

AirSpacefighters. Rett's wingpartner in the 114th. (JTN3 Stratagem)

Atira
Senior Sergeant, Platoon leader for D-troop.

Avok
AYE-vock

A full Yixolryn, rank of Commander. Used to serve under Iheolon, later made "commandant" of the farming unit Complex 63 on the Epnocian main continent. Avok and Rett have history, and not the good kind. (JTN2 Gravity)

Bhayorn
Bee·orn

F-troop; doubles as Med's assistant. Pam thinks his name (as she interprets it) is entirely appropriate to his appearance, since he looks more like a bear than a humanoid. (Except for those lovely green eyes, of course.)

Branwud Labonne

Branwood Lah-bone-eh

A Zetinorian trooper at Complex 63 assigned as School Warden and also a liaison between Commander Avok and many of the complex residents. (Among other things.) (JTN2 Gravity)

Bressim

From Rett's past. Bressim was a bully four years older than Rett, and often targeted her or would egg her on by targeting younger, weaker children. At age 12, Rett completely went postal on him after Bressim endangered Ariam. The story of Rett and Bressim will be featured in the JTN Prelude: *Rett's Story*.

Briealun

Bree-allun

AirSpacefighters. Assigned to the 114th shortly after the Aurora invasion. She, like Rett, is a native of Treetop Province. (JTN3 Stratagem)

C'zleni

Sea-slenny (it looks funny, but it's the right sound)

Drill captain, riding instructor at Aurora Base (JTN3 Stratagem)

Centra

Colonel, AirSpacefighters. CO of the 114th (JTN2 Gravity)

Chihakiru

chee-hakee-ru

FlightControl/FlightOps officer, 114th AirSpacefighters (JTN2 Gravity)

Darbey

F-troop member, with Rett at the battle for the Wide River Gap bridge.

Deeclar

One of Rett's childhood heroes; a firejumper pilot from Branch province who also flew difficult missions with AirSpacefighters (piloting troopjumpers) that earned him two Freedom Stars.

Dinnold
Sergeant, an R-troop squadleader who probably doesn't want to hear another "toasted bun" joke, ever, ever again. (JTN2 Gravity)

Druden
F-troop member killed in action during the battle for Complex 63. (JTN2 Gravity)

D'lano
dell·ah·no
Captain, 52nd Division. Infantry Liaison/coordinator for F-troop. (Convergence JTN1)

Etron
Aey-tron
114th AirSpacefighters squadron commander

Evard
Eh·vardh
SubColonel, replaced Col. Mott as 52nd Div CO. A crop farmer before the war. (Convergence JTN1)

Evetez
Eh·veh·tes
Lieutenant, Special Forces. He was in Rett's training platoon and, at first, always doing things that got her into trouble. They became close and fast friends. In Gravity, JTN2, Evetez is given command of a new task force designated Easy Force, containing the units F-, B-, R-, S-, and D-troops.

Ewayn
YOU·uhn
Sr Corporal, member of F-troop.

Farley
Daughter of Lans and Restalya. (Convergence JTN1)

Fortlan
Youngest of Lans and Restalya. (Convergence JTN1)

Frgerrizolont

Something like *Ferger-riz-olont*, make sure you growl when you say it. AKA Commander Stinky, or "that Coalition officer that almost ate me for lunch" according to Rett. This alien was commander of the garrison stationed at Complex 412. An extraordinarily gifted scientist, he was experimenting with darklight laser technology in-between snacking on the more humanoid troopers under his command. (JTN2 Gravity)

Gerrale

JER·aa·lee

F-troop, a squad second mortally wounded at Wide River Gap. (Convergence JTN1)

Gulanai

Joo-lan-eye

A farmer, life mated with Shemet and Zairynthe. Mother of Shannai.

Gulimethe

Joo-lee-meth-eh

Baby sister of Shannai, aka "Guli". (JTN2 Gravity)

H'leelem

huh-lee-lem

TRANS serviceperson at Aurora Base. (JTN3 Stratagem)

H'tenneck

huh·ten·eck

A native of Aurora continent of Epnoce and F-troop's youngest member. At age fifteen, he hid aboard a Coalition transport from Epnoce with intelligence gathered from the civilian resistance. Unable to return home, he was allowed to enlist and after Basic, chose to try for Special Forces. A whiz with gadgets.

Iheolon

i·HE·o·lon

Troop commander. Half Yixolryn, half-humanoid, he is

dangerous, intelligent, and quite mad. He's obsessed over Rett and anyone else he can't break down.

Jaq Pym
zJak (or Jack, he probably won't mind.)
A Coalition trooper from Zetinor Prime who defects before the battle for Circle. (See the entry on Zetinorians below.)

Jayord
Specialist, F-troop. Carakenne's mission partner for the attack on Complex 412. (JTN2 Gravity)

Jessek
ZHESS·ek
F-troop. One of the platoon's top five sharpshooters and close with Steffi and Mikel.

Kaitan
caai·TAN
Member of F-troop.

Kalebetha
Maintenance worker, Complex 63, mother of "Blaze" aka Spacemarine Lt. Kalenthi

Kalenthi
Lieutenant, Spacemarines. (JTN2 Gravity)

Kallet
Son of Kalenthi, sister to Kalenthi (JTN2 Gravity)

Kennet
Pilot, 114th AirSpacefighters (JTN3 Stratagem)

Kentrez
ken·tres
Eldest son of Lans and Restalya. (Convergence JTN1)

Kraym
Crayhm
Co-second of F-troop and Ariam's lover. He has an unusual

non-psi talent to buffer negative moods. He likes to throw himself at closed doors, an odd hobby for such an organized person. (No offense, big guy.) (Convergence JTN1)

Kytrasian
Kai-trah-sian
One of the first humanoids to make contact with Ice Beasts. Associated with Ice Beast doe **C'pret** (*Sea-pret*) (JTN3 Stratagem)

Lenna
Sergeant, AirSpacefighters. Jumpmaster on troopjumper (JTN2 Gravity)

Lans
Operations manager at Branch lumber mill. (Convergence JTN1)

Mahrhys
Ma·russ
Long-time second-in-command and XO to Major Yidnar of the Special Forces.

Massithe
Massi·(d)a
Military Police operative stationed in Branch. (Convergence JTN1)

Mikel
my·KELL
F-troop. Used to be a building maintenance technician in Circle. Best friends with Jessek and Steffi.

Mordell
Senior Sergeant, Platoon Leader for S-troop

Motuk Iheolon
Yixolryn sleeper agent planted on Nyorfias and disguised as a Nyorfian type humanoid at least thirty years before the war started. Cousin of Tyndal Iheolon, brother to Sclamuse Iheolon

437

Nauskova
Noss-kofva
XO/Second in command to Colonel Reve of the 21st Infantry.

Nerrah
ney·RAH
F-troop. One of the top five sharpshooters and the longtime lover of Trebor. Nerrah was a sculptor and artist before the war and her work had a large following both insystem and offworld. Like Rett, Nerrah and Trebor were part of C-troop.

Newi
see N'wessar.

N'galler
A Voi under Iheolon's command, a real nasty piece of work. Rett kills him in JTN1 Convergence, but his name isn't mentioned until Avok brings it up in JTN2 Gravity.

Nhoz Palen
Also known as Xonomer, the Ravener, and The Black King. An agent of Darkness and Pheasyce's opponent in the Game of Balance. (JTN3 Stratagem)

Nitraym
nee·TRAY·uhm
Sr Corporal. An F-troop squadleader and leader of the chemical/demolition personnel. Some readers think his name has something to do with "Nitro", and the truth be told, it's just a happy coincidence. I didn't even think about that until someone pointed it out.

Norlah
Lumber grader at Treetop Lumber, lifepartner with Rafe; neighbor of Rett and Ariam.

N'wessar
nu·ee·szahr
A Military Police operative stationed in Branch. Nicknamed

Newi. Kraym's best friend in their wild and crazy youth: together known as the "terrors of Bolle's Marsh". (Convergence JTN1)

Ohmara

Ohm-arah

Soldier from R-troop, killed in action in the battle for Complex 63 (JTN2 Gravity)

Olanzar

R-troop, injured during battle at the pipeline on Aurora continent.

Olvero

A young child, son of Valera and Ulorath, from Complex 63 (JTN2 Gravity)

Onelya

Captain, Special Forces, Commander of Lightning Force, another special strike team. (JTN2 Gravity)

Pam

(aka dimwitted alien mindforce)

A woman from Earth. The entity Pheasyce merges Pam with Rett, and we find out why later. Pam has a great imagination, likes to write stories, and takes care of seven horses. She doesn't dare mention to Rett that she has more than one name because Rett freaks out enough when Pam tells her oddities of Earth culture. (But we'll let you in on it: it's Pamela Catherine Marguerite Bertina Ptarski. Try saying that three times fast.)

Pheasyce

Fee·ah·sigh·chee The "deity" protecting the delicate balance between Light (true good) and Dark (true evil) in the Nyorfian system. Pheasyce is neither male nor female, but it was easier to assign her a gender, perhaps she was female in her last life. Pheasyce is a Guardian of Balance, and has no solid physical form.

Pipano

Pih·pah·no nickname *Pip*. F-troop. Pip is a demolition specialist with an arm and aim that would turn any ballplayer on Earth (in any game where balls are thrown objects otherwise unattached to living entities) green with envy. Probably the oldest F-troop member in age, Pip will tell you it's proof of his pyrotechnic talent—not his age—that he has no hair. (And you just never mind he still has eyebrows.)

Prill

Military Police operative stationed in Branch. (Convergence JTN1)

Quessel/Ionis

Two Voi (reptilian alien species) who are part of Commander Avok's thug detail. (JTN2 Gravity)

Rafe

Longtime operations manager at Treetop Lumber.

Restalya

ress·TAL·yah

Lifepartner of Lans, teacher at Branch primary school, mother of Kentrez, Farley, and Fortlan. (Convergence JTN1)

Rett

rhett

Sr Sergeant, F-troop platoon leader. A mountain bred logger's kid from the backwoods of northwestern Main (Treetop Province). She has a burning desire to know why the deities chose to merge her with a dimwitted alien mindforce named Pam.

Reve

Ree·veh (very soft exhale on the eh)

Colonel, 21st Infantry Division. Rett and Ariam's father.

Rhozev

Row·seff

F-troop, better known as Med. A healer-empath, his talent lets him know immediately when anyone in his range is hurt or sick. Med's had the fortunate experience being widely traveled (offworld) and having studied under healers from other GTC member worlds. He prefers a homeopathic, holistic approach whenever possible. (If Med is being nice to a patient, it's not considered a good sign.)

Rimms
Junior Sergeant, B-troop, Sgt Semage's long time third-up.

Safkas
Young girl at Complex 63 (JTN2 Gravity)

Sclamuse Iheolon
A sleeper agent, planted long-term on Nyorfias. Brother to Motuk. A skilled scientist, Sclamuse created poisons, diseases, drugs, and devices before, during, and after the war.

441

Semage
say·MAAge
2023rd Special Forces, B-troop platoon leader, and one of Rett's first and best friends.

Shamos
SHAH·muus
Major, 52nd Div, Exec.

Shannai
Teenage girl from Complex 63 (JTN2 Gravity)

Sharpeye
A call sign for a pilot from 114th AirSpacefighters (JTN3 Stratagem)

Shemet
shem-et
A farmer. Shannai's blood father, life mated with Zairynthe and Gulanai, Complex 63 (JTN2 Gravity)

Shenyver
shen·nu·fur (rhymes with Jennifer)
B-troop's medtech. (JTN2)

Soonjei
MP, Epnoce MainCommand, and drill/skirmish/sparring aide (JTN2 Gravity)

Steffi
STEH·fee
F-troop. She, Mikel, and Jessek are very close.

Tasheesh
aka Tash
In same Special Forces training unit as Rett, Evetez, and Semage. Find out more about Tash in the JTN Prequel, *Rett's Story*.

Thalom
Teenage boy from Complex 63 (JTN2 Gravity)

Tianorius
TEE-an-or-ree-us
The Zetinorian Guardian of Balance.

Torleyne
Specialist, R-troop. (JTN2 Gravity)

Tovadan
TOE·vah·dahn
nickname-*Tova*. Rett and Ariam's brother, killed at the beginning of the war. He was contact-empathic and saw (visually) people's emotional auras as visible colors.

Trebor
trah·BOR
F-troop third-up (third in chain of command). Rett insists he is the best shot in the system, if not the quadrant, maybe even the entire GTC. He was in C-troop with Rett and Nerrah. Before the war, he taught architectural design at the university in South Point. In Gravity JTN2, he moves into second-in-command of F-troop.

Ulorath
Olvero's father, life-partner to Valera, Complex 63 (JTN2 Gravity)

Utahe
YOU·tah·hee
C-troop platoon leader, killed in action at Azurebay. C-troop was the unit to which Rett was first assigned after her training.

Vinzk
vinsek
MP, drill assistant, skirmish/sparring aide (JTN2 Gravity)

Wik
A Unethi, personal bodyguard to Commander Avok. (JTN2 Gravity)

Wilkath
Captain, MP, In charge of the MP drill aides, skirmish/sparring aides (JTN2 Gravity)

Worren
war·run
F-troop. Squadleader and sharpshooter. He was a dairy farmer in Centerland Province, very near the Wide River Gap, before the war. While he was in Basic training, his family was killed, and farm destroyed, by Coalition troops.

Yidnar
EED·nahr
2023rd Special Forces commanding officer. Worked for the Department of Interplanetary Affairs (DIPA) before the war. (Would you believe he was a *lawyer*?) He loves fishing. Loves it. And he can tell a whopping fish story with the best of them, too.

Zairynthe
zai-rinth-eh
Shannai's second father, life-mates with Shemet and Gulanai (JTN2 Gravity)

Zharré

Tshar-ray

12-year-old Kyarta girl, enslaved to an officer under Iheolon's command. Liberated after the battle for Aurora Base. She is the last of her kind. There will be more about Zharré in an upcoming side-story. (JTN3 Stratagem)

Zhent

Zshent

Squadleader from C-troop, the unit to which Rett was first assigned. He'd been captured by the Coalition and implanted with a device; he was under its influence when Rett was forced to kill him in self-defense. You will be able to read more about Zhent in the JTN Prequel.

Zlotfyr

Tslot-fire

A peppy older citizen who gives his effort to the war driving military personnel stationed in Branch around on errands. (JTN2 Gravity)

ICE BEASTS (JTN3 STRATAGEM)

H'bris
huh-briss Sgt Tris

H'chan
Huh-chan Sgt Rett

H'jin
Huh-jin One of the first Ice Beasts to make humanoid contact, with a man named Tennar.

H'mert
Huh-mert Sgt Mordell

H'poll
Huh-poll Sgt Trebor

H'sol
Huh-sol Sgt Atira

H'tan
Huh-tan (aka Kraym) Sgt Ariam

H'tero
Huh-tea-ro (aka Killer) Jaq Pym

H'ting
Huh-ting Semage

H'vren
Huh-vren
(aka "Ranger"). Major Yidnar

H'wan
Huh-wan Lieutenant Evetez aka MYOTS

H'yaris
Huh-yah-ris Corporal Carakenne

ORGANIZATIONS/ALIENS
AND OTHER PEOPLE THINGS . . .

AirSpacefighters

Flight division of the Free Army, running planet-based and space-based operations.

B-troop

Sergeant Semage's platoon.

C-troop

Rett's original unit, which she joined right out of Special Forces training and served for seven years. C-troop under SrSgt Utahe was annihilated in the course of leading off a successful joint operation with 88th Infantry Div. and Seacorps units to secure Azurebay. At that time, Rett was second in command. Rett, Trebor, and Nerrah were the only survivors of their platoon. But, that's another story.

Easy Force

One of several special attack units formed for the Epnocian campaign. Lt. Evetez is given command, with Rett as his XO and Combat Team Leader (in addition to her duties as F-troop platoon leader.) Easy Force contains the platoons F, B, R, D, and S troops.

F-troop

2023rd Battalion, Special Forces. F-troop is SrSgt Rett's platoon, formed shortly after the decimation of C-troop. (In case you were wondering, Nyorfian military units are not designated in alphabetical or numeric order. Why? Uhm . . . one of the mysteries of life? As soon as Pam finds out and tells me, I'll let you know.)

Free Army

Collective term for entire military. The Free Army formed only in the year before the Yixolryn Coalition invaded, when the Nyorfian council felt the threat of invasion was getting high. Up until then, Nyorfias and Epnoce only had a very loosely organized citizen militia.

GTC

Galactic Trade Commission. Huge, united network of races, worlds, and solar systems. As a member system, Nyorfias turned to the GTC for help when they were invaded by the Yixolryns, but also being out on the frontier of GTC space meant they were a long way from help. By the time GTC forces arrived, the Yixolryns had the Nyorfian system blockaded. Only one Nyorfian space station, Brenekar, remained outside the enemy lines. The AirSpacefighters and Spacemarines on Brenekar fought with GTC forces to break up the enemy blockade and establish their own protective perimeter. But that, too, is another story . . .

Kyarta

Kyarta was a world with a very strong population of psi-talented individuals, mostly mindspeakers. They Yixolryn Coalition ended up destroying the homeworld and most of the population with it over two hundred years before the timeframe of these stories. They took a few of the young children, hoping to use them as genetic material or breeders to add psi talent into their race. (They have not been successful.) The Zetinorians had contact with the Kyarta and had tried to help them, but were too far away.

MainCommand

Nyorfias' version on the Pentagon. MainCommand isn't a place, since those involved change location frequently. Rather, it is a collective of the most experienced individuals the Nyorfian system has in military matters.

MainTech

The center for technology and scientific development and research.

MilitaryCentral

Familiar name for the Branch military base, since it is the central operations hub on the main continent.

Prenzzirhim

A Zetinorian term for a spirit guide.

Seacorps

Naval division of the Free Army. Although we don't see much of the navy, Seacorps' role cannot be underestimated in what might seem a mostly land/space based war. More on Seacorps in *The Nyorfias Files, A Compleat Guide.*

Spacemarine

Soldiers specializing in space battles.

Standard

Universal language, systems of time, weights, and measures used by Galactic Trade Commission member worlds. Nyorfians did not always use Standard, but converted to it completely since joining.

Unethi

Alien race aligned with the Yixolryn Coalition. They have tentacles for grasping as well as locomotion and spongy purple feelers on their "heads" as sensory organs. Not too much is known about them. They are rumored to originate from another far, far, *far* away sector of the galaxy.

Voi

A reptilian alien race aligned with the Yixolryn Coalition. There are quite a few Voi in the invasion force and wherever you find Yixolryns, you're sure to find Voi sucking up to them.

Yixolryn

Yeeks·all·rin

The alien bad guys.

Zetinor Prime, Zetinorian(s)

*ZEH·tee·nor*also *Zetinorian Ze-ti-NOR-I-an*

Zetinor Prime was taken over by the Coalition and subsequently destroyed. The exact number of Zetinorian natives left is unknown, since Zetinorians give off various pheromones that Yixolryns cannot tolerate. Zetinorians are humanoid with reddish-bronze skin and unusual hair. Unlike most humanoids, a Zetinorian's hair is alive from root to tip, sensitive to heat, cold, and touch, and marked with a pale central crest that runs from the center of the forehead all the way down the spine. Yep, that far.

PLACES

Aurora
Continent north and east of the main landmass on Epnoce.

Azurebay
A town, East Ocean Province, NNE Main, Nyorfias.

Barrens (the)
A desert region in South Point province that also hosts the biggest, deepest canyon on Nyorfias, known as The Rift.

Bolle ('s)
bo·lay (s)
Town and large swamp on east bank of Centerland Lake; also a family name of original colonists. Bolle's Marsh is the area Kraym and Newi came from.

Branch
A northern province of Main.

Cadie's
kha·dee
Third highest peak in Treetop Province, also a family name from the original colonists.

Cascadale
Town in NW Morrey's Peninsula (western Main); family name from original colonists.

Centerland
Centralmost geographic area of Main.

East Ocean
Province in northeast part of Main. Semage comes from Azurebay, the provincial capital.

Epnoce
EPP·noss
Sister planet to Nyorfias.

Hundei

HUN·dee·eye

Name of river and inlet near Azurebay in East Ocean Province. Also a family name from the original colonists.

Hunterdon

County in central New Jersey (United States, Earth.) Where Pam lives.

Main

The name of the huge Nyorfian main continent. Nyorfians don't waste too much time thinking up frivolous names for things or places when a perfectly ordinary term will do. For example, the main continent on Epnoce is also called "the main continent". Okay, that's not the same as Main, but it does show that Nyorfians are willing to wait for the perfect name to come along in its own time (or else they prefer to save their imaginations for other things).

451

Morrey's Peninsula

Westernmost province of Main, and home to one of the largest active volcano chains on the continent. Morrey is also a family name from the original colonists.

Nyorfias

NOR·fee·us

(Nyorfians, Nyorfian) Name of the main planet in the system and collective term for the population living on both worlds.

Seaboard Island

East central province of Main.

Skyraker Range, Skyrakers

A range of huge and dangerous mountains in Branch Province.

South Point

Southern province and also the name of the provincial capital.

Treetop

Northwestern province. Where Rett comes from.

THINGS

azurium

Rare element found only in Nyorfian system, more commonly compounded with metallic minerals. It is rarely found as pure crystals, and highly valued for even more uses (including decorative ones) when it is. Rett, at age fourteen, finds an azurium crystal cracked into halves, which she gives to her brother and sister. (JTN1)

backlash

Any retro action.

bubblehead

Also bubbleheaded. Silly, scatterbrained. See *Evetez* (just kidding)

camo

camouflage.

chewie bird

Avian species common to coniferous forests of northwest Main, scavengers. Garrulous, bold, and brightly plumaged.

chillbumps

We call them goosebumps.

comunit

Any small personal communication device.

dirtsiders

What people who spend most of their time in space call people who spend most of their time on a planet's surface. (JTN2)

dunos

due·NOSS

A large grazing mammal. It's perhaps as large as a moose, but has a single spatulate horn in the center of its forehead. So maybe like a unicorn/rhinoceros moose. Common to the northern forests of Main. It looks clumsy and its manner of crashing through underbrush promotes that image, but it actually is an agile, speedy creature.

ego-merge

Who put the peanut butter in my chocolate? Or, when there's a girl with another girl in her head. A rare phenomenon documented to have occurred only four times or so in 500 years of Nyorfian history—most of these occurrences in the two hundred years prior to the war. From Convergence JTN, you, dear reader, should have guessed a certain Guardian of Balance was behind these events. More on ego-merges will be explained in The Compleat Guide.

fingerlength

8 cm or about three inches.

handspan

20 cm or about 8 inches, the LENGTH of average adult hand from wrist to end of longest finger.

jumper

Applies to a variety of short to medium range surface-skimming and VTOL aircraft.

kitbag

In which one carries personal gear such as clothing, hygienic articles, etc.

knotroot

A large, thick, twisted rhizome that grows anywhere there's open space. Can be eaten raw (when small) or cooked. Leaves and stalks are also edible.

kurra

(like curry) Tree-dwelling rodent common to northern forested areas.

logheaded
stubborn. (And almost every other word in the thesaurus that goes with that.) Often used to describe Rett.

logheadedness
stubbornness. See above.

longcone
One of several varieties of everbearing coniferous trees native to Nyorfias, so called for the long seed cones (with yummy edible nuts) that sometimes reach three handspans in length.

martun
A small scavenger animal common to almost any wooded area over the northern sections of Main.

medjumper
Air ambulance.

medtech(s)
A generic term for doctors and paramedical personnel.

mindspeak
Nyorfian term for telepathy.

nightwing
A nocturnal avian species common to the more "temperate zone" of Epnoce's main continent.

nullgravity
Low gravity (there's always gravity, even in space, but when the effects are nulled enough to float things about, Nyorfians apply this term.).

outworld (er)
Anyone or anything not from your home world/system.

pcom
The variety of tiny personal comlink used by Special Forces.

pourstone
Like concrete, cement.

railtube
Underground transit tunnel.

redseed
Redseed berry, bramble fruit common to Main.

rover
Any of a variety of surface vehicles (hovercraft) all electrically powered.

Talent
Psi ability. Anyone with measurable psi in the GTC is defined as Talented. The most highly talented are called Adepts. The Yixolryn Coalition seeks out Talented Nyorfians in the attempt to breed the tendency into their own race . . . or at least breed it in to people they can control. So far, they've not been successful. Note: Rett's talent to see energy from nonliving and living sources isn't considered a psi ability.

tenday
Ten Standard days, four tendays a month, thirteen months a year.

tiffed
In American, this means *pissed,* as in *pissed off.* In the Queen's English . . . uh, how about anything from irritated (tiffed) to furious (really tiffed). (To UK/Ireland when you're pissed, you're drunk. Among Nyorfian soldiers, drunk is *stupid* or *zoned.*)

tiffing
See above.

transuranics
Radioactive elements.

troopjumper
Jumper with minimum of comfort and maximum of armor to move troops in/out of combat zones.

troopshuttle
Like a troopjumper, except designed for travel between planets or space stations. According to experts (namely the Spacemarines), traveling via troopshuttle is barely one step over going as cargo.

vichroxite
Rare element valued for interstellar spaceflight technology. Unlike azurium, vichroxite is found elsewhere in the known galaxy (just not enough of it, which of course is why it is rare. Hmm.) Nyorfias has several good deposits in the Skyraker Range.

* * * * *

I HOPE YOU ENJOYED THIS story. The best thanks, next to fan mail, that any author can ask for is an honest review at the review venue of your choice.

ABOUT . . .

AUTHOR AND COVER ARTIST
TERRY ROY

TERRY ROY HAS WRITTEN UNDER several nom de plumes: Terran Moffat, T.M. Roy, and Sharona Troy. Her primary career is as a book designer, technical writer, editor, and graphic artist. By any other time she's a fiction writer, artist, illustrator, and anything else life demands she must be.

In 2003, Roy's novel, *Discovery*, was a finalist in the 2003 EPIC Awards for Best Science Fiction Romance. She prefers to write adventure stories in sci-fi settings, some of which have been over twenty years in the making.

She was lost in a wormhole for a while and stranded in North Dakota for eight years, but found her way back through the event horizon into the Pacific Northwest. A random tesseract then transported her back to the Upper Midwest where she now resides in the Minneapolis-St. Paul metro area with an opinionated Quaker parrot named Apple and a rescued Senegal parrot, Sir Hugo the Naked.

When she's not writing, formatting, or drawing, she is campaigning to save the honeybee, gardening, "putting up" food, and when she can afford it, flying small airplanes.

She likes hearing from her readers. Feel free to drop an email to terzap@gmail.com or visit her Facebook pages:

Author page: https://www.facebook.com/Teryvisions/